CORRAG

ALSO BY SUSAN FLETCHER

Oystercatchers

Eve Green

CORRAG

Susan Fletcher

W. W. NORTON & COMPANY

New York · London

For information about permission to reproduce selections from this book,
write to Permissions, W. W. Norton & Company, Inc.,
500 Fifth Avenue, New York, NY 10110

For information about special discounts for bulk purchases, please contact
W. W. Norton Special Sales at specialsales@wwnorton.com or 800-233-4830

Manufacturing by RR Donnelley Harrisonburg
Book design by Helene Berinsky
Production manager: Julia Druskin

Library of Congress Cataloging-in-Publication Data

Fletcher, Susan, 1979–
Corrag / Susan Fletcher.
p. cm.
ISBN 978-0-393-08000-1
1. Witches—Scotland—History—17th century—Fiction.
2. Jacobites—Fiction. 3. Glencoe Massacre, 1692—Fiction. I. Title.
PR6106.L48C67 2010b
823'.92—dc22

                                        2010025743

W. W. Norton & Company, Inc.
500 Fifth Avenue, New York, N.Y. 10110
www.wwnorton.com

W. W. Norton & Company Ltd.
Castle House, 75/76 Wells Street, London W1T 3QT

1 2 3 4 5 6 7 8 9 0

CORRAG

I had an unexpected request the other day; there had been two bad landslides where the bulldozers have been working on the slate banks. Someone . . . said it was because the workmen had been disturbing the grave of Corrag. Corrag was a famous Glencoe witch . . . One point of interest about her is that in spite of reputed badness, she was to have been buried on the Burial Island of Eilean Munda. It was often noticed that however stormy the sea, or wild the weather, it habitually calmed down to allow the boat out for a burial. In the case of Corrag the storm did not cease till finally she was buried beside where the road now runs. By the way, in the Highlands, islands were used for burial very widely. Remember wolves remained here very much later than in the south.

—Barbara Fairweather
Clan Donald magazine, No. 8
(1979)

More things are learnt in the woods than in books. Animals, trees and rocks teach you things not to be heard elsewhere.

—Saint Bernard
(1090–1153)

Jane

I can't think of a winter that has been this cruel, or has asked so much of me. For weeks now, it has been blizzards, and ice. The wind is a hard, northern one—it finds its way inside my room and troubles this candle that I'm writing by. Twice it has gone out. For the candle's sake I must keep this brief.

I have news as foul as the weather.

Edinburgh shivers, and coughs—but it whispers, too. In its wynds and markets, there are whispers of treachery—of a mauling in the brutish, Highland parts. Deaths are often violent there, but I hear these were despicably done. A clan, they say, has been slaughtered. Their guests rose up against them and killed them in their beds.

On its own, this is abhorrent. But there is more.

Jane—they say it was soldier's work.

Of all people, you know my mind. You know my heart, and if this is true—if it was soldiers' hands that did this bloodiness—then surely it was the King who ordered it (or I will say the Orange, pretending one, for he is not my king).

I must leave for this valley. They call it wild and remote, and it's surely snowbound at this time—but it's my duty. I must learn what I can and report it, my love, for if William is behind this wickedness it may prove his undoing, and our making. All I wish, as you know, is to restore the true King to his throne.

Pray for my task. Ask the Lord for its safe and proper outcome. Pray for the lives of all our brothers in this cause, for we risk so much in its name. Pray, too, for better weather? This snow gives me a cough.

The candle gutters. I must end this letter, or I shall soon be writing by the fire's light which is not enough light for my eyes.

In God's love, and my own,

Charles

One

I

"The Moon is Lady of this."

of Privet

Complete Herbal
Culpeper
1653

W hen they come for me, I will think of the end of the northern ridge, for that's where I was happiest—with the skies
and wind, and the mountains being dark with moss, or dark with the
shadow of a cloud moving across them. I will think of how it is when
part of a mountain brightens very suddenly, so it is like that rock is
chosen by the sun—marked out by sunshine from all the other rocks.
It will shine, and then grow dark again. And I'll stand with my skirts
blowing, make my way home. I will have that sunlit rock in me. I will
keep it safe.

Or I'll think of how I ran with the snow coming down. There was
no moon, but I saw the morning star, which they say is the Devil's
star but it is love's star, too. It shone, that night—so brightly. And I ran
beneath it thinking *let all be well let all be well*. Then I saw the land
below which was so peaceful, so white and still and sleeping that I
thought maybe the star had heard and all *was* well—no death was

coming near. It was a night of beauty, then. For a while, it was the greatest beauty I had ever seen in all my life. My little life.

Or I will think of *you.*

In my last, quiet moments, I will think of him beside me. How, very softly, he said *you* . . .

SOME called it *a dark place*—like there was no goodness to be found inside those hills. But I know there was goodness. I climbed into its snowy heights. I crouched by the loch and drank from it, so my hair was in the water, and I lifted up my head to see the mist come down. On a clear, frosty night, when they said all the wolves were gone, I heard a wolf call from Bidean nam Bian. It was such a long, mournful call that I closed my eyes to hear it. It mourned its own end, I think, or ours—as if it knew. Those nights were like no other nights. The hills were very black, like they were shapes cut out of cloth, and the cloth was dark-blue, starry sky. I knew stars—but not as those stars were.

Those were its nights. And its days were clouds and rocks. Its days were paths in grass, and pulling herbs from soggy places that stained my hands and left their peaty smell on me. I was damp, peat-smelling. Deer trod their ways. I also trod them, or nestled in their hollows and felt their old deer-warmth. I saw what their black deer-eyes had seen, before my own. Those were its days—small things. Like how a river parts around a rock and joins again.

It was not *dark.* No.

I had to find it—darkness. I had to push rocks from their resting place, or look for it in caves. The summer nights could be so light, so full of light that I curled up like a mouse, hid my eyes beneath my hand so I might find a little dark to sleep inside. It is how I sleep, even now—tucked up.

I will think this way. When my life is ending. I will not think of musket shots or how it smelt by Achnacon. Not of bloodied things.

I will think of the end of the northern ridge. How my hair blew all about me. How I saw the glen go light and dark with clouds, or how he said *you've changed me,* as he stood by my side. I thought *this is the place,* as I stood there. I thought *this is my place*—mine, where I was meant for.

It was waiting for me, and I found it, in the end.

No rivers for me, now. No bogs.

Now I am in chains. I'm in a half-dark cell with shackles on my wrists, and wet straw to lie upon. A cracked bucket. Bars.

And it snows. From the little window, I can see it snows. It's been months, I think, of snowing—of bluish ice, and cold. Months of clouded breath. I blow, and see my breath roll out and I think *look. That is my life. I am still living.*

I like it—snow. I always did. I was born in a sharp, hard-earth December, as the church folk sang about three wise men and a star through their chattering teeth. Cora said that the weather you are born in is yours, all your life—your own weather. *You will shine brightest in snowstorms* she told me. *Oh yes* . . . I believed her—for she was born in thunder, and was always stormy-eyed.

So snow and ice is mine. And I have known some winters. I've heard fish knock beneath their ice. I've seen a trapdoor freeze so it could not go *bang,* though they still took the man's life away, in the end. Me? I'm a hardy thing. People die from the cold, but I haven't. I've not had blue skin, not once—a man said it was the evil fire in me that kept me warm, and *bind that harlot up.* But it was no evil fire. I was just born in snowy weather and had to be hardy, to stay living. I wanted to live, in this life. So I grew strong, and did.

Evil fire. Harlot.

That half-bird half-whore that lives by the burn . . .

I have many names. Never mind my hardy ways—it was my looks which brought the word *hag* out, at first, with my eyes like ghosts and my tiny size. My mother's nature did not help. She of the wild nights. She who threw back her hair, who lay on the leaf mulch in evening woods to breathe in its smell and soak up its age. She'd come home with dirty hands, a dirty face. *Her daughter's no better . . . Worse, I daresay.*

Vile matter, she is. Devil's hole . . .

And there's *witch.*

That word. It's never far away. I know its weight, and the mouth's shape when it says it. I know how folk spit with it, throw stones, hiss or grapple at me. They cross themselves and lock their doors, and cry *witch! Witch!* Like I am the plague or worse than it. Like my simple passing-by is a curse upon them, a danger, a proper woe in their lives. Like I am not a person—no feelings, no heart. No dreams in me.

Witch . . . I have tried to not mind it. I've tried so hard.

I have tried to say *it does not hurt,* and smile. And maybe I can reason that *witch* has been a gift, in its way—or look at my life . . . Look at the beauty that *witch* has brought me to. Such pink-sky dawns, and waterfalls, and long, grey beaches with a thundering sea, and look what people I met—what people! I've met some sovereign lives. I've met wise, giving, spirited lives which I would not have done, without *witch.* What love it showed me, too. No *witch,* and I would not have met the man who made me think *him, him, him*—all the time. Him, who tucked a strand of my hair behind my ear. Him who said *you* . . .

Alasdair.

Witch did that. So maybe it's been worth it all, in the end.

I WAIT for my death. I think *him,* and wonder how many days I have left to think it in. I turn my hands over, and stare. I feel my bones under my skin—my shins, my little hips—and wonder what will happen to them when I'm gone.

I wonder plenty.

Like *who will remember me? Who?*

There are one or two, maybe. Like Alasdair. Like his brother, who never quite trusted me, for I was English-sounding, and strange-looking. I had my lonesome ways.

And Gormshuil. She'll remember me. What a mind she had, tucked inside that hairless skull—what sight, what knowing . . . *Blood comes,* she said to me. *A man will find you. A man will come to you, and see your iron wrists, your small feet.* What were those words? I brushed them away, as she said them. I thought it was henbane talking, or some half-had dream of hers.

But blood was spilled, in Glencoe, like she said. Blood did come.

A MAN will find you.

I hear these words, now.

A man will find you. Iron wrists.

Some things we know. We hear them, and think *I know*—like we've always had the knowledge waiting in ourselves. And I know. She was right. There was a light in Gormshuil when she said *iron wrists*—a wide, astonished light, as if she'd never been so sure. Like how a deer is, when it lifts its head and sees you, and is scared—for it knows you are real, and breathing, and that you've crouched there all this while.

So I wait. With my shackles, and dirt.

I wait, and he comes. A man I've never met is riding to my cell.

When I tuck up in the straw, I stare into the dark and see my other lives. I see the bogs, the glen. But I also see his face.

His spectacles.

His neat, buckled shoes, and leather case.

The Eagle Inn
Stirling

Jane

I write this letter from Stirling. It is poor ink so forgive the poorer hand. Forgive, too, my bad humour. My supper was barely a crumb and my bed is damp from the cold, or the previous sleeper. What's more, I was hoping to be further north by now, but the weather remains unkind. We've kept to the lower roads. We lost a horse two days ago which has stolen hours, or days, from us. It's a wildly unsatisfactory business.

Let me go back a while—you shall know each part, as a wife should.

I left Edinburgh on Friday, which seems many months gone. I am indebted to a gentleman who leant me a sturdy cob and some funds—though I cannot give his name. I hate to withhold truths from you, but it may endanger him to write much more; I will simply say he is powerful, respected and sympathetic to our cause. Indeed, I glimpsed an embroidered white rose on his coat which we all know says Jacobite. *We drank to King James' health and his speedy return—for he will return. We are few in number, Jane, but we are strong.*

My thoughts were to make for a place named Inverlochy, on the Scottish north-west coast. It has a fort, and a settlement. Also it is a mere day's journey from this ruined Glen of Coe. The gentleman assured me that its governor, a Colonel Hill, is kindly, and wise, and I might find lodgings with him—but I fear the snow prevents this. I travel with two servants who speak of thick blizzards on the moor that lies between the fort and here. They're surly men, and locals. As I write they are in the town's dens, drinking. I don't trust them. I'm minded to insist we take this snowy route, no matter—for we have ridden this far through such weather. But I cannot risk another horse. Nor can I serve God if I perish on Rannoch Moor.

So tomorrow, our journey takes us west. Inverlochy must wait.

We are headed, now, for the town of Inverary—a small, Campbell town on the shores of Loch Fyne. The coast has a milder climate, I hear. I also hear the Campbells are a strong and wealthy people—I hope for a warmer bed than this one that Stirling provides. There, we might fatten our horses and ourselves, and rest, and wait for the thaw. It sounds a decent resting place. But I must be wary, Jane—these Campbells are William's men. They are loyal to him, and support him—they would not take kindly to my cause. They'd call it treachery, or worse. So I must hide my heart, and hold my tongue.

Wretched weather. My cough is thicker and I worry my chilblains might come back. Do you remember how I suffered from them in our first married winter? I would not wish for them again.

I feel far from you. I feel far from Ireland. Also, from like-minded men—I write to them in London, asking for their help, in words or in funds to assist me, but I hear nothing from them. Perhaps this weather slows those letters. Perhaps it slows these letters to you.

Forgive me. I am maudlin tonight. It is hunger that troubles me—for food, for warmth, for a little hope in these hopeless times. For you, too, my love. I think of you reading this by the fire, in Glaslough, and I wish I could be with you. But I must serve God.

Dear Jane. Keep warm and dry.

I will endeavour to do the same, and shall write to you from Inverary. It may be an arduous journey so do not expect a letter in haste. But have patience, as you have other virtues—for a letter will come.

In God's love, as always,

Charles

II

*"The black seed also (helps) such as in their sleep
are troubled with the disease called Ephilates or Incubus,
but we do commonly call it the Night-mare."*

of Peony

I wait for it—death. My own, fiery one.

Or perhaps it waits for me—tall, dark-wearing. Perhaps it stands beside the others who it has already called away—my mother, the MacDonalds, my big-bottomed mare. Their bodies are worms—but their souls are free, untied from their bones, and their souls are waiting for me. *The realm,* Cora called it—*where we all go, one day. Our death is a door we must pass through,* and it seemed a good thing by how she spoke of it. Calm, and good. Part of life—which it is.

But I was wrong to think it was calm. Or I was wrong to think it always happened that way. I was a child, with a child's mind, and I thought all deaths were by lying down, closing our eyes, and a sigh. Only when I killed the pig and it squealed did I think *it can hurt. Be bloody, and sad.* That was an awful lesson I learnt. After it, I was wiser. Cora said my eyes turned a darker shade of grey.

It can hurt. Yes.

And I have seen more hurtful deaths than I've seen gentle ones.

There was the nest which fell, and all those little feathered lives were licked up by the cats. In Hexham, a man was put in stocks and had stones thrown at him until he was dead—and for what? Not much, most likely. Also, there was Widow Finton, and I don't know how she died, but it took a week to know that she was gone—they smelt the smell, and found her. A door we must pass through? I believe that part. I believe it, for I have seen souls lift up and move away. But not all deaths are peaceful. They are lucky, who get those.

We do not get them. Peaceful deaths.

Not us who have *hag* as a name.

Why should we? When they say we worship the Devil and eat dead babes? When we steal milk by wishing it? We have no easy ends. For my mother's mother, they used the ducking stool. All the town was watching as she bobbed like a holey boat, and then sank under. I imagined it, in my infant days—out in the marshes with the frogs and swaying reeds. I crouched until my nose was in the water and I could not breathe, and I thought *she died this way,* and *would it have been a simple death? A painless one?* I doubted it. I coughed reeds up. Cora grabbed me, cursed me and plucked frogspawn from my hair.

Then there are the twirling deaths. Like the ones the Mossmen had. I saw these ones—how they put the rope on you like a crown that is too big, and your hands are double-tied. Like you are king, the crowds hiss or cheer. And then there is the *bang,* and maybe some go quickly but I've seen the heels drumming, and I've thought *what sadness. What huge sadness there is, in the world.*

And pricking. A dreadful word.

That is a fate they save only for us—for *witch* and *whore.* I've been afraid of the pricking men for all my life, for Cora was. She shook when she spoke of them. She made herself small, and hid. *Part of a witch does not bleed,* she whispered—*so the church says. So men prod our women with metal pins, seeking it . . .* I asked her *how big? Are the pins?* And she held out her hands, like this—like how fishermen do, when telling their tales.

A door, Cora said, *that we must pass through.*

Yes.

But not by painful ways. No death should be like that.

WITCH is a dying word, I know. I've known it as long as I've known my own name—*witch* will make you hunted, *witch* will shorten your days. And they hunted me, and hated me, and my life will be done by the month's end, I am certain of that. They will rope me to barrels, and make me flame.

Fire. To cleanse me. To burn the demons out.

Outside, they gather wood. I hear them drag it through the snow, and the nails going in. Inside, I look at my skin. I see its scars and freckles. I feel my bones, and I roll the skin upon my knees so that the bones beneath them *clunk*—back and fro. I follow where my veins run along my arm and hands. I touch the tender places—inside my legs, my belly. The pink, wrinkled skin between my toes.

⋯⟷⋯

I am fretful, tonight. Afraid.

Tonight, I breathe too quickly. I walk up and down, up and down. I run my fist along the bars so that my knuckles hurt, and bleed—but the hurt says *I am living,* that my body still has blood in it and works like it should do. I talk to myself so my breath comes out—white, white—and when I sit, tucked up, I hold my feet very tightly and I rock myself like children do when they have plenty on their minds. I try to say *hush now* to me, to calm me, but it doesn't work. For surely it hurts? Surely it is a pain beyond all knowing, and a slow death, too?

And such a lonesome one. *Fire . . .* And when I think it, it makes me wrap my arms about me, and I wail. My wail has an echo. I hear the echo, and think *poor, poor creature, to make such a sound*—for it is a desperate, dying sound. It is the wail of such a mauled and mangled thing, with no hope left, no light. No friend.

I pull at my chains. *Don't let me die.*

Don't let it be by burning.

I rock back and forth like this.

STILL. I have a comfort. It is small, but I have it—I whisper it into cupped hands.

People live because of me.

They do. They live because I saved them—because I listened to my soul's voice, to the song of my bones, the words of the world. I listened to my womb, my belly, my breasts. My instinct. The howling wolf in me. And I told them *make for Appin!* And *go! Go!* And they went. I watched them running in the snow, with their skirts hitched up, and their children strapped on tightly, and I thought *yes—be safe. Live long lives.*

There. It comforts me. It takes the fear away, and makes my breath slow down. When they tie me to the wood, I will say *I have saved lives,* and it will be a comfort and I will not mind the flames. For what if that's the cost? My life for their lives? What if the world asks for that—for my small life, with its lonely hours, in return for the lives of three hundred, or more? I will pay it. If it means they are living, and if it means the stag still treads the slopes, and the herrings still flash themselves in the loch, in summer, and if it means the people still play their pipes and still tell their stories of Fionn and his dogs, and the Lord of the Isles, and if the heather still shakes in the wind, and if it means that he—*him, him,* with hair like how wet hillside is—is still living, and mending, then I will pay it. I will.

Does he live? I think he does. In my darkest hours I worry he is dead—but I think he lives. I see him by the sea. On his side, he has the poultice of horsetail and comfrey, and he unpeels it. He sees he is healing, smiles, thinks *Corrag* . . . He presses the poultice back on.

SEE? I am calm now. I can see his dark-red hair.

I must sleep. It partly seems a waste of final hours, of breath. But even as I think of life, and love, and the stag with his fine branches, I have Gormshuil in my head—how she said *a man will come*.

I think he comes tomorrow. My days grow less and less.

LET him come. Let him do his purpose, even if it hurts. Even if it's pins, or his turn to say *whore,* or *hag*. For I am still living. Ones I love are still living, and so what pain can come to me? What is there to fear?

Lives mean far more than deaths ever do. It is what we remember—the life. Not how they died, but how warm and bright-eyed they were, and how they lived their lives.

The Argyll Inn
Inverary
26 February

Darling Jane

You will be glad, I think, to see where I write this from. I have made it safely to the town of Inverary—though there were times in our journey when I doubted that we would. It was arduous, my love. It was wild with blizzards. We passed such dark, desolate water, and the wind howled like a demon at night. I thought of the stitched kneeler my mother made—remember? It says "So we say with confidence, 'The Lord is my helper; I will not be afraid. What can man do to me?'" (Hebrews 13:6)—and it is His doing alone, His loving care, which brought us to Inverary, in the end.

It is an attractive town, despite the weather. Placed on the edge of Loch Fyne, it has an air of money and civility which is welcome at this time. My lodgings here are warm, and dry. They are by the water, in a coaching inn which seems lively by day and more so at night. My rooms have a fire, and a window which looks out across the loch and its clinking ice—(I take a rather childish pleasure in seeing such coldness, whilst I am warm. I write this, and see the blueness)—and I wonder at the hardiness of these people, who live amongst such mountains and wind. The Campbells are also generous men. Their allegiance may not be my own, but I have eaten well in this inn, and our two remaining horses which have served us so well seem as happy as I am, for the food and rest. I confess to being better in my spirits, than I was. I have even eaten venison, Jane. I am still picking my teeth from it, but it is a good, restorative meat.

On to my purpose.

I have heard plenty of Glencoe. In the corners of the inn, it is all they speak about. I dined, and overheard such things that chilled me—the Chief, they say, was shot as he rose from his bed. His lady wife was injured in such a manner that she died, naked, out in the snow. Her rings, I hear, were bitten from her hands, so that her hands were mauled most savagely. Dreadful, despicable deeds.

I know this from my landlord. You'd smile, I think, at him—he has the reddest hair I've ever known, and red cheeks. He brims with words, and I have been in Inverary for a mere afternoon—four hours, at most!—yet he has already accosted me more than once. Even as I arrived I felt his stealth. He said, staying long? *I replied that I, like all travellers, am at the Lord's mercy, and that He and the weather will decide on my length of stay. I think he will pry, Jane. But this may prove of use, in its way. For he pries with me, does he not pry with others? He may know plenty, in time.*

Thinking this, I asked very casually, is that infamous glen in these parts?

How he liked that! He came near, said aye, what remains of it. Burnt and butchered, it was. *His eyes blackened, and he leant closer in.* Mark me, *he said*—it is no loss. Those that were cut down in that glen will not be missed ... *He caught himself then—for I am a stranger to him, so he said,* what is your name, sir? You have not given it.

May God forgive me, Jane—for I spoke falsely. With my true purpose in mind, I did not give my own name—rather, I fashioned a name from scraps that we know. I used, my love, your unmarried name. For what if they had heard of me? And my teachings? And my Jacobite ways? I could not risk the townsfolk learning where my sympathies lie.

Charles Griffin, *I told him.* Reverend.

Reverend? And what it is your purpose? You are far from home, friend.

I said I've come to spread the Lord's loving word in the northern, lawless parts. For I hear the Highlands are full of sin.

They are! To the north of here? Catholics and criminals, dishonest men . . . *He polished his glass, shook his head.* Brimful with cruelty and barbarous ways. They shame us! And, *he said, a finger raised,* the north is full of traitors. Ones who plot against the King.

William?

Aye, King William. God protect him. Thank the Lord he came across—a well-named revolution, was it not?

I took a sip of my ale. I would call it far from glorious, but did not say so.

He said, do you know of the witch?

I was surprised at this—who would not be? I swallowed, said, no. *I know that this country—indeed, our own—has been troubled in the past times with the matter of witches, and other black deeds on which I do not choose to dwell. But this was brazen talk. He said* there's one here in Inverary. She is chained up in the tollbooth for her malicious ways. I hear, *he said,* she crawls with lice, and her teeth are gone. She faces her death for her evil. Sir, she was in Glencoe . . .

Jane. My dearest.

We have spoken of this matter in the past, you and I—in the gardens in Glaslough, by the willow tree. Do you remember? You wore the blue shawl that makes your eyes bluer, and I talked of enchantment—so we spoke of witchcraft, by that tree. I know we disagreed. Men of my faith and profession know of it—of the Devil's work. We know there are folk who serve him—perhaps not by choice, but they do. It is bedevilment, and a threat to a safe and civil nation. Some say no-one who meddles in such a way must be allowed to live, and so must be purged by fire or water, for their own sake. Plenty think this. You know that I am with them? That such women cannot be endured? It worries you, I know—my feeling on this. But do we not have enough foes at this time, Jane? Do we not have enough to fight

*against—other faiths, and false kings, and wars—without being troubled by
such Devil-lovers too? Who truly knows their power? If there is a God, there
is a Devil—and there are both, as we know. There is enough wickedness, my
love, in this world. It favours the pure parts of it to rid ourselves of the black.*

*I know your heart. I remember. Your blue eyes filled with water. You do
not believe in* witch, *or rather you don't trust the men who call it out—I
know. You think such women are ill, perhaps. That they suffer delusions, or
grief, or fear men. You said you felt sorry for such creatures—in your blue
shawl, beneath the willow tree.*

I love that trusting part of you—that faith in ones you have not met.

*But there is evil, Jane, in this world—I promise it. It casts its darkness
everywhere. It hopes to choke virtue, and decency, and I will spend my life
fighting to prevent this—as my father did. There is a righteous path. My
life's purpose is to return all men to it—for us to walk, once more, in God's
light.*

*I hope I stay briefly in this town. It is merely a resting place, before I head
north to this ravaged glen. This witch was there, my love. She was at the
murders, and saw them with her eyes. I am not keen to visit her, or to spend
time with such a cankered, godless piece—nor do I wish to get her lice. But
I must remember my cause. If she was at these deaths, then she must have
her uses. She will have seen the redcoats—and any word, even a witch's, is a
better word than none.*

*It is late. Past midnight—my pocket watch tells me so. I will conclude this
letter with assuring you how much I miss you. They are small words. But
to look out of my window is to see Loch Fyne, and the sea, and I look west
across it which makes me think of you. I tell myself that Ireland is across
that water. You are across it, and our boys, all that I love in the world beside
God.*

Keep strong. I know my absence asks much of you, and you endure a hardship by being alone. Forgive me. I ask this, but I know that I am forgiven already, for your faith and love of God is as mine is. I have slept in damp beds and I will talk to witches for His glory and for James, but I also think of you as I do it. I hope I make you proud.

It still snows. I might grumble at it, but it looks soft and beautiful with you, my wife, in mind.

My love to you, from across Loch Fyne, and all that is between us.

Charles

III

"This is a common but very neglected plant.
It contains very great virtues."

of Comfrey

The gaoler knows me now.

He knows how I talk in the dark. How small I can be when I curl myself up—so small that he thinks I've done magick, and gone. *Filthy witch* he says, when he finds me. *I hope they do you slowly . . . I'll be there to warm myself.*

But I also know him. I know his sideways eye, and that chickweed would help the leaf-dry skin on his hands that flakes, when he moves. Those hands get worse in this weather. I know he drinks—for his breath is all whisky and old meat, and I've heard him snoring when there is daylight outside, or at least a paler sky than night. I think whisky is his best thing of all. I know his footsteps, too. I know he has a limp, so he drags his left leg. No one else walks like that—like the sea coming in. Also, his keys jangle. It is the only music I hear in this tollbooth—no birdsong, no pipes. Just his keys, and his heavy left leg.

I know the sound of him, walking.

This isn't him walking.

These are the footsteps of a man who is not him.

Come in. Sit down?

I see that look that you give.

They all give me that look, as soon as they see me for the first time. It's my size, I think—how small I am? I know I am tiny. I've been called *mouse* and *little bird,* and *bairn,* though I'm none of these things. The doctor came in and could not see me in the gloom. He was cross, shouted *there is no prisoner in here!* And then I shifted my chains so that they clinked, and I whispered to him *oh there is . . .*

Come in from the door. See how locked up I am? Most of the thieves they put here do not wear chains like I do. They are put behind bars, and that's all. But I have chains because of *witch*—they think I might turn into a wind, and blow myself away. Or make myself a frog, and hop out through the door. But also, I am chained because of my smallness—my arms like twigs, and my thin body. Stair said I might slip through the bars, *so chain her. Shackle her up, and tightly! This one mustn't go.*

Therefore come in from the door. I cannot hurt you.

There is a stool, by that wall.

I KNEW a woman who dreamt of you. She was half-mad, and as tall as a man can be. In a light, soft snow when the snow did not fall, but lingered in the air, she spoke of you to me. *A man* she said. *After the bloodshed, he will come to you.* She talked of my iron wrists, and called you *neatly done.* She did not talk of spectacles but I imagined them, and I am also right about your shiny buckled shoes. About your wig's tight curls.

What a look you give. The look I know.

It says *damned slattern. Keep away from me.*

So I knew you would come. Gormshuil was her name. She had the second sight, though I did not always believe what she said, for she loved her henbane too much to trust her words. Once, she put her finger to my chest and said, *a wife!* As if she saw one in me—that I might become a wife. I told her *no* . . . I shook my head, stepped back, but she sang the word as she drifted away—*wife! wife!* through the glen.

That's the henbane for you—as strong a herb as I know. Too much can kill you, and speedily too. But I believed her when she told me, sir, of you.

It's your purpose for coming that I don't know.

Others have come. You are not the first, sir, to sit on that stool, or frown at the walls. Several have come. And their reasons have been so plentiful, and strange, that it is like plucking herbs—none are the same. To save my soul from Hell's unending fires, is one. I think my soul is fine, but many try it—to make me speak of God and repent my wicked ways. There were belches from the priest who came to me, like croakings from a toad. He talked to me like all churchmen do, which is like I'm not human, or at best a simple one. Are you a churchman? I see the cross about your neck, and your dislike of me has a high, Godly air. I reckon a thousand Bible words live in your head, and are spoken very solemnly. But save my soul? Maybe not. You don't sit like the others did. You don't stare as hard. The priest belched, and stared so intently that I stared back and he hated that—*a staring witch-called piece,* he said. And he hated my talking. I know I can talk. But I don't see many people so I talk plenty when I do.

He called me *harlot,* and *quarrelsome,* too. Said my chatter disrespected him, and that the day I was burnt like a hog on a spit would be a good day.

So I get them—churchy ones. Who think that by cursing me they are better men.

And lawmen. They have come. But what law is that? I've seen no trial, sir. I've seen no proper fairness—for when did fairness say its name in law? None of our women ever heard it. If a bird squawks as much as once, then cook the bird, or drown it, or maybe string it up and kick away the stool, so it may not squawk again—that is the law. *Law,* I think, is like *hag*—it is said so much we are blind to it. Its heart, which is the truest part, is lost, and a wicked lie sits in its heart-shaped place. I'm not the squawking kind, and never was. But that's no matter. Here I am—chained up.

And doctors. There has been a doctor. Just one—a man with his own lice who looked at the wound where the musket caught me. He said it was healing so fast it was the Horned One's work—which it wasn't, of course. It was horsetail with some comfrey boiled up and pressed on. He might do well from comfrey himself for he had very rank sores from his lice. One was all pus and will only grow worse. He was no true doctor.

And then there were the rest. The townsfolk from Inverary who just wanted to see—to see and smell a witch, a *Devil's whore.* They threw stones through the bars at me. They pressed pennies into the gaoler's hands, as they left, and handkerchiefs to their noses, and I reckon I've fed him well. He must have bought many bottles with what he's made from *that witch who was in that damned glen.*

She was there? In Glencoe?

Aye. Saw it all, they say. They say she knelt and did her spells there.

Called in the Devil?

Oh aye. All that blood and murder . . . The Devil was there, right enough.

A man called Stair, as well. He has come. He has sat where you are sitting now. He looked upon me as a wolf looks on a thing it has stalked too long, but has now.

That is all I have to say on him.

Reverend Charles Leslie. I feel I know your name.

Leslie—like the wind in the trees, or the sea coming in . . .

I saw you flinch at *witch*.

Oh it's a dark word, for certain. It has caused its damage across the months and years. Many good people have been undone by it— married and unmarried, beautiful, and strange. Women. Men.

What did you have, in your head? With *witch*?

I know that all people have a certain creature in their head, when they hear it—a woman, mostly. Pitch-dark and cruel, crooked with age. Did you think *she will be mad, this witch*? I might be. It's been said. I prattle, I play with my hands and bring them up to my face when I speak like this, as a mouse may with its paws as it eats or cleans itself. My voice is shrill and girlish—this has been called proof, for they say the Devil took my lower voice away and ate it up to make his own voice deeper. Which is a lie, of course. I am small, so my voice is small, too—that's all.

And spells? Oh they've tried to pin a thousand things on me—a splinter in a finger, or an owl swooping in. They pinned even more on my mother, but she was a wilder one than me, and beautiful, and brave. A calf with a star on its forehead was her doing, and so were the twins which were as alike as shoes. Cora said, once, that a black cock crowed by a church door so they took it and buried it—the cock, not the door. Buried it alive, too, so that she heard its scrabbles as they held it down. *The Devil sent it to us,* they hissed. And Cora unburied the cock with frantic hands that night, but it was too late—it was earthy, and dead. She buried it again but gently, and in a better, secret place.

I hated that story. That poor cock which did no harm—it was just

black, and passing by. But Cora said all people bury what it is they fear—*so it cannot hurt them. So it is kept from them, locked up in the earth or in the sea.*

Does it work? I asked her. *Burying a feared thing?*

She pursed her lips. *Maybe. If it is done justly, and with an honest, hopeful heart—which it wasn't with that rooster, I can promise you that.* She shook her head, sighed. It was a waste of a fine, cockerel life.

So what townsfolk say we do and what we truly do are very different things. I have cast no spells. I've never plucked out gizzards or howled at moons. I've never turned into a bird, skimmed a night-time loch, or settled on ships to make them drown. I've not kissed obscenely or eaten dead babes, and I don't have a third teat, and nor do I laugh like broth when it's left to boil over and ruin the fire, and ruin itself for the broth tastes bitter, then. I've never seen the future in a rotten egg. I never laughed at murders, or called murders in.

I've not summoned anything. I've only asked—prayed.

Pray. Yes. I use that word, too. I pray—not in church and with no Bible, but otherwise I reckon it's probably like how you pray, which is with the heart's voice talking, not the mouth's.

DEVIL-*child,* they've called me. *Evil piece.*

But Mr Leslie, I will tell you this. When *witch* was first thrown at me, as I passed through a market, Cora led me by the hand to an alleyway and sat me down, and wiped my wet eyes, and said *listen to me. The only evil in the world is the one that lies in people—in their pride, and greed, and duty. Remember that.*

And from what I have seen of this world, this life, I think she was right.

My telling? Of Glencoe?

Mine?

Why mine? There are others who, I'm sure, could tell you more. If you are after the truth of that night, of the snowy glen murders, then go to them that survived it. Go to them who live to bury those that do not, and ask for their stories. They know more than me, on many things—like who killed the MacIain, and who ran his wife through. Whose voice said *find his damned cubs!*

Why mine? And here, too, is a question, Mr Leslie—why do you want to know at all? No one else has asked. No others care that so many people died in the glen. They were MacDonalds. *Why grieve for MacDonalds?* is what they say—for they stole cattle. Burnt homes. Ate their foe.

Barbarous clan.

The gallows herd.

Glencoe? A dark place . . .

I think most are glad that those people were stabbed, and robbed. Like they deserved what happened to them—for their outdoors life, and their language, and their dress were all a blight on the nation, a canker in the rose. So Lowlanders say. So Stair says, and the Campbells. So does this Orange Dutchman who seems to be king.

KING . . . That brightens you.

I reckon it's a word to hang with *hag* and *law*—a fiery word which can kill a man, if whispered wrongly, or in the wrong ear. But most folk like it. Most folk have a man they call *king,* and fight for—and such fighting . . . Two men, with two different faiths, and look what that does? It splits up the world. It makes nations narrow their eyes at themselves, and seethe.

Always eyes and ears, in the dark.

James is your fellow, I think.

Jacobite? I know the word. The MacDonald men were those—*that Jacobite clan. Those wretched papists in Glencoe.* They wanted what you want, sir—to have James sail back from France and take his throne again, and for all to be as God meant it to be. They fought for that. They went to Killiecrankie and flew his flag, and killed William's men, and rallied, and sang, and plotted against the Dutchman in their wild, blustery glen, and I was asked by them *who is your king, English thing? Whose flag do you stand under?* That was in the Chief's house. There were beeswax candles, and a dog with its head on its paws. And I said I didn't have a flag—that nobody ruled me. I said *I don't have a king.*

That brought a silence to the room. I remember that.

But it's true. I think kings can only cause trouble. Too many men die, in their name. Too many fight, and kill, or are killed—and so I think of loss with that word *king.* With *king,* I think of lost things.

So much is gone. So much. All for kings, or a shiny coin.

And I remember so much . . . The dog's name was Bran, and the snow lay itself down on every branch of every tree, that night, and I kissed a man—there was a kiss—and I remember so much! I know plenty. And if I do not speak of what I saw, that will also be gone.

Stair called me *a meddling piece,* but he also said *you must have seen such things, through those long lashes of yours* . . . In a soft voice. Like he was my friend which he never was.

That's why he'll burn me, I think.

Get rid of the one who saw it all.

The one who saved people, and ruined the plan.

She who remembers all things.

Yes I will give you my telling.

You say *tell me what you know—give me names! Soldiers' names.* And I will. I will tell you of the Glencoe massacre, and what I saw—of the musket fire, and the screams, and the herbs I used, and the truth. The truth! Who else knows it, as I know it? I will tell you every part. And I promise you this, Mr Leslie—it will help your cause. It will help you to bring your James back, for what I have to tell makes the Highlanders look wise, and civilised, as they are. It shows their dignity. It says the King we have now is not Orange, but blood-red. I promise you that.

And in return?

Speak of me. Of me. Of my little life. Speak of it, when I am gone—for who is left to tell it? None know my story. There is no one left to tell it to, so speak of it from your pulpit, or write it down in ink. Talk of what I tell you, and add no lies to it—it needs none, it brims with love and loss so I see it be quite a fireside tale as it is, all truthful. Say *Corrag was good.* Say that she did not deserve a fiery death, or lonesome one. All I've ever tried to be is kind.

Is THIS fair? A fair bargaining? Sit with me and hear my life's tale, and I will speak, in time, of Glencoe. On a snowy night. When people I loved fell, and died. But some, also, survived.

It is *Corrag*. Cor-*rag*. No other name but that.

My mother was *Cora,* sir. But her most common name was *hag* so she joined them together like two sticks on fire, to make my name. That was her way. Her humour.

But *Corrag* is also what they call *a finger* in the Highland tongue. I never knew it till I walked into those hills. Many folk have pointed theirs at me, so it's a fitting name. Also, it's fitting that some mountains are called the word—the tall and snow-topped ones. There is the *Corrag Bhuide* which I never saw because it's far north of here. But they say it is beautiful—mist-wearing, and wolf-trodden. It's all height and wonder in my head.

WHO would believe it? A churchman and a captured witch, helping each other like this? But it is so.

The world has its wonders and I will speak of them.

Dearest Jane

*I have plenty to tell you. There is much to write, for today was full of
strangeness—so much strangeness that I wonder where to start. Have I
not met sinners before? I have. When I was still a bishop, I met plenty of
them—thieves and fornicators, and do you remember the man they strung
up for having two wives, and blaspheming? That was a foul business. I had
hoped to never step near such wickedness twice, in my life. But I wonder if I
have met worse.*

This afternoon, I sat with the witch.

*I think I wrote a little to you of how they say she is: savage, dark-
hearted, and with lice. He—my landlord, who is the sole source of all I
know, thus far—assured me she was quick-tongued and hot-tempered, or so
he had heard. I asked* how hot-tempered *and he said* very, I hear. She is
the wickedest person that has been in that cell—and that cell's seen
some rogues, sir! *And he filled up a tankard.*

*I took my Bible, of course. I do not like being near wickedness, and I
confess to you that as I walked through the snow to the tollbooth, I felt an
apprehension in me. A nervousness, perhaps. So I recited as I walked, which
heartened me. "But the Lord is faithful, and He will strengthen and keep
you safe from the Evil One" (2 Thessalonians 3:3—as you know).*

*Let me tell you of the tollbooth where she is kept. It is near the castle,
in this town. It's a sombre prison, certainly—half on the ground and half
beneath it. It was built, I am told, to keep the Highland cattle-thieves before
they were hung up on Doom Hill, and perhaps it was anxiousness on my
part, but I thought I smelt cows there. It has the smell of a byre—dung and
dampness. Also, the odour that comes from soiled bodies and fear—the gallows at Lawnmarket had a milder form of it. I wonder if this is death's smell,
or the smell before death.*

The gaoler belongs, I think, in the cells as much as the ones he locks there. He curses. He reeked of ale and vices, and insisted on undoing my leather travelling case. He thumbed my inkwell and quill. He glanced at the Bible as if it bored him—I'll pray for his soul. Then he coughed into his hand, wiped it on his coat, and held out that hand for some pennies. Seeing the witch is-nee free, *he said (so they talk, in this country). I gave over a coin, and he smiled a brown smile.* The last door? That's her.

The corridor I walked along was not fit for even beasts. I was careful to touch as little as I could. The walls were wet-looking. I am not sure what I trod upon but it was soft, and soundless.

As for the woman herself—Jane, I wonder if even your motherly heart and goodness would feel any warmth for the wretch. I thought she was a child, when I entered. She is child-sized. I barely saw her at all, and thought the cell was empty. But then she shifted in her chains and spoke. You might read child-sized *and feel tender for her—but Jane, she's a despicable thing. Her hair is knots and branches. She is half-naked, dressed in thin rags which are crusted with mud and blood and all manner of filth (the smell in her cell is unpleasant). Her feet are bare. Her fingernails are splintered and black, and she gnaws on them sometimes, and I partly wondered if she was human at all. I was minded to turn, and leave. But she said* sit. *And I felt the Lord beside me, so I did not leave.*

I sat—and then, in the gloom I saw her eyes. They were a very pale grey, and gave her a haunted expression, as the dying get. Her stare was brazen. She stared, and said she had expected me—which I doubt. If she knew I'd hoped to visit her, it can only be through prattle—for news is swift, in small towns. Even prisoners have ears.

She herself can prattle. The landlord was right about her tongue, for she talked more than I did. She rocked with her knees to her chest like her mind was half-gone—which it may be. She is witch, and therefore deserves no sympathy, and I give her none, but I will say she has been poorly treated in her time—there were bruises on her arms, a reddened crust above one eye, and there's a blood-stain on the side of her. The shackles have also broken her skin. I wonder if these wounds will kill her before the flames do. (I'll also add this—that she is bruised and cut, and mangled, but I saw no bites on her. So rest yourself, Jane—do not worry yourself on lice.)

She may have been pretty, once. But the Devil takes hold of a face as much as he does the soul, and she is filthy now. Woe is on her features. This also makes her look older than I will say she is. If she is older than our eldest son, Jane, it can only be by months.

So, in short, Inverary tollbooth is a very foul place. Foul, too, is its inmate whose high, girlish voice spoke of kindness and good deeds—but I am not tricked by that. The Devil was speaking. He hides his nature in lies, and when she said I cannot hurt you *I heard his voice very clearly. I thought,* I will not be fooled by you. I know who you are. *He speaks through this half-creature in a feminine way—and it is better for her that she is burnt, and soon. The flames will purge her soul. The fire will clean her of wickedness, and to be purified in death is far better than to live in this manner—un-Christian, defiled.*

It was good to leave. I stepped into the snow, and filled up my lungs with fresh air. I wondered if I'd ever met such a wretched human, as her—and I was minded to not return. But Jane, I am intrigued—for she spoke of Dalrymple, the Master of Stair. His is not a name you know. But he is a Lowlander. His hatred of the Highlands is as famous as his love of himself, and fine things—and he is William's wolf. He prowls Scotland, in the King's name. In short, if he had a hand in the Glencoe murders, then is that not proof? Of William's own sin?

For all her unpleasantness, this witch may help our cause.

So I will not be discouraged by her smell, or strangeness. I will endure her, and use her for her knowledge—no more than that. For I believe she may indeed have news that brings James in. I have given her my true name— which I hope I will not regret. But who might she tell? She will die soon.

She has promised to speak of the massacre and what she knows, but only if I listen to the years of her life, beforehand. A tiresome task. Who knows what horrors or filth she has seen? But she said no one knows my story. *She said* William is blood-red, not orange—*so I agreed to her request.*

A curious arrangement, indeed. It is not one I could have imagined when I wrote to you, in Edinburgh. But God works as He chooses—we have our tests, and He has His revelations. This is an unearthly winter. I will be glad when spring comes.

My love, with this knowledge, and with there being no hasty thaw of snow, I think I may be in Inverary for longer than I thought. Perhaps two weeks, or more. Therefore, if you find the time to write a small note to me, it will reach me here. It would be a joy to have your words. It is the closest I can be to you—and as always, I wish to be close.

Charles

Two

I

"*Called also Wind flower, because they say the flowers never open but when the wind blows.*"

of Anemone

How would you like my words? I have so many of them. Like a night sky is starry, so my mind is shining with words. I could not sleep, last night, for thinking. I lay on my straw and thought *where do I start, with my story? How?*

I could speak of the night of the murders itself—how I ran all breathless from Inverlochy with the snow coming down. Or how the loch was dark with ice. Or Alasdair's kiss—his mouth on my mouth.

Or further back?

To before the glen? To my English life?

I will start there. I'll start in a town of clover, with my mother's glossy black hair. For it's right, I think, that I start with my early days—for how can you tell my tale, if you don't know me? Who I am? You think I am a stinking, small-sized wretch. No heart in my chest. No skin on my bones.

Yes I will wait a moment.

A quill, ink, your holy book.

Is it a goose's feather? Very long and white. I have seen geese flying at twilight, and I have heard them call, and those are good moments. They happened in England, in the autumn days. Where were the geese flying to? I never really knew. But sometimes their feathers would undo themselves, and float down into the cornfields, and Cora and I would find them, take them home. She couldn't write, but she liked them. *So long and white . . .* she'd whisper, fingering it. Like your quill.

And a small table, that unfolds?

You have brought plenty in that leather bag of yours.

There is the saying, sir, that witches are not born at all.

I have heard such lies—that their mothers were cats, or a cow whose milk had soured so she heaved her curdle out in human form. A fishwife once said she hatched out from fish eggs, but she cackled, too—she liked the whisky too much. Then there was Doideag. She swore she grew like a tooth on a rock, on the isle of Mull—and she believed her own story, I think. But I didn't. That one lusted for henbane, like Gormshuil did. Fiercesome pieces, both. They smiled when they heard of a boat being wrecked—and I asked *why? It is awful! A boat is gone, and all those lives . . .* But I reckon they smiled at what they knew, from years before—loss, and sorrow. That's why.

A tooth? On a rock?

Not me.

I had a mother. A proper human one.

She was like no other human I have ever known. Her eyelashes brushed her cheekbones. Her laugh was many shrieks in a line, like how a bird does when a fox comes by it. She wore a blood-red skirt, which is why she wore it, I think—for when our pig died, his blood didn't show on it at all. Nor did berry juices, or mud. When she spun on her toes those skirts lifted up, like a wing—as if she might fly far away. Cora lapped up the morning dew, cat-like. She rustled with all the herbs she'd picked, and she told future times, and most of the men looked twice at her as she passed, and smiled. The blacksmith was in love with her. The baker's boy would follow her, put his feet where hers had been. And Mr Fothers loathed her—but I won't talk of him just yet.

There was something to her, is what they all said, later. I call it magick, and boldness. But some people are scared of these things.

Cora . . . All of north England knew her name. I ran away when I was nearly a woman, and for many weeks I still heard tales—of a red-skirted beauty in the border country. How she stopped the church clock by pointing at it, or shed feathers in pheasant season. This was her. I knew it. Lies, of course—who sheds feathers? But there is only ever gossip on the brighter, wilder lives.

Cora bewitched them—that is how they put it. She courted men with her beauty, and nature with her soul. And she courted her own death too, in the end—for the last tale I heard was how the wind caught her skirts on the gallows, and twirled her round and round.

SHE, also, was human-born. Her mother was no fish egg—she was a Godly woman, with rubies in her ears and a twisted hand. Cora was blamed, for that twisting—for her birth came in with a lightning strike which set fire to the house, and burnt her mother's hand as she pushed the door to flee. *An ill-luck child. Cora*—who moved like a spider. Who did not crawl as bairns do, but scrambled—all legs and eyes. She scrambled in church, one Sunday, so that she scratched the pew with her fingernails and the mark was a cross downside-up. *A sign!* they all cried. *Satan's work!* When the witch-hunting fever came to them, as it did, it was her mother they took to the ducking stool.

You have fornicated, they told her, *with Yon Fellow* (for they feared saying his name, but didn't fear murder, it seems). They said her hand like a hoof was His mark on her. *Proof,* they tutted, *of your sin.*

What hope did she have? Not even some. My grandmother, who was a God-serving woman all her days, was taken to a dread pool outside the town. Her husband tried to save her. He tried, but who can undo *witch*? So he stood and wept as they undressed her. He called out *I love my wife* when she was in her shift, and she called back *and I love my husband, very much.* And then they tied her thumbs to her big toes so that her chin touched her knees. Then they dropped her in. She floated three times. On the fourth time she went under, and that was her end.

Cora saw this. She watched it from the bridge with her witch's eye.

Later, she would swear to me *there is no Devil, only man's devilish ways. All bad things,* she hissed, *are man-made . . . All of them!* And I know she saw her mother when she said this, sinking down.

Afterwards, her father found an inn and never left.

As for Cora, they all hoped she might turn her face to the Lord and be saved by him. My mother? No. She had that lightning in her heart, I think, and it could not be stilled. She took to church falsely, smiled to hide her fire. She used the cross round her neck to crush flies and pop out apple seeds, and other casual deeds which had naught to do with God.

She ran from the town when she was old enough to run fast. Six or seven years old—no older.

THIS was her wandering time. These were the days and nights which made her the creature she was, in her heart—owl-wise, cat-sly. She prowled in the dark. She slept in lonesome places where no soul had been, for years—caves, forests. A dank waterwheel. She stood by the sea, and crouched in bogs, and she met other people on her wanderings—other hiding people. Witches. Rogues.

I learnt my herbs, she said, *from those people. I picked them in those places.*

So Cora learnt herbs, and she grew. She grew tall, and wide-hipped. She took her red skirt from a gooseberry bush it dried upon, as she came into Cumberland. Then she wore it to market for eggs and bread, where a woman said *thief! 'Tis my skirt!* So she moved on with no eggs, or bread. She lived as gypsies live—selling cures, and people's future times. She did not always speak the truth, for bad futures did not pay well. I think her purse jingled. She could talk very well when she buttoned her wild tongue, and only used her other.

A troublesome piece.

So she was called at her birth and so called, too, once I was born. She was definitely that—troublesome. But was she made to be? By others? Maybe—for if you kick a dog for barking it will only bark more, in the end.

I've wondered if I take after her, that way. I know some would say so—*troublesome hag.* But I have saved trouble too, yes I have.

———

So I am English-born. You know that from my voice.

Thorneyburnbank. A long name, and a fitting one—for its burn had thorns to its southern side. There was also an elm wood, and field so brackish that the cows were haunch-high when they fed on its clover. They did that in the spring—it was sweetest then. Their milk, too, was sweeter, and the village was happier for the sweet milk. More hats were raised in the street, at me.

Not many knew of our village. Most knew of Hexham, though—with it being near the wall that the Romans made. Hexham's abbey had bells which rang from the south, and if the wind was also southern we would hear them. I remember it like that—the cows in the marsh, and the bells ringing. It's a pretty sight, in my head.

But it was not always pretty. And Cora was not fooled by pretty, gentle things. She was tired of wandering, that's all. How many years can a person walk and walk, and sleep on bare earth? She was tired by now. She'd thought to try Hexham for a wholesome life, since she'd dreamt of its name very clearly—but the gaol upset her, I think. *Justice* was a word she scowled at, and was black for. The gaol hissed it to her—or at least, man's meaning of it, which was Jeddart's justice, mostly. She'd seen plenty of that, in a dark pool. She looked for less people to live by, for less people can mean more sense.

A hearth. A proper sleeping place.

A den for her feral heart.

THE border country had a wild and unbridled way of life. It was filled with unkind weather, and as many ghosts as there was rain in the sky. There were rains so heavy the burn came up and ate the bridge like a fish does a fly—rain on rain. That meant trouble for the bats, too— for there were some bats that liked the bridge for roosting, and hung upside-down from it. We put our pig in the cottage with us one early spring for the mud was too thick for even a pig. So three of us snored at night, and sat by the hearth but not so close that we might smell pork roasting.

Winters could kill folk, there. They froze the earth so that all things in it—beasts, bushes—froze too. I knew the story of Old Man Bean. They only found his boots.

Reiving weather, Cora said. *Oh yes.*

Reiver, Mr Leslie. *Ree*-ver.

That was a whispered word. An old one, too. She knew it. She knew that in *reiver* there had been spoiled homes and outrageous foraging, and cattle stolen away into the northern woods. She'd heard these stories of olden days, but she'd seen it too—in her head, in the strange roamings when her eyes went wide. *Their hats,* she said, *were shiny-shiny . . .* She called them *crook-hearted, and cruel.*

Cora told me, as a bedtime tale, that these reivers had ridden on moonless nights, and damp autumn ones when the cattle were fat, and worth reiving. The air might have had thick, swirling mists in it so they came forth, like ghosts. They'd charged onto farmsteads with their bonnets and daggs, roaring for what they had no right to have—hens, coins, leather. They maimed as they chose and left homes burning, so that if the night began itself moonless it ended fiery, full of light.

I thought of them when I was small. I thought of how I might fight them if they came for our pig, or three scrag hens. I thought I may fight them with a flaming cloth tied to bones, or stones. I fell on this distraction—I liked it more than working hard. But one day Mother Mundy spied me burning turf as March-wardens did. She beckoned me. She was a grizzled old crone whose teeth were gone, save for a peg or two. She told me of a night in which she'd been young and fair, unknown to any man, but was made known to a reiver as the thatch burned above her. The town raised hue and cry, she said. She was left extremely hurt and mangled, but with her life. *I was lucky* she slurred—*others were slew . . . Oxen gone and horses too.* She said I was to keep her secret safe in me. She said she'd told no other soul in all her years, not even her man Mundy who was a long time boxed under the earth. He'd stepped on a nail, or so I heard. It turned his blood bad, and that took him.

I don't know why she told me of the reiver. I only half-caught her meaning, but did not forget.

Most were gone by my birth. They did their crimes before this Dutch Orange king, or the witch-hating one. The red-haired queen was on the English throne when they fought with most splendour or the least shame—whichever you'd have it. Before the war people called civil, when no war is such. They were caught and banished, or strung up like rats, so that these northern parts could sleep well on autumn nights.

The second Charles king talked of border peace then. But he was wrong, as kings can be. There was no proper border peace. The sons of reivers and their sons were still alive. They were fewer, but vengeful. And when my mother first came to Thorneyburnbank she knew the last reivers still rode out at night, and lurked in blind turnings, for the witch in her could smell their blades and fires, and sheep fat. She could hear their hobblers' teeth upon their bridles in the dark.

Wise Cora.

She was. For she reasoned that if a village had one eye on the Scotch raiders, they would not say *witch* so much. *Folk need a foe,* she told me*, and they have their foe already. See?* I saw. Some people fight Campbells, or papists, or the English, or women who live on their own. But Thorneyburnbank? They fought these night-time marauders, these varlots. These Mossmen.

A week before an unknown lady with a blood-red skirt came into the village, a farmstead was reived. A dozen geese were thrown in a sack, and stolen. Local men rode after the sound of a dozen white geese in foul tempers, but the Mossmen knew the windings, the places no-one knew. The geese were gone, plucked, roasted before the men had saddled up, most likely. And the farmer had no beasts now, except for an old bull.

So when Cora slipped through the falling light, with her tangled hair, she heard *halt! Stay there! Show yourself!* She wept. She talked of her own bereaving ten miles away—her lost cows, her dead man. *May I find shelter with you? In the Lord's name?* Cora could jaw well, and lie better. And the men saw her prettiness, and how long her lashes were—how she looked from behind in those skirts of hers.

So she lived in Thorneyburnbank with its wild, cold wind and singing water.

Our cottage was by a burn. It was a reedy, whispering burn which met the river Allen and later the river Tyne—rivers meet rivers like fingers meet hands. It was so close to the water that its floor was marshy, and its roof was bright with fish that had jumped, stuck. Cora found it half-lost to holly and liked this, for holly is said to hold the lightning back. So she let the holly grow. She swept the floor of fishes' scales and she went to church—for to not go to church was to shine a light upon her. It was darkness she wanted, and peace.

This is how she was in the beginning. Tidy, and quiet. She made her pennies from reeds and rushes for thatch—for there were many growing by the burn. And there is always a need for rushes in a land where the wind is hard, and so are the men who come raiding.

She sold them in Hexham, and smiled at men. She was as sweet as a pear, or let them think it. Cora wore her cross on its chain, to fool them, and she took Christ's body into her mouth on Sundays, kept it under her tongue for an hour or two until she could spit it out. What a piece. Who would have known that as she was seated on her pew, with her head bowed, she thought of full moons and thumbs-and-toes tied?

It is a shame Cora did not stay pear-sweet—for she did not.

She was always a night-time lady. The wolf in her howled for night air, and so she took herself away into the unknown parts. If she was seen, she'd say *I am a widow. I grieve out in the darkness* . . . and this would satisfy them for a while. But it was an odd grieving—lifting her skirts, throwing back her hair.

I won't talk too much of it. Nor did she—snapping out *hush up!*
What I do is what I *do, not you* . . . before running bright-eyed into the
night. All I will say is what harm did she do? What trouble? She had a
beauty which lured men to meet her by the Romans' wall, and they
grappled in the gloaming or held each other back. They sought themselves, somehow. And when the sky lightened, she re-tied her bodice,
shrugged, and wandered home with the birds singing about her, and
her hair undone.

I never knew my father, Mr Leslie.

Nor did Cora. Or not for more than a moment or two.

I know this says *whore* to you. *Slattern. Old jade.* They are names
she gave herself sometimes, and laughed, and how she is remembered
in Hexham is as a *witch* and a *whore.* They think it's right that they
stretched her neck like they did. But I don't think these things.

What she did, Mr Leslie, was not bad. More badness was done years
before, when she was a little one—in a river, with her mother snared
like a bird.

Cora had her feelings on love.

Do not feel it, she told me. She took my wrist, or my chin in her
hands and said *Never feel it. For if you love, then you can be hurt very sorely
and be worse than before. So don't love,* she said. *Do you hear me?* She made
me repeat what she said.

That's a sad story, is it not? It is to my ears—a woman as fair-faced
as Cora being afraid of love. So don't call her a *whore,* thank you. Not
my mother. She found her comfort in deep-furred cats, and the moon,
and the fireside, but also in kisses from unknown men. Who did this
hurt? Nobody.

We all need our comforts. Things which say *hush* . . . and *there,*
now.

So her belly swelled. It fattened liked the berries did. But what filled her head? Some fierceness. She took off her cross and stepped out from the cottage of fish and holly as she was—not a widow, but a woman of bad weather. A person who did not like *God*. His word was *justice,* she said, and what a ripe lie that was, with its trapdoors and screws.

Mr Pepper in the church spoke of forgiveness. On the Sabbath he said *we are all from the Lord*—but folk ignore what doesn't suit them. They hissed, *her? With child? And without a man by her side?* They brought their rushes from someone else after that—a lazy wife who cut them wrong, so they cankered. But this wife prayed and read the Bible, so her bad reeds were better than clean ones from that slattern in the dark-red skirt. It did not matter. Cora had her means. She told future times in Hexham's wynds and shadows. She gave herbs to the women who needed it—fern, lovage. It's always the women.

That was a merciless winter. One of frosts and white breath. Old Man Bean left to hunt the pheasants and was not seen again. Cora knew the cold called out to the Mossmen. They came for food and wood to burn, and a Scotchman with a yellow beard stole two cows away, and a dog, and a kiss from the milkmaid. Cora was glad. It was all eyes to the north once more, and none on her belly like a bramble fattening up.

Oh she loved the Mossmen. She tightened her fists with glee at the sound of their hooves on the frost—*da-da, da-da*. She loved their moonless nights, and the smell of their torches flaming as they rode. And on Christmas Eve, as they galloped to Hexham with their backswords held high, my mother took her body out into the yard. She roared with two voices. She steamed in the dark, and I fell onto the ice.

Witch, she called me, for she knew it would follow me for all my days.

Then, she cradled me, kissed me. Said *but Corrag's your true name.*

THAT was me. My beginning.

I lived on old fish and sour milk, for months. If I cried, she lay me down amongst the reeds and I would sleep—maybe it was wind sounds, or the wet. *Ghost baby* she called me, because of my eyes which are pale and wide. I crawled in the spring-time elm wood. I walked in the next summer, by the cherry tree. Later, still, I'd sit on a fallen log by the church and ride it—my wet, wooden horse. I had ivy for reins, and a saddle of leaves.

Autumn was also good for mushrooms. She showed them to me like she showed me herbs—*this one is for sickness. This brings poisons out. And these ones . . .* she'd say, twirling a stalk before my eyes, *are for supper! Let's run home and cook them!* And we would run, hair out.

Still. Winters were best.

And they were hard ones in Thorneyburnbank. A duck froze on the burn—it squawked until a fox came, and left its webbed feet in the ice. There were icicles we sucked, Cora and I. The millpond could be walked on, and once, a tree broke from all its snow and buried a cow—they had to dig for it with spades and hands. All night they dug, and the cow lowed so crossly that they did not hear the Mossmen taking horses from the forge. Also, one winter, there was a wooden box— put beneath the yew tree, and not buried, for the ground was too dark, iron-hard. The box was broken by dogs and crows who knew meat when they neared it. Poor Widow Finton. But she was dead and never felt it. All things must eat.

I saw the crows again in Hexham square.

That was the day they hung the Mossmen by the neck.

Five of them. I was maybe twelve years old when Cora came to me, her eyes on fire, and said *this is bad, very bad* . . . She meant for us—but not so bad that we stayed away from it. She knotted my cloak, and we trod through the snow to the town. And the sound! There were more folk in the square than when the judge came, or when the Christmas market did. All jeering and jabbering. I climbed on a barrel to see what they saw, which was the word *scaffold*. Five ropes in neat circles. It chilled me in a way no snow had done. And the crowd laughed at the men who stood by their ropes with their hands trussed up behind. *These* I thought *are Mossmen.* Just men with scars, and sad eyes. The yellow-bearded one was there. He saw the crows, like I did—perched on the scaffold, cleaning their wings. I felt so sorry for him. I thought I could hear his thumping heart, his quick breath, and the crowd cheered when the ropes were put over the Mossmen's heads. *Bang* went the door, and *bang* went the next, and *bang* and *bang* and the last man was crying for mercy. *Sorry for my sins,* he pleaded, and shook. And maybe the door was bolted still or the cold had frozen it, I don't know, but it didn't open—so they took him to a rope that had a Mossman hanging from it, and they cut the dead man down and strung the live one up and used that rope again.

Folk need a foe.

Cora muttered this. She also said, *I should have known . . . For did you see the bats? Did you, Corrag? All gone* . . . They'd flown away the day before. They'd streamed out from beneath the bridge with their leathered wings, and not come back—and Cora said that creatures do this, before a death. Like weather, they feel it coming. They sense trouble in their wings, their paws, their hooves—and flee.

Foe . . . she said. She scattered bones by the hearth that evening, tore herbs so our cottage smelt green. I knew what troubled her. All my life, she had sung *let them raid!* But they did not raid as they hung with the frost on them, and crows pecking by.

. . .

LATER, Cora fell on the floor and arched her back up. She had the second sight this way—the sight I didn't have. I knew to stay by her, and stroked her hair until it passed.

When she sat up, she whispered, *do I have a gallows neck?*

It was late. I was sleep-heavy, and she looked strange to me—fear, I think it was. She held up her thick, black hair, said *do I? Say the truth.*

I always did. So with the hearth being the only sound, for the burn was frozen and the owl was silent that night, I said the truth to her. She knew it, too.

A pretty neck, but yes—it was gallows-made.

⁊ﹸ──◀▆▶──ﹸ⁊

Spring came in. Water sounds all over—the burn roared with snow-melt. Up came the clover in the marshy parts which made sweet milk, and cattle fat. This is when I took the knife to the pig and killed it—a terrible thing. I think I was taken with some spring madness, or it was the Mossmen's deaths in me. I don't know. But Cora was cross. She said why kill it in spring when we had made it through the winter, and was I a simpleton? The meat did not sit well in my mouth, or my stomach. Poor pig.

Full of shame, I ran away. I hid in the elm wood all day, crouching by a log, and when I rose up in the dusky half-light I did not see the log, and fell. *Pop!* A neat sound by my shoulder. Then, a pain—a huge, hot pain, so that I stumbled back to Cora with my right arm very mangled, and my shoulder pushed high up. I wailed, as I ran. *The pig's revenge* said Cora dryly, and she pressed my bone back in its proper place. *Pop* again. And marjoram was laid upon it, which can help.

And things grew. The crops grew well, that year. That made Cora's purse clink, for women were making babies with all that corn in them.

Mostly it was feverfew, for the easy birth. Comfrey dried up old milk. She sent me out for fern, also, and told me how to cut it—with a single slice, and thinking kind thoughts. Fern has its dark powers—for the secret cleansing of a woman, shall we say.

And creatures made babies too—calves, and chicks that went *peep*. There was a striped cat too whose teats were like thumbs, who purred when I stroked her. She was good. But one day, with dandelions blowing, I saw her lying on the ground. There was a bucket by her, and Mr Fothers in his hat. He was staring at the bucket, and then he marched away—and I thought *why is the striped cat so still? The lovely striped cat?* I straightened my back. *So very still . . .* And then I thought *run!* I had such a fear in me that I threw my dandelion away and ran, and in the bucket I found water, and five dark newborn kittens mewling for their lives. Their paws scraped the metal. Their eyes were closed, so I pushed the bucket over, said *wake up! Don't die!* They rolled into their mother, who was dead and not purring now.

Cora, when I carried them home, said, *what happened to them? So tiny . . .* And in a lower voice she hissed *who did this?* For she had a proper hatred of people drowning things.

We fed them. We laid them by the fire and dropped cow's milk on their tongues. I sang ancient songs to them like they were my own, and Cora said *how dare that man? How dare he? A life is a life—each life . . .* She narrowed her eyes at his name. She kicked the kettle and it bounced outside. But she softened when she stroked the kittens, and felt their grainy tongues against her hand. Mr Fothers hated creatures but we never did.

They lived—all five. They were meant to drown on a dandelion day but they did not. Instead, they grew into quick, ash-coloured cats with eyes as green as mint is, and they rubbed against our shins, tails up. I liked how their gentle heads would butt against my own. In time,

they sniffed out the fish in the thatch. I remember them that way—
high up in the rafters, crunching the bones of the stranded fish, their
noses silvery with scales.

MAYBE I should not have saved them—those cats. They brought more
than dead mice to the doorstep, in the end.

Mr Fothers started it. Maybe he didn't like how I saved those five.
Cats, he said? *Green-eyed?* And he spoke bad words about me, like how
I squatted in bogs. Like how, one twilight, I'd shifted into a half-bird
and screamed my way home from the elm wood. *Her right arm was a
wing . . . This is true.*

So it went. Small things which once meant *reivers*—no moon, or
worms in the miller's flour—no longer meant *reivers,* for the reivers
were dead. Who, then, caused this? Where was the blame? People were
quiet, at first. People bit on their tongues.

It was *king* that made it worse. The proper trouble started then—in
the year that King James fled away to France, and in his place came
the Orange, Protestant one with his very black wig. He sat on the
throne still warm from James, and England called this *glorious. What a
revolution!* they said. But Cora didn't think so. She sucked her bottom
lip. She looked at stars for a long, long time. One night, I tugged her
sleeve. I asked, *what does this mean?* And she shook her head, said *trouble,
I reckon—that's what it means. Kings always do.* And it did. For *king* makes
blood boil over. It makes the air feel thick, and strange, and so just as
the wind span the weathervane, so eyes turned to look at the cottage
by the burn with its holly and bog-water.

Slowly, there was more.

Small doings. A calf was born with a white star on its head—neat,
and clear. Very pretty. But curious, too, so it was talked of—*a marked
calf . . .* said the men. *How uncommon.* And then Mr Dobbs, whose field

the calf was in, took to sneezing all day and all night. Cora said it was the air being full of flowers—but no one else thought so. And an owl screeched down from the church tower at midnight, and the cherries from the cherry tree were tarter than most years. A rat was seen on the half-moon bridge. And in late summer, when the air was heavy with heat and no wind, and the skies flashed with a storm, Mr Vetch's affections moved away from his wife and onto the fair-haired buxom girl who sold ribbons, in Hexham. Mrs Vetch was distraught. *He's lost his mind,* she wailed. Out in the street, wringing her doughy hands, she wailed, *it's a bewitching! A madness! Surely, it is . . .*

We watched this. Cora and me.

That word . . . she whispered. And she glanced up at the rumbling skies.

It took a day or so. But *witch* came in.

Whore, said Mr Fothers, as my mother walked by.

In church, Mr Pepper did his best. He said *we are God's children and He loves us all the same*. But it stopped nothing. It did not calm Cora, who stood outside at night. She said *what is coming? Something comes . . . I feel it.* Then Mr Fothers said that Cora stole his grey mare when the moon was full. He said the horse sprouted wings, and they flew to the Devil and back. A flying horse? A flying lie is better. But he locked the mare up every full-moon night, and rode a brown cob instead. It kicked out at shadows, and snorted—but Mr Fothers preferred to risk his neck on the brown horse than his eternal soul on the mare.

HATE her? Cora? Oh he did.

I don't know why. Her beauty perhaps. Her power, and her knowledge of the world, which was so strong that I felt it, as she passed—it brushed my skin, like breath. Maybe he heard of her meetings with unknown men by the Romans' wall and he longed for that—to be such a man. To untie her bodice in the northern dark. But how could he? Being married, and church-going? Nor would my mother have let him. She said he had a chicken's look about him—with a loose chin, and a look like everything was worth a peck or two. *Foul man* she called him. *Fowl*.

I see the goodness in most people, for most people are good. But his was hard to see.

He drowned the striped cat in a bucket. He threw stones at me. His wife was meek as a duckling is, and once she bought groundsel from Cora for a bruise that was damson-dark. It was hand-shaped, too— Cora told me. Mrs Fothers blushed, said she had fallen—*clumsy me!*— but we knew this wasn't from falling. The poor lady tried for hemlock once but Cora didn't keep it. That's a very final herb—it kills you, and not kindly. Cora felt very sorry for Mrs Fothers' lonely life.

These are proofs of Mr Fothers' wickedness.

He beat his grey mare also.

And he killed my mother. I know it—here, inside.

I shall bring this all together like if I was sewing.

William sat on the throne. He was a wheezy king, and like he'd sent his wheezing out on horseback to the north, a consumption came up northern parts. Word came up of people dying foully in York. Cora said she had no herb to cure it if it came to Thorneyburnbank. So we waited. It never came to my knowing. But Mr Pepper fell down dead in church—from a tired heart, most likely—and folk muttered *pest*. Cora was restless and stood waist-deep into the burn. She eyed me very strangely and had no sleep in her.

They buried Mr Pepper under an oak which dropped its leaves on his box, like it was crying. And the new churchman who came in wore eye-glasses above a dark moustache. He was young and had the look of rats in him—all whiskers and quick-moving.

Ah said Cora seeing him.

There is worse than pestilence in our mortal world. There is falling from the sight of the God. There is the Devil's work. There are those who know the Devil's ways and is it not our duty to cleanse the earth? To rid it of such sinners?

Then there was a baby which came out blue, and dead.

Also, a hare was seen in the fields, washing its ears, and the moon rose behind it so that the whole village saw it—a hare, and a full, white moon . . .

Cora sniffed. She took me in her arms.

She kissed me over and over, and in my heart I thought *not long now.* For I had also seen the starlings flying west—a ball of them, rolling far away from us—and we slept side by side in those last few nights. Our hair tangled up, and blue-black.

A DOG barked in the village. And that night, Cora pushed the cats from my bed, grasped my hair in her fist and said *Wake up! Wake now!* I woke. I saw her eyes were very wide. She pulled me from my bed by my hair and I cried out, and was scared.

She said, *take my cloak. Take this bread. Take this purse, Corrag—it has all my herbs in it. Every herb I ever picked, or knew, is in this purse, and it is yours now. Keep it safe. Promise me?*

I looked at the purse. Then I looked at her—into her eyes which were shining.

And Corrag, a horse waits—outside, in the marsh. She grazes there, and you must take her and ride her. Go north-and-west. Ride fast, and hard, and you will know the place that's meant for you, when you find it—and on finding it, stay there. She put her hand against my cheek. *My little ghost baby . . .* she said.

The dog's bark came again, but closer.

I said, *are you coming too?*

She shook her head. *You are going alone. You are leaving me now, and you must not come back. Be careful. Be brave. Never be sorry for what you are, Corrag—but do not love people. Love is too sore and makes life hard to bear . . .*

I nodded. I heard her, and knew.

She fastened her cloak on me. She smoothed my hair, put up its hood.

Be good to every living thing, she whispered.

Listen to the voice in you.

I will never be far away from you. And I will see you again—one day.

I wore her herby purse about me. I wore her dark-blue cloak which dragged on the ground, and I hid crusts and a pear in its sleeve. Outside, in the cold night-time air, I found Mr Fothers' grey mare hock-high in the rushes. I mounted her, and looked to the cottage with the fish in the roof and the holly and my mother stood before it, red-skirted and black-haired, with a grey cat sitting by her, and that was my mother. That is Cora for always now.

Ride, she said. *North-and-west! Go! Go!*

We galloped into the dark, over heath and moor. I took the mare's mane for she had no reins on her, or saddle. I saw the ground beneath us rushing by. I was all breathless and afraid. At the Romans' wall we rested for a time. The world was very quiet, and the mist was less. The stars were out and I never saw such a starry night—it was like all the sky was with us as we went north, and all the earth's magick also. I spoke to the wall. I told it of Cora, and I told it I was scared. *Keep us safe?* I asked it. *I am scared.* I think the mare heard me for her ears were forwards, and her mouth was very gentle when she took the pear from my hand.

We crossed the wall by a lone sycamore.

Then we rode amongst trees for a very long time. I don't know when we crossed into Scotland, but it was somewhere in those woods. I patted the horse, and saw that all I had now in the whole world was a cloak, a purse, two crusts of bread and Mr Fothers' old grey mare.

<hr />

This is my final stitch tonight.

Cora. Who thought the pricking men might take her but no, the gallows did.

I don't know this for certain. But I think they snared her that night, and a few weeks later they tied her thumb-to-thumb. I think she said nothing. I think she was strong, and defiant, and knew the realm was waiting for her so why be afraid? I don't think she was afraid. I think she shook her hair free from the rope around her neck, and looked up at the sky, for she always looked up at the windy autumn skies. And then the trapdoor banged twice against its hinges, and she heard a crunch in her ears, and I wonder what she saw, in her last mind's eye—if it was me, or her mother sinking under.

I also think that Mr Fothers saw it. I think he went home with a quietness inside him that had no name, and it grew in the weeks that followed. He saw Cora's cottage be lost to the holly and storm-water. He thought of her with newborn calves or cherries, or with a lightning bolt that lit up the fields very briefly so that all things looked white and strange.

He found his stable empty and thought *Cora did this.*

When her cats slunk by him, his heart creaked open like a door.

Dear Jane

I am tired tonight, my love. Not in body, as such—as I was when we rode here, through the drifts and wind. But my mind is tired, which some may say is a far greater fatigue. I was grateful to leave that cell, and looked forward to the peace that a good fire and solitude can bring—and does bring, as I write this. I am glad of the hearth—a little light and warmth. I am also glad of this proper chair, for that three-legged stool that I perch upon in there is low, and may trouble my back, in time.

I was also glad of a meal. I did not think I had an appetite, after such an unsavoury place, but when I ate it restored me. Sometimes we are hungry when we think we are not.

You are, I am sure, anxious to hear of my latest encounter with the witch. I will tell you of it—but I will use less words than she did, for she talked more than I've ever done. I preach, Jane—I have preached, and written my pamphlets, and have I not been called the orator of the age? A generous name, perhaps. Yet I wonder if I have ever spoken as much as she speaks. Her talking is like a river—running on and bursting into smaller rivers which lead nowhere, so she comes back to her starting place. I listened to her and thought, is this madness? *How she uses her hands asks this question, as well—for she is rarely still. She talks with her hands up by her face, like she's catching her words, or feeling them as she speaks them. Can you see that? I am not one for description. My strength is in sermons, and not in decorative talk.*

I think this is what has tired me—her manner of speaking. It is chatter.

But also, what *she speaks! I am glad you were not there, my love. Such blasphemy! Such wicked ways! She sat there like a beggar—all rags and large eyes—and told me of so many ungodly things that I felt several feel-*

ings, amongst them revulsion and rage. Her mother sounds a dire piece—slatternly, is the kindest word. She (the mother) saw some unkind sights in her youth, but it does not excuse the wrong path she walked along in such a wanton way. Herbs are not to be dallied with. Prayer is the best cure, and a true physician—not this greenish alchemy that I won't abide. And this woman told lies, and hid her false face behind a church smile! She took the communion to hide her debauched ways.

I do not recall her name. I do not wish to recall it—for it is poisonous. But I'll say that the world is well to be rid of her.

Corrag defends her, of course. What harm did she do? I was minded to say plenty—an unfettered woman brings much trouble in. But I held my tongue.

I think this is why my mind is so tired, my love: I have endured an afternoon of rambles and offences which were of no benefit to our Jacobite cause. How can an English childhood bring James to the throne? Or some gabble on half-drowned kittens take William away?

Still. She promises she has news to help us—on Glencoe, and the deaths. If so, it is worth the endurance. And how else might I fill my afternoons, in such weather? It snows even more, now, Jane.

My landlord has the fine trick of appearing from air, spectre-like. On the stairwell this evening, he expressed shock at finding me upon there—when I am certain he was well aware. We exchanged pleasantries. But as I turned I heard and how is the wretch in the tollbooth? Helpful? Foul-smelling? They say she can turn into a bird . . . I was polite, Jane, but did not indulge him—not tonight, for his interest is rather tiresome, and the hour is late, and your husband is not as young as he was.

I will say this much more on Corrag. For all her wounds and tangles, and her squalid condition, and for all her prattling, her wickedness, and her restless hands, she can tell a tale. She has an eye which sees the smaller parts of life—how a tree moves, or a scent. It means I felt, briefly, as if I was in *this Thorneyburnbank where she lived. But I'll call this bewitchment—and resist it. It is further proof of her sin.*

Moreover, I hope this will not offend you, but her hair is like your hair. Not in its knots or thorns—of course not. But it has the same dark colour, the same length. I think of your hair's weight, when I last untied it. I watched her twist a strand of it about a finger, as she spoke, and I imagined you as a child—before we met. If our daughter had lived, I am sure she'd have had this same hair.

I will write more tomorrow. What would I do, in these hours, if I did not write to my wife? I would sit in the half-dark, and dream of you instead. If I did not have you at all, I would imagine the woman I'd wish for, as wife—and she would be you. Exactly as you are.

I marvel at your patience. I worry that you, too, worry—for my health, and protection. But do not be troubled. Am I not protected? Do I not have a shield? "The Lord himself goes before you, and will be with you; He will never leave you, nor forsake you" (Deuteronomy 31:8).

Write if you can.

Charles

II

"It is commonly found under hedges, and on the sides of ditches
under houses, or in shadowed lanes and other waste grounds,
in almost every part of this land."

of Ground Ivy

Last night, she was with me. When you had gone, she sat on the
stool and looked at me with her shiny bird-eyes. I said to her *I
spoke of you to a man today* and I reckon she knew. I thought of all the
things which belong to her, which make me think of her when I see
them, or hear them—thunder, rope.

Every herb I ever used, Mr Leslie, has had my mother in it. She
taught them to me. In the elm wood she plucked them, rubbed their
leaves. She boiled their roots, pressed their stems, and she said *do not
think that the small leaves are not useful. Sometimes they are the most useful
leaves of all* . . . I know what I know about leafy plants because she
knew them, and passed them on.

So when I saved lives, Cora saved them.

When I cured an ache, or sealed up a wound, Cora also sealed it.

NEVER *love* is what she told me. Sometimes I thought *then she surely
does not love me? If she says "do not love"?* I know she could be black-
tempered. I know that mostly she was daydreaming, and had a half-

smile to give—but sometimes a cloud came down upon her. It made her hiss in the cottage. She would run out into the rain to curse, and roar. She hated the word *justice,* and churches, and tore at her nails, and she smacked me, too, sometimes. When I said a bad word against her she put a teasel in my mouth and said *chew,* so that I'd learn the soreness of such words—and I'd think, chewing teasels, *this isn't kind.* I also thought *this isn't her* . . . Not the proper Cora.

Do not love . . . But I think she did love me. I think so. For she combed my hair at night, and when my shoulder popped itself she'd kissed it, said *poor old bones* . . . And one winter in Hexham we caught snowflakes and ate them, left our shapes in the deeper drifts. We sang old and naughty witch songs on our way home, and that was good. There was love in that.

But there was no other love—not for people, sir. She loved no man. Instead, she packed her heart away and let them take her like bulls take their cows—sighing onto the back of her neck. She never met the same bull twice. Nor did she ever meet them by day, in case they were handsome, and what if her heart broke out, and was free? I blame the ducking stool for that.

Ride north-and-west. Don't come back.

They may not sound much, to your ear—those words. But she did not have to say them. She could have let me sleep, on that night of dog-barking. Or she could have mounted the grey mare with me, and we could have fled together into Scotland, and forests, with our hair flying out.

But she said *ride north-and-west*—because she knew she would die.

She knew they would follow her—hunt her till they found her, and on finding her, hang her, and whoever she was with.

Be good to every living thing she said.

She died alone. Which was better in her eyes than dying with her daughter by her side.

. . .

Miss her? Sometimes. Like how I miss the soft, dreamless child's sleep that I once knew but don't, now. And I wish her death had not been murder, and I wished for a time that we'd had a better, true goodbye. But she is in the realm, now. It is a good place to be.

She said her own goodbye, much later.

It was dusk, in a pine forest. I looked up to see her ghost passing by. I knew she was a ghost, for ghosts are pale and very quiet, which she never was in life. She trod between the trees and glanced across at me. She looked so beautiful, and thankful, and this was her goodbye.

I thought of her at the Romans' wall. With the stars and silence. With the mare working quietly on the pear.

I thought of her too in the forest. There were small sounds like the wind high up, or a pine cone dropping down—and I thought maybe these sounds were Cora, like she was speaking to me. I listened for a while, thinking *is it you? Are you there?* And the wind shushed the trees which was like *I am here. Yes.*

I thought of how she'd crouched in wynds, selling herbs and secrets.

How she loved blackcurrants.

But what good are backward glances? They do not help. They cannot be helped, or do any proper helping. I had her with me. *I will never be far away from you.*

So I said *on with it*—I had to. I knew a life awaited me.

Mr Leslie. I am glad to see you.

I thought perhaps you'd not return today. For I know how my talking can be. I was always one for going on and on—for saying so much a person's eyes grow fish-like, and dead. Maybe it's the lonesome life I've had. I've been mostly out of doors, on my own, with no soul but my own to talk to—so when I have a person with me I talk and talk and talk.

Was I that bad? Were you tired last night?

I am glad that you are here again. With your folding table and your goose quill.

I know you do not care for what I tell you very much. What does a James-loving man want Hexham for, or grey mares, or Mossmen? He doesn't want them, I know. But I will give you what you need, in time.

⁕———⫶⫶⫶———⁕

The forest, then. The mare.

Mr Fothers' mare, the grey one he'd called *bewitched,* his *grizzled old nag.* He had locked her up with every full-moon and given her no water to drink, for Mr Fothers thought water called the Devil in. So she'd licked the walls, whinnied for rain. We took a pail to her, Cora and I. One night we held it to the mare and she sucked and sucked the water up. She blew hard through her nostrils, scratched her rump on the doorpost, and Cora said *she's too fine a horse for him.* Which was true.

Now I rode her.

I was on her back. *Me.*

I looked down. I had not fully looked on her before. I had patted her nose at the Romans' wall, and I'd pressed my cheek to her neck and clutched at her mane as she'd galloped. But we were not galloping now. We were treading through a forest, and I saw that she was a pretty horse—white-coloured on top, but with brown flecks on her hind parts and belly like she'd trodden on soft apples and they'd burst, speckled her. I felt how she swayed. She was wide like barrels, so my legs stuck out.

And she was tall. Maybe not to most people, but I am tiny-sized—
so she was big as a house to me. The ground seemed far, far down. I
learnt, in time, how mounting her was best to run a little, grab her
mane and heave. If she minded this she never said so. She might even
hold her foreleg up for me to step on which could be useful in hurried times when folk were shouting *witch*—and later I'd find hay or
fistfuls of mint and offer them to her, kind thing. I think my clamber-
ing up was far better than a fat man on her back with whips and spurs.
I'd once seen him jab her in the mouth so much with a horrid metal
bridle that her mouth frothed pink and her eyes rolled wild. Wicked
man. All I did to her mouth was fill it up with pears.

Nor was she quiet. I learnt this in those trees. She whickered at
things that pleased her and at things that did not. She blew through
her nose when I patted her, and sometimes she snored in her deep,
horse-sleep. And most of her life she was eating—brambles, nettles,
dock—so most of her life her belly grumbled at itself with all that
food inside it. Food makes air as we know. She could be very noisy
when that air found freedom. It's not decent to speak of this but she
could toot.

Yes I talk fondly. So would you.

Creatures do not care for *hag* or *witch*. It is what makes them so
wise and worthy—how they only mind if they are treated well or not.
That is how we should all live. The mare shook off *witch* like it was a
fly or a leaf that fell on her. She kicked the ones who tried to hurt me,
and she had a way of rubbing her head on my shoulders when I felt
lonesome. This made her nice to be with.

I was glad of her. I rode her through the forest and told her so.

I called her *my mare*. I put a kiss on my hand, pressed my hand to
her neck.

Not Mr Fothers' anymore, but mine.

. . .

WE WENT deeper in. What else might we do? *Don't come back* said Cora, and *north-and-west*. So we went deeper in.

It rained. It was *drip drip drip* from the branches, and *suck suck* from her hooves in the mud. We sheltered by upturned trees, or in a ruined cottage which was only mossy stones. And for eating we ate what we found—fir cones, and tree-roots. Berries. I took ants from tree-barks with my thumb, whispered *sorry* to them, ate them up. One day I fell upon some mushrooms which swelled like froth from the cleft of a log and I picked them, roasted them in garlick leaves and it was a meal of sorts. It tasted like Hexham—a man had sold them there and we'd bought a penny's worth, Cora and me, and gobbled them. So I thought of her, as I ate them. The mare ate dead-nettle and moss.

They were dark and wet days. When I think on them I think *sad,* and *dark,* and *wet.*

I did light fires, sometimes. It was hard, in all that dampness, to light one that didn't hiss or smoke blackly—but I did it once or twice. Once, we found a clearing that had a stream in it, and moss of such bright greenness that it glowed. There, by my fire, I unfolded Cora's purse. I laid them out, on rocks. There were hundreds of them—all tied with string, all with different natures and smells, and properties. Some were fresh, and still soft. Others seemed so old that they powdered, to my touch, and I wondered if she'd found them when she was much younger—in her own wandering times.

I thought *some herbs might be older than me.*

Mallow, chervil, goldenrod.

Campion and eyebright—which is rare, but worth looking for. It brightens eyes exceedingly.

I gathered them up, one by one. I folded them into my mother's cloth purse, and fastened it, and I said *these are her whole life's gatherings* to the mare, who listened carefully. So did the trees, and the gold-green moss.

I put the purse under my cloak, to keep it safe.

Then the mare reared. She whinnied.

Then I heard a bird go *flap flap flap* so I turned my head, thinking *what is . . . ?*

And I was grabbed.

I was grabbed very roughly, with an arm on my throat so I could not breathe—I could not breathe for the arm was so strong and I kicked, and grappled with it. The horse snorted. That bird went *flap.*

I could not breathe at all. My eyes sprang tears, and the arm lifted me clean up so my feet were off the ground and I had a small, cold moment where I thought *I will die here*—but then I thought *no I will not.* I was cross. I tried to scratch the arm but my fingernails were bitten so I reached behind to feel for this man's face or ears or hair. I found his hair. I pulled it very hard which did nothing, so I fumbled with his face and found his eyes. I pushed my thumbs right in. Eyes are soft. It felt like they burst under my thumbs and there was a yell, a holler, and he dropped me. I scrabbled away and heaved in air.

He wailed *my eyes my eyes!*

The mare squealed, and I coughed thickly. The man moaned *my eyes are bleeding, she's blinded me*—and so I knew he was not alone. I turned. Three of them. Three more men came out of the darkness like thoughts, but I knew they were real—they were muddied and strong-smelling, and in jerkins of such thin leather and so laden up with rusted blades and ropes that I thought *I know your kind . . .* I remembered. I saw a frosty morning. I saw five ropes swinging.

I stared at them. I looked at each face as I crept back towards the mare—one had a plum-coloured face like he was half-burnt, and he beckoned to me.

Give us your purse and we'll not harm you.

I shook my head. I was keeping Cora's herbs for always—for all my life.

We saw it. Give your money.

I said, *I have no money.*

He spat into a nettle bush. He stepped towards me more. *No one travels with no money.* Then he took a dirk out and growled again *your purse.* I heard his tongue's accent which was Scotch—I knew it well enough from peddlers on the roads who'd beckoned me. I'd bought a silver mirror from a Scotchman once because it was so pretty and Mother Pindle saw me do so. She'd spat out the word *Scotchman* like it was *whore* or *plague.*

I have no money!

He smiled quickly, like I was a joke to him. Then he came at me, lifted me right up and pushed me back against a tree. He struggled with me, seeking my purse so harshly that my teeth rattled, and I roared at him, and smacked his head.

Ha he said, finding it. Cora's purse.

He tugged it free and opened it, and out they went—radish, dock, lovage, fennel, comfrey, elderflower, sage. All over the forest floor.

I wailed. I dropped to my knees to gather them. It was like my mother was sprawled on the floor too, and for a while there was silence—just me saying *no no no . . .*

Take her horse, then.

I screamed. I ran to the mare who was head-up and walking back-wards, not liking this at all. I grabbed her mane but some Mossman had my leg so I could not mount her and the mare tried to carry me off, good girl. But the man had my boot, so I was stretched like on a rack and the ground was lying under me, and I knew I could not hold the mare much longer. I also knew that if I let go they would take her so I screamed *I'll curse you all! I will summon the Devil and he'll not like this at all!*

Well that was a fine trick.

They let me go like I was on fire. I hit the ground, scrambled to my feet and turned with my back to the mare and my arms stretched out like I was hiding her from them, keeping her safe. These four men could only stare at me—or rather three did, for the fourth was still crouching and saying *my eyes*. I slowed my breath, stared back. It was like all the forest had heard me, all the birds and insects, and I thought then, too late, that maybe saying witch-like things was foolish. I was running from witch-haters, and there were no doubt plenty more in this country. Rats can cross walls, after all. But it was said now. It was done.

Witch?

They looked at each other.

They looked down at the herbs, understanding them now.

There was a small hush, so I heard all our breathing and the rain going *drip*. Then they muttered in their own Scotch words. They looked on me for such a long time I felt hot, awkward.

I didn't say *yes I am*—for I've never called my own self *witch*. I held my tongue and scratched the mare's neck how she likes, to calm her.

How old are you?

I pouted. I was cross because they'd troubled her and because they'd made Cora's herbs fall out of her purse, and now they were treading on them, which was a proper waste and sadness.

This winter will be my sixteenth I said.

What's your business?

What's yours? Saucy of me. I can be, and that's Cora.

The plum-faced one considered me. *An English girl? In a woman's cloak? On a stolen horse?*

Maybe it was the softness which had come into his voice. Or the half-light. Or maybe it was my lonesomeness that made me talk to him—I don't know. But I said *my mother sent me away. They call her a witch, and hate her, and she will die soon, so she told me to flee north-and-west away from Thorneyburnbank so that they might not kill me, too. I* looked at the ground. *These were her herbs. They are mine, now—to sell, I think, and to keep me safe. They are all I have in the world—except for my wits, and my mare.*

This all came out in a rush. It was like my words were water and out they came, and now what? We all stood amongst my words like leggy birds in a stream. I was breathless, and a small part of me felt like being teary-eyed because I thought of Cora dying, but I wouldn't let them see it.

I thought *fool* to myself. No-one likes a chatterer. It's best to keep your mouth tied up, but I never did it.

It was even stranger, what was next.

They did not come to me. They did not grab my purse or my mare. It was like they were creatures who put their claws away because I had shown my proper face—like how the air is always better when the storm's come in and gone. We all looked upon ourselves, brushed our clothes of rain. I straightened out my skirts and tried to make my hair less of a thatch.

The plum-faced one said *hanging is a greater sin than most folk are hung for.* Like he was trying to comfort me.

I sniffed. I said *yes.*

He looked at me. *I know Thorneyburnbank* he said. *Near Hexham? Does it have a cherry tree?* And then he looked so sad, so empty and sad that I felt sorry for him, and had no fear at all. He looked about the ground at my herbs, and he said *what can you do? Can you mend?*

Some things.

Can you mend his eyes? For the poor one on the ground was still bloodied.

I said *I reckon so.*

How about sewing? Cooking?

These were not my best things but I could do them. I said *yes.*

He nodded. *Mend his eyes,* he said. *Mend my cough and that one's foot and sew a jerkin or two, and we'll give you some meat. And you can rest a while.*

He helped me to gather Cora's herbs, and put them in my purse.

I FOLLOWED them through the trees. I walked with the *drip drip* and my mare blowing her nose, and I whispered to myself, to her, to what it is that sees us and hears us—God, or spirits, or the hidden self, or all these things—*this, now, is my second life.*

It began as Cora's ended.

My second, galloping life.

———

They were ghosts, Mr Leslie.

Not spectres made of mist, and air—not lost souls. Just ghostly men. The last of their kind, for reiving days were gone. I'd thought all the Mossmen had been hung, or sent away. But here they were. With their sweat and goatskin boots.

They took me to a clearing of moss, and damp. A goat's leg boiled in a pot. A lone hobbler dozed beneath a tree, and three hens pecked in the dirt. The evening light was dusty, like it is in barns, and when I looked up I saw the evening star, shining through the trees.

Here. Some of the cooking water was given to me, in a cup.

I thought of how I used to be—of what I'd believed in, a few hours before, which had not been these things.

I MENDED his eyes that night. I was glad of the eyebright, and pressed it on with flaxweed, and said *hush, now,* and laid them on his lids. Then I also took a splinter out from a heel. For the cough, which rattled like pins in a pail, I took coltsfoot and warmed it up in milk. I said *sip this tonight, and your cough will go directly.* There is no herb better for the chest.

I ate a little goat's meat, which was good. The fire crackled. My mare dozed with the hobbler, side by side.

We've met ones like you, said the plum-faced one.

Like me? I looked up.

Runners. Hiders. These woods are full of folk who are hunted for things—small and big things. He put goat in his mouth, and chewed. *For a still-born child. A wild heart. Faith.*

I nodded. *My mother's heart is wild.*

He looked up. *But she doesn't run with you?*

No. Because they would follow her. They would follow her, and find her, and find me too. It made my eyes fill up with tears which I think he saw.

We are the same—you and us. You might think we are not, but we are. Our ancestors are mostly dead by the hangman's doing. We also live by nature's laws—which are the true laws. He shook his head. *Man's laws are not as they should be.*

I agreed to this. I ate.

We're Mossmen, he said. *My father's father was a reiver, and my father was—and I am the last of them. But where they raped and burnt—and I know they did, God forgive them—I've only ever taken what I needed to, and no more. An egg. Perhaps a lamb. And only from the rich.* He eyed me, as if he wanted me to nod at this. Then, to himself, he said *they call us murderers but I've not killed a soul. Not even hurt one.*

Like Cora, I said. *They blamed her for a baby that came out blue.*

Not her fault?

No.

The fire lapped on itself. I heard the mare's belly rumble, which was the hay in her.

Thorneyburnbank . . . he said. *Yes, I know it. Clover. It had the sweetest cattle when I was a boy. A half-moon bridge. That cherry tree . . .*

They were good cherries.

He nodded. *They were. My brother liked them. He liked all of it.*

The whole tree?

The whole village. With its fat cows. Its stream full of fish. The folk too . . . He threw a piece of grass into the fire. *My brother said they were sour. That they were sour to each other, and that thieving from sour people was less sinful than thieving from the good.*

Some were kind I said, sharply. I thought of Mrs Fothers with her hand-shaped bruise. Mr Pepper who had never minded Cora's ways, or mine.

He wiped his chin with his forearm. *Some. There's always a star or two, on dark nights, I'll say that. But . . .* He looked into the fire, then. He looked so hugely, deeply sad that I wanted to ask him of it—but I did not need to ask. He said, *we took from there. When I was younger, we took some geese from there. Then my brother wanted more, so he rode back for two plump cows. He took them from a farmer who beat his herd with sticks until they bled, which wasn't good. I was there. I helped him.* He held up his fingers. *Two cows. We never took more than we needed, and never left a person with nothing at all.*

What then? I asked this. But I think I knew.

They rode out a third time. He shook his head. He was quiet for a long time, so that I heard the wind move high above us. I smelt the pines, and the smoke. *Hung by the neck in Hexham. Three years ago, this winter.*

I saw it. I was there again, and saw it—the crow waiting, and the crowd's cheer as the doors went *bang.*

Was his beard yellow?

He glanced over. *Yes. You saw?*

I did not tell him I often saw it, in my head—the one, small bounce when the rope reached its end. *They were all your men?*

My brother, an uncle, three friends.

. . .

HE said no more on this. He said no more at all that night—only *you can sleep soundly here,* which I believed. And I did sleep soundly—beneath my mother's cloak, breathing night-time air.

But no, there was no more, on those deaths. I know some people think that to talk of others dying is not right—that it makes them die a second time. Maybe he thought his brother died a new death that night, by the fire, with goat's meat in our mouths. He had looked so woeful. He'd rubbed at his eyes. And thieving is wrong—even a hen, or turnip or two—but not much deserves the scaffold, and these men never did.

I'm sorry I said.

He nodded. *We took two cows and they took five lives.*

I don't think to talk of how people died makes them die twice-over, though. I think it keeps them living. But we all think different things.

He was the one I knew. Him with the reddish bloom on his face which I reckoned came with his birth—and which no herbs could fade. It ran from his brow, over one eye. It was plum-coloured, and shiny, and Cora would have liked it. She liked differences. She said true beauty lay in them.

The other Mossmen kept in shadows, or slept, but the plum-faced one stayed near me—as if he wanted to. Maybe he did. Maybe he felt closer to his brother by being with a girl who'd seen his bad death. I don't know.

Are you coming? he'd ask.

Where to?

Into the forest, always. He trod old paths. He led me to streams which silvered with fish, and we gathered berries there, and fire-wood. *This,* he said, *is how to catch the fish*—and it was slowness that did it. He moved his hand so slowly that the fish thought it was weed until it scooped it up, into the air, with *there! See?* He showed me how to smoke it, and lift it from its bones. I whispered *thank you* to the fish, as I ate it—and the Mossman smiled a little, said *Corrag—it cannot hear you now.* By the fire he showed me how to skin a rabbit, how to use its fur. We mended the small roof which we all huddled under, in hard rain—with moss, and thick branches. He showed me how. And one day I said *do you know about mushrooms at all?* Which he did not. So I took him out to the dankest parts and gave him their names, showed him their pale, velvet underskirts—and I was glad of this, for I felt I'd been taking more than giving, and I like giving more.

And he was the best for stories. He had many—so many. Maybe he knew that I loved strange and wild tellings, for when we picked this-tles out of manes together, or shook trees to bring the grubs down, or sat by the fire with broth, he'd speak of them. I'd say *tell me of . . .* And some tales were of such wonder that I could not breathe, with them. Unearthly, whispering tales—of red-coloured moons, or a boy who spoke more wisdom than any grown man could, or of a green, north-ern light in the sky. Of an eggshell with three eggs inside it. He spoke of how he fell, once, with a wound and woke to find a rough tongue licking his blood away—a fox's tongue. *A fox?* I said. But he was sure of it.

He had reiving tales in him, too. Not his own—for he said he had never reived in the true sense of it. *But my father, and his father, and his . . . Their times were brutal times—hiding, raiding, creeping in the dusk, fighting with March-wardens, breaking free from cells . . . They burnt all the farmsteads they reived from so the night sky was orange. Filled with sparks.*

Like the sun had come early, I said. But what I also thought was *why?*

Why would a man choose such a life? To butcher and burn? To hurt other souls. It made no sense to my small ears, and had no good in it—I said so. *There are other ways to live.*

He sighed. *Aye—perhaps. But it was always the way in these parts. Such hatred in the air . . . You could smell it in the wood-smoke, and hear it in the wind . . . Still can. A Scot may cut an Englishman down but he'd give his own life for the Scot by his side, and so it is in England, also. That hasn't changed in my lifetime. Nor will it. There's been too much fighting and slyness to ever clean the air of it.* He shook his head. *Politics . . .*

This made me think. In the dusk and in the dripping trees, I said *Scotland* to myself. If it was not for their accents, this place felt like England to me.

Slyness?

He turned his eyes to look at me. He narrowed them. *You don't know much of countries, do you? Of thrones? Loyalties?* He shook his head a little. *If you're going north-and-west, my wee thing, you should know more than you do.*

WE SAT by the fire, that night. I stitched at a jerkin which was half-undone, and as I sewed he told me what he called *must-knows,* and *truths.*

Scotland is two countries.

I pricked my thumb. *Two? Scotland? Two?*

England says one. But England's wrong about that. Highland and Low-land, he told me. *Like two different worlds.* He threw on a pine branch, and out came its smell—sweet, and like Christmas.

Which one is this? That we're in?

These are the borders, he said. *Which is its own country too, in many ways. But they lead into the Lowland parts not far from here—and the Lowlands are green, and lush. More people live in them. They are civil people, too, or so they like to say. They say they're more learned, more wise of the world than the rest. They speak English as we do. 'Tis the regal part—the Queen Mary who is dead now rode to her Bothwell's castle, near here, and there is Edinburgh which is reekie and tall but that's a true city.* He shook his head. *I'll never see it. Carlisle's as big as I'll see in my life.*

That's big. Cora said so.

But not like Edinburgh is. They say its castle is so high that you might see London from it. It's where they hung a bishop from the palace walls, and every new king or queen rides the Royal Mile so the crowds may cheer and wave at them.

I don't like kings I said.

I'm not too fond myself. But most Lowlanders are favouring this new Orange king, and—he pointed—*you should remember this.*

I scowled. It was the Orange king's wheezes that had helped to put *witch* on Cora, and I sewed very firmly. I tugged my needle through.

But the Highlands . . .

I glanced up.

They are another world. I have never seen them either—they are far, far to the north and I'm too old to see them now. But they say it's a properly wild place to be. Wind and rain, and bogs, and wolves calling. And 'tis a fiercer folk who live in that wild land, for it takes a hardy soul to survive it.

Hardy?

Aye. Savage. No laws—or not the laws that Lowland folk live by. They have their own language. Their own faith. He sipped from his broth. He found a bone in it, plucked it out, looked at it. Then he put it in the fire, said *they are hated.*

By whom?

Lowland hates Highland like horses hate flies. You'll see that, soon enough.

Why?

He shrugged. *For being lawless. For having their Catholic ways. They say the Highland parts weigh this nation down . . . That the clans are barbarous.*

They scrap amongst themselves, is what I hear—and there are many known
rogues up there. Even I know of them—me! Down here! The MacDonalds,
mostly.

Who?

A clan with as many branches as a tree has. The Glencoe ones are spoken
of plenty—their flashing blades . . . Thieving.

I did a stitch. I thought of how little I knew of the world. Of how
far away my old life was, with its holly, and frogs in marshes. It seemed
a good life, briefly—that Thorneyburnbank one. I had known it, and
its people. I'd not met a person who spoke a language of their own.
This life, now, seemed harder. More shadows to pass by.

I was quiet for a time. Then I whispered *what of us? Of people like*
me? What does witch *mean here? They hang them or drown them in pools,*
where I'm from. Or they try them by a judge, and do not kill them—but they
are called witch *for forever, then, and have stones thrown at them all their*
lives.

He watched me. How he looked at me made me wonder if he'd
ever had a child at all—for it was the kind of gentle look a parent
gives. It was partly sad. Maybe he wished I might have more than
this—more than *witch,* and sewing jerkins in a wood. He rubbed his
plum-red patch with the heel of his hand. *There were fevers in my youth,*
I'll say that. Witch-hunting times—as there were in the south. They burnt a
woman in Fife and in the market square they trod on a wetness that must
have been her. Her body. Maybe he saw my face, for he said very quickly
that was east. That was out in fishing villages, where it's been worst. So don't
go east.

How is north-and-west?

He drank, chewed his broth. He swallowed. *Aye. That might be best.*
You may be safest in the wild parts—for Highlanders are hated more than
you'll ever be, I think.

I nodded.

I wanted blowing skies. To be where wolves still called.

RIDE north-and-west, Cora had said. She'd had the second sight, maybe, and knew. *Don't come back. North-and-west.*

Aye, I said, like he did. And I mended the jerkin, so he looked smart in it.

Sir, I tell you these things so you know, too. You need to know—how Scotland is. Maybe you do know—how it is two countries, with low parts hating high. Civil hating savages. Cities hating glens.

Highland and Lowland. Write that down.

Write also, of this.

That it was as I lived with those Mossmen that my mother died. I saw it in my head. I was knelt by a pool, drinking from cupped hands, when I saw my reflection and I thought briefly it was her. The water flashed about her. Light flashed about her neck, so I knew. I knew her time was done.

Here is what I think. That a rope was placed tenderly over her head, by tender hands—like the hangman half-loved her, and did not want her gone. Her hair blew about her. Her thumbs were tied neatly behind her back, and in the last few moments she looked up at the sky and thought *it is so beautiful . . .* I also looked up. I saw the swaying trees, and the grey clouds rolling by. I breathed in, as she breathed in. I closed my eyes.

Mr Leslie, I sent all the love I'd ever had to her. I sent it to England, wanting it to find her so that she might die on the scaffold feeling loved. By me.

Tell her I am living. Tell her I am safe.

That night, I saw her ghost.

She came into the clearing with her thumbs untied, and her red skirts rustled as she came. She was in the realm, where no harm is. She looked across, and smiled.

So yes, I know she is dead. I know the river claimed her cottage in the months that followed, that all traces of her life are gone—except for me.

⁂

I was with them for three months—for three moon-turns. Three times, I saw it grow from a thin, pale crescent through the trees above my bed to a heavy fruit-like moon, which I might pluck, and hold. I mended those eyes in September; it was frosty by the time I left, with my belly full of meat and their songs in my head. For they sang old thieving songs by that fire—of love, and lost love.

He taught me many things. Scotland was two countries—two faiths, two tongues. How to skin a rabbit with one pull. He gave me a dirk, for keeping. He gave me *the MacDonalds are a savage sept,* to also tuck away.

But maybe the best thing I learnt was this: that we cannot know a person's soul and nature until we've sat beside them, and talked. For *Mossman* once meant *trouble.* Now, it means sadness, and goats.

What if I had not met them? We can always ask those things. If they had not seen me and my purse, what now? I might have been bolder in Lowland parts, and found my death that way. I might have not found the Highlands—not ever. Not found *him,* or Glencoe.

Alasdair. There he is, now. In my head.

Did I know he was waiting? Did my heart feel him, even then?

That is fanciful talking, I know. But as soon as the plum-faced Moss-man said *Highland* to me, I thought *there . . . There! That is the place!* Where the people are wild, and the trees are wind-buckled, and there are lochs which mirror the sky. Where men live crouching down, waiting. Where I might live as I am.

Go there. Move on.

AND I did. In the end, I slipped away.

A quiet night-time wind moved the trees, and made me think *north-and-west*. Of my mother's eyes.

I knew I had to go. So as the first frost settled, I rose up. I pulled my cloak about me, beckoned to my mare. I looked at the four men sleeping on the ground. They were under their cloaks, breathing—and I listened to their breath for a time. I said *thank you*. I put *thank you* in the air, and hoped it would hang there, so they might hear it when they woke to find me gone.

I laid heartsease by him with the plum-coloured face—for it is rightly named, and strengthens the heart, and comforts it. He was the best to me.

And we galloped.

I had no reins for her, so I clutched her mane, said *go!* Out of the forest, over white-crusted fields, and under a sky of so many stars that I smiled a little, as I held tight. I felt her warmth, heard her snorting as we went, and I knew that this was a true witch's leaving—by night, and secretly.

Sometimes we have so much to say, we cannot say it. Sometimes it is best we do not say goodbyes.

Jane

I grow more familiar with this town. Every morning, after my breakfast of smoked fish, I take a walk about it with my coat buttoned up, and my muffler on. I am careful, of course—for there are sideways winds on this coast, and they are strong enough to unsteady a man. I am careful too of the snow. It gathers in corners, and on roofs. I keep away from porches in case a gust of wind drops a weight of snow on me—which would assist neither my cough nor my humour.

Despite the weather, it is a handsome place. My walk takes me past a castle and a fine church, and the market place is of such a size that all of the townsfolk might be there, and still move freely. (In its centre, there is a barrel or two, and wood. This will be the prisoner's burning place, in time—although who knows when it might thaw? I wonder if it ever will.) I will also add that there are also some elegant homes in fine positions on the loch's edge. There must be money in Inverary—or in being a Campbell, at least.

On this morning's walk, which took me by the castle, I thought about the name. Campbell. What do we know of clans, you and I? Not much—and not enough. What I know of this country is newly-learnt, and tender. It was the Edinburgh gentleman who first warned me of the Highland parts—of how its tribes fight amongst themselves, hold tight to their grievances and reap their revenges many years on. He talked of the Campbells. He called them two-sided, *I remember that—like coins, they have two faces.* Charles, he said, that evening, you must know this: that the Campbells are seen as either shrewd and self-serving, or they are seen as wise on the matter of betterment, and how to extend what they own. You will hear both views, on your journey. *He assured me that they own much of the western parts, and—he pointed his finger to the ceiling, as he said this, to ensure I marked him—they are never on the losing side . . .*

So one either loathes a Campbell, or admires them. They are either friend or foe.

They are both to me, at this time. Perhaps that sounds strange—but isn't it so? They are genial hosts, and I was greeted on this morning's walk (as Reverend Griffin, of course) which is always heartening. Manners, I think, are proof of a civilised man. But they are foe in that they are William's men, and see no crime in a Dutchman taking a foreign throne. Nor is there any denying their sharpness in the dealings—they pry, and I feel every penny I give and word I say is remembered. I would not choose to fight a Campbell, Jane, in arms or mind.

Friend and foe, then—both.

My landlord speaks highly of the Campbell clan. He calls his people honest, and Godly—a light in the Highland darkness *he said.* The northern ones are barbarous, heathen. I pity you, *he added,* and your task. I doubt you will make them decent with words. Or by other means! *He polished a glass, shook his head.*

I asked my landlord of the Glencoe men again, and he laughed through one side of his crooked mouth. He said if we are the light, then those MacDonalds are mostly the dark! Their chief? As tall as two men, with a bull-hide coat and a cup he kept for drinking blood. The Glencoe MacDonalds were the worst of all of them. *He spat.* You will not find many grieving for that den of thieves.

Jane, I will add that not all are dead. I came upon mutterings in the inn which said that some MacDonalds survived that murderous night—many did. Indeed, my landlord assures me (with narrowed eyes) that plenty scuttled up into the hills. How they survived, I cannot say. It is a wonder

*they did, by all tellings—for the weather was as merciless as the murderers, it
seems.*

*Still. Some found safety. A fisherwoman picking over the shore this
morning hissed* some got to Appin, sir, *which is a coastal town to the
north. It is Stewart ground (more clans!)—for these Stewarts, I hear, are also
Jacobites and are sheltering their brothers at this time. Perhaps I make for
Appin, when the snow lifts up.*

*I passed this on to Corrag. I spoke of Appin, of survivors being there—
and she gripped the bars and shook her chains, and said* who? Which
ones? What are their names? *She looked feverish, and her eyes flashed.
She gasped, too, when I said* I have no names. *It was the Devil, I think,
that made her cheeks flush as they did.*

Find their names, *she told me.* Do the sons live? Their wives?

I have barely written of her, in this letter.

*She remains as she was—still talking, still small. Still a prisoner, and
rightly so—for she has told me of thieves, and broken men. She spoke of
raiders that live in the borders' woods who she rested with a while—learning
tricks from them. She says coltsfoot will help a cough, as mine is, but what
trickery is that? The Devil speaks such things. My thoughts on her have
darkened. I must not be swayed by how she seems kind—for surely, she lies.*

*Still—I will admit again that she has a manner of speaking which could
charm a lesser man—a less wary man. Perhaps it is her girlish voice, or
her words (I don't know which—both?) But she spoke of her life in those
border trees and when I walked back from the tollbooth, through the snow, I
believed that I smelt moss, and damp earth. I thought I trod on pine cones.*

Witchcraft, this. I will not be fooled.

*I will add that I worry for the horse. The chestnut cob that the gentle-
man in Edinburgh was good enough to lend me is not in full health, which
is a true concern. I went to the stables, and he carried a hind hoof, in the air.
I do not know why, as yet. But I will find a blacksmith. A costly business,*

I fear—but I will be requiring a horse when the weather clears, for it is a mountainous and inhospitable journey north, to Glencoe.

A letter, my love? I long to hear your voice, which I know I cannot do. But to read your words would be the same. I can imagine your writing—its slant, its long stems—but would ask that you send me some of it. Indulge me? I am missing my wife.

C.

III

*"The leaves put under the bare feet galled by travelling,
are a great refreshing to them."*

of Great Alder

You are back. You are—and do you know any more of Appin? Of who is there? You mentioned it so casually as you left, last night, so that all I thought of in the dark was *who is in Appin? Who made it there? Who is safe?* I have barely slept. I have had a thousand imaginings of what may have happened, since that bloody night and now. I know that the blizzards and mountain routes will have unpicked them. Killed more than the muskets did.

Do you have names?

Please listen for them. Ask? And if you hear names of people still living then pass them to me? Every night and each morning I think, *let him be safe. Let him be mending.* The others, too—*let them all be safe.* But I think of Alasdair most of all.

I SEE it still snows. Is it heavier?

Maybe it will never stop. Maybe it will snow on and on until we cannot move for it, and we freeze, and that is that. Only the people like me will survive—the ones who like coldness, or do not feel it at least. We shall live in snow caves and be blue-skinned, and black-eyed. Maybe.

But that's a strange dream I have. It won't be like that. *Spring always comes* is what Cora said, nodding—for she never liked snow. She liked the warm weather much better. The green shoots.

Spring always comes. Yes.

But I reckon I won't see it. I hear them drag the wood for me, even through the snow. They wait for a thaw, I think. When it thaws, they will come for me, and burn me on that wood—for snowy weather's on my side. My weather. It will be when the birds sing again, and the buds show themselves, that I will be gone.

Just ashes. A blackened skull.

MAUDLIN talk. But I am allowed a little of it, I think. To be burnt . . . I have never burnt a single living thing, and never would—no matter of its nature or what it had done. Never.

How can lives burn lives? What part of them has no feeling, that they can say *burn her,* and then turn on their heel, leave before the burning smell weaves into their wigs? I never understood it.

But I am not like most people.

That winter. That long, blue-lit winter that we moved through, her and I. She broke ice with her hooves. She crunched out over frosty fields and kicked the snow up, and was very startled when a bough dropped its load on her back. She whinnied, charged away. I fell from her, into a drift, but the mare came back and sniffed about for me. I think she was sorry, for her ears were forwards. She always put her ears forwards when she was glad to see a thing.

I sucked icicles. I saw some eerie, moonlit nights. Sometimes the sky was so clear that I put my cloak across her back, as she slept—for she felt the cold more than I. She was foaled in the summer, long ago.

We rode through old reiver valleys.

Drank from moats of castles.

And we moved mostly at night, for these are the emptier times. I said *north-and-west,* in her ears, and we set out under the stars. We trod carefully in dank places. We held our breath in them—or what else lurks in such dankness? *Not much that's good,* I thought. But we galloped, too—out over the open, snow-covered wastes, and the drifty valleys, and under bare trees. She liked it. When had she ever galloped before? Being locked up, and thrashed? She put her ears back when she galloped. I felt her strain beneath me, heard her breath, so that whenever we slowed back down to a walk she had mucus in her nostrils from all her galloping. She snorted through them. She blew her nostrils clean, and scratched her face on her leg, and I said *well done* and *good girl.*

I nearly lost her this way.

Not from the mucus, but the galloping.

Near the Hermitage castle, where dead Queen Mary had untied her skirts for this Bothwell man, the mare sank in a bog. All bogs were hard with frost, or had been. We had gone over them with our manes flying out—but this bog was not frozen. We plunged right in. I slipped off her and climbed onto some rocks, but she, being a heavy horse, was stuck. I wailed. Her legs and lower body was lost in the mud. I took her mane, and pulled.

Please don't die here I told her.

She whinnied.

Climb out! Heave!

She rolled her brown eyes and her nostrils went in and out, in and out. She sank deeper down.

Please don't . . .

But she didn't die. I went to her. I murmured gentle things to her until she was calm. And when she was calm I put a little mint on the rock in front of her, which she smelt, and tried to reach with her lips. Then I went behind her with thistles in my hand, and a roar in my mouth, and I smacked the mare so hard that my hand tingled, my throat broke in two, and she was so shocked at the smack and the sound that she hauled herself up, and was free.

She found the mint and munched on it. Shook her mane.

I was fierce with her, for a moment.

Then I wasn't fierce at all. I hugged her boggy neck. I thought *do not love her,* for I had promised it—but I liked how she searched my hair with her lips, and left drool in it, and I was glad she had not died, in that bog. I wondered if the heart could be ordered, in such a way.

She was grey on top, and mud-black below. When I looked back at her, it was as if she was floating—a half-horse creature, sailing through the dark.

We moved through the gloaming most of all—the times that are neither day nor night. Cora called them the *betwixt-and-between times,* when the world is stirring or it is setting down. When the light is strange, and your eye can think *what is that? Moving?* But nothing moves out there. Dawn and dusk are always softly lit. Their shadows are thin, and to ride through these shadows on my mare felt like breaking them—but they sealed themselves again, in our wake.

Cora also said *the veil is thinnest, at this time*—that the wall between this world and the other, magick world was weakest. She breathed, *you can reach, and touch it . . .* I never felt that, when I was small. But out on the mare, I felt it. Treading through mud, with deepening skies, and birds coming in to roost, I felt it in my body *I am not alone. I am seen,* I thought, with the sunrise.

You look at me as if I'm senseless. Like I've blasphemed.

I only meant to say that those are my favourite times.

And what ones I saw. What dusks and dawns. We saw them from strange places, for we slept in some uncommon beds, her and I. Rocks, barns and islands. An empty badger's sett which made me musky for days. Once, I slept in a tree, and I felt Cora was with me that night.

Are you there? Are you with me tonight?

I am with you every night. Or so I dreamt she said.

And we slept, too, in a church. It was empty, and ruined. There was ivy where the roof should be, and a pigeon in the font. Our forelocks were stuck down after three nights of rain, and so when we found the empty church we both said *yes. Here.* I laid down on a pew, and rested. I fingered the old singing books, and looked at the calm, wooden face of Jesus on His cross—and I thought what a gentle face He had. Gentle—when so many ungentle things had been done in His name.

It was a peaceful place, and dry. The mare let out a little wind by the altar, followed by what made it, but these are natural things, and I don't think the church minded. It was giving shelter. Shelter and love is what faith is—or so Mr Pepper said.

Which church? Which town?

I don't know. There are so many different churches. I know this King William is of one faith and hates the other, and James is of the other and hates what he is not, and so aren't they both the same? In this hating?

It was nature's church. That's what I call it. Mother Nature's church, for her brambles wrapped round the pulpit, and her sermon was soft pigeon calls. Her hymns were beetles clicking over wood.

More churches should be like that church, maybe.

WE kept from towns. You ask for their names like I rode through them, or stayed a while. But I did my best to keep away from where people were, and *witch*.

When I met people it was mostly by chance. It was by coming to a place where two paths met and on the other path would be someone. We'd slow, eye each other. But most night-time travellers do not want to be seen, and so are happy to pretend to have seen nothing, as well. I met a man and his wife, running. I did not ask why, but her belly was round—perhaps she was not his wife. I blinked kindly at them, gave a small smile. They did the same. We did small exchanges, too—herbs for an egg, or a crust of bread. And we said no words, but on the edge of a wood, where its trees met a field which was grey with moonlight, we wished each other well, with our eyes. *Hide well. Be safe.*

I also saw a man on a rock, one daybreak. He was sitting with his legs tucked up, and looking east. I sat myself beside him for a while. I felt his sorrow, and when he spoke he said *they say my mind is gone* in his Scottish voice. He did not look at me. His eyes were on the sun coming up, which told me his mind was not gone at all, that he was like me—sometimes so amazed by a sight that all he could do was stare. So we watched the sun come up together, and heard the distant bells ring in Christmas Day, and we shared the stale bread I'd found in the church, and some wine.

And Covenanters? Did I tell you of them? I saw them, in a wood. Don't ask me what they were, for I don't rightly know. But I reckon they were one faith being hunted by the other. I reckon they were people who were frightened for their lives because of who their God was, so they did their praying to Him very secretly—in trees, and at night. Not much could find them that way. Only owls, and a fox or two. And me, of course—an English thing with a half-sad face who saw beauty in a leafless tree. Who had no-one to tell of these people in woods, so their secret was safe, with me.

ON, and on. We had our brave times. Those were when we'd pass a sign for carrots or fresh milk, and want some. So I'd lick my thumb and clean my face with it. I'd tidy my hair, and knock on a door. I'd smile. I tried a Scottish accent to the carrot-selling man, and he blinked, shook his head, said *pardon?* When I used my proper voice he stepped back. But still, I got some carrots—maybe voices do not matter if there are pennies to be had.

In fog, we came to a farm. I came through the mist in a mist-coloured cloak, on a mist-coloured horse. And I tried to buy some oats, for my mare was looking thin. The farmer's wife stared beadily, said *what's in that purse?* I looked down. Some leaves were spilling from it, which she saw. I had no words. I shrugged. She said *if you have cures in there, I need some.*

What for?

Nightmares. My boy has so many he fears sleep, and has grown ill.

And I helped her with that. I gave some peony, and spoke of its virtues, and she nodded and gave us some oats. But later, as I groomed the mare with thistles in a wood, I heard *there she is! Witch! She cured my wee boy! Witch! Witch!* How unfair. What a kindness returned. I could not see her, for the fog—but it was surely her. And the mare sighed, lifted her foreleg so I might climb aboard, and I said *go—as best you can in all this fog.* She went. She saw the way. And we did not knock on doors, after that.

We drank bog-water. We slept in old byres.

We passed a ditch, thought of settling down in it, when a twig snapped and the mare reared up. A boy was crouching in there. *Why are you hiding?* I was cross with him. He did not say a word. But in the fields I heard dogs, barking, and he whimpered at the sound, and I knew he was frightened for his life. So I said *climb on. Quick!* The mare waded through a river with us. It was fast-flowing with snowmelt, and loud, and her hooves clattered on the river's rocks. But the boy was safe from the dogs, after that, and was gone.

On a very wet evening, as we trudged through the mud, we heard a gasping sound which was not rain. I looked about, frowned. And there, in a hedgerow, was a hare—snared in wire. It was bleeding at the neck, and I dropped down from the horse to tend to it. I said *poor you, poor you,* prised the wire away, and it cut into my fingertips so my blood mixed with the hare's, but at least it scrabbled free. Off it went, long-legged. And I wrapped my hands in dock leaves for a day or so.

***

I still have scars from that snare. See?

I have more scars than that—for a running life has its wounds. It has its wire and rope. It has the stones thrown out with *witch,* as I ran, and most stones were only fast air by my ear, or a thud on my mare's behind—so that *witch* stung more. I have scars from a dog that tried for me.

But a running life has its lonely times—such lonely, long ones—so that I think the soul's wounds are the worst of all. I do. To pass homes, as we did. To hide in the woods as a family passes by on the road, laughing. A family! What one had I known? I'd been happy enough—Cora and me, and the pig before I killed it. Our scrag hens. That had been my family life—no father to speak of, and no family name. Just *Cora,* just *Corrag. That red-skirted woman by the burn, and her child* . . . And had I minded? I'd never minded. We were as we were, her and I. But I held the mare's nose as I stood by her, and I watched.

This was a true family passing by—parents, and brothers, and children, and wives.

I scratched the mare's neck, as they went on their way.

Maybe she felt it, too. She would see fields of horses, or a stable-door, and put her ears forwards at them. She never called out. But she'd put up her tail and dance on her toes, and once I took her over to a bay filly in a barn. They pressed noses, and breathed. They rubbed their rumps on the wall, side by side. And I was sorry she had to leave her friend—but she did. We had *north-and-west* to do.

It is being lonely—that night-time, running life.

Like a twilight I came to. It was feather-grey, and red. I thought *look at the beauty* . . . But the mare was busy with the ground nuts, so I watched the sky alone, and I knew that that moment—seeing the shadows grow long on my own—was how Cora's life had been, also. She'd lost her parents, and run. And she'd run and run. And I hoped that she'd had a twilight or two with a person beside her, hand in hand—not all of them on her own.

So YES, the heart has its scars. It has its spaces, so that I wondered if it whistled when the wind was strong. I wondered if it leaked, on rainy days. A heart with holes in it.

In rough, open country, on a full-moon night, I was thinking of hearts, and witches. I was looking up at the moon, as I rode, and dreaming my dreams. When I heard voices.

The mare heard it too—ears up. I slid down from her, and crept towards the sound. Through some hawthorn bushes and past a fallen log, I saw firelight. It was a warm, good glow. By it, I saw a rabbit roasting on a stick, and a group of men were sitting by the rabbit, drinking ale. They were not like usual men—for they were redcoated, with shiny boots on their feet. They had yellow breeches.

Soldiers. I spoke this under my breath, into the leaves.

Why here? I didn't know, or cared to. If they had been sitting very soberly, and talking in a measured tone, I might have dared to venture forth, and ask for a taste of their rabbit in return for a herb or two. But sober was not the word—not at all. They were passing a bottle of some such about themselves, and they drooled, and one said *shall I say why they have whisky, and drink it so much?*

Why?

For the Devil drinks it. He drinks a dram each evening . . .

They laughed. *He's a Scotsman.*

The Devil? A man from Glencoe, most likely!

They laughed.

'Tis being unfair to the Devil, sir! The chief of that sept is far worse than him . . . A butcher, he is. And that valley is worse than all his flames!

I trusted no part. I did not like this talk of the Devil, and I did not like the sound of this Glencoe place. For all their bright buttons and scarlet coats, I thought *do not show yourself to them. Turn. Let them be.*

So I turned.

But as I did my skirt caught on a bramble, and I pulled the branch as I left so that it strained, creaked, and then let go of me. It jumped back to its starting place, and rustled.

The laughing stopped. There was silence. Then I heard short, hard words, and a growl, and metal drawn out, and they were getting to their feet.

One of them looked up, and saw me. He had red eyes from the drink and the fire, so that his face matched his coat, and he said *well, well.* An English voice. An English voice in a Scottish field, and he came towards me. I answered him. I said *keep away,* so that he heard my own voice, and said *she's English* to them. *An English girl so far north . . . Well, well.* And he came at me.

He fell through the hawthorn bush. I hurried away, but he reached, and found me, and his weight came down on me so that I fell to the ground. I scrabbled. I screamed, and tasted earth. I screamed again, and *no no please no* and when he put his hand on my mouth to silence me I bit him very hard, so he let go, and I pulled myself out, stood up.

My mare was whinnying, and I leapt onto her back. But I was pulled back down, straight down, and I fell very heavily so that I lost my breath. The weight came back upon me so that my cheek was in the grass, and my chest was breaking, and I heard *shh. Hush now—I won't hurt you* . . . He said it very gentle, like he meant no harm. But I knew he meant harm. He licked my ear, said *ye be good for me now* . . .

I would not be good for him. I would not be good for him or his friends who were cackling by the fire, and I wished I was stronger—I wished I was tall, with claws and sharp teeth, so that I might rise up and kick him away. I wished I was a true witch who could do magick or bring the sky down with rage, and I thought of Mother Mundy who a reiver had climbed upon, and the thatch above her had burned as he did, and I thought how mangled she was, and the soldier was working under my skirts, now, and saying *that's right,* and I hated it, I hated it, and the mare hated it also for she was rearing up and snorting, and I thought *not this! Not this way and not with him, and not here*—and I would not let him grapple with my skirts anymore. He was pulling me, so that I slid, and I thought *I will not let him find me, I will not let him* . . . I closed my eyes. Gritted my teeth.

Pop.

A neat sound.

A hot, huge pain. In it came. It flooded me, and slowly I began to roar with it. I roared, and screamed, and his hands stopped. His weight came off me. He stood back, said *what the* . . . ?

I staggered to my feet. I stumbled with my shoulder high up, like a wing, and my arm swinging freely, and all the time I roared like I had done in Thorneyburnbank, in the elm wood, long ago.

God save me, he said. At my shifting shape.

Then, he said *a witch* . . .

I wailed. I clung to the mare with my left arm. I hung on her side, said *go! Please go!* And she'd never carried me like that—half-on, and roaring like that. She turned her head, briefly, to look. And as she looked, the soldier came back with his hands, and whisky-breath—and he clawed at her. He grabbed her tail, and pulled. It made her squeal, and kick with her legs, and she put her ears forwards, snorted and carried me fast fast fast into the northern dark.

How we galloped. How we went, that night—but on other nights, too. How the mare was, with her ears back and her neck stretched far, far ahead of me, and her mane between my fingers, and her hooves striking rocks and mud, in the dark. I held on tight. When we galloped, I kept my head low. I put my cheek by her shoulder, and looked down at her foreleg, flashing white, white, white. Or I watched the grasses rush by, felt the river splash up at us and the branches catch my hair. If there were stars, I might look up. But also, when she galloped over moors, when my mare was at her wild, midnight fastest and the air was cold, and the moon was full, I might close my eyes—and with her warmth against one cheek and the wind against my other, I felt a magick in me. I thought *go* to my mare. I thought *faster! Faster!* And briefly, it did not matter that I was dirty, or tired, or I had no meat in my belly; it did not matter that they called me *witch,* and I had no safe place to be—for I was galloping on my mare, through a cold and unknown landscape, and I thought *I live. I am living, and alive.* My mother was not. Others were not. But I was—and I was so glad of my mare, and I smiled into her shoulder as we galloped through the night.

Over moors, and through forests. A beach, too—we galloped on the sand with salt in our hair. And we galloped up the sides of hills so that, as dawn broke, we seemed higher than all other things, and we were black shapes against the spreading sky.

We'd slow down, at first light. We'd catch our breath, and rest a while. We looked back to see the shiny, broken water, and birds coming back to where we'd chased them from. The paths through grass, where we had been.

⌖────◆────⌖

Quiet, now. You have no words to say.

The shoulder? It does that. It leaps out at its own bidding, but I can force it too. I can make it unclick and lift up, like a wing. And later, when the mare had carried me away, I slid down upon the floor and knocked my arm against a rock—*pop,* again. And so my arm was righted.

I cried a little at the pain. I cried at what had happened, and what had nearly come to pass. I cried, too, on seeing my mare's tail—for it was mostly gone, tugged out by a soldier's hand. But she nuzzled me, and scratched her nose on her foreleg, and I patted her. I pulled her rabbit ears.

Who loves a horse, in this age? Who loves a creature? I loved my mare, who galloped for three hundred nights with me. Who nuzzled my pockets for mint, or pears. Who stared very firmly at things, sometimes—a tree, or field's gate—as if they might say *boo* at her. I loved her—I knew I did. And I knew, by loving her, that the heart could not be ordered, and the head could not keep it down.

Do not love—but already I did.

She was my best friend ever, I think.

She took me to Glencoe.

Tell me, Mr Leslie—how do you love your wife? I think you love her greatly. You have spoken of her every time you've sat there on that stool. Your handkerchiefs are embroidered by her, I think, and your inkwell is silver-topped—a gift? It is very pretty. You said my hair is like her hair, and I've seen you watching, when I twist it—like this.

I knew what I was. When I first stood in the marshes, and heard the frogs croak, and saw the clouds moving, I knew. *Different. Lonesome.* That it might be hard to find love.

But I knew I would find it. I always knew.

As the soldier had worked away at me, and my mouth had filled with mud, I'd thought—I'd *known*—*I will love a man with all my heart, one day. He will hold my hand.* And it would not be this soldier that took me, or made me known. Not him.

And I say this: what creatures we are. What powers are in us—in all of us. What we already know, if we choose to spend some time with ourselves. What a deep love we can feel.

LEAVE me, now? I am lost, tonight. Lost with it all.

I will tuck myself up with the man I found, in the end. His name was Alasdair. He had hair like hillside when it is wet, and the ferns are old—deep, earth-red. He saw the beauty of an eggshell, and loved his son. Once, he said *you* . . .

Come back? Tomorrow?

I will take us to the Highlands. To height. To blowing skies.

My love,

I am joyful. It snows, and I am far from what I love—but I am joyful. What a joy (it is too weak a word for how I felt) to see your neat handwriting, to touch the bottom of the paper where the heel of your hand would have rested, as you wrote it. I imagined I could feel your body's warmth from it. I could not, of course—but in such a climate as this we can often dream of warmth, and think we feel it. As you know, I miss you very much.

I read your words in my chair, by the window. I had a view of the hill, and the north-east of the loch which is still thick with ice. I stoked my fire, pulled a rug about me and unfolded your letter—and it was as if you were speaking them to me, in that room. Once, I asked you not to say darling*— remember? I thought it took all dignity and solemnity away—the qualities my father said a man must always have. I scolded you for* darling*, once. I was a fool to do so. Youth brings in such foolishness. Age, and absence, has changed me, for as I sat in my chair, I was grateful for the word* darling*, in ink. How did I ever think it took dignity away? The word itself is dignified, I think—for love is an honest, dignified, God-given gift between a man and his wife. I am blessed by it. I smoothed the word with my thumb.*

I love that we are not the same. Some men wish for a wife who agrees with her husband, always—most men, I think. Not I. You are the wife I want, and no other, and Jane I love, deeply, how you see the world with your wide and dark-blue eyes. You reprimand me, I think? I will accept it. I can be zealous, I know, and selfish.

You write, perhaps the word "witch" harms her, and your cause? *How you speak of the prisoner (I shall use this word, instead—for she is a prisoner, is she not? It is not wrong to call her that) is how I knew you would, for you've never liked the term. Yet still, you surprise me with your eloquence, and truth.* She is a human, as we are, *you wrote,* but if we do not nourish or water a living thing it will twist itself, and rot. *You are right, my love, and I am ashamed that I forgot it, or did not see—for I did not. I heard* witch, *and I saw her, and I was reviled. What did I write, in my letter to you? Of disgust, I recall. I will ask for the Lord's forgiveness— for does He not teach tolerance, and that no lost soul was always lost? "For he hath not despised nor abhorred the affliction of the afflicted" (Psalm 22:24—it is one of the torn pages in your Bible, where the moths found it. I trust it is still readable. One day, I shall buy you a new, uneaten one, my love—when I am on Irish soil again, which will be a good day).*

So I must not see her as a witch, or a half-creature. She is ill. And perhaps, as with so many illnesses, a little care is half the remedy. Her lonesomeness and matted hair, and how she talks to herself are all parts of her twisting, from lack of love. It is indeed a wonder that she is not savage, and cruel.

I'll say, Jane, that any cruelty in her life seems to have been done against her, rather than by her. But these are early days.

Such tenderness in you. I glance down on your note and see if she speaks of loneliness, then she is poor indeed, *and they are tender words. You have not met Corrag, yet you talk with such measure that I feel you have—that you visit with her on your own, and neither of you tell me. Perhaps you cross the Irish sea weekly, take a lantern and your violet scent into the tollbooth, sit on that stool . . . I know you do not. But I also know that women keep secrets between them. Last night, I heard Corrag speak of a winter sunrise—of its pink skies and silence—and I think you would have loved to hear such words, to have seen such a sky. You are my little bird. You sing, and fill the house at Glaslough with your singing—even when you do not say a word.*

Here is a truth that you have taught me: that if it was you, Jane, who played with your hands as you spoke, and whose voice was high-pitched, I'd think it delicate, and enchanting. Yet because it is a prisoner who has done, and does, these things, I call it madness. It is wrong of me.

Do not be blinded by James, dear one. Do not assume God's will. *You write far better than I do—and I was the student, the essayist. I read these words and pondered on them, in bed. Do I assume His will? His purpose for me? I cannot tell. But you are right to remind me of the need for a humble, open mind. I have always thought that James's restoration was— is—my reason for being in this country. It is, after all, the reason that Ireland has banished me, called me a traitor for not accepting William as king. But I may be wrong, in thinking it. He—our Lord—moves in wondrous ways.*

"I am like an olive tree flowering in the house of God; I trust in God's unfailing love for ever and ever" (Psalm 52:8. Again—perhaps the moths had read it. They are well-read, Christian moths).

I am sorry to hear of the weather, in Ireland. Does it sound absurd, to say I miss such rain? I miss all weather save for snow, and ice. If I were in Glaslough I would walk out in the rain, feel it on my face. Then I would return, to you.

Of course, I will listen hard to her. You're right—we all have our stories, and right to tell them, to have them heard. You do not see her as a wretch, and I must borrow your eyes. I know the thought of her death troubles you. In truth, I wonder if it does not trouble me somewhat, also. It did not, when I first found her—I was minded that Devil-worshippers should not be suf- fered to live. But I do not think she is one. She blasphemes, which is a sin, and she has known some thieves in her days. But is this worth murder? I cannot say. Moreover, she had been treated very poorly by soldiers. I will write no more on this, lest it distresses you—but I am glad to say she was not hurt in the way they tried for. Even prisoners do not deserve such things.

Dark times, these. There seems so little light—in the minds and hearts of us all. My Bible, and your name bring light to mine. I will confess, too, that

*there is something in her character—her love of living, I think, of being in
the world—which lightens my step a little, when I walk out into the snow. I
would call this* bewitchment. *But we have banished such words, now.*

*Thank you again for your letter. I cherish it, and will carry it with me.
Would it be selfish and shameful to ask for another? If you find the time?*

    *My love to our boys. Remind them that a father in Scotland does not
mean a father who cannot punish, or reprimand. I hope they treat their
mother as she deserves to always be treated—with love, and awe.*

Charles

IV

"Moonwort is a herb (they say) will open locks and unshoe such horses as tread upon it . . . Country people, that I know, call it Unshoe The Horse."

of Moonwort

In these empty hours, when you are not with me, I look upon myself like I am new to me.

My face. My chest. And my arms—with their veins, their scars from thorns or an old, English cat. I look upon my legs like they are not my own. They are marked, muddied legs. I clutch my toes, some-times, too. I rub each one, and feel the tender skin that hides between them—secret skin. I think, *my toes.* I call them *mine.*

I put my thumb to my neck, and hear my heart. It beats, it beats.

And I breathe in, out. In. Out.

I am sure the gaoler says *madness* when he sees me—feeling myself, watching my cold, white breath as it steams, and vanishes. *Witch,* he says. But he does not know why I do these things—why I hold my hands before me. These hands. Which are small, Mr Leslie, but think of what they have held, and brushed against—what herbs, and rocks.

I have always looked upon myself like this. It was *witch* that did it. In the elm wood at Thorneyburnbank, or sleeping on a low-tide beach, I'd look at my body like it was marked, somehow. Like it was newly-given.

Why am I so small I asked Cora. For she wasn't.

She shrugged, said *you are like my mother. She was small.* But all things are small when they're tied thumb-to-toe.

Still.

I look upon myself far more in these dark days and nights. I look with old, wise eyes—for I know that in the Mercat Cross they are bringing wood in, hauling it slowly through the snow. Rope. Tar. I know they do this, that they do it for me. I look on myself, sir, for I cannot believe I will burn, and be gone. That my skin will blacken, and open up. That my hair will flame up.

This pale, soft skin between my toes will be the first to burn, I think. These parts.

Was Cora like this? As the rope was put about her neck? Did she feel how strong she was—how alive? Was her heart so fierce in her ears, beating like a drum, that she could not believe the drop would come, the *bang*—and she would be gone? The chief of the MacDonalds said he never felt more living than on the eve of a battle, with his sword across his lap. I believe it now. I believe that when we think our life may soon be done, and our bodies broken up, we see every part of us. All the little hairs on my arms. My wrinkled bits.

Cora and an unknown man made me. I come from them.

But also I come from the wind and sky and earth and trees, and what it is that made these things. I have always thought it. But I say it now, for it comforts me.

I need comforting for I am afraid, tonight. I know they bind the barrels up.

WHAT will comfort me? Your face, which I know now. It is a better face than most which come into this room. I know its looks now, and what they mean. This look, now. The one you are giving me. It is sorrow, a pity which you try to hide—for I know you feel you should not feel it. Not for a witch. You think, maybe, *I am a reverend and I hate all sinners,* and so you tell yourself *burn her.* I know. But I see pity in your eyes, and I think you soften to me. I saw the sadness when I talked of my toes, on fire.

I am not so bad, am I? Not a *hag,* or a *wicked piece.*

My mare, also, will comfort me. I can see her. In this half-light. I can see her so clearly that I am on her, I think—with her dappled shoulders beneath me and her thick, pale mane. *Good girl.* I hear her fleshy nostril sounds, and when I leant down and said *go!* she always knew, always—and she went. She'd jump forwards, shake herself, go.

I CRIED, after those soldiers. I cried at my sore shoulder, and the rudeness of it, and the strength of them. I cried at what they wanted—at what I had, and did not have.

And of course I missed Thorneyburnbank, then—of course I did. I missed the marshes, and my childhood bed, and the cats in the eaves with their silver-tipped tongues. I missed Mother Mundy's beady-eyes, and her tales. The holly, which caught my hair as I passed. I missed these things, as I rode into the Highlands, for I thought *they were safe days! They were known* . . . And aren't there days when all we seek is safety, and warmth, and a meal?

But, I told the mare, *those days weren't truly so safe* . . . Not with Mr Fothers and his narrow eyes. *Not with folk need a foe* . . . And maybe it was this that I cried at, most of all—that nowhere I had ever been was safe.

So when the land began to rise, and the ground grew rockier, and as the water which I drank from tasted thick and cool with peat, and the earth which I knelt in as I drank was black on my knees, and as the lochs had mist upon them, and the birds soared by the peaks, and as the castles became smaller and in darker, higher, windy spots, and as the homes became less, and the horses too, and as I climbed down from the mare to cross a river which had had no bridge for miles and miles and I could see none ahead, so that I thought *has anyone even been here before?*—I did not feel scared. Not at all. I stood waist-deep in the river and said *Highland*. I knew.

And yes, they had been called *brutish*. They had been called wild, and untamed. And hadn't their people been called *barbarous*? I stood in a river, on a summer's night, and said *what can be more brutish? Than what I have known?* I told the insects that I'd been grappled at, and spat upon, and chased, and called *witch,* and my mare had been hurt, and my mother was dead.

We crossed the river, and went on.

And as the dawn broke, we came into the Highland parts.

❦

How can I speak of it without saying *wild*? Or *beautiful*? I had never seen such beauty. Cora had promised me that beauty was in differences, in the sights that most folk did not like, or was fearful of—she'd said *for are not all other things very dull?* She'd liked the egg with two yolks in. She'd liked that star-marked calf.

And as I rode out across Rannoch Moor, I thought of her. She would have danced, in it. She'd have lain down and clutched the peat, pressed it to her face. She'd have plunged her red skirts into the lochs, and tugged up the reeds, and chased the deer with her arms stretched out—for here was her soul's home. No people. For people said *witch,* and tied thumbs-to-toes. Here, there were pools so still that there was a second sky in them, and a lone bird skimmed the water so that there were two birds. When there was wind, it rattled the heather. It came about the boulders and the side of hills like water—shaking itself, shrill, almost white. It whistled through the cattle skulls, and my hair beat itself like a wing on my cheek, saying *fly fly fly*, and when the wind moved away again, I heard bees. I heard the soft tread of deer, and their teeth on the grass, and I liked them. I liked their reddish, thick bodies, and their crowns on their heads like they were the true kings of the world—not a wheezy Dutchman. Not a Stuart hiding in France.

I heard the *lap lap* of loch water, and the *puck* fish made with their mouths.

North-and-west, always. And I nudged the mare on. She felt the wind in her half-tail, and went.

WE slept against rocks. We stood on high places, and looked out. I wondered how we looked, the mare and I—standing side by side on those peaks, with the breezy weather in our manes and our skirts blowing out. I wondered what saw us. I scratched her ear. *Good girl. Old thing.*

And as I said that, I knew it was true. I knew she was old. I had known it since I first hauled myself on her back, with Cora crying *go! Go!* For I remembered her days as a foal. I remembered her sniffing the wind, in her field. I'd been in Cora's arms, picking pears with her, and my mother had said *shall we share a pear? With the little horse, here?* So we fed her. She'd been thin and long-legged, but she'd already got her brown-speckled rump and rabbit ears. She'd snuffled, found the pear. I'd seen my face in her polished eyes, and she'd seen hers in mine.

Those were our young, English days.

I told her this. That I'd always liked her. That we'd always been friends—her and I.

And as if she also knew, in her heart, that she was old now—that her early life of beatings had made her old too soon, and she had galloped for so long with me that her bones were stiff and sore. As if she knew that our journey was almost done, she lowered her head, and blew a long breath into the grass. She still had a foal's nosiness, and still skittered at leaves. But her ribs pressed out, and her back sunk down.

ON A day of flashing skies, I looked into her eye. It had the whole moor in it—all its light, and sky, and water, and I thought her eye looked sad. Like she did not want to leave it. Like she knew the realm was near her, now.

I stroked her. I said *I know.*

I did not ride her on her last day. I walked by her, held back branches for her, and sought out good rocks to shelter behind. I gathered herbs as we went, and fed them to her, and she chewed as we walked. *Good girl.* Never had there been a better girl than her, in all the world's days. And the summer sky rumbled, and the wind picked up, and as a raindrop fell very fatly on her neck, and another, and another, and the wind picked up, I made a promise to her—that I would find her a proper resting place now. A bed. A roof. For how fair was it, to keep saying *north-and-west*? Not fair anymore.

Thunder came in.

And my head was by her head, as we walked, and her hooves clicked on the stones, and down the rain came and plopped into the mud. It hit our heads, and flattened our hair, and the mare went dark-coloured, and she hung her head low, and we both stumbled as the rain grew worse. It hurt us. The sky flashed and growled.

Poor horse. Her last hours in this life were wet and cold ones. She sank deep into bogs, and dragged her soul also, and I called to her *we rest soon!* But where? I saw nothing, I saw no place to warm her and she was old, my little mare was old, and the rain was very painful and it blinded us and the wind charged at our bodies and I had no wish at all but for some safety.

I prayed. I called into the rain *please let us find shelter. Please.*

I shielded my eyes from the rain, and peered, and just when I thought *there is nothing. We are done for,* I saw a small, stone hut.

It was not much. Just a rough and battered hut—but it had a roof on it and three-and-some stone walls, and I said *there!* We hurried. I pushed the mare from behind, so that she went in and shook herself, and I knew, as we entered it, this was her dying place.

INSIDE there were nettles and some moss. The floor was dry. I pulled moss down from the stones and gathered old heather to make a soft place for her and I said *lie down there*. She blew very hard. We stood, the mare and I, and let our ears hear how the storm was some muffled now. I smoothed her wet coat. I told her she was safe in this sheiling with its thick walls and moss and she could sleep.

And the grey mare I called *friend* gave a sigh that was as deep as all the seas and valleys. Her knees made a sound like pebbles do and she came down. She fell onto the moss and then rolled back very gently with her head laid down amongst the old heather, and her speckled body filled itself with air.

I lay down also. I put my hands on her belly and spoke to her. I told her our stories. I told her all our best stories—like the ruined, leafy church, and the forests, and the frosts we had galloped on, and the rushing rivers she'd carried me through. Of the hare, in its trap. Of the boy we'd taken away from dogs. Of the night we had spent in a cave, her and I—sleeping nose to nose on its floor.

I said *do you remember . . . ?* And her eyelashes fluttered, like she did.

And she gave a breath, a very long, tired breath which said the realm was waiting now, and she was going there. Her lower lip trembled. I put my face by her face. I put my breath from my own nostrils into her nostrils, and I looked into her shiny half-closed eye. I did not want her gone. I remembered how she'd munched hay in her stall on full-moon nights and carried Mr Fothers against his bidding into ditches after bramble leaves and plums. I thought of her tooting, and how she knew *go!*

I did not want her gone at all. I thought *please stay* . . .

But lives must go. Lives cannot stay.

I called her *good* then. I called her *good lady,* and patted her coat. I spent her last night with my head on her belly, and in my sleep I saw what she had seen in her final drawing out of breath—a river with a lone bird standing by it, and a field of hay.

She was cold when I awoke. I combed her mane of knots and thorns and laid it neatly down. I put a kiss on her nose. Outside the sky was pale and there was no more wind, no more rain.

I knew I could not lie there, missing her.

No magick brings the dead back, and I think the newly-dead need quietness to say their own farewells in, to leave their old earthly shapes behind and slip away. I believe this very much.

The rain had made small lochs as clear as glass is. The air smelt clean. I washed my face in a burn and drank it, and saw how the sky lightened pinkly in the eastern parts. It was good and peaceful watching. I gave an honest thanking to whatever sees us in such times, a thank you for her ways and an asking to now keep her well. When I looked back across the peat I saw the hut's shape in the darkness. She'd had no better resting place in all her days—even Mr Fothers could not have filled his stable with such soft moss or heather—and it was my comfort that she died in a very fine horse-place.

I watched. And as I watched, her ghost came out into the morning air. She shook her mane, grazed.

I headed north with silvery horsehair on my cloak.

I was twenty days on Rannoch Moor. The wind was less at night-time and so I travelled then, for the moon was waxing and gave light enough. I came to know bogs, in the dark. I used stones to cross them. I ate roots. Some stalks have a nectar in themselves that you suck upon, and this was enough for another fist of miles. But my cloak picked up branches and thorns, as I walked, and my body felt so tired from a year of *north-and-west*. I stood very still in high places. I crouched by lochs which were dimpled with rain, and heard their dimpling, felt it on the backs of my hands, and I thought *I am meant to be here. I am meant to see this rain.*

I was done with roaming. By a rock with lichen on it I said *I will walk for one more day. And where I am in one day's time, I'll stay.* This was not a spell. It was just a tired soul speaking. I told this to the moor, but the moor already knew.

You have been patient. How many days of my chatter have you sat with me for? And you never said *on with it, Corrag* or *I am full.* You will be glad of my next part I reckon—for it is my arriving. It is the proper start of it.

Kind Mr Leslie with your goose-wing quill.

Listen. I came to the glen on a full-moon night when the mare was gone. There was still magick in the world, and still wolves in lonesome places. The Covenanters were nearly done with, and William was newly-kinged and making his wheezy Protestant noise, and *Jacobite* was an infant word still wet from its hard birth. Men I loved were still living, as were men I did not love. I'd not yet breathed a stag's breath in. I thought I was wise when no, I was far from it.

I came like the queen of rain and wind, of tiredness, with a skirt so mud-hung that I was twice as heavy. I dragged branches behind me with moss and spiders on. These spiders had made their cobwebs in my hair at night, so moths were caught in them. My hair was wings and whiteness, and I felt their legs upon my face as I walked. I wore thistles on my hem, and held some. My bodice creaked with frost and mud. It was no pretty creature that fell into the glen.

But I did fall into it. And I stood in Glencoe and thought *this is the place.*

Is it not the name you've been asking for, all these nights?

Glencoe, Corrag! Speak of Glencoe . . . It is Glencoe I am after . . .

And I will speak of it. I am speaking of it now.

This is the place. I was certain. For the heart knows its home when it finds it, and on finding it, stays there.

My dear Jane,

*This note will be briefer than my last to you. It must be—for the clock says
it is far later than I would like. The fault is mine, for having left the tollbooth
I did not return immediately to my room. I was thoughtful, and I walked,
and found myself in the town's square. It is where they will burn the prisoner, when the thaw begins, and I looked upon the timber that gathers there.
They have tried to cover it with cloth, for the snow still falls. There was also
a notice nailed to a post which said* witch *and* trial by fire. *There is no
date—it merely speaks of the first clear day, and less snow.*

*I have expressed my feelings on ones who are not our faith. But it would
be a hardened man—a callous one, I dare say—to see the wood gathered
there and not feel a little moved by it.*

*It is past midnight, and the candle is low. Corrag (I have not thought or
called her* witch *since your letter, my love) spoke of the Highland region this
evening, and of the wild moor that lies before Glencoe. I did not write down
a word of her story, for I was also lost on it. I did not write because my ears
and eyes were on the windy moor, not the paper. She can give such accounts,
Jane—she cannot read, nor write herself, and when she counted the days that
she spent on that moor she used her fingers and toes. Yet she can talk. She is
gifted with words, and I will not call that witchcraft. I will say it is a talent
God gave her, when He made her, and before she stepped away from His
name.*

My landlord, who saw my late return tonight, said has the whore in
chains confessed herself? Conjured the devil for you, yet? *And he
made a sound in his throat—a rasp, like he may retch. I think he hoped for
news—for tales, to tell the drinkers. But I was tired, Jane, and I said* she
has not.

Nor has she. She talked of Rannoch Moor, and her words were fondly done. She spoke of a death, out on its hills—of a horse, which she felt affections for. A beast is a beast, as you know. But I think this horse was the only life which stayed with her for a year or more, which was not taken from her or called her hag, and her eyes were very moist when she spoke of the death. She has had, I'll agree, a lonesome life.

Jane, she reminds me of you. Not in lonesomeness, of course (for you have never seemed it, nor will our boys allow it) and not in appearance (except for the hair—its thickness, and how it falls). But Corrag delights in the tiny parts of life we mostly do not see, for hurrying—a bee in a bloom, the sound a fish makes with its mouth. And I know, too, that you love such delicate things. You listen to birds singing, and do you remember our excursion to the coast, when our boys were barely born? You brought a sea-stone back with you, and when I asked why you said, I would have missed it—*as though my enquiry was strange to you. I thought of this, tonight.*

I thought also of my father. I asked myself what he would have done, when offered a three-legged stool in a cell before this girl. Would he have softened, as she says I do? I know the answer, of course. He softened at neither deaths nor births, and he'd never have softened at witch. *He'd have hastened her death or done it himself.*

My love—I also have been thinking of our loss. I confess that our own quiet death lies in my head and heart, tonight. For a year, nearly, we have not spoken of our daughter dying, and I understand why—what mother would choose to speak of such a loss? But I assure you here, in ink, that I have not forgotten. Do not think I have forgotten.

Forgive me. You suffer enough from my absence, and I do not wish to cause you any more.

I will put some light in this letter.

Corrag's tale has brought us to Glencoe. I trust that tomorrow I shall hear more of these MacDonalds—and from one who is not as topped up with bias as the Campbells are. Or if I do not hear of them, I am sure I will hear of the glen, and its hills. All I hear from my innkeeper and the rest I speak to is what a dark place. A nest of thieves.

So I hope, that from tomorrow, I will be given such news that I might write a far better letter to London—not asking for funds (or not only) but assuring that this massacre was ordered by our present king, and that I may prove it. I may prove it. The thought lifts me. It lightens this, does it not?

I will write now, as always, of you. Are you well? Do you see my hand-writing and feel as I do, on seeing your own? I hope you sleep knowing that I will come back to you. Jane, I shall.

Tomorrow I will write again. I will return to the square, whose snowy pile of barrels and wood will haunt me far less, by daylight. I will feel less sore at seeing them, and know myself again. And I shall take the cob to the blacksmith's—for even though I have not much to pay him, the horse is in pain and will only grow worse. It will be warm, in the forge, at least.

The candle is gone. I will end this, and undress in the firelight.

I am far away, but with you.

Charles

Three

I

"Esteem it as a jewel."

of Black Elder

I love that I was there. I love that I saw it before the trouble came—that I trod in the glen, and washed myself in its burns. I love that I closed my teeth down upon its berries when it was only *den of thieves*—no worse than that. Most folk will never see it. Most the world will never even know its name, or write it—or if they do they will speak of its badness, of its hurts, of its deaths and betrayal. They will say *Glencoe? There were murders there* . . . and say nothing more, for what will they know? Not how, on summer days, the clouds moved their shadows along the valley floor, over the cows and the heather, over the lochs, and me.

Before it was bloodied, or snow-thick, Glencoe was lit by moon. It was a quiet, night-time valley which I crept into, with mud and moths in my hair. It was height—such height that to see it I tilted my head so much that my mouth opened a little, and I held my arms out so I might not fall. I looked up, up. Up.

It was cool air, with the sea's breath. It had the thick, earthy smell of plants at night, and water, and water sounds, and as I stood there, breathing it, I knew in my whole being that this was the place my mother meant when she stood by her cottage, still living, red-skirted, and said *north-and-west, now! North-and-west!* I knew it was the place that my mare had seen, beneath her white lashes, and galloped for. I'd had no reins on her, so how could I guide her? Steer her? She took me where she chose to, and she had chosen this place.

When the plum-faced man or any soul had said *Highland* I'd thought, *yes.* Like a deep, female part of me knew more than the rest. How can I explain it? I shall leave it unexplained. All I know is that when they said *it is a wild place* or *they have savage ways,* I thought *there. That is where I must be. Go there.*

Can you see it? In your mind's eye, which is our sharpest eye? A valley of such narrowness, and with such steep sides that it is like walking into a hand, half-closed. Some would say this frightened them— that it was a fist of rocks. Some said the mountains were so high they might fall down, and crush a man. But I never felt that. I felt Glencoe was kind. It was an open hand that I could lie inside, and it would keep me safe.

It wants me here is what I told myself. For did it not call?

I brushed through the grasses, and drank from a pool.

Then I lay down amongst the rocks, brought my mother's cloak about me, and closed my eyes, and slept.

I slept all day. I slept, and it was not daylight that woke me. It was a cow's breath. She sniffed wetly, and beyond her shaggy head was rocks and evening sky.

Rocks and sky. They are small words. To say *it was rocks and sky* sounds like it wasn't much. But it was. Rocks can have a thousand colours in them—grey, brown, purple-grey, dark-blue. They can have moss and lichen on their sides, and heather, and birch trees, and water-falls, and marks where waterfalls have been. There can be caves and loose rocks which tumble, and deer treading neatly, and a perched bird. I saw these things, as I sat there. I saw the different colours, and shapes against the sky. When I stood, and moved down through the cattle, I put my hands upon a stone beneath the northern ridge, and felt it. It had an old warmth, and a wisdom. It was rough, like a tongue. And like all the skies I saw there, it was a blowing sky.

I WALKED. I made my way further down into the dark, evening glen. My skirts dragged their branches, which dragged their own branches now. It was a noisy load to pull which grew louder with each step as it gathered more leaves, more peat and stones. I looked back on my trail. It was tatters and cow muck, and I turned to rid myself of it but by turning so my skirts did—I turned like a dog who seeks its own tail. I could not reach the branches. I stretched, but they moved away as I stretched. For a moment or two I turned, and turned.

I stopped, considered this.

A spider hung down from my hair on its thread.

Above me, a pale evening mist came down very slowly, rolled into the glen. And as I looked at it, I heard a sound. It was a sound I knew, a sound all wild places have, if you listen long enough—a river's sound, as it drops from a height. I went on, and the sound grew louder, the heather dropped away, and I came to bright, falling water.

Like glass, I thought. How it flashed, and smashed onto rocks. How clean it looked. How it broke.

I undressed. I lay my purse down and untied my cloak. My bodice was knotted, and stiff with old mud, but my fingers picked at it, and I stepped out of my skirt which I had not stepped out of in months. My boots came off, and my hose did. Then I looked down at my shift. It was grime, and sweat, and blood, and horse's drool was on it, and this was my old life's story. These were my old life's stains.

I pulled my shift off so that I was fully bare.

And I stood, naked. I had not been naked for a full year, or more, and I closed my eyes, felt the mist on me. I was like that, for a time. I was very still, feeling it—air on me, and wetness, and how my skin tightened at the draught that falling water makes. It made me feel some tearful. I did not know why—the water's breath, maybe? Like I recognised it, or had missed it? Like my body was grateful, and hugely so? Maybe it was Cora. For I knew she would have done this, if she'd been standing there. She'd have torn off her skirts, opened her arms.

I trod to an alder tree. There, I took the spiders from my hair and hung them on its leaves. One by one I did this. I said *there you are* . . . And when all the little lives were off me, I held my breath, and I stepped out under the waterfall. It was so cold and strong that I gasped—I cried out. It was the strongest water I had ever known, for it hammered about me, onto me, far harder than any rain had done. It nearly hurt. It nearly bruised, but I let it fall, for it felt like proper washing—like all the old days were being washed away, like all traces of fox dens and bogs and galloping and grief were coming off me, now. I stood in the waterfall. I felt my hair fill up.

When I was done with the thundering, I swam. I jumped from the waterfall into the deep pool. I floated like a star. I pulled my clothes in with me, and I washed them one by one—soaking them, rubbing the stains against rocks and picking mud off with my thumb. I hummed to myself. I cleaned my fingernails with thorns. Birds flitted over, and the sun came through leaves, and it was a fine, private washing place.

The Meeting of the Waters is its proper name. So I was told, later.

When my skirt was a new colour, and my bodice was cleaner, I hung them out on rocks. It was fully dark, now—or nearly so. A thin moon was above me, and trees, and I lay down. I spread my hair about me, tucked up my knees.

I laid myself down, too. Spread my hair out, and put the cloak across me so that I was less bare. I thought, *my third life,* sniffed, and smiled. I looked up at all the rocks and sky.

THINGS come to us like gifts. They do. Gifts come, and we must take them—for they are the world saying *here—this way* . . . The waterfall was a gift. So were the cows, with their warmth and kind eyes. I knelt beneath the mothering ones and put their teats in my mouth, and there is no better taste than fresh, warm milk after months of cold eating. I was a human calf, that way. The cow would look down on me as if thinking *who is . . . ?*

I have a list of gifts, from that time. The creak of a flower closing up. Finches' wings.

And *crunch* . . .

On my fourth night I heard it. I was resting in a thicket of birch and blackthorn trees and on the shores of sleep when I heard a treading sound. Up I sat. I stared hard into the gloom. What was this sound? My heart beat, and beat. I knew. I thought *footsteps!* But there were many of them—many feet, working through the bogs. Heavy feet. Slow ones.

It was the cows. But it was not the cows wandering. They were walking very firmly now—in a long, solemn line. Mothers and calves together filed up the side of this mountain very carefully, moving round the rocks and hollows, maybe pulling tussocks up for eating as they passed. Their coats were silver-black in the moonlight, and I thought I saw their eyes flash, and I thought *where are you going?* For they walked with purpose. They walked like they knew where they must be.

I followed them. I stood up but kept low, and went. The cows trod neatly into a gully between two mountains. There was a stream in the gully, and birch trees. I felt the trunks of these trees, as I passed. We climbed, and the gully grew very thin, and I thought again, *where are they going?* For there were two huge boulders at the gully's end. *There is nowhere to go!*

But there was. The boulders had a narrow path through them.

I was amazed. I was wide-eyed, and the cows passed through the boulder like ghosts, swinging their tails. I followed. And by following, I found my home.

I called it *the lost valley,* at first. For it was hidden away. It was a small, grassy field tucked up between two mountains, and guarded by rock. Who could have known it was there? How might I have found it, without those cows?

Birch trees, and water, and a starry sky.

Made for a witch-called girl, I thought, *who wants to rest, and be safe.*

WE ALL need a house. We all need shelter and a hearth, in the end. This is what had made Cora come to Thorneyburnbank and live in a hut with holly in its doorway and fish stuck in its roof, and what made her be church-going for a time. As for her grey-eyed daughter it meant a home all handmade herself from stone and reeds and heather in a lost Highland valley that was guarded by two boulders, and where stolen cows were kept. Where she found a proper peace. Where the wind rocked the birches at night, and that was a good sound.

Coire Gabhail is its proper Gaelic name. Try that. *Corry Garl.* It's the strangest name I've heard of, but it's a strange language—or it is to an English tongue. All these throaty words like music. This talk like the river—fast-moving, deep. *Sassenach.* That's what they called me, in Glencoe. *It is Gaelic for English,* or so Alasdair said—*for aren't you?*

English? I was. They all threw out the word like it was a curse, at first. But then, later, they said it as if it was a precious word. They used softer voices. They would put their heads on one side, say *Sassenach* . . .

Coire Gabhail.

The Lost Valley.

But soon, I called it *mine*. On the eastern side of the valley, I found a half-circle of high stones. Amongst them there was room for me to spin and stand, and lie down fully—so I smiled, and knew. Day by day, I made a shelter there. I used my dirk to cut up turf and heather, and I knew the cow droppings had some strength to them when dried so I hauled their doings up into my skirt which was like a basket and carried them up to my stones. I made a roof like the Mossman had done, a year before. Here were walls. They did not smell—no more than just a soft cow-smell which I never minded. Most places smell of that.

And I crept up onto the slopes about my home and looked down upon it. I saw it from heights, and said *home* to myself. I found a herb or two, in hollows, and in the glen, I found a peat-patch which was freshly dug. By it, peat was drying. It had been cut, and stacked, and I glanced about myself before taking a piece or two. For I needed fuel, like all people. I needed to cook, and be warm.

That was a fine home. It even had a window of turf that I might roll up and down as I chose to. I had a part of roof that was very thin and almost bare so my smoke might find its way outside and not fill my place with choking—but not so thin the rain might pour in. I made it, and was so proud.

Look I said to the cows, when it was done. They were not very sure, but I was.

I will be happy here I said as I sat cross-legged on my floor under my thatching with the rain drizzling out on the cattle and rocks. I watched the rain. When it was too dark to see it, I listened to its sound.

ON A day of crisp leaves twirling down from trees, I came upon a hind on the slopes of a southern hill—dead, and freshly so, and warm. I felt sad at seeing her, with the arrow in her flank—but I also saw her uses. Very carefully, I took her hide away. I used my knife, and cut it—and this was messy. It was sad, and bloody—but she was dead already, and her death would be all the sadder if it led to nothing at all. So I hauled the hide back. I dried it for days in the early autumn sun. In time, I lay it on my floor.

I took a little meat from her, too. Just enough. I roasted it, and ate my first meat in weeks and weeks. I followed it with blackcurrants— and these brought Cora to mind.

I thought of Cora plenty in those days. Maybe it was because I wasn't running, now, or because I had a home which had only me in it, or maybe it was warmth and good food waking the sleeping parts of me up—I'm not sure. But I thought of them both, on the braes. A year after Cora had swung on a rope, and I cried. At last, I mourned her passing. Against a rock with lichen on it, I sank down and cried for her. I cried for her death, and the life that had ended too roughly, too soon. I cried for all the others who had gone, as she had gone.

I cried, too, for the mare. In my hut, I remembered her velvety nostrils, her bristly chin, her eyes. I let my sadness out very noisily, and wiped it on my arm. And afterwards, in the hush that followed it, I smiled—for it was her life I thought of, not her death. It was her whickering life, with its moors and ripe pears, and I was lucky to have seen it, to have shared it with her.

Early days, those. Quiet ones.

Was I mending myself? I think so. I was tying a knot in the old, past things—for so much was lying ahead of me. So much was to come.

You look sadly at me. Why sadly? Look what I found. Look where I lived, and where I called home. Go to Glencoe. Stand amongst its peaks, and you will understand—what a gift it was, to live there. What a gift, to follow those cows. I had milk, and a fire, and a deerskin to sleep upon. And if I called out my name the rocks gave it back to me. *Corrag* . . . The owls called it out.

Lonesome? Me?

Never, and always. That was *witch* for you—that one word. When was I not a bit lonesome inside? I mostly was. Seeing true, natural beauty can lessen it, because sunsets and winter light can make you say inside you *I am not alone*—you feel it, through such beauty. But it can worsen it, also. When you want a person with you it can be a sore thing. Sometimes you see this beauty and think *it is not as lovely as them*.

And poor? You think I was poor, in Glencoe? Far from it. No pennies, no. But when did pennies make a person truly rich? Folk seem to fill their lives with favours or a title or two—as if these are the things which matter, like happiness lies in a coin or two. Like the natural world and our place in it is worth far less than a stuffed purse, or a word like *earl* or *duke*. Perhaps, for them, it is. But that's not my way and never was. I was at my richest as I sat cross-legged amongst the last of the foxgloves, watching a plump-bodied bee live his life. He pushed up inside each flower so that his bottom peeped out, and his droning sound was muffled, and then he'd slowly creep back out with a louder hum, and powdered wings. From flower to flower, he went. I was watching him four hours, and I reckoned I was richer for that wandering bee than a fistful of gold could ever make me.

Poor? Not poor. Lonely? A small part.

STILL. There was magick in that place—I promise it.

I felt it everywhere. I felt it in each tiny thing I saw—each stone which shifted under my heels, or each raindrop. I had time, now. Time, until now, had been as thin and as scarce as a windblown web—fluttering by, very brief. My second life had been *go! Go!* And when had I had the time to lie on my belly and watch a snail make its way across a leaf, leaving its moonshine mark? Never. I was running too much. I was galloping over mud and wild land, with the mare snorting hard, and any slow times were spent with her—picking the nettles out of her tail. No snails. No hour upon hour in the rain, watching a leaf's middle become a rain-bright pool.

I had never liked *witch,* and still don't. But if ever I deserved the name at all, it was then, I reckon. It was having my hair fly in the wind as I stood on the tops, and how I crawled through the woods where the mushrooms grew. It was cloud-watching and stag-seeing, and spending long hours—full afternoons—by the waterfall that I'd bathed in, watching the autumn leaves fall down and make their way seaward. They bobbed and swirled. I said *magick,* one day. In the gully that led to my valley, I stopped. The wind was in the birches, and it felt they were speaking. If they were speaking, it was *magick* they said. *Magick. Here.*

I found it everywhere. I hauled myself onto the tops and sat upon them for hours, just looking—like a queen might look at her kingdom and think *it is good*. It was all very good. I learnt the glen's shape, this way. I saw its long, thin nature, and how high its mountains were. In the west, if I squinted, I saw a shining sea. I learnt the glen's colour, too—reddish-brown, with old ferns. Leaves were turning copper. Hours and hours were spent, just sitting there on the tops.

And coming home, one evening, I heard a distant roar. I stopped. I thought *what is that?* Not thunder. Not a drum. I looked up, to where the roar came from—and on a peak I saw a stag. He was bellowing. He was dark against the greyish sky, and I saw his wide branches, and how his breath steamed out. I thought *is this a welcome? To me?* Maybe not. But I chose to think it was, for the lonesome part in me had been stirred by sitting there, high up. My hair had blown across me. The loch had shone with dying light, and I'd wished another living thing might have seen it too. None had come. But here was a stag, looking so fine. *He welcomes me,* I thought. And he roared again, with cloudy breath.

I THINK, also, I healed. Those early Glencoe were days like no other days. As though I had found where I'd been looking for, for years and years, I felt myself soften and tend to myself. I think I had not grieved, till Glencoe, or be kind to myself. I don't think I had sat down and thought of Cora, and truly allowed myself to be sad. I'd been so stern with myself—but amongst the brown ferns, and the air, and the goodness that is felt in clean, wild places I became more gentle, and remembered her. I cried for her there. I cried, too, for my mare.

All the things I loved were amongst me—rivers, rocks. Creatures. Wind sounds. And I was grateful for them. I was grateful, for amongst them I could mend the wounds inside—the losses, the sorrow. My soul, where it was bruised, could be fed and cared for in my hut, on the peaks—and who does that? Which people take the time to care for their souls, these days? I reckon not many. But Mr Leslie, hear this: I think that maybe in our lives—in our scrabbling for food, in the washing of our bodies and warming of them, in our small daily battles—we can forget our souls. We do not tend to them, as if they matter less. But I don't think they matter less.

Still. What stays the same? What does not change?

I had been in the glen for a month, no more. And in came a brown-coloured day. I remember it—the leaves blowing off, and the ferns turning soft, and a deep autumn-red. Most don't like such days—their damp air, and their brownness. But I never minded them. Why should we mind them? The birds liked the pools they made in fallen trees, and they make for greener grass in the months that follow them. They make silvered parts in cobwebs. Mist is a thing I'll miss, when I am dead—walking through it, smelling it.

I went walking. I wanted berries, and a day on damp, autumn hills. And I thought I might see the stag again, or more stags, or an eagle or two.

I saw none of these.

But I saw houses.

Houses came. Or I came to them—for as I was wandering west, along the top, I paused, looked down. Chimney smoke. It rose up very steadily. It was black, in the half-light, and I sank down onto my heels and stared. *Of course.* How could I be surprised? I reasoned that a glen of such clean, fast water, and with cattle grazing in it, and berries ink-ing up on bushes must have people in it. Others must have found this glen and thought *yes. Here.*

And there they were. A single house, by the loch. I sucked my bottom lip, thought *one house is not so bad.* But when I sighed, and looked west towards the sea where the sun was going down, I saw more—more chimneys, more small, low houses with no windows. Many more.

People. Which meant trouble.

It worried me. It kept me awake, picking my thumbs. I searched my head for all the old words I had heard about the Gaelic folk—and I searched for good things, not bad. But what good had I heard? *They are barbarous . . .* Not much.

There is no devil, said Cora. *Only man's devilish ways.*

And I sniffed. I thought *that doesn't help.* But by my fireside, with an owl calling outside, I also thought *Cora would not be afraid of them. She'd be as she is. She'd not fear them at all. She would go down. She'd peer through their doors and not care if they saw her. She'd throw back her hair. Swing her red skirts.* I told the cows this, and they listened. *Am I not her daughter?* I said. And they stared.

So at dawn, I crept down. I passed through the boulder, and went down to the glen. I scurried to the lone house by the loch, and eyed it from a birch tree. I heard no talking. I heard no footsteps. But I heard a man snoring, very thickly. Also, a dog yawned—the quick, high whine, and I heard it flap its ears. So I stepped a little closer. I breathed in the smells of the place—peat, wet wool, meat, the dog, unclean people. I smelt chickens, too, and when I was so close to the house that I could touch its walls, I heard the *cluck* of a roosting hen. There she was, in the thatch. Her eyes had the milky film on them that hens' eyes have, when they're sleeping, and I thought *when did I last have an egg?* Very quietly I reached up to her. I slipped my hand beneath her feathers, and felt a firm warmth. I clutched it, pulled. She broke into a squawking, and the dog woke up, and I ran.

I ran and ran, with my hair flying. I ran, and I cooked the egg up, and I curled up on my deer's hide and pulled my knees to my chest. I felt so close to something. But what? I didn't know.

Theft? No! I have never thieved.

I went back to that house in the evening and left herbs there. I left a little oak there, for if it is burnt and its vapours are breathed in, they can help the snoring. I put it under the hen. Maybe, I thought, the wife would check for eggs and think *our hen is laying herbs, now?* And maybe she'd prize the herb above a hundred eggs, if it meant her man stopped snoring, and she could sleep better. I hoped so. I liked that thought.

I became a bolder creature. Knowing the rocks, and the best hand-holds, and the animal sounds made me bold. Knowing the homes, the herbs, the views. Where the best sitting places were.

I had took more than an egg, I confess. I'd lifted a pot from a house, one night—a house to the western end. In trees, I'd found some houses which were nicely done—with a window or two, and a cleaner smell. And I'd peeped through a door, and seen a dozen pots in there. They had so many pots, and I longed for just one. I left all-heal for them—which is a fair exchange. Does its name not say what a virtuous herb it is? And now I was eating mushrooms and blackberries, and boiling up roots, and warming milk, and I'd made a good stew from a rabbit or two. I had a little belly from it all. I prodded it, when I bathed—a new shape, and softness.

I had also found a rock below the northern ridge which I liked. It was small, and on its own. When I sat against it, it fitted the shape of my back, and there was such a view from it that I could look for hours. Autumn was rich, and wild. And it was as I sat there, with my hood pulled up, that I saw people.

At last.

Men. Three of them—moving in a line along the river's edge. I kept very still. I did not take my eyes off them. Sometimes they went behind trees, but not for long. Three men in colours that were like the hillside—earthy, damp-coloured. They had belts which flashed, and I thought, too, *they move fast.* Faster than I ever did.

I thought *where are they going?*

Then I thought *I know where.*

They turned, and made their way between the two hills. They went up into the gully which led to my valley, so that I said to my rock, and the air, *no . . .*

I ran.

I did not want them finding my home and ruining it, tugging at its walls or burning its roof. I did not want them spying on me, with my herbs and small fire. How I'd laid out my treasures in a corner of my hut—a pebble like an egg, the mare's thrown shoe, an owl feather, my few coins. My basket of berries was in there, and what if they ate them? They had been a whole day's picking. I ran with my skirts tucked into their top.

I was afraid, yes. But not of them. Not of these men being savage or cruel like the soldiers had been, for I think I knew they were not. I was afraid of them making me leave where I'd found, of my home being lost, and where would I go? I was tired of wandering on, and on. My mare was dead, my heart was tired, and I had walked into the glen thinking *here is the place, here is where I'm meant to be.* I did not want to leave. I liked my rock. I liked how I could sit by my hut, in its doorway, and see the deer on the slopes. I liked the stars. The taste of its water when I cupped my hands, and drank. I did not want to leave it.

I ran thinking *no.* I would not go.

I saw their footprints as I ran up the gully to my hut.

I came into the valley and saw them, standing there. Outside my home. One was walking round it, testing its walls with the heel of his hand. A man with a beard like a fox's brush was dipping his head, looking in.

My skirt rustled as I walked across to them. They turned and watched me come. My heart quivered, then, for they were huge men—three huge men, and I remembered the soldier's hand on my ankle and how he said *hush now . . .*

The man with the orange beard spoke to me. But not in English. He spoke in the Highland tongue—so that it was babbling in my ear.

I stared. Blinked.

We all looked upon each other. They spoke between themselves. He turned to me again and said *who are you? Where are you from? You speak English?* I had the thought that none did, in these parts.

He tilted his head at my voice, like how birds listen for worms. *From the Lowlands?*

No. Thorneyburnbank. Near Hexham.

England?

Yes.

He turned, spoke in Gaelic again. The other two men were much older than him—grizzled, broad men, like when wood is left out in the seasons. They had that weathered look. Years of squinting in sun, and snow, and rain. I have never seen bears, but I have seen them in my head. These men were like bears, I reckoned. Hands like paws.

My heart was beating fast and very hard.

There's been talk of you, he said.

Of me?

Of a black-haired faery stealing pots and eggs from our tacksmen. Of some half-woman, half-child skinning a hind freshly killed by my cousin— he needed that hide, and would have set upon you if he'd known you were human. Our cows have less milk, since you chose to milk them. You've built this—he kicked the wall of my house—*on our land, in a place no-one knows of but us, and now we find you're English.*

A bear said *Sassenach . . .*

I saw myself, then. I saw myself as they saw me—a tiny, snag-haired thieving thing, with a hovel made of cow-dung and fish drying in its eaves. I saw my dirty hands. I thought *what to say*—but what could I say? I knew they thought *witch*. I knew that I could lie, but lies unpick themselves and that's some cleaning up. There have been too many lies.

I have come north to be safer, I said. *To have a quiet life. To make a home here.* I tried a half-smile. *I mean no harm.*

They watched me. They muttered Gaelic amongst themselves, and I waited. Speaking with the cows had been a simpler thing.

A safer life? Here?

I've seen trouble before. I've had a life of trouble in the south, with witch being said and stones thrown at me. I shrugged. *I was told north-and-west, so I came here . . .*

The tallest and greyest bear snapped out Gaelic words. These older ones spoke no English, I reckoned—only the red-haired one did. He spoke over his shoulder to them, with his eyes on me.

Witch? We have enough of them.

Like the cattle, we shifted on our feet.

You have plants in there. In your house.

Yes.

Herbs?

I nodded.

He thought on this, for a while. He looked up at the clouds. He talked in that watery language to his friends, who said it back. And then, in a voice which sounded like he had had enough of me, and better ones to speak to, he said *take less milk—there's one of you and far more than one of us. And herbs to eggs is no fair trading—not from a man whose hens are old, and lay less and less each week.* He thumbed my roof like it was poorly made, or very well-made—I was not sure which. *Give us no bother and we'll give none back.*

I agreed. I said I'd drink less milk—I had just been very hungry, but not now.

They turned to go. But the red-headed man said *your name?*

Corrag.

What?

Corrag.

Your full name?

It is just Corrag. I have no other name, for I never had a father.

He considered this. *I'm Iain MacDonald—and I do have a father, and he's the chief of our clan. This is our tacksman of Achtriochtan whose eggs you've garnered, and this is Old Man Inverrigan—it's his wife's pot I see sitting on your fire. No more thieving, Sassenach. If it's the quiet life you truly want, we'll not meet again.*

And they walked away from me.

I thought *MacDonald?* I felt my belly tighten. I think my eyes widened like how water does when a stone's thrown in, and I pushed myself onto my toes and called after them *where is here? Its name?*

As they were about to drop away from view, Iain MacDonald with his beard like a fox-brush and his shrewd eyes called back, *Glen of Coe. And your roof won't last the winter.*

Then they were gone. All that was left was their footprints, and their smell which was how most of them smelt, for what else was there? To smell of? Wet wool, and cows, and peat-smoke, and sweat.

The owl called its name, after this. The stream which came down the mountainside by my hut said *Coe . . .* all the time. The wind in the trees and the rough, sudden flap of a hare's hind leg on its ear, scratching it, which I heard one dusk by the birch trees said *Glen of Coe Glen of Coe.* I heard it in the stag, when he roared from his rock above my hut—*Coe,* he said. His breath steamed, as he roared.

Fear?

No. I have felt it. I've known fear very well—like when the drunken man grappled me, or when I knew my mother's feet were treading the air, turning, and then growing still. But I was not afraid of *Glencoe.*

I spoke of it to my hearth. I whispered it—*Glen of Coe.*

I've heard *fate* talked of. It's not a word I use. I think we make our own choices. I think how we live our lives is our own doing, and we cannot fully hope on dreams and stars. But dreams and stars can guide us, perhaps. And the heart's voice is a strong one. Always is.

Listen to it, is my advice. If I give no more of it, take this as all I have to say on life, and how to live it (for is my life not nearly done?). Your heart's voice is your true voice. It is easy to ignore it, for sometimes it says what we'd rather it did not—and it is so hard to risk the things we have. But what life are we living, if we don't live by our hearts? Not a true one. And the person living it is not the true you.

That's just my way of thinking. Not many think this way.

Is IT late? Yes.

It's so dark I barely see you. Just your white wig and your goose-wing quill.

Darling Jane

She talks of gifts—of the world being rich with them, and we must know them when we see them. For her, it was a waterfall and a valley hidden from view. Jane, I feel a gift has come to me. He is the blacksmith, with a beard as thick as the seaweed on this coast, and just as long. He, like all I have met in this town, is genial, and good at his work—but as he stood in his apron with the sparks about him, I thought I had found a man with a little sadness to him. When I mentioned Glencoe and its murders, he shook his head in a melancholy way.

I go too fast.

His forge is a mile or so outside the town—and therefore, in the snow, it was a lengthy walk. (Have I expressed how glad I am, of my coat? I have not had a coat better, and I am glad of the day we saw it, you and I. It keeps my cough from worsening, I'm sure). But the forge stood at the lane's end, and glowed, and we could hear the metal being worked, and the smell was a sour one of smoke, and iron. It might have daunted a lesser man. Indeed, the cob was wary, with his ears switching back and forth.

Yet there was warmth in the place—in its fire, and the heat of sweaty toil, and beasts, but also in the sincere and honest welcome that I received from the blacksmith himself. Perhaps he is not frequented by many. Perhaps (and this is more likely—for he spoke of a family, and conversed freely with me) there is less work in this weather than he would like. Not many folk are travelling, of course. Less travel must mean less need for a horseshoe, or a fixed gate.

He shook my hand, and patted the cob's rump as he examined him. He complimented his strength and condition, and I found myself implying that the horse was my own (or rather, the horse of Charles Griffin. How these falsehoods grow, Jane. But all for a cause, and a noble one). It seems that all four shoes are beyond mending, and new ones are required. There also seems to be a swelling of some kind, in a hind hoof. I fear this will be costly—but no talk of fiscal matters tonight.

Like Corrag, the blacksmith is gifted with words. He has the soft Scottish accent of these parts, and I wonder if a lifetime of being near beasts has softened his voice further—his voice had a musical tone. Bent over, with a hoof against his knees, he said I think I know you, sir. Are you not the Irish gentleman who has come to tame the northern clans?

I agreed that I was, and he clucked his tongue. He called it a sorry business—all of it.

I asked him, what was, sir?

Glencoe. *He looked up.* The dreadful deeds that came to pass in it, not three weeks ago. You have surely heard of the murders?

I said I knew a small part—the men were killed by their guests, as they slept. Soldiers, I think? Perhaps it is all gossip that's come by me . . .

He wiped his hands on his apron. Aye. It flies, right enough. But so it should—a sin like that . . .

A sin? *This brought me closer. I stood at the cob's end, by his tail, so that I might hear the blacksmith better.* Sir, *I said,* I have heard some say that such barbarity was deserved, by these men. *I held up my hands, added,* I know little of these parts, and have formed no thoughts myself as yet . . .

They were an unruly sept, I'll grant that. Thieves. Rebels. But—*he winced, tightened his face.* The soldiers slaughtered bairns, they did. A boy! A wee boy was run through.

You were there? *For he spoke so clearly, so boldly.*

I was not. But I shoed the horse of a soldier who'd been there. Last week he came to me. Nice black mare—good blood in her.

A soldier? On his own?

He shook his head. Several of them, but they all stayed out in the
lane, and shivered. Only their captain came here. And I will tell you
this—they had blood on them, on their breeches and shirts. And
musket-shot and peat. And I know about the wee boy being slain
from the captain's own words, sir. He saw it, and was marked by it.

Marked?

The blacksmith tapped the side of this head. In here. He was haunted.
Troubled. I reckon they were fearful men.

Fearful?

He rose, straightened his back. I tell you this for you are not a
Lowlander. Not a Scot. You'll be standing amongst us with different, foreign eyes—and I know you hope to spread God's words up
in those wild parts. So hear this, if you will: what barbarity they may
have done as a clan did not deserve such killing. And such killing
had troubled those soldiers—I swear it. Glencoe hung on them.

*Glencoe hung on them! It is a worthy expression, is it not? I wanted to ask
more, but as I tried to he said,* this beast is worse than I thought. See
here? This blister? *And we spoke about the horse, and the weather. A blizzard picked up for my walk back to the inn. If such weather chills me in a
town—with venison, a reading chair and a fire to comfort me—how might it
chill me in a desolate glen? In Glencoe?*

A dark place, *he'd called it, patting the horse.*

But Corrag does not call it such. She assures me it shone with light.

*So to bed, my wife. I retire. What should I think of these murders? I hear
so much. Good men killed, as the prisoner would say? Or did good men do
the killing, and rid the world of sin? It is hard to know, truly. What I feel
confident of, Jane, is William's part—for it was certainly his soldiers in that
glen. And who orders the King's soldiers, but the King?*

As I blow out the candle and tuck the blankets about me, I think of the creature sitting in her cell, in her chains. How can she not feel such cold? She tells me she does not. She says we all have a weather that we are our brightest in, and winter is hers.

I wonder on our weather, then—yours and mine. For ours is the same, I think. I think we are summer creatures, when the path through the woods is sunlit, and scented, and the boys are playing about us. I think those are the times of greatest joy, in my life.

I miss you, and ask for your forgiveness—for I know that you will fold this letter up, and move through the house on your own. I will return, soon.

Charles

II

"... also, if you tie a bull, be he ever so mad, to a Fig Tree,
he will quickly become tame and gentle."

of Fig

Well. Did Iain MacDonald walk back to your lodgings with
you? In your head? Him, with his hair so red that he had the
fox's look—orange, more than red. In sunlight it was on fire with its
brightness. He had the same orange marks on his hands, and across his
nose—and I knew of herbs which, my mother had told me, would
take these marks away. I did not think them unsightly, though. I see
freckles like the sun that fell on them. Dappled light.

They say that he has his father's colours in him. Before he took
to being white as snow on his head, the chief of the Glencoe men—
the MacIain, is what they called him—was also fox-orange, on fire. I
thought, too, *they have the same nose.* I also reckoned they had the same
speaking manner, which was blunt but not unkindly-said. They did
not say *witch,* but they said I must not trouble them. *We have trouble
enough* the Chief said.

But the MacIain's second son was not like them. Not in looks.
They said he took more of his mother in appearance—the blue eyes,
and not as tall as Iain but broader, and stronger, and bolder in the way
he moved so that he seemed taller, to me. His hair was red, but not

his brother's orange-red. It was darker. *Like hillside,* is what I thought. Like the wet, autumn hillside—old ferns, damp heather. I thought of his hair when I grasped branches or tufts as I ran. I said *Alasdair* when I was high-up and looked down upon all that dark-red, and deep-brown.

Your shoes are wet.

Just on the toe.

Is it thawing? A little? Just a small part. I thought it might be, for as I thought of them all last night, as I thought of their plaids and wet-wool smell, I heard a *drip . . . Drip . . .*

I must talk, then.

Of the MacDonalds who lived there. Of the glen, and the feet that walked upon it. Many of those feet are gone now, dead—so I must talk of them. It makes them not dead, or less so.

It was Iain who said to me *no man born outside the glen can truly know it.* I saw him on the braes, not long after the autumn came in and the leaves were falling down. He was squinting when he said it, for the sun was low. I saw the lines on his face, the old scars. *Not even you.*

But I did. I did know it. In time, I came to know how every mountain looked against the sky, and what their colours were. I climbed them with my skirts tied up. Where there were deer-paths, I took them, and where there were deer-hollows I lay myself down. I learnt their wind sounds. Their herbs.

I think I know it, I said to him. Sassy.

He shook his head, turned. *Be careful. I won't say it twice, to you.*

Careful—which all women are, by nature, who are not quite like the rest.

I was careful. I knew I must be, for wild places are not kind to things which think them easy. In Thorneyburnbank, Old Man Bean had been lost to a biting winter wind, or a fox or two, for he'd sauntered out too casually. In the Highlands, it was the rocks which awaited. Many gullies could be false. They could beckon and have the look of a path to other valleys by way of streams, or birch, so that men may wander up them—but these were foolish men. So many gullies led only to rock. Or, worse, they led to no rock at all—only drops of air, and mist. I nearly went this way. I was scrambling above my hut, singing under my breath, and fell, and it was a birch tree that saved me. Pebbles fell down and down, and I clung to the branch, and I saw my thatch of moss and stones far, far beneath me, between my ankles which dangled like fruit. I was glad of that birch tree. I hugged its bark, smelt it. I'd remember it, on passing. *Birch of the Saved Life.*

I'd hear stories. Not all folk had birch trees by them, when they slipped, and fell. Iain said bodies of their enemies might be washed downstream, in snowmelt—a Campbell, or a Stewart of Appin when the Stewarts were their foes. *We'd have heard none of him since last winter*—and there was the rotting reason why. They took a dead Breadalbane man, strapped him to a cow that had been taken from him, and they led the cow back to its old grazing place. I hated that. Poor herder, to look up and see his kin rotting on a cow's back. But who was I to speak? To call this cruel? I was English, and alone. I was living on their land—and I had seen cruelty, and known of crueller things.

You can't know it. Don't try to, if you like your life such as it is.

Oh, Iain could be quick with me. He could use the same voice with me as he did his dogs, or the cattle, and he looked at the sky when he spoke like the skies mattered far more to him. He thought I was untrustworthy. I think he heard my English voice and hated it, at first—for it meant *Protestant,* and *William,* and many English things. Battles fought, and yet to come. Lives gone.

England?

Yes. And I'd seen his face when I'd said that.

BUT I did know the glen. I did. Show me their shapes and I'll tell you their names. I gave my own names to the mountains, before I knew their Gaelic ones. In those early days, I began to venture out—climbing and crawling on autumn braes, and I named them from what I saw on them, or from them. Deer, or ragwort. A wildcat, which hissed. *Aonach Dubh* is its proper name but it was always *Cat Peak* to me.

This was how it was. It's how it still is—my childish names against their Gaelic ones. At the glen's eastern end, by Rannoch Moor, there was a mountain which was darker than the rest, in colour—black in storms, and shiny—so it was *Dark Mount,* sometimes. Then, when I trod upon an arrowhead, lying in its peat, it nicked my heel and bled me, so I called it *the Arrowhead* after this, for a time. Later, I knew the ones who lived on it. I knew their dirt and sadness. I knew how the wind caught the soul up there, and shook it, so it was *Gormshuil's Mountain,* also. I called it all these things.

What? Alasdair said, when I told him. *Dark Mount?* He half-smiled, half-frowned. *It's Buachaille Etive Mor, to us . . .*

Maybe. But I liked my names better.

And further in, as the glen's sides grew higher and higher, there was *Thistle Top,* for it had rustled with them as I'd sat on its peak, and the pass beneath it which led into more hills was *Pass of the Hinds,* for I saw so many treading through its peat, their ears back, their eyes half-closed against the wind. In the winter, a bird flew up from the heights at the western end—a white, stocky bird. I never saw it twice, but that made it *White Bird Peak.*

The Pap, too—for that hill was woman-shaped.

A waterfall became *Grey Mare's Tail,* as it was just like hers had been.

And the ridge. If Glencoe is ever known for its mountains alone, I reckon it's the ridge that most will know. What a ridge. Huge, and dark, and notched like teeth. It ran the length of the glen's northern side—and it was *Northern Ridge,* for a while. In my head, I thought *I will walk upon the Northern Ridge,* or *the Northern Ridge is frost-topped today.* But this changed. This changed as I ran beneath it one early evening, and looked up. There, at that moment, I gasped. I stumbled. It became *Ridge Like a Church.* That was its name. To me, it was that. For how like a church it was! Not in its colour (for it was brown, mostly, not the grey of church stones) and not for its shape, as it did not have a tower to it. I called it this for its grandeur. It was so grand . . . It had the grandeur which can stop a person walking, which can stop their tongue and make them feel both drawn to it, and scared. I was in awe, I think. That evening, I felt tearful at its height, and age. I looked up, and nearly trembled. And I'd dip by it like I dipped by all churches— thinking *it is not meant for me,* and not wanting to know it better, but still feeling its long, cool shadow on me, as I went. I could see very clearly why others might be bound with love for it. Why they might never take their eyes from it, and serve it all their lives.

This is why I called it *Ridge Like a Church*. It made me feel tiny. And it made the glen a sanctuary, of sorts, which also fits its name—no soul could ever climb it. It was too high, too steep.

Aonach Eagach is its Gaelic name. I know that, now. Alasdair taught me their names, and when he spoke them to me, he used his hands— as if feeling each word as it came out. We were by my fire. His hair was dark-gold, in its light, and he said *Beinn Fhada, Bidean nam Bian, Aonach Dubh* . . .—pinching the words, with his thumb and forefinger. *Your turn.* And I tried them, in my own mouth. His words in my mouth.

But I taught him my names, too.

The three, rolling hills on the southern side, which looked very squarely at the Ridge Like a Church, were my favourite hills. I lived amongst them. My own hidden valley was tucked behind them, and so I often found myself climbing up, up, on these three peaks. I came to truly know them. I lay in their hollows, and licked their waterfalls. I spoke my secrets to their winds, which carried them—so they knew me, too.

The Three Sisters, I told him, shyly.

They have their own names. I told you . . .

I know. But I call them this.

Months later—months, Mr Leslie—I heard the MacIain tell of a fine white hind he had shot, as a boy, in the windy heights of Beinn Fhada, and whose skin he still wore, even now. I said *Beinn Fhada?* For a white hind has magick in its heart—or more than most. And he'd drained his cup, waved his hand like my words were flies which troubled him, said *the eastern sister. Of the three.*

I smiled at that, thinking that they might not be too trusting of my Englishness, but look—they liked my English names.

So Iain had found me. Him, and those two bears. They had sniffed, growled, tied *Sassenach* on. They'd spied my herbs, and left.

People change a place. A place's air is different when three men have passed through it. Their footprints stayed by my hut for weeks, and their wet-wool smell lingered, and so did their words—*your roof won't last.* That troubled me. I circled my hut that evening, testing it, peering in. I'd done my best, and it had served me well—for the turf and branches and dung had kept me dry enough. The thin part of the roof had let my smoke drift out. I had been happy. Warm.

But within days, a frost came in. I woke in the night—not from coldness, for I do not mind the cold. But from a strange light inside my hut, which was bluish, and unknown. I crawled on my belly to my door of hanging turf, lifted it. And there it was—my first Highland frost. Ghost-blue, and still.

It was beautiful, to my eyes. The mountains looked down on me, and glinted. But it also made me think that he was right—my roof would not do. It was too thin. Rain would come—driving, sideways rain which is the common Scottish kind, and a steady rain, too. And snow. I feared lying under my hind's skin with dreams in my head only to have the roof fall in on me, with an arm's depth of snow. I may not mind the cold, but I mind being woken rudely. We all need our sleep.

So on a frosty October morning I went down, into the glen. I crept into the woods, by the river Coe, and gathered more branches. I bundled them up, hauled them back. And this was hard doing, so I paused to rest a while. As I rested, I looked up. And on the slopes above my gully, there he was—the stag. His branches. He was eyeing me from a different hill and he had a single hoof held above the snow, as if he'd been walking when he spied me, and stopped. There we were, watching.

I counted his points. Five on the left side and four on the right.

He flicked his tail, trotted away.

I dreamt of his crown, that night. Under my new, thicker roof, I dreamt of his branches, his shining eye. And it was a deep dream, I think—for when I woke in the morning, I found more footprints in the frost outside my hut. I crouched, and looked at them. Human footprints. My hand was small against them, and I could smell wet wool.

It made me glad of my new roof, and my thickened walls.

———

There was also a hill called *Keep-Me-Safe*.

My name for it—of course. Named on a starry-sky night, for as I passed beneath it I looked up and asked *keep me safe? I am afraid.*

It did, too.

I was half-asleep. I was listening to the fire lick itself, and I lay on my side, tucked up. Outside, an owl called, and I shifted. The owl sounded far away, like wakeful things do when you are sliding into sleep.

Sassenach!

There was a bang on my turf door which made the hut shake.

I yelped. I had been soft and warm. I'd been dreaming, and now I was scrambling to my feet with my hair snagging on the thatch, and I heard a horse snort outside. *Sassenach!*

No good news comes in the night-time with a bang on the door, and a sweating horse—and I fell outside to find Iain MacDonald on my threshold again with his hands on his hips from his hard ride. *Your plants,* he said.

I rubbed my eyes.

What are their purposes?

Which? I asked. *They have many purposes. Toothaches, nightmares, the fluxes. The gout, the hiccoughing, the—*

Wounds? Hard ones. To the head which bleed profusely and cannot be stopped?

I looked at his eyes. I understood this, now—this bluntness of his. His speed. I said, *yes.*

Get them.

I was quick, for I know what my herbs are. I took horsetail, bugle and some chervil, and said *who is ill?*

My father.

The Chief?

Aye.

And it was as I climbed onto the garron with him, in front of him, and held on to the oily mane, that I thought *merciless.* I remembered *their chief is savage-hearted, even to Highlanders,* and we clattered down the gully, and west into the glen. Mud came up, from the hooves. His horse snorted like my mare had snorted, and I was afraid, Mr Leslie—my heart was fast, and my hands shook, and as we galloped under a starry sky I looked up at it. I looked at the trees. We passed a broad, pale mountain I'd never seen before, and I asked it *keep me safe?* Then, like a ghost, it was gone.

HE TOOK me to the very western end. There were lights ahead that grew brighter, and as we rode I smelt peat-smoke. We passed homes on either side—chimneys, hearths, dogs. People. I saw figures in the half-dark, and they saw me go by. I clutched to the mane, held my breath.

Keep me safe. Be with me.

The horse slowed, and tossed its head. Iain MacDonald dropped the reins, and slid down to the ground, and I slid too which pushed my skirts up so I struggled with them to make myself decent, and pulled them back down. Patted my hair.

He said *come.* Like I was a dog to him.

It was the biggest house I had ever seen. In all my small life, I'd not seen a house as tall, or as glowing as this. It was such a wide, strong house that I wondered how it could be in a glen—not a city, or in Hexham. How could it be here? It was mostly stone. But its windows had glass in them—proper glass, like in the Lowlands—and its roof was deep-blue slate. I stared. I could smell pine trees, and knew they were about us. I could hear how water is, when a wind catches it, so I knew that the sea was behind me, unfolding in the dark.

I looked. I did not move.

Iain was ahead, and when he saw how I stood he hissed, *come!* And he knocked twice on the door and pushed it, and was gone.

I thought of *go!* Of all the words I know, I know *go* very well. *Run away.*

But I followed him—I did not run. I took a few, slow breaths, and smoothed my skirts, and I crept towards the door. My hand was scared to push it, but my head said *Corrag—push the door. The world is with you, and Cora is.* I did push it. And if it was the biggest house I'd ever seen, then the door opened up onto the biggest room in all my days. It was how the King's rooms must have been—oak panels on the walls, and more glass, and silver cups. There were antlers all about it, and a cow's horn strung up by a leather strap, and a wolf's skin lay down on the floor with its teeth still in, and holes for its eyes. There were proper beeswax candles, which gave out a bright light so that I squinted. A roaring fire. Mirrors. The candles' honeyed smell.

I smelt dogs, too, and sweat. Meat. Liquor. I smelt old leather, and amongst it all a smell I knew but could not name—a metal smell.

Co tha seo?

A voice. I blinked about me. There were a dozen folk in there, or more. I shielded my eyes from the candlelight and saw a dozen faces— half-lit, or fully-lit. They were lined, and weathered, and their eyes were all upon me—they stared, and stared.

I stepped back.

Iain spoke. He said *here.*

And I thought, *blood.* That was the smell—blood, fresh blood—and Iain took my shoulder very roughly, and said into my ear *there! Go to him. There.*

I did not want to look up, but I did.

There he was. Him they called *the MacIain,* but I had heard him called a hundred other things. *Butcher,* the plum-faced one had said. The soldiers said *the Devil was a better man. He eats his own foe, does he? Slayed a hundred men . . .*

He sat, with a cut on his head.

I stared. I did not want to go to him, but Iain pushed me. *Go!*

I went to the wound. And as I came to it, as it became clearer to me, I forgot his size, and the glass, and the candles, and I forgot the dozen faces—for the wound was wet, and red. It streamed its redness down the side of his face and onto his chest. His shirt was sodden, and the rest of his face was very pale. He eyed me. Those eyes were blue, but red-rimmed. I could see the little veins in them. His lips unsealed themselves.

You're the English thing he said. And then, to himself, or maybe to the people at his side he whispered *is she a child?*

I looked at the wound. I thought *look on the wound, and mend it,* and as I peered at the tissue which was very neatly sliced I said *your son sent me.*

My son? Which one of them? Which son?

Iain took off his coat, shook his hair. *She has herbs. Hers is the hut in the Coire Gabhail.*

A blade had done the wound. It was such a clean, deep, straight wound that I made a small noise, like I had been wounded too—for it would have killed most men.

Yes he said. *An inch deeper and I would be dead, I think.*

I moved myself, to see each part of it. It hung, like a mouth, and I could see the sides of veins, and old dirt in it. Was there a bone? I saw some white amongst it all. Some would have paled and fainted at this, but not me. Not hardy me.

I need liquor, I said *and water. More cloth. Clean cloth. A needle and thread.*

The chief growled *get these things! Get them for her or I will die here!* There were footsteps, and hurrying. He turned back to me, with shrewd eyes. His moustache was glossy with bleeding. His face was striped with old wound-marks, and he had a lost tooth from a fist, or a musket's butt. *Mend me,* he said. *If you do not, you yourself will need mending.*

What an order. What a thing to say. I might have wept with fear, but

I did not. I thought of what trouble I'd seen, and survived—trouble that was worse than a bloodied, very tall man with sharp words. *I will survive this,* I thought—*I will.* A lady's hand placed a bowl of water by me, and strips of cloth, and a candle. I thought *I will mend him,* and I tied back my hair in a knot. I poured liquor on the wound to make it clean. He winced, and hissed, so that I said *excuse me*—but what other way was there? None. Then I laid my herbs out, ran my hands across them. *Privet,* I wondered. But it was too mild—and a womanly herb, which works best for women's blood. I breathed in all their scents. I closed my eyes, thinking, and there was silence in the room behind me. None said *faster.* They waited—like they knew that the right herb is the answer. It is the most vital part.

Rupture-wort. I lifted it, said its name. I powdered it very roughly, dropped a little in water and said *drink.* He did. He took it, swallowed. He closed his eyes, then, and I dabbed at his wound which ran from his ear up to his crown.

The fire crackled, but there was no other sound.

Who did this? I asked.

Iain said *that's not yours to know.*

I was quiet for a small time. Then I said *when? That matters. I must know when this happened to know the right way to heal it. The herbs.*

This afternoon. He was down at Glenorchy.

How many hours?

A new voice came. A new man's voice. It came from the shadows to my right and said, *three hours. No more. I was with him.*

But I made the man pay for it, did I not?

You did, Father.

He said *ha.* It led to a small, pained cough.

I muttered to myself *three hours?* It was such a deep wound. It was running so freely that most folk would have died within one hour, or less. Three hours—and he still bled. I did not know how much more blood he had left in him. He was a huge man—as he sat, his head was the height of my own head, and his chest was five times as broad as my own—but his skin was pale, and we all need our blood. *He bleeds too much,* I said.

I took a cloth, soaked it in a paste of horsetail and bugle. I tried to press it on. I pressed hard, but my hand was so small against the wound. It could not staunch all of it. Such a tiny hand.

I said, *I need a person's hand. A hand?*

Someone came by me. I felt their shadow, their body's warmth, and I saw a hand held out. I took it—a broad, man's hand, his right hand, and I took it, pressed it hard against the poultice. I spread the fingers out, pressed the thumb, and I saw how marked the skin was—bruises, and old scars, cuts which had half-healed themselves into darker, puckered skin. I saw the fingernails. One was black, from a blow of some kind. One was torn. I said, *keep your hand there. Like that.*

Like this?

I did not glance up at him. My mind was on the wound. My own hand held a needle in the candle's flame to make it clean, and to move it better through the flesh. Then I threaded it. It took a small while, for I trembled a little from it all. But I sucked the thread's end, and, in time, I pushed it through the needle's hole.

Let me see it now. I whispered it.

I gently lifted the man's hand, and looked. There was less blood. It still bled, but less quickly. That's a sovereign herb for bloody things.

So I sewed the Chief MacIain. I did it slowly, with my smallest stitches. I breathed very softly, and thought of nothing else but *mend him, sew him up,* and the fire made its sound.

It was a quiet room, now. Folk nestled back in their chairs, or against the walls. The man at my side stepped back, into the shadows, and the room hushed itself. I breathed. I thought the Chief was asleep, for his eyes were closed and his breath was very steady, but as I sewed he spoke. He said, *I hear you seek safety. That you came here for that.* He laughed a soft, slow laugh.

I sewed.

Have you found it? Here? Look at the blood on you . . .

He opened one eye. I looked into its blueness. I saw the fire reflected in it, and the candles on the walls.

It is safer than most places is what I whispered.

Ha, he said. *A beetle hides with beetles, does it? You think you're less black amongst other black things?*

I did not understand this. He wheezed, and I let him. His wife lifted a cup to his lips and he drank, and when he had swallowed he said, *what have you heard, I wonder? About the MacDonalds of Glencoe?*

I let him settle. Then I pushed the needle back into his skin, and sewed again. What might I say? Always the truth is better. *That you thieve. You fight.*

We all fight! All clans thieve! If we did not steal cattle, our own would be taken and we would starve! And if we fight more than most it is to save our glen—for men have always wanted our glen as their own, and come with their knives to claim it. He muttered at this. *Campbells, mostly. Always an eye on their pockets . . . And they have sworn their love for a different king to us.*

There it was. *King.* One of my dread words. What good ever comes from saying it?

You've heard us called papists, have you not? Ha. That Popish clan of Glencoe . . . We are not wealthy men, but we have anger. Vigour. Faith! He thumped his chest. *We have hearts that would fight to the death, and that is true wealth—that is.* He settled back. He coughed a little, pulled his plaid about him. *They wanted me dead, so they took a sword to my head. But I'm still living. And my sons have their swords in their hands . . .*

I did not speak. This was not the time to do my prattling.

But the Chief leant forwards very slowly, tilted his head, said *And you? Who is your king?*

The room shifted itself. His wife was sharp in Gaelic, and I wondered if she also hated talk of kings. Maybe all women hate it for they know where it leads—to their men riding out for it. Making them widows for *king.*

I have no king, I said.

None? We all have a king. William is on the throne. You do not think he is your king?

I looked at my needle. I thought for a moment and said *neither matters. Not to me. None of them believe what I believe. None would want me living.*

Kings matter, he said, carefully.

Not to me.

They matter as God matters. Who he asked *is your god?*

I have no god like most people have a god.

The Chief unpeeled his second eye. He stared. His stare was fierce, and hot, and the fire hissed, and I wondered how this had come to be—me, in the Highlands, sewing a chief with beeswax candles on the walls. He breathed to me, *no god?*

Behind me, Iain said *she's alone, sir. Not living with the others.*

Which others? I asked.

But the Chief said more loudly, *no god? None?* He winced. *Last summer we rode out to the Pass of Killiecrankie—myself, my sons here, my tacksmen and cousins. We fought with our hands for King James against red-coats with muskets, and won. We won! We fought for him, and killed for him—because of his faith, our faith. We lost Bonnie Dundee on the field, and may the Lord save his soul—but he died for his king, and for God, and gladly so.* I felt so small in his hard blue stare. *What do you live for? What would you give your life for?*

I did not speak.

For these limp herbs of yours?

I had no words. I could not think of words, so I said very quietly *you do not know me, sir.*

I do not! I do not know you! Yet you are living on our land! Ours! In a house of moss and dung with feathers by the door! You bathe in our burns and steal eggs from our hens and now you say you have no god?

My eyes pricked. I had no words at all now. I was never good at being shouted at.

Like he saw this, the MacIain settled back. He held out his hand for more whisky. He kept very still as I sewed, and sewed, and in time he gave a wry smile—a knowing one. *Witch?* he said. *Ha. Witches and Scots . . . We have both had our hammers, have we not?*

That was all he said to me.

He kept his eyes closed and said no more. He slept, I think, in his chair.

I WASHED my hands in a bowl. I gathered my herbs, and untied my hair. When I turned, there were two men standing by the door. They were both red-coloured, both tall.

Iain said, *Alasdair will take you back.*

It's raining, he said.

I looked at him, then. I looked at this man for the first time—at his dark-red hair, the rough, reddish beard on his jaw, and how his hair fell near his eyes. I looked at the height of him, and breadth, and I saw how thick his legs were, from a life of hills and riding hard. I saw his mouth. I saw his eyes—deep-blue. They looked at me through his hair, and his stare was bold, unblinking, and like no stare I'd known in all my life— hot, strong—but also, it was like I did know it. Like I'd somehow seen these eyes before. I stared, back. Then I looked down. I saw his hands. I saw the torn nail and the scars, on his right hand.

I whispered, *no.*

Iain breathed out, as if tired of me. *It's late, and it's far. He'll take you on a garron.*

No, sir.

I wanted to be on my own. I wanted night air. To walk through the rain on my own, with my thoughts, and to clean my face in a midnight pool. Like witches do.

I'll walk, I said.

Iain stepped aside, let me pass. *Must the wound be looked upon again?*

I nodded. *In a day or so.*

Then we will expect you.

And I left. I trod past the houses to where it was dark, and cool. I knelt by the Coe and drank from cupped hands. I stood in the rain, took down my hood and said *it's raining* like he had said it. *It's raining. It's raining. It's raining . . .*

All night it pattered on my roof, and turf door.

⸎⸻◁▷⸻⸏

We have days which change us. I believe that.

I believe that the world changed for Cora when her mother was sunk down. I think also that the calf with the star on its face undid her, and changed her—so she had two such days.

Me? I reckon I've had a hundred of them, a hundred days which made me think *I am different now*—different to what I was before. *North-and-west* changed me. The soldier did. The five kittens drowning changed me in some way, because I felt what was right and wrong so clearly that it made me strong, and clear-minded. Rannoch Moor's wide space spoke to me, I know that. So did the mare, and her dying. So did many things I saw—mostly night-time things.

You. I think you have changed me, too. Until you, Mr Leslie, I thought all churchmen wanted me tied up by the neck, with my feet mid-air. I had run from such men. Crouched low. Do you want me dead? Maybe. You're so proper, with your buttons, and your neat buckled shoes. But if so, you hide it. You sit here, in this cell—which is a plenty more than others do.

Yes you changed me. Gormshuil told me *he will come* and look— you came.

That night did too—change me.

That wound, and the dog which slept by the fire, and those candles in their silver holders on the wood-panelled walls . . . *It's raining*, and *who is your king?* They all changed me. Made me better. Made me what I am.

And what am I? Some might say a snag-haired lonesome thing, with the Devil standing by. A wretch. A waste of breath and life. But I am not.

IN THE day that followed my first visit to the house, I took myself away. I roamed south, across the blowy tops, and down. I found another glen this way. Its loch was glass with stillness. Its fish were so plentiful they swam into my hand, and I took a few of them to eat or store for winter months—but most of them swam on. I felt their fins against my palm. I saw their pink and gold.

Such gifts, I thought, at the water's edge. *Every day.*

And in the evening I trawled my skirts back to my little hut, and found two chickens there. Two. Pecking the earth by the hazel tree.

So I had my own eggs, maybe. A *thank you,* or a *sorry*—in brown-feathered form.

⁜

I was made for places, as you know. I was asked by the MacIain *what would you give your life up for?* And I said nothing. But at that moment, sewing him, I would have said *for this world,* I think. *For kindness. For the simple, daily moments that we stop seeing, but should not—a pan as it boils, or how a flower is more open than it was the day before. Because I truly love those moments. I love such places as a marsh, or a cave.*

I'd have said this, if I'd been brave enough. If the words had come.

But I didn't say them. I never did. What I said, in the end, was just one word—and later. By my fireside, I said it. *Him.*

I KNOW. So soon, Mr Leslie—so sudden.

But with my knees to my chest I knew, already—*him. Him. Him.*

My love,

We are fully in Glencoe now, the prisoner and I. It has taken seven nights, and I have sat upon a stool which plagues my back as I write, but now she unfolds the glen for me, and she unfolds the men and women who are maybe dead now, or maligned. No matter that I am in the half-dark, and she's on wet straw—she has laid the glen out for me with all its mist and hillsides that I felt I was there, on its rocks. She does talk well. Once, I thought she talked too much—too richly, too carelessly. Certainly, she can talk at haste. But even here, Jane, at my bureau, I believe I can hear the rain.

She speaks of the MacDonalds. Furthermore, she speaks of the MacIain, who is well-known in this country. If you have not heard his name (which I should think you haven't. Why would you? Few men's fame reaches our small village, does it? Long may it stay so—Glaslough, with its hedges and birds and its lack of trouble), then let me tell you he is the worst of them. He did butchering in the Campbell lands and took to raiding boats that were moored off the west coast, and I hear he was a man of such savagery that he drank from the skulls of his foe. Some rumours are truer than others, of course. But of his prowess in battle, and the loyalty he inspired there cannot be doubt. Nor that he was tall—I hear he was a giant.

I have not met a soul here in Inverary who was not afeard of him.

Yet—yet!—Corrag tells me that she saved his life, in a fashion. She told me, Jane, that she was summoned to stitch a wound on his head, after a skirmish. She tells me he said mend me or you will need mending—*which are brutal words from a brutal man. He roared, it seems, on kings, and faith, and I have long heard (as all Scotland has heard) how fiercely Jacobite he was—he and his clan. I shall not recount how she mended him, for she spoke of these herbs that she lives by. But she did sew—and wasn't I always* astonished at how much can be saved or bettered by a stitch or two? I will call her brave, if nothing else. Small, and well-meaning, and brave.

These herbs, Jane. How am I to see them? I have always seen a witchery in finding cures in plants. Yet she said, once, that if herbs are made by God, then their qualities are God-given and have no Devil in them. There is a sense in her words. She is yet to have hurt a living creature, save for those she takes for food—and she seems sorrowful each time she speaks of a fish she has smoked. I feel, in short, she is kind.

In matters of duty, I am growing well-informed. My papers are many, now—for I write plenty of what she speaks of, and as you know (and see) my handwriting was never as small as my father might have hoped for. Before I retire each night, I read through the day's words—for they all paint these men for me, and the Highlands, and her own life. She spoke of a raid at Glenorchy, and I know this is true for I have also heard it spoken of (in Stirling, I caught word)—it was a ripe and savage looting. It seems to be their way, as I know a Glen of Lyon suffered also, at their hands. Not a home was left unburned, as I hear it, in that glen—and it was done at the year's close, too, so a perishing time to be mauled. The west Highlands seem brimful of tales of feuds, raids and misdeeds.

I have written a little of the Glencoe sons. The MacIain had two, Jane— both red-headed, spirited men. I have written (I can see it, now, as I write this) "did they survive the night?" For who knows? None know, for certain. I am minded to think they both died, for would they not have been sought out? Struck down? For there can be no denying that William would want this clan stamped out, their bloodline gone.

Jane—a month ago, to call a mountain A Ridge Like a Church, as she does, would tread near blasphemy, in my eyes. I'd have condemned it. But she spoke very tenderly—her sight is very tender, in that she sees and feels what we have mostly forgotten to see. She says that she felt humbled by the ridge, *as she feels humbled by a church. Grandeur, was her word. She may not know it, but she has her Godly ways—indeed, she speaks better than some men of my profession that I might write of.*

What a simple creature she is. How lonely.

I feel that we walk by the ridge, her and I. On clear days, we see eagles.

Charles

III

*"[Its leaves are] broader at the bottom than they are
at the end, a little dented about the edges, and a sad,
green colour, and full of veins."*

of Hedge Hyssop

There is always the thought in me that you will not return. Even
now. Even now that we speak as friends do, or nearly. I no longer
think you may prick me, or spit, and I trust you now, but I watched
you put your coat on in the evenings and fasten your bag with its ink
and good book, and think it may be my last sight of you. That you
will not come back.

So I am glad when you do—come back to me. It is a good thing—
and what good things are there, in the life of a thing that waits for
its death? Not too many. I have my comforts, but they are memories,
mostly. They are my own comforts which I must find, and bring back.
How you duck into the room is a comfort to me, and I will confess
that I never thought a churchman might bring a sense of ease to me,
but you do. I want you to know that.

I thought it last night, and I said to the straw and the spider in its
web that if you came back to me, I would tell you. That you are a
comfort. That I am glad, when you walk in.

. . .

YOU are tired. I worry I tell you the wrong things—do I? Tell you the wrong things? Do I speak too much, or not enough? I can hurry to the end if you wish it, and then you may sleep or be on your way, and I will understand it and not see it as any broken vow—for I have learnt from the MacDonalds what passions can burn in a man. What eagerness is in them, for *king,* and *faith.*

When I knew them more, and felt to be one of them, or nearly, I heard the tacksman of Inverrigan pray for James to return before he prayed for his family's health—like James mattered more. But maybe James did. For what we believe is what shapes us, and our lives, and Angus MacDonald of Inverrigan with his freckled face thought all the world would brighten with a Stuart on the throne. That James's return would heal his family of shivers and aches. So *restore James to his seat, and shine the light of the Stuarts back into Scotland so it may chase away the dark,* he said, with his eyes closed, on his knees.

You ask *what is Inverrigan?*

It was a handful of houses. It was a few homes in the woods, by the Coe. That was how the MacDonalds of Glencoe lived, sir—not in one settlement, but in a few smaller ones. Each one had a name. *Achnacon* was the houses by the river's bend, where they say the warrior Fiann once kept his hunting dogs. *Achtriochtan* was on the valley floor, by the loch where a water-bull slept, and this bull would creep out on full-moon nights to graze, and shake himself. It wasn't true, of course. A water-bull? But myths can be so strong they feel like truth. And the men at Achtriochtan could tell a myth well. They were called *bards* and *poets,* and sat close to the fires. They had a Killiecrankie song and one for their kin who fought for Montrose, and ones against all Campbells, and ballads on where they came from—for all Highlanders know that. All were Gaelic songs. I could not sing one for you but maybe I could hum.

Carnoch, too. That was the biggest handful of homes. It was by the sea, and smelt salty, and faced the setting sun. The MacIain's house was there. His sons lived near it. It was, Mr Leslie, a fine place to be.

I say *was*. It *was* a fine place. For none of them exist, now.

It makes me so sad to say it, and think it. But the last time I saw these homes, they were on fire. They were flaming in the snow, and blackened with smoke. Soldiers ran through them, saying *any left? Any left? None must be left!* In the woods, at Inverrigan, there were nine people outside it—trussed up and dead. Snow came down on freckles. Snow settled on their eyes.

WHERE was I with my telling? I had stitched the Chief's face, I think?

I can still see it. His nose, and missing tooth. He is dead, now. They shot him in his bedchamber, as he dressed to meet his guests. He was calling for wine to be brought to them, for he always said *am I not a good host, Corrag?* and when he turned his back they shot him. So he is dead, and gone.

But two winters ago, he was living. And I was walking on the wintery peaks of Glencoe—using my hands to haul myself up onto rocks, and leaving my footprints and handprints in the thin snow. From the Three Sisters I could see the whole world, or it felt so. To the north, over the Ridge Like a Church, I could see peak after peak. Snow after snow.

I took myself to Carnoch with my cloak tied up, and my feet were bound with rabbit skin for the ice was sharp as knives. I had my herbs pressed to my body and my breath was like a cloud, and I had spent a whole night taking knots out of my hair. I'd combed it with a thistle, and scrubbed my face.

Be calm I told myself, as I went.

Be calm, and be kind.

The village was smaller by day. Smaller, with more mud in it. Through the mist, I saw faces which came to stare at me—at my grey eyes, my small ways. Dogs growled. Children called out.

The lady answered when I knocked on the door—her hair greyer in the winter sun, and her face with more lines. She looked down on me. She tilted her head as if her mind was saying *who is . . . ?* But then she knew. She smiled. At me. She smiled at me, and when had that happened? I could not recall a smile at me.

Corrag she said. *He is better. Come.*

He was in the chair like he'd never stood up, or left it. The dog still slept with its head on its paws. Still candles, and still a fire, so that I could think *is this a dream? It is all the same.*

There was Gaelic spoken.

Then he said in a deep barrel-voice, *Ah! My nurse is here.*

He had a colour to him that he'd not had before—a pinkness to his cheeks, and where his eyes had been red they were not now. I bowed my head. I almost did a curtsey, for how does one greet a man so tall and strong, and with such a voice?

Sit he said. *Take this clot of nonsense off my head and tell me how mended I am.*

I did. I nestled by the dog, by the MacIain's knees. Reaching up, I unpeeled the poultice of rupture-wort and horsetail, and looked. The stitches were very black, and not very neat, but they had held. The skin about them was ink-blue from bruises, and still swollen up in parts. But there was no yellow or blackness. I could see and smell no infection there, and I sat back from him and did a smile.

It looks better I said, *than it did.*

Ha! Better? My head was cut in two. To look any worse would make me a dead man.

It is swollen, and sore-looking. But it smells as it should, and there is a crust coming.

A crust?

This is good. It will knit the skin together.

Lady Glencoe and I made a new poultice by the fireside. She pressed down the herbs so their juices came out. I wondered if she had ever had *witch* thrown at her, for she had a knowing look to her, and knew the way of plants.

The dog stretched itself, and turned, settled down.

Thank you for my hens I said.

Ah. The hens. You need not take my cousin's eggs now.

I blushed. *No.*

I am the MacIain, he said, waving an arm, *who butchers and bludgeons, as they say—but I have a heart, also. I am not without gratitude where gratitude is due.* He let me lie the poultice down upon his wound, closed his eyes. *I wonder if you saved me the other night, Sassenach. I know the wound was deep, and I've seen men die from less. I've had my rough dealings before, and survived them. But I'm not young, and that wound . . .* He opened those eyes. *I was also sharp-tongued with you. I know I was.*

You have strong feelings.

I do. He straightened his back. *Yes. But that was not the time to show them. The hens are a gift.*

I nodded. I knew this was him saying *sorry*—a proud man's way, which is not saying the word itself but treading about it. *Thank you.*

Ach, he said, *thank my son. He took them to you. Went out in this weather with a flapping hen in each hand. Left his wife and fireside to climb the heights with a blizzard coming down . . . But that's him. That was always his way—fiery, and foolishly so. He'll learn, or he'll die—one or both.*

I heard this. As I did, I thought of Iain's quickness with me, his fox-sharp eyes. I said *I am grateful to Iain for it. I'll care for those hens.*

He shook his head, drank from his cup. As he swallowed he said, *It was Alasdair who carried them. Am I mended?*

I did not answer him. I put my herbs away, and told him I would return in a week or more to pick the stitches out of his skin, but he straightened his back in his chair—he was taller than me, just by sitting.

You will come back sooner, he said. *You will eat here. Drink. I want to know more of my English nurse—of what she knows. You will come back sooner.*

I backed away, and made noises like an unsure child does.

I am not asking, he said.

I thought *be high, be wild.* For I knew no other way. I had always been for places, and I knew how places were—so I took myself to the places I knew would soften me—air, rushing water. I sat very still in thin, wet snow and felt it fall upon me. I thought *he left his fireside. He left his wife.*

You are for places, Corrag—not people. Remember that.

But as I took a path back down towards my hut, I found some brown feathers drifting on the snow. I stopped. They rolled themselves slowly, and I thought *from my hens*—for they were the same brown, and softness. I knelt down, touched them. I pressed one to my hand. And I knew that Alasdair had come this way.

I CARED for those hens. I did. Their natures were gentle, and they tilted their heads when they looked at me. Their eggs were big, and cream-shelled.

In the evenings, I lay a little grain down for them. And one evening, as I watched them go *peck* and stretch their wings, I thought *grain . . .* I did not have very much of it. I'd gathered seed-heads all autumn, and these were feeding them well. But it would not last. I did not have very much at all—only my herbs, which were for curing, not eating.

I looked about myself. A few fish smoked in the eaves and I had some mushrooms. An old berry or two. I was not worried for myself, for I could live on air pretty well—but these hens were a gift. They were mine to care for, now. And I did not want them hungry.

I'll look after you, I told them.

I talked to the hens for a while. And because I was talking, I was not listening. I was thinking of the hens, and nothing else.

I smelt a smell. There was my peat-smoke, and herbs—but there was another smell. It came in quickly, as if it had been blown in, and the hens flinched as I did. We all turned around.

I thought *rotting.*

It was the odour of a rotting plant, or even meat that worms had found.

I moved to my door, thinking maybe a creature had died outside in the early frost and I was smelling its death, and if so I must tend to it in some way. I went out.

A woman stood there.

I made a sound, I think, for I had heard no footsteps or skirts on the ground. And in frost, all sounds are heard! Even a leaf falling down. A bird cleaning its wings. I said *how . . . ?*

Say your name she said.

I stared. I stared at her height, and her thinness. I stared at her, and I wondered her age, but could not tell it—she was weathered and lined, but this can belie an age. It says more of the manner of living than of how long one has lived, and so I stared, then, at her hair to look for some greyness. But she did not have much hair. I saw a shawl of filthy wool. Also, she had a very tight mouth, as if made for spitting. I knew her kind—or thought so. Sour piece.

Say yours I told her.

She narrowed her eyes. Her nails were all tangled in that shawl of muck and grime. I didn't see her teeth, for her lips were so puckered—

but I put a penny on them being pegs. Oh yes I knew her kind. She was what all folk see, when they hear *witch*—unclean, ill-mannered, fearful things. She is what brought the word *witch* in.

I would not give my name. I waited.

I know you she said. Beady-eyed bird.

And I know you. Which was a lie of mine. I did not know her—yet I thought that I had sensed her, had thought in my bones that I could not be the only hiding soul in these parts. *She does not live with the others,* Iain had said to his father, in the beeswax candlelight. I'd heard this, as I'd stitched. I remembered this. *The others.* This woman.

This bony creature with her privy smell walked towards me, then. She passed me, bent down and crept into my hut.

I squawked. I followed her, saying *this is my home! You cannot walk into my home like it's your home!*

She could not straighten herself inside it, she was so tall. But she tried. She lifted herself until her hair with its leaves brushed the roof. The fish I was drying shed a few scales.

Ah . . . she said. *Herbs.*

Like Iain had said. Like the only thing that mattered to any person in this glen was herbs. *Yes.* I said it sharply.

Which?

Which?

Herbs, she said. *Which herbs?* I heard her voice properly then. It was a soft Scottish voice, and she spoke like the MacDonalds did—like English was not the tongue she was born with. Like she had learnt these English words.

Where are you from? I asked.

Do you have henbane?

Where, I said, *are you from? Tell me. Where are you from, and where are you now living?*

She eyed me. Maybe it was the firelight on her, or how she stooped as an old woman would, but she looked less fearful then. More human. I saw a sadness in her, briefly. Like a bird's shadow it flitted over her, and was gone.

Moy. 'Tis not near here.

I nodded. *And now?*

On what they call the buachaille. The pointed rock at the east.

I knew it. It was the black, pointed mountain at the east of the glen. It was where I had trodden on an arrowhead, and where I'd seen an eagle preen its feathers on an alder branch.

I did not ask why she was in the glen. Not why she wasn't in this place called *Moy,* these days. I thought *she is hiding.* For most folk I've met in my life that live alone are hiding, from other people.

Do you have henbane?

I said *ha.* Folk only want henbane because of what it does—which is that it stupefies their heads, and makes them dream whilst they're awake, and I've never wanted that. Cora told me. She said it owns you, once you try it—that you seek it again and again.

Despite her puckered mouth, and her stink, I felt for her, then. I thought *poor her. Being as she is.* Plucking her shawl and looking for that herb.

I have henbane.

And her eyes grew wide, and a peg-toothed smile came.

So, Mr Leslie, in my hut, on a winter day, I gave a woman called Gormshuil a fistful of henbane so that she shook as she took it, and whispered to it as if it could hear. *Yes . . .* But I did not give it freely— no, sir. I gave her a price for the herb. I asked for some grain to feed my hens upon, and which I might make a broth from.

She flinched. *Grain?*

It is a fair bargain, I said. *Henbane is harder to find than grain, I can promise you.*

I watched her go. She made no sound, and the mist soon took her and she was gone. I thought *I will get no grain for this*—for what was trustworthy, in her? I doubted that she ate. I doubted that she found much joy in the world, or beauty, or that she treated people well. I half-doubted she had ever been there, in the mist—for she had been so ghost-like. But her smell lingered.

I did get grain.

Two days later, she came to me with a sack and her fish-eyes. Grain was in it. I peered in, smiled, and when I looked back to thank her she was gone, and a crow was in her place. Some folk say witches shift their shapes into new creatures, when it suits them, and I know this is a lie. I know it can't be done. It is only when bones misbehave themselves, or when the falling sickness comes and women twitch. But the crow had a look to it. It tilted its head, cawed at me twice, and I fancied it was *thank you*, or *see? Grain for you*.

It flew. I watched it fly. And when I looked down at her footprints in the snow, I wished they were not her footprints. I wished they were someone else's.

⟡————⬧————⟡

Say what you will. Say *old hag*. She looked it, and smelt like one. She was an old half-human creature who suited the winter weather—not in the way I suited it, for Gormshuil was not winter-born and saw no beauty in a naked tree. No. She suited winter for she had no green shoots in her—no hope, no love, no dreams. She was as thin as sleet can be. As sly.

I told myself, sometimes, that she had been a child once. A daughter, and a wife.

Once, I told my hens, *she was happy—once. I must remember that.* But like it is hard to see a winter field and remember it in flower-time, so it was with Gormshuil.

· · ·

WHY do I speak of her? Because she lived. Because by living, she altered the world as we all do, and who is there to speak of her? So I speak of her. And in time, perhaps you will—for she played her part in the murders, sir. Her name is worth writing down.

We all have our stories, and we speak of them, and weave them into other people's stories—that's how it goes, does it not? But she did not speak of hers. She was reeky and lonesome, and when I think of her I see henbane in her teeth. She lived on a pointed mountain. She crouched by a fire with two other women whose minds were half-gone, and whose hearts were sealed up. And what life is that? A sadder one than mine was. Far more so. Full of winter nights.

Gormshuil of Moy. You will hear many things said of her, and all bad. But not many people, sir, are all bad.

Those winter nights. I'd look out at the huge sides of snowy rocks which grew about me, and I'd see their eerie colours—grey, black, blue. Then I would go inside, where my fire spoke to itself. But still, I felt them. In my hut, I was still aware of the mountains looking down on me. I could feel their height, and darkness. I thought of their age, of what they had seen, and as I tucked up by my fire I thought *they glow* . . . Like living things. Their frost glinted on me, and their breath was icy-cold.

Some people hate such thoughts. They stay away from mountains like mountains mean them harm. But what I say to myself when I see a mountain or a starry sky, or any natural thing which feels too much to bear, is *what made this, made me, too. I am as special. We are made by the same thing* . . . Call it *God,* if you wish. Call it *chance,* or *nature*—it does not matter. Both the mountains of Glencoe and me are real, and here. Both the moon which is full tonight and you, Mr Leslie, are here, and shining.

IN THE days that followed Gormshuil, and her sack of grain, I saw Alasdair again. I was high up, looking down. He was by my hut, and then he circled it as if I might be hiding there. For a while he was still, thinking. He had no blades with him, and no hens. Just him—with his plaid, his dark-red hair.

From my hiding place, I watched him go. He trod down through the gully and back into Glencoe, and I could see his marks left in the snow.

I went down.

I touched the rock I'd seen him touch. I heard the sounds he'd heard—the stream, my hens—and I thought, *come back to me.*

My love,

*I will talk more of the blacksmith now, for he has given me plenty which
I have written down, and much of it will prove of interest to my Jacobite
brothers in London, and Edinburgh, and elsewhere. I wrote all afternoon,
and wrote a little more on my return from the tollbooth. My hand is a little
sore with it—but not so sore to keep me from writing my thoughts and love
to you.*

*My love—the cob, I will assure you, mends well. Indeed, I rather feel
he's liked his time in the forge, for he has a curiosity that I do not recognise.
He searched my pockets with his lips which he has never done previously—
perhaps the man (or a child of his? I think he has many) has been befriend-
ing him with sugar, or mint. I wouldn't advise it, but he is a good horse who
has served me well thus far.*

*And if a child has befriended a cob, have I befriended the child's father?
I may have done. It seems a long while since I have met a man as honest,
humble and amiable, as this. The blacksmith was eager to clean the stool
before I sat upon it, as if I was quite some guest—which I am not, clearly.
I am merely myself. But I was treated well—and in such a climate and in
such times I am grateful for it.*

*I complimented him on his work—for the cob seems far happier with his
feet, than he did. And the blacksmith thanked me. He said,* I take pride in
what I do. Kingdoms are won and lost, on a horse's shoes.

Indeed, *I said.* A man's pride in his work is Godly. I have always
said that.

He turned a glowing piece of iron in a fire, said not too much. For it
can be a vice, sir.

A deadly sin, as we know.

We nodded, and thought on this for a small while. The chief of that clan was known for it. For pride. For too much of it. Did you hear that?

I said, no, sir.

Och—*he brought the iron out*—a proud man. Pride killed him in the end, I'll tell you.

Pride? *I was minded to think that thieving and butchery was what killed him in the end—that he was punished by soldiers for a lifetime of uncivil ways.*

He said—most do think that. And that clan's savagery is what routed them out, right enough. But their pride, sir . . . The MacIain was a proud man to the last. He'd not swear an oath to a Campbell, and that's what made trouble for his men.

I asked about this oath. For I have heard whispers of it, Jane, but no more than that—and here I felt I might be told far more on it.

An oath. Of allegiance. Did you not hear of it? *Then he shrugged, said* perhaps being Irish you did not. Our King William ordered it. He might have his follies but he is no fool—he knows who the Highlanders serve, and that they plot against him. So he called for an oath to be sworn here in Inverary, by the first day of January. That all rebel clans might pledge their faith to him, and only him. Denounce their Jacobite ways.

I leant forward. And if a clan did not pledge it?

They would feel the King's full force upon them, as traitors do. And because the old chief MacIain would swear nothing to a Campbell but hatred, he rode to Inverlochy instead. Which was the wrong place. No oath could be sworn there . . .

I rose, then. I stood, and came towards him. So they swore no oath? The MacDonalds were killed for not swearing an oath?

They swore it, sir. They did. But . . . *he shook his head*—they were six days late.

See? I learn more, daily. I learn more about this country, its ways and laws.
More about William, and none of what I learn goes in his favour—it all
goes in ours.

How hated that Glencoe tribe must have been, to be mauled in such a
way! How strong and impressive a people they must have been, to have war-
ranted such hating. I can only think that there were smiles in London and
Edinburgh when they heard of this lateness in taking the oath—for is this
not treason? An act of defiance against this Orange king? If they needed a
reason to maul them, here it was. If they sought an excuse for routing them
and taking their land, then yes—pride gave it. Six days did.

I walked home from the forge feeling alive, Jane, and hopeful, and I am
minded to write to King James himself, in France, to tell him of what I have
learnt, thus far! It feels such news. It puts blood on Dutch hands.

But a blacksmith's word is not enough. He was not there, in the glen. He
did not know the MacDonalds or live amongst them, and he did not see the
murders with his own eyes.

I am a different man to the man who rode into Inverary, shivering and
old. I wrote of my hatred for witch. *I wrote scornful words, and damning*
ones, and did I not support her coming death? By flames? I am different,
now. The thought of her death troubles me—I cannot lie, or pretend other-
wise. Corrag speaks of goodness, largely, and beneath the knots and dirt and
blood I see how delicate she is, how frail. She speaks, too, of her fondness for
a man called Alasdair—the Chief's second son, and a rogue of some stand-
ing (though not in her eyes). What a tiny, lovesick creature she becomes, when
she mentions his name.

I am lovesick, also, for you. We are alike, then—the prisoner and I. We wish
for the touch of one who is far away, and in our quiet times we both think of
their face, their voice. Do you miss me, as much as this? And do you think,
my love, of our loss? Our daughter comes to me each night, as you do. My

greatest fear is that you grieve on your own—that you weep for our dead child in the dark, and alone.

My heart is with you. It is nowhere else—it is with you, and does not leave your side.

What strange days these are. I worry in them, and change. I have spent much of the day with my Bible on my lap. "The Lord says, I will bring my people back to me. I will love them with all my heart" (Hosea 14:4). What does this mean, now?

   Ever-loving

                                                              Charles

IV

I have been fretful, all night, about my hens.

Such hens. Good ones—pale, egg-coloured. They roosted in the hazel tree when it was mild, and closed their eyes with that milky, skin-like lid that chickens have, so that I wondered if they also had the sight—some second sight. In winter they nestled with me, indoors. They clucked as they slept.

Last night, in my cell, I said, *what of them now?*

I said it into the dark, so my voice came back off the walls. But truly—what of them? It still snows a little. Not as much as it did, and the snow is the watery kind—but it is still snow. Are they living? Alasdair's hens? In winter, I fed them what I had gathered in the leaf-fall months—stalks, pods, seeds. A little fat. But now I am here, with chains on my wrists, so how can I feed them?

I fear they are starving, up in the hills.

And my goats! In time, I had goats. Three of them—with tiny teeth, and lips which burrowed into my pockets, and they scratched their heads on brambles, and where are they now? Now that my fire is out, and their shelter is gone?

I tell myself *they are living.*

I say *they are just as they were. Yes.* The hens scratch under the snow. The goats, knowing I am gone and will not come back, have made their way up, up. Into the heights. They tread along the peaks with their eyes half-shut against the wind, and their coats turning white with flurried snow. They will survive. My goats will have baby goats, in the spring. Their babies will have babies of their own.

Maybe in the years to come, there will still be goats in Glencoe. Not many, but some. They will crop the higher slopes. And maybe if a person says *goats? Here? Wild goats?* then another will say to them *ah . . . Yes. They come from the goats of Corrag. She was a good woman who died in a bad way, and who did not deserve her burning. But she died. And these goats come from her goats, so let us remember her when we see them. Let us watch her goats, and rest a while . . .*

I would like that. I indulge myself in these dreams, in the dark.

I will hope for them to be so.

A FARM? No. But it came to feel like I had more than I needed—rich, in that way. I had two hens, three goats, and an owl that told its secrets to me on some moonless nights. I had spiders that weaved, in the darkness. The stag, too, with the branches. He came back, and back.

The world breathed about me, folded in and out, and what more could be asked for? *What is better? Than being this much in the world?* I asked this, as I watched the frosts settle down, or the smoke curl up from my fire.

Nothing is better I told myself.

There were days when I saw no people—not even one—and I said *nothing is better. Nothing is better at all.*

. . .

I DID not want to go back to Carnoch—and I did want to. Both.

Amongst their beeswax candles, the MacIain told me this—*we have always been a fighting clan . . .*

He was mending. He had rested, and drank, and the howling wind and weather had kept him by his fire so that he was flushed, bright-eyed. The room at Carnoch was full. It was fuller than it ever was, with maybe three dozen in there, and the air was scented with honey, and wet wool, and peat, and I could smell the hounds which scratched in the corners. I could smell people, too—sweat, and their whisky. I thought, *I breathe MacDonald breath.*

Always fighting, he said, filling his cup. *And these hills have been fought for since man first found them, and wanted them. The Irish were here before us. A man called Fionn with his warriors, and dogs. They fought many thousand men to save the glen—and when the Fionn men died, it is said the mountains grew upon them, and that even now they sleep with their swords beneath the rocks and earth. One day they will rise up again. Fight for what needs fighting.* He slowly brought his cup to his lips, and drank.

I imagined all these sleeping men.

He swallowed. *Iain Og nan Fraoch took the glen for his own, in time. He came from the islands. And he was a fine MacDonald . . .*

All are! said a voice. They laughed.

But are we not the finest? Of all MacDonalds? In how we live and fight? The room settled down. Their faces stared at the Chief, and the Chief stared at them, and when he looked back to me he said in a softer voice *we are named for him. We—the MacDonalds of this glen—are called the MacIains, for we are sons of him. Young John of the Heather sired our line in this glen—with its woods and hills, and so many fish in the rivers that all he did was dip his hand . . . They say that on winter nights you may hear his dog, barking.*

He could tell a story well, that man. That chief.

Everyone listened. Those people had heard this tale all their lives— of who they were from, and what legend is. But they listened like they had not heard it before, like part of their faith was to hear the tale of Fionn and his dogs. There were stories of Norsemen and Irish kings. A doomed love. Battles. The peat shifted itself, as it burnt.

I can hear the peat shifting. Can smell it.

BRING the stool nearer? I have much to say about them tonight— these *papists,* this *damnable sept.*

It was the last night in December. In my little valley, I was drinking from a pool of cracked ice, like a cat—crouching down, my hands flat. I heard a horse's nostrils, and turned, and it was Iain. He was astride his garron with a dead hind strapped behind, and he said *you are summoned. To Carnoch.*

I sat back on my ankles, wiped my mouth. *Tonight?*

Yes. Tonight.

Is it the MacIain? His wound? Or a new one?

The man scoffed. He shook his head, and he spoke very slowly, as if I were a simpleton—*no . . . It's Hogmanay. The last day of the year? You've been asked, so you'll come.*

So I went. How could I not, when I lived on their land? Drank from their cattle? So I freshened myself with water, and I crushed some rosemary in my hair to be sweet-scented, and I went to the great Carnoch house, where the river met the sea. I knew my way to it, now. I passed the peak called Keep-Me-Safe, and trod beside the Coe.

There were more people in that single, oak-walled room with its fire and beeswax candles and whisky and glass than I'd seen in all of Hexham, or in all my travelling days. I could see nothing but people, at first—waists and bellies and forearms. I was brushed by their plaids, got trodden on, and they were laughing and drinking and I thought *leave. You are not for here. Go back outside to the ice, and sharp air.* But as I turned to go a fair-haired lady came by me, and smiled. She took down my hood. She said *don't hide those eyes . . .* And she smoothed my shoulders, winked, moved on.

After this, I felt I was seen. With my hood down, I felt they were turning, and looking down at me. My cheeks grew hot. I gave a shy smile to the man from Inverrigan, but he only stared. A cup-eared boy called me *faery,* as I passed, and an elderly man smacked his toothless gums as I slipped by, like I was for eating, and I wished I hadn't come at all—for there were so many people, and so little air, and why had I come? I wasn't a MacDonald. I was dirty-nailed, small.

But the MacIain came. He strode through his people, gathered my cloak in his fist and said *my Sassenach! My English doctor who has no king . . .* And with one hand, he lifted me into the air.

All night, I sat by his side.

The other folk sat on the floors, or on chairs, or on the great table itself which brimmed with food and whisky cups. But he'd lowered me onto a stool by his side and said *should I not feed my healer? Keep her well? Ha!* From there, I peered. I looked upon the faces. The bear of a man whose egg I once stole carved up a leg of roasted deer, and laughed. There were children from Achnacon, squirming and fighting with sticks, and two women were whispering with linen curraichd on their heads, and Iain was kissing a rosy girl by the fire and a half-drunk man was playing a pipe and two men were quarrelling in Gaelic until their wives made them stop and Bran the dog was chewing a bone and a huge bear-man called MacPhail fought a man outside, so they both came in bloodied, but then they shook hands and drank. I stared and stared—because there was so much to see. So many lives.

Alasdair looked over the rim of his cup at me.

The MacIain said *have you ever seen such a people? As these?*

I said *no.* It was truthful.

No gatherings in England? No fine house like mine, to gather in? He was pleased at how I shook my head. He grinned, said *there is no greater clan than this . . . We are small, but we fight with heart and honour.* With his hand raised to silence the room, he said, *we have always been a fighting clan . . .*

And he told me of heather, and Fionn.

THERE were bannocks and barley-cakes and cheese and atholl brose. There was the hind, roasting, and more ale than I'd seen, and a cup of corn whisky which Lady Glencoe pressed into my hand and said *drink.* I nodded, brought it to my lips. But it made me cough from smelling it.

And there was music—the lively kind, which they danced to, and clapped to, and some pottery was broken to a cheer which made Bran bark out, and I saw Alasdair laughing with men, and children drowsed on their mothers' laps. A bristly man came by me and said, *a dance, wee beastie?* He held his hand out. But I did not dance. I stayed sitting, with my whisky. I saw the colours whirl, and the plaids swing, and when the jig ended the MacIain called out Gaelic words which hushed the room down. They settled—on chairs, or on each other. And a softer music came. It came from the fair-haired lady who had said *don't hide those eyes* to me. She stood in the half-shadows, held her hands across herself, and sang in such a frail, ghostly voice that it made my skin tighten, and my eyes felt strange. It made me think of Cora—for she had sung, once.

It was a Gaelic song. But it was a love-song, I knew that—from how she sang, and how they all listened with glistening eyes, like my eyes. *Love of Scotland,* I thought—not of a person, but of a place of air and wild land. Its rocks. I felt it was this, and when it was done, she seated herself by Alasdair. She pulled his arm about her, nestled against him. He kissed her hair.

I looked down. Bran put his head on my knee, and blinked, and I told him he was a very fine dog, a very fine dog indeed.

THE clock struck as I patted Bran, as the candles burnt low.

1691 was the year, now. And the MacDonalds of Glencoe raised their cups, and said a prayer—which I reckon was like how most prayers are. I reckon they asked for God's help this year, for a good harvest, for health, for courage in war. All hearts ask for these things, in their way—no matter of faith, or language.

I asked for them too. I sat on my stool and asked the world for food for my hens, and love, and good skies, and to keep these people safe—for they'd never thrown stones, or said *hag* at me.

For a while it was a quiet room. But then the pipe roared up, and the MacIain shouted *more whisky, here!* And there was more dancing, more songs.

I LEFT. I gathered my cloak about me, and slipped away. It was late, and I longed for my hut—its hush, the hens.

I ducked under the door and put my hood up. I heard my name.
Corrag?

He was in the doorway. He had come up behind me. One hand was on the eaves like he was testing them for strength, and he rested his forehead against that arm. His other hand was by his side. He said *are you leaving?*

Yes.

He looked very boldly at me—not blinking. *We've never met,* he said. *Not in a proper way. Nor did I thank you for mending our father. We* all thought that was his end, with that wound, but . . . He smiled. *I'm Alasdair Og.*

Og?

Aye. It means younger. Named after the MacIain.

He is Alasdair, too?

He is. He put his head on one side, as he looked. He saw me trying out *og*, in my mouth. He said, *you're Corrag, I think?*

I am.

There's been plenty of talk about you, did you know?

I hadn't known this but I wasn't too surprised. Women like us cause tongues to chat in shadows, and always did. Maybe I blushed. I know I gathered my cloak about me, as if to leave, for my own tongue was unsure of what to say to him with his blue eyes on me.

But he spoke. He said, *what brought you here? Of all places?*

Your brother said I was summoned—

No. He smiled. *Not here. What brought you to the glen?*

I also smiled, at that. I nearly laughed. I looked away and shook my head, for it seemed like an old story, now, and a strange one—too strange to speak of. Not to him, with his hair like that.

A long tale? Too long?

Yes.

He nodded.

We shifted for a while. Alasdair looked up to the eaves, smoothed his hand across them. Then he brought that hand down. He leant against the doorframe, and I wondered if I should turn, and go, for there was a long silence between us. Behind him, they were dancing again.

Did you eat enough? he asked. *There is plenty . . .*

Yes.

More silence. He breathed in. *So where did you spend your last Hogmanay? Not in a Highland glen, I reckon—not with that voice.*

I straightened. I looked sternly at him. Was he teasing me? Did he know the true answer, and was mocking me? His brother could mock, I was sure of that. His father, too. I eyed him, and searched for a wry smile or a raised eyebrow—but found none. He was looking at me like he truly wanted to know.

So I said, *I was on my grey horse in the Lowlands. We passed an inn at midnight, and heard them cheer. It was a full moon, and we galloped out across a low-tide beach that night, and did not stop till sunrise, and that's what I did.* I shrugged. *We galloped. Under more stars than I'd ever seen.*

He was very still. All the noise and dancing was behind him, and he was still. Just looking. He had the bright eyes which made me think that he could see it, in his mind—that beach. Its mirrored sand.

He opened his mouth to speak—but as he did this, an arm came about his waist so that he turned his head, and the fair-haired girl with the singing voice came to his side. She was taller than me, and more shapely. She had the shape a woman's meant to, and she pushed herself against Alasdair, said *you*—prodding his chest with her forefinger, and smiling—*are letting the cold air in . . .*

Then she turned to me. She beamed. She did not frown at my knotted hair or my ragged skirts. She said *I am Sarah. And I am glad of any new woman in this place—too many men! All these men . . .* Such a smile. Bright, and clear.

We all smiled. We smiled away, wished each other a fine, healthy year, and I tightened my cloak and turned, slipped away into the dark.

In the gully of birch trees I paused, briefly. I felt the night air. I breathed it.

I slept with a hen on either side of me.

This was winter, then—my season. My weather. And what a wild, Highland winter that one was. Ice creaked, and the flakes of proper

snow did not fall, at first—they hung, mid-air. They drifted about my
head as I walked back from the glen, with peat in my arms. When I
saw myself in darkened pools I saw my snowy hair.

Seeing it, I thought *this is the start.*

It was. These thin flurries did not last. Five days after Hogmanay, a
wind blew in. It threw snow against the northern ridge, and howled
up into my valley so that my roof shook. Skies swelled and raced, like
sea-skies do. And I wandered—for wasn't winter always too magick to
go unseen? I had never feared it. So I wandered where I knew there
would be beauty—to half-frozen water, or to the heights where deer
were. They sat against rocks, blinked in the wind. I saw a white hare
running—so fast and snow-coloured it was like wind, or a flurry of
flakes, and only its black eye and the pads of its feet showed it was not
these things. *A snow-hare* . . . I had never seen one. I looked at its tracks
when it was gone. I was spun in the wind when I crested peaks, and
when I lay down I caught flakes on my tongue. These things. Small,
and safe things.

But day by day, there was less snow. Slowly, there became more
water noises, and the falling burn in my valley grew loud, and strong.
I drank from it—not on my knees, or with cupped hands, but by
clutching a rock, leaning in and opening my mouth. I smiled as I
drank. I tasted old winter. I drank new spring.

Day by day, green shoots showed themselves. The snow grew dimpled and up they came—comfrey, and motherwort. To see them was
like seeing friends again. I crouched to them, thought *who needs people?
People aren't always like this*—by which I meant meek, and kind, and
soft to touch. I gathered them, dried them. Or I powdered them up,
or put them in salt. Or I let them grown on, in the earth.

It was in these watery days that Gormshuil came back to me. She
appeared like a tree on the top of a peak—very thin and straight. I
watched her come down, and as she drifted nearer I saw her thinness,
the deep-blue veins beneath her skin. Despite her smell, I worried.

She was dead-looking, so that I said *will you stay? Have an egg or two?*
It's right to offer kindness to a soul less well than us. But she did not
want eggs, or warmth, or a friend. In a frail, girlish voice she said
henbane . . . And I freely gave it. I asked nothing, in return.

Gormshuil, I said, *if you ever need food* . . .

But she shook her head. She smiled, for the henbane was in her
hand now, and her skin was as thin as a moth's wing, and she said *you
are like a wife* to me—*a wife! A wife!* And she whispered to herself as she
walked over the rocks, as if her mind was gone. *I am no wife.*

It was not just her that came.

The birds sang and sang. They perched on the hazel tree and sang,
or they washed themselves in the snowmelt, and as I was washing my
cloak in the burn one afternoon I realised that I'd missed such music.
In the snowy depths, I'd only heard an owl. But spring was near, and
here the birds were. I sang along with them. I scrubbed my cloak, and
hummed.

And as I wringed my cloak of water, I noticed the birds had
stopped. No singing.

I thought *Gormshuil is back.* But no.

On the north slopes, where the snow still was, I saw the stag. He
was very still, and looked like a rock. But his branches were very broad,
and pale, and I could see his tracks which came down from the tops.
He stood, watching. I also stood and watched.

Are there no others with you? I asked.

He seemed alone. He seemed thin too, from the winter. His fur had
the mottled look that comes with age, or thinness. He heard my voice,
and one ear went back. I thought *he is beautiful,* for I had not seen a
living deer so close, and here he was—thick-coated, and his mouth
steamed with heat, and grass. There were a hundred colours in his fur,
and his stare was hard, and his crown was held high. For a while there
was nothing but him and me, and the burn.

Then both ears went back. His chest and forelegs moved themselves, and he turned neatly in the snow. He surged up, away from me
and back to the safe, high parts, and I said *where are you going? Why?*
For I had not moved, or spoken.

He saw me, I think.

I stumbled. I had not heard a person coming across the grass. All
that water noise, and the swaying trees, and my own talking to the
deer had meant I had not heard his feet, or his plaid against his legs. I
steadied myself, put my hand on a rock.

Sorry, he said, one hand held up. *I disturbed you?*

I shook my head.

He waited. He waited until I had smoothed my skirts, and caught
my breath.

Here, he said. He held a basket out. A cloth was upon it, and when
I peeked beneath it I saw meat—dark, and salted.

Venison. We had more than enough left from Hogmanay. He smiled at
how I must have looked—there was so much of it. *But maybe don't
show your friend.*

I frowned. *Friend?*

Him. He smiled, nodded at the stag who was a shape against the
sky, still watching us, one ear forwards and one back.

<hr />

Alasdair Og MacDonald. That was his whole name.

But I have others, he said. *Red—for the hair, but also in battle, for I've
been bloodied by the ones I've killed. I can fight well. I reckon it's what I'm
best at, in most ways. Down in Argyll they call me a scrapper, for a brawl I
had with some Campbell men when I was a boy. I broke my bones, but I broke
theirs too. Scrapper . . . I've heard that enough. Pup. Spare.*

I tended the fire as he spoke. It was mid-afternoon, with the January light growing old outside. He sat by the doorway to my hut—half-in, half-not. The hens pecked near him.

Pup?

My mother says I answered less to a name than a whistle, as a boy. Said the dog knew Gaelic better.

I liked that.

We have many names, as a clan. The MacIains, or the Glencoe men, mostly—but if you ask a Lowlander . . . He grimaced. *Then there are names which have hatred in them. A papist tribe. That gallows herd . . .* He rubbed the heel of his cuaran into the ground.

I said, *I know.*

Our names?

How names can be. I have plenty. I am Corrag, firstly. But I've been called other things more often than I've been called that. Hag. Witch. Devil's piece.

Sassenach.

I eyed him. *I don't know what that means.*

English, he said, smiling. He looked up from his cuaran, met my look. *It means English. Which aren't you?*

Yes, I said. *I'm from Thorneyburnbank. It's a village with a half-moon bridge and a cherry tree. There was the Romans' wall near it, and such wind . . . I was born there. I was born on a very frosty night.* I saw that frost, and other frosts.

But you are here now, he said.

I WARMED some meat in the pot, and put herbs in. I had a little stale bannock, and added this, and I had no way of serving it but to pick from the pot with our hands. Why might I have dishes? It was only ever me.

I said *I have no dishes.* But he did not frown, or mind.

How is your father?

Alasdair ate. He ate like men do—quickly, and without looking up, and using the bannock to dig into the meat. I watched his hands, as he did this. *He is well. He is sore-headed, I think—but more from Hogmanay than the wound. Still his fiercesome self.*

I looked at the fire. Gently, I said *I heard stories.*

Of him? Oh aye. There are plenty of them. He's the best-known High-lander since Bonnie Dundee, most likely. 'Tis his height and how he looks, firstly. Then there is his fighting. You've seen an old man in a chair with a dog by his feet, but the MacIain has scalped a dozen men in one fight, on his own—it's true. He raided Glenlyon so quickly they all escaped barefoot, if they escaped at all. Some burnt in their homes. Alasdair eyed me. *He fought some English, too.*

English? Because they were English?

Because they moved with the Campbells, down in the south. We've always been hated by that clan, and seen as foe. Seen as trouble.

As thieves?

*They'll say that. But all clans steal, see? Even Campbells do. No—*he chewed—*it runs deeper than that. It runs into God, and politics. Into how we see Scotland, and what we hope for it. Feuds,* he said, *don't die quickly in these parts.*

I was quiet. I thought a while, then said quickly, beneath my breath, *so much hatred here.*

He glanced up. *No more hatred here than elsewhere. You know this. You've been running from it, have you not? Feared for your life?*

This was true. *But I've never hurt a person. I've never fought.*

Never fought? At all?

I shrugged. *Not with my hands. Not with blades.*

He blew out his cheeks at this, sighed. *That's fair. They are little hands, and would not do well at fighting.*

Not like his. I looked across at them. I knew his right hand—its half-moon scars, its marks. I saw how it tore the bannock, and remembered how I had spread its fingers out upon the poultice and said *press. Like that.* It felt a long time ago.

Maybe, I said, *there will be no hatred, one day. No dark. No fighting.*

You believe that? He shook his head. *For as long as there is envy, or greed, there'll be hatred. For as long as William sits on the throne.*

William? You hate him?

He hates us just as much! For we won't call him king. We won't bow to him, or be ruled by him, and he knows it.

Because of faith?

Aye because of faith. Because he's not of ours, nor of our nation. He is ashamed of the Highlanders and calls us trouble, and barbarous, and a yoke on his throne, but has he ever met us? Come to our glen, or any glen? He has not. He narrowed his eyes. *I speak to you in English. Do you know why?*

I didn't.

Not all of us can speak it. The older folk can't. But the MacIain was sent to London, as a boy—he was forced to, for the government says if the clans lose their language they might lose their faith too, and that will be a good day in their eyes. He shook his head. *They want to breed us out, Sassenach. Change our ways and break our backs. We must keep our old language—talk Gaelic more. And we must ride out against this king and all who serve him, and cut them down if we must . . .*

I listened to this. I sat by my fire with the hens, and I watched the light darken, behind his head. I wondered on its colour—this light. Not grey. Not deep-blue.

I said, *you have cut many down?*

Aye. When I've had to. When there have been quarrels or insult to the clan. I fought at Killiecrankie and took a few with my dirk on those braes.

I felt a deep, long sadness. I listened to the valley, at that moment—to the hearth, the sound of him eating. The wind. I thought of how far that wind had come, of the trees it had passed through, the birds it had borne.

He was looking at me. *You say nothing,* he said. *What is in that mind of yours?*

That you came here for this—to tell me of wars. Of the men you've killed. To make me feel I was wrong to have ever come here—to have come north-and-west . . .

I came here with venison, he said. *To give it to you.*

I nodded, blushed. *I know.*

We sat as we were. The fire tended to itself, as a cat does, and we both seemed to watch it—the red, and how the peat glowed.

He said, *your name? It is a strange name.*

It's from my mother. She was Cora. That was her true name, but she had hag *thrown out at her so much that she sometimes thought that was her name, instead. She joined them to make mine—*Cora *and* hag. I saw his face, thinking. *She had a strange humour. She laughed when I was born.*

Do you know what it means? In our tongue?

Corrag?

Yes. Do you know?

I looked up from the fire to his face, for I didn't know. I did not understand him. *It has a meaning?*

He raised a finger. In the half-dark, he lifted up his forefinger and slowly pointed at me—at my face, my eyes. *It is Gaelic,* he said, *for this.*

For finger?

For finger. You have a Gaelic name, Sassenach. So maybe you were right to come this far.

MR LESLIE, do you remember how I said that moments change lives? Small moments? I think that was one. How Alasdair lifted his finger.

How he looked, in the twilight that had moved in, behind him. He
was a dark shape, a dark face.

When he left, I thanked him. *For the meat,* I said.

I hope it lasts you. There is plenty.

*Did you save enough? For your wife, and family? I can live on far less
than what you've given me.*

We have some, Sarah and I.

I nodded, smiled.

We did our goodbyes, which were small.

Look. See? My finger. Not much to see. It is tiny and muddied, and
its nail is torn, and it's some crooked from how I grasped rocks and
heather to haul myself up onto tops like how my toes are crooked.
The mare bit me once, thinking I was food, and there is a mark upon
my finger still from a tooth of hers—there. She never meant it. It bled,
but I had knotgrass in Cora's purse back then.

Corrag means *finger.*

Do you know what they said? The ones in other glens who'd heard
of me and my name, but had never met me? They knew of my herbs
and ghost-grey eyes, and how I trod the braes in windy weather, and
they said *Corrag? Ah . . . Because she curses by pointing. She points at a
person and it turns them into stone . . .*

You'll hear that. It's what they will tell you—the Camerons from
the north, and maybe a Stewart or two. There's the man called Breadalbane who said he'd heard my finger had light at its tip, and it hurt
folk—like lightning can. But he was half-fool. What will you say back
to them?

Say no. *She never pointed—not at people, and she never cursed. For I*
never have.

. . .

I LOOKED at my finger, after that. I saw its wrinkled parts, its lines, and thought *how can that be my name? My proper name?*

I did not like it. Not my name's meaning, nor my little hands.

But I like both things, now. I know them, and like them.

Corrag? Why Corrag?

Because she was brave. She showed the way.

I know I must be grateful—and I am.

But I miss him, Mr Leslie. All my waking hours, I miss him. At night, I dream of him, so that I think I'm by his side, or sitting by that fire as he talks and eats his meat—but then I wake, and miss him. I miss him all the more.

DO NOT leave me yet? I know it is late. But talk of Ireland, and its skies? Of your sons, and wife?

Maybe I will dream of them.

Talk me to sleep.

My love

I cannot thank you enough for your letter. Just to see your handwriting again soothes me, and when I read it I feel as if you are here in Inverary, with me. I wish you were, as you know. When I read my Bible in the evenings, by the fire, I look at the second chair in this room which I have never sat upon, and imagine how you would be if you were sitting in it. Embroidering, perhaps. Or with a small novel on your lap. I have seen many sights, Jane. As a bishop, as an exile—but I have seen the greatest of them as a husband.

    I told her so.

    Tonight, she grew fretful and I think she cried, in the dark. It was not her death that troubled her so much (she can grow very anxious on that, of course)—rather, it was her life, I think. Mostly, she sees the good in the world, the light where there is dark—for who else can have a soldier try to defile her (you will understand my meaning—the worst way a man can defile a woman) and afterwards talk of a slowly-setting sun? She sees beauty where we mostly pass it by. But tonight, she was heavy-hearted. I think sometimes she unfolds all her losses and stares at them, in the dark.

    She said talk to me of Ireland, *as I packed my quill away.*

    So I stayed a while. She was the listener and I spoke to her. I told her of how our boys grow, daily, into strong and educated men, and how your singing voice is the sweetest sound I know. I gave her Glaslough, with its ivy and gardens, and I told her how the lanes are very full with flowers in the spring, so she said which flowers?—*but when have I ever known which flowers they are? I said* my wife knows them. *And to this she smiled a little, said* women do. Yes.

    She asked me of you, Jane. I did not describe you to her too greatly—for perhaps it would be like telling a little flower on a rock what qualities a rose

has. It would not seem fair. But she asked me such questions as what makes
you love her? *And how could I answer? I have no starting place.*

*I write this, and I hear a drip. It is outside, and comes from the roof down
onto the other roof beneath me—the kitchen's roof, I believe. It is, I think,
the slow start of spring, and I know this means that her death grows near.
They are hauling the wood and ropes to the square, and my landlord assures
me that that wicked Devil-child (his words, not my own) does not have long,
now. A week, he says, at best—(they prefer weekends, for burning. It brings, I
think, more people out).*

    *I also asked him who the sheriff of this town is. Who, I asked him, might
take an oath for the King?*

    The name he gave was Ardkinglas.

    *So I will find this man and speak to him. He must have been one of the
last men to have seen the MacIain before his slaughter, and it will interest
me to hear his account of him.*

*I will retire with your letter. There is a patter of rain against the window—
rain, not snow. So yes, surely I will be riding north, within the week.*

                                                       C.

V

"The flowers are white and very small; later come the little cases which hold the seed, which are flat, almost in the form of a heart."

of Shepherd's Purse

If you have never been to the Highlands, sir, then you will not know of deer.

There were many in Glencoe. Just as there were men who burnt turf and climbed high, so there were deer. Horse-high and nut-coloured, they trod in a line through marshes so that I might follow their path, and not sink down. They were shapes on peaks, staring. As I slept in my hut, they grazed outside—for I heard the sound of the grass being cropped very neatly, and their droppings pushed up between my toes at dawn.

They were wary, too. They had grown to be—for hadn't they had a hundred lives of arrows shot into their rumps, or a blade pulled over the throat? They had. So theirs was a wary way of life. I might be humming on the spring-time hills with my skirts tucked up or picking herbs when I'd come across a herd of them on some far-off hill, and they'd have heard and seen me long before I saw them. Necks straight up, ears forward. They could fix you with such a stare! Far harder than any scolding. A deer and I might lock eyes on each other and stare for a long time, both thinking the other might have some trick to them.

Deer—I'll say the hinds, most specially—could stare for so long you thought maybe they were not deer at all, but rocks shaped like them. Then I might lift a foot or tilt my head and they would be gone. *Trot-trot* with their pale behinds.

The hinds and their calves had a tidy way.

The stags were less neat. Their necks were hedge-thick, and heavy. Sometimes they carried strings of drool, or had moss in the branches like they'd been in a battle or two. They lost their branches, too. In spring, their branches broke off and died, and new ones grew, and they took on the shape the old ones had. I came across a perfect half-branch on Keep-Me-Safe, and I took it back to my hut. At night, it cast a shadow. I hoped the stag who'd shed it would have a long, good life.

Also, they roared. I had heard it, in my early days—I'd thought that single stag had welcomed me. I'd never heard such a sound as that deep, breathy roar. *Why?* I asked Alasdair, once. And he'd spoken of the stags fighting each other, locking their antlers together like hands.

Fighting?

For hinds. To win them.

Even the deer fight in Glencoe, I said to myself. Rolled my eyes.

So yes—many deer. You will see how many, when you are in Glencoe—or if not, you will see their neat hoof-prints in the bogs, and their dung like currants will press themselves into the arch of your foot. You'll shake your foot, to be rid of them.

MY STAG, I think, saw me. I think he spied me when I first came to the glen—trawling my skirts, with moths in my hair. I think how I made my hut was reflected in his eyes, for he was very watchful. More watchful than the rest.

I searched the tops of hills for him, after that. Scrubbing my pots in the burn, or scrubbing myself very naked in the pools that snowmelt made, I would run my eyes along the peaks—in case. I might see groups of stags, grazing. But he was not with them. I knew this, for I knew his strange, uneven branches. I knew the oily deepness of the fur upon his neck.

Maybe he is gone. Maybe he is dead.

But he came back.

I was drying water-mint in the sun. It grew richly on the sides of Loch Achtriochtan, where the water-bull lived and rose up at full-moons. I saw no water-bull, but as I pulled the herbs up I felt a pair of eyes, and there he was—on the top of Cat Peak, looking down. Under my breath I said *hello* . . . And like he heard me, he took himself away.

But back by my hut, with the mint laid out in a row like washing is, he returned. I straightened my back. The sunshine was bright, so I shielded my eyes to see him, and I watched how he trod very carefully down the sides. He came nearer. He flicked his tail twice. The slopes of Cat Peak can be very loose, but he did not slide at all.

I said *hello* again. He stopped.

He had seven branches on the right side and five on the left—so I knew it was him.

For a good while we looked upon each other. I took in his brittle hooves, his pale mouth, his eyes. I also saw his nostrils open and close, and very slowly he brought his head down, leaned, so that I thought *he smells the mint. He smells it* . . .

I crouched, picked some.

Here, I said.

Up went the head. He looked very boldly, as if offended by me. His nose smelt the herb, we stood like this for a long time—me with my arm held out, saying *here,* and him with his head held high. I hoped he would take it. I felt my body long for him to come closer to me, for him to take the herb from my hand. *Just once. Take it* . . . I wanted to feel his warmth on me, for him to leave drool behind. Like the mare did. Like all creatures do.

Here . . .

But stags are wild things. He was wilder than most—on his own, and with branches like that. I knew he wanted the mint, but I knew that the ground between us was huge to him, and airy, and I was too human, so he turned on his back legs again.

He went up and over, out of sight. I looked down at the little green leaves in my hand and felt sad, briefly. But I also knew he would come back—for I saw in his eyes what he wanted. I knew the look.

Spring was good, Mr Leslie. It is good for all souls, and for herbs, and all plants which had been sleeping over winter. I ducked out of my hut, breathed, and raced up onto the peaks which snow had kept from me. I lifted rocks. I found betony and yarrow, and beetles, and in the woods by Inverrigan I found tansy which I had not seen since Thorneyburnbank. I crouched down by it, felt its leaves. I made me think of Cora. I remembered being a child, and with her. She always said that tansy-leaves were as soft as rabbit fur—and this said it was a kind plant. It was best for sun-burnings and joint-aches. It made me sad, for I missed her. But also, there she was—in a scent, in herbs. She was real again, and with me. I found her in many places, in such weather.

I found other people, too—people whose faces I began to know.

The children from Achnacon with their freckled skin hung upside down in an alder tree, as I passed it. They hollered to me. They swung their arms, and I said *are you bats? In that tree?* They spoke no English, and giggled. Their hair brushed my own as I walked underneath. And as I lifted water from a bend in the Coe, I spied the old man from Inverrigan fishing with his boys—very still, like wading birds. And by the Ridge Like a Church, I saw Sarah. She caught my wrist, said *how are you?* Asking it like she meant it, like she wanted to know. I sat with her for a time. She stroked her belly, and closed her eyes when the sun came out from clouds, and smiled. *Sunshine,* she breathed, *at last.* And so we basked a while, her and I.

I told her, *I am well. Very well. Fine.*

All folk seemed well, in those weeks.

On a day of green buds and bright water, more cows came. I was beating my deerskin with a stick, to rid it of winter's dust, and heard hooves on rocks. I turned. In they came—a dozen black cows, drooling grass. MacDonald men came, too. They were muddied, and red-cheeked, and blowing hard, and smacked the cows on with their hands, and I thought *whose cows . . . ?* For they were stolen cows. Being kept in a secret valley, so they could be found and taken back. I knew their ways, by now.

I watched them. No Alasdair. Just the Gaelic-speaking men, the ones like bears. They did not look at me. They passed so near to me that I felt their draught, smelt their sweat—but they did not speak a word, and I felt heavy-hearted, at this. *Why won't they smile? Greet me?* I stood with my hands by my side.

But as they were leaving, the one with the scar which ran down his chin, clefting it, turned as he walked, so that he walked backwards for a time. And as he walked backwards, he raised his hand. He raised it to me. I raised mine.

It is the small moments, sir, which change a world.

———

I was barely left alone, in those months. I barely saw a day without a person in it, which I sometimes liked but also, sometimes, I wanted peace and hush. I could not step out of my clothes to wash myself, for fear of eyes. I had not much to hide—bones and whiteness, mostly—but it still isn't right to be looked upon like that. It is a private time.

A man with a splinter came to me, held up this thumb, and I healed him.

Bran found me, panted, lifted his leg on the hazel tree. But he was gone again, soon after—and no person was with him. Or if a person was, they never came down to my hut. I looked up at the braes, but all there seemed to be on them was rocks and tufty grass.

I liked it—to see lives. To have lives come to me. But I told my reflection in a peaty pool *you are for places, Corrag. Do not love. Do not look for him, in shadows. Do not whisper his name.*

So I also took myself away. I chose a breezy day to walk towards the moor. Rannoch Moor—on which my mare had died, and where I'd seen her ghost walk out. Where I'd wandered like a bride of rags and grief and tiredness, and I'd never seen Glencoe before. Where I'd had a different life.

I stood at the glen's western end, and looked out at it. I saw its bees rising, and its blowing sky. And I took myself onto the mountain which stood by my side, looking out—the *Dark Mount,* maybe, or *the Arrowhead,* for I still had a mark on my heel from the wound. But I thought *climb up! Think of the view . . .* It was hard climbing. I scrabbled, and used my fingers. In places, I saw the heather far beneath me, between my feet, and it made me say *keep going! Go up!* And I imagined the joy from the peak, when I made it—the air and sore limbs, and the view, the view!

But I did not feel joy, at the top. Instead, I smelt a smell.

I slowed. There, on the top of this black, jagged mount, was Gormshuil.

I gasped. I put my hands upon my hips and said *you? Here?* For what a climb it had been! I'd clung, and jumped, and swung my way up. And she was three times my height and four times my age, and ate nothing that I could see, and yet here she stood with her lacewing's skin and her threadbare cloak catching the wind. She said nothing. She only stepped aside. And behind her I saw a shelter of stones, and a low hearth, and bones, and old cloth. And two other women, sitting there.

I stayed for manners' sake. I crouched upon a stone, and smiled at the new faces. They were as thin and pale as Gormshuil—but both younger, I reckoned. One had a very damaged face—its bones had been broken in past times, for her nose was flattened and her jaw was not straight. Her lower teeth protruded, and so she slurred as she spoke. *Doideag,* she hissed. *From Mull. An island—south* . . . And she pointed. The second girl did not speak. She looked at her toes, with her chin on her knees. She had more sadness upon her than I had ever seen, maybe, and Gormshuil hissed *that one has no tongue.*

No tongue?

She has a tongue but does-nee use it. Can-nee. Shock took words from her.

Shock?

A boat went down. Laorag. From Tiree. And all the ones drowned about her, and clawed at her hair, and she swam with dead men's hands on her skirts . . . All sank down but her.

It was no good thing, to sit upon Dark Mount with these women of such strangeness—of such wild living that even Cora would not have cared for it. Amongst their hearth were gnawed bones, and feathers, and their privy was upwind so its over-ripe smell came down to me. There was no proper sleeping place—only rocks, and a bundle of muddied cloth. No green, save for my henbane. I saw it, sitting on a stone.

Gormshuil eyed me. It was like she did not know me—like maybe she knew me, but maybe she did not. *You have a different look* she said, as if it displeased her.

I frowned. *No.* I looked the same.

She did not. She looked worse, I reckoned. She had sores by her mouth. At the corners of her lips there were red crusts which flaked when she spoke—and this was the winter's doing. I thought how comfrey would help her.

You are different, she said. *Seeds are being sown all over, and up they come through the earth . . .*

Strange talk. I shook my head at it. Doideag's mouth made a sound like Bran's did, when he licked himself—she ate something, in her hand. Her jaw was very twisted, and her cheeks were sharp from broken bones.

I said, *this is fine weather. I've seen more folk in the past two weeks than in my whole life, I think. Fishing in the Coe. Weaving. I've seen the boys practice their swordplay, and—*

Gormshuil said *foraying.*

Foraying?

Aye. Stealing. Being reckless in the south. 'Tis what they do . . .

She knew these things. She pushed her tongue into the gaps where her teeth had been, as if she was thinking hard—and maybe she was. But hers was a grizzled brain. It was clouded with henbane, and age—I was certain of this. *They'll take and take. They'll bring more cattle here. Turf. Horses . . . It will do for them, in the end* she told me—*this theft.* She raised an eyebrow and tightened her hand about the herbs. *The youngest is a thiever. Yours.*

Mine?

Yours. His seed grows, and his thieving does. Glen Lyon cows, these ones. Found in the river, drinking, and he took them—at dusk. Oh there had been trouble with him. Wild hearts. All flaming like his hair is, and he was shackled up in Inverlochy for his ways, last summer—and it took the Queen to free him. The proper queen! She won't last long. She's stronger than her husband but a plague will carry her . . .

Gormshuil, I said, *what are you speaking of?*

She eyed me. *You know . . .* Then, *a small candle is brightest in a place with no candles . . .* And she looked away from me, out across Rannoch Moor where the shadows of clouds raced over its rocks, and she watched this. *You will come to me,* she said, *when there is a wolf.*

I shook my head. *A wolf?* This was proper nonsense, now.

When it calls. You'll come back . . .

A wolf? A thought took me, then. *You have the second sight?*

Wolves won't last. No, no . . .

I shifted. *Do you have it? The sight? Gormshuil?*

She was lost to me, after this. She stood, and wandered over the stones and dirt, picking at a dead bird and whispering under her breath. I watched her do this. And I sensed a power to her, then. Perhaps it was the henbane, addling her brain and filling it with dreams. Or perhaps it was her height and old bones which made her seem oddly wise.

I DIDN'T know. I couldn't tell. But as I dropped down from stone to stone, and made my way home, I came across the man of Achtriochtan, digging peat in the glen. I crept up to him. Very quietly, I said to him, *the cows? In the hidden valley? Where were they stolen from?*

He understood enough. *Glen Lyon. South-east.*

And how could she have known that? With her broken, half-drugged life?

I tucked myself up very tightly by the fire, that night.

⁕───⬦───⁕

Second sight. Even you, sir, have heard of it—how a person can know of future times—can see them, and be certain. Cora had fits, on the floor. She'd arch her back, and when it had passed she'd clutch her head, say *I think I have a gallows neck,* or *be wary of marked calves . . .* She saw *north-and-west* this way, I think. Saw her rope, and *go!*

Sometimes Cora had sold them—her seeings, her second sight. She'd come back from Hexham with a fistful of pennies she'd spend on food, or a ribbon for her hair. But not Gormshuil. She sold nothing. She kept from the houses and hid in the heights, and the MacDonalds had their stories of her—of a glaistrig, who wailed on full-moon nights. The leaver of faery-shot, in the grass. Lady Glencoe spoke of the *bean nighe*—a woman of mist, who'd wash her clothes in the Coe on dark nights, and her name meant that death was nearby. I heard this, and knew it was Gormshuil they spoke of. I said she *is real, not mist-made. I've met her, and she has a sour smell.* But beliefs can be stronger than facts, sometimes. *Stay away from her, Sassenach,* said Lady Glencoe. *Death's in that one.*

A witch. A seer. Crone.

But Gormshuil was a human. They all were—they were people of bones and blood, with a heart hidden inside. Doideag scratched, and sneezed. Laorag of Tiree had her monthly courses, for I saw them on her skirts as she drifted by in her upright way. And once I found Gormshuil spying on a Cameron man from a distant glen—he came to Glencoe, sang as he went, and she followed him for a time. Why? I'll guess. I reckon she wanted a hot, private act with him—but never asked, or tried.

I talk too much on this.

What I say is this. That despite the second sight, and the reeking, and the wild life, they were still human things. They had still been daughters and sisters, and wives, and so I'd watch them with their henbane eyes and think *what happened? What hardship came by?* For no-one lives such a life by choice. No one lives on a mountain unless there has been some kind of sadness—a hurt, or a loss, or fear upon fear.

Doideag was mangled by fists, I thought. A man, or men, had brawled with her and left her for dead—for I saw the shape her bones had, and I heard how she clicked when she walked. The girl from

Tiree was so heart-sore and lonesome that it took out her tongue, and she suffered such dreams that I thought I heard her calling out, one night—in pain. Dreams of lost boats.

And Gormshuil? I'll never know. But she took henbane to deaden all echoes of it.

Once, I heard her say *love* . . . That was all. She said no more. But how she said it—slowly, with a lazy blink of her red-rimmed eyes—made it sound like she wished it had not found her, and passed her by.

Look what it did to them. Look what people did.

But what good are words? I counted the days where I did not see Alasdair.

I looked for him on the peaks. I wandered through the woods, and when a bird flapped up from the bushes I thought *him?* But it was not him.

Still. He came, in the end. He came down from the slopes of Cat Peak, bringing down pebbles which I heard first. They were like rain. They pattered, and as I turned I saw the pebbles bouncing against rocks, and knocking into the cows, so that I thought *what is . . . ?* And when I looked up, there he was.

He said *I've been away. Too long, I think.*

His hair was brighter from sunshine, and he seemed broader to me. And in his pocket he brought out the thin, blue-dappled shell of an egg. Half of it. It still had the whitish film inside it, and a small streak of blood, and I knew a bird had flown from this. It had broken from it, flown away. He put it into my hand.

. . .

WE WALKED. We did not stay by my hut, for the afternoon was warm and slow. Insects hung in handfuls, and the cows swung their tails as they grazed.

We'll be moving them soon, he said. *We'll move them onto Rannoch Moor for the grazing. Your valley is too small for so many.*

My valley?

Aye. Yours.

We took ourselves to the Meeting of the Waters. Once, a thousand years ago, I'd washed my cloak here and hung cobwebs on trees. Now, the waterfall did not thunder or mist as it had done, for the snow had melted and there'd been no rain.

He said, *how have you been?*

Very well. Busy. Spring means herbs, so I have been gathering.

He nodded, but I wondered if he'd heard me. His eyes seemed far away.

My mother taught them to me. She had wandered all over, and picked herbs that she passed . . .

He said, *I was wrong to speak as I did, last time. I spoke too strongly. It's my way, and I must mind it. Women don't care for war stories . . .*

Not this woman. I gave a small smile to him. *I'm for healing sores, not making them.*

He nodded. *I will remember that. Perhaps you run, and I fight.*

Perhaps you should fight less. There is plenty of it, and it helps no-one's cause—not that I can see.

He smiled, looked away. *Your nature is not like mine. It is not like any-one's here. I saw that, as you stitched our father. You're more for cowslips than claymores, I think,* he said. Teasing me.

More for eggshells.

Aye. I saw it and thought of you.

I smiled. I watched his hand on the grasses, and wondered why my nature was always my own—why I was always alone in it. Cora had been like me, had she not? But none here, and none for a long time. *Your brother dislikes my nature,* I said.

Iain? It's not dislike. It's distrust.

Distrust? But I mended your father.

You did. I know that. Our father knows that. The clan, he said, *knows that. But look at you. Listen to you! There was talk for a time of you being a spy, Sassenach.*

For whom?

This Dutch king. The Campbells. Sent in with those eyes of yours and your girlish voice to tame us, or to hear what we may be plotting. To send back news on this Jacobite clan . . . You spoke of having no god, and no king—

I'm not a spy.

I know, he said. *I know. But I've never heard a person speak that way. Our whole clan fights and lives to bring King James back to the throne. We are all for kings, and you . . .* He gave a long, heavy sigh. *Understand my brother's ways. He will be chief of this clan, one day, and there is so much we risk in these times. So many shadows . . .*

We listened to the waterfall. We listened to the silence that comes when two people want to speak, but neither does. There was such light on the water, such brightness, that it was hard to think of shadows, or of enemies, or war. It was hard to believe in my old lives, with the ash-coloured cats, or the red winter sunrises that took my breath away. They seemed so long ago, to me.

Sarah is with child, he said. *She wondered it a little after Hogmanay but she is certain now. It grows quickly. She's—*he held out his hand, showing her belly.

I smiled. *I know.*

You do?

I shrugged, pointed at my eyes. *I have these.*

You do.

We nodded at each other. And in silence, we walked back to my hut through the birdsong, and flies. I searched through my herbs for motherwort, which is a true female herb. It mends sickness and worry, and is kind to all parts, and I gave it to Alasdair. I said *she may boil the leaves, and sip it. Or burn a little in the fire and its smoke with settle her. It's from the Ridge Like a Church. There is a rock which it grows about.*

He smiled, bemused. *From where?*

I told him, then. I blushed, and told him my names for the hills which I walked on, and loved, and knew the shapes of. I listed all of them, and he listened, smiled. It made him stay a little longer—for he settled by my fire, and taught me their proper names. Rather than leave, with the motherwort, he stayed and whispered *Gearr Aonach* to me. *Aonach Dubh. Sgorr na Ciche.* He said their names very slowly. He used his hands, as if pinching the words as he said them.

Your turn, Sassenach.

Aonach Dubh.

I tried. I shaped my mouth as he shaped his. By the fire, we said the same words.

HE STOOD, as it grew dark. He took the herb, and turned slowly in the doorway. He said, *is there no man you've left behind? No husband?*

No.

He shifted, looked down at the herb. *And have you been safe?*

I did not know his meaning. I blinked. When is a person truly safe?

As you travelled, he said. *You're small, and on your own, and you don't believe in fighting . . .* He moved his jaw. He had words he did not want to say.

I understood him, then. I knew what he was asking. The sun was very low, and we were both looking very keenly at the motherwort, and the tiny hairs on the tips of its leaves, and I remembered the soldier saying *hush, now . . . You be good for me.*

I said, *not always.*

Where? Were you least safe?

I sniffed. *The day before I came to the Highlands I was hurt.*

How hurt?

Not badly. Not as much as he'd tried for.

He tensed. I saw his shoulders tighten, and he blew out a sharp breath. He said, *you'll be safe here. You will. I promise it.*

We were never good at farewells, him and I. They were always the same—standing, moving stones with our feet, before he turned very quickly and went.

I WONDERED why he asked me. I picked at my nails, and twisted my hair. I lay in the dark with my plump old hens and thought *why did he ask me?* And *she is with child.*

My nature's like no-one else's, he'd said. *But I'm still a human, and I feel human things.* I knew what beauty was, in a person. I had seen it, in the way a woman fastened her hair under her cap, tucked the fair curls in—and I was dark-haired and had no cap. The day before, I had lowered my head to drink from the loch and risen with weed and water-snail on me. All day I hadn't known it. The snail had swung in my hair, like fruit. It put a silvery wetness on me, and I'd carried it over the Three Sisters so that it saw things no other snail would see.

I turned onto my side, tucked up my knees.

My heart said *him, him . . .* But my head told it to stop prattling, for what was the point? *Go to sleep, Corrag. Stop feeling what you feel.*

Those wide eyes of yours. Looking through your spectacles, as if I was the whore that they all said I was—for *whore* hurries after *witch*. What a dread word. What a wire, to bind a girl up with—for once it's been held against you, it leaves its mark. I have it marked upon me. I still feel its cut.

Whore. How much it makes me think of my English days, where our grey cats stretched themselves, and my mother returned at dawn, half-dressed and flushed. *Whore* was a stone thrown at her. *Whore* was murmured as she walked with me, hand-in-hand, through the streets, and *whore* was what she said once, to herself—she whispered it, looking at her face in a looking-glass. She was so sad-looking, then. She touched the skin by her eyes—like this.

It is a word said in fear—always. For only the strong-willed, wise-hearted women defy such laws, I reckon. And all the folk of Thorneyburnbank feared Cora—for they knew that she knew herself, and was living a life they did not dare, and maybe the others wondered, deep down, what a moonlit night on the moor was like, with the wolf in them calling out, for their own wolf was caged by themselves, and half-dead. Cora, then, was *whore*. They knew what lifting up those dark-red skirts could do.

But I am me, am I not? My mother's child, yes—but also me. And you have sat with me enough times to know that I let my wolf run free in other ways. By sitting cross-legged on a night-time mountain, and waiting, waiting, waiting, waiting, until up comes the sun, and day.

You know that I'm for places. But I'm for people most of all.

I wanted love, Mr Leslie. *Do not love,* but I wanted to—I wanted to find it, and the right kind of it. I'd say to myself *I am not lonely*— and mostly I wasn't, for there is such a solace in how trees move, and rain, and my mare and hens have been good friends. But I would feel the space beside me, from time to time. I'd be lying in the heather, turn my head and consider the heather next to me—its colour, how scented it was—and wish there was a person lying on it, looking at the clouds with me.

Haven't I always tried to be good? To all living things?

Gormshuil called him *yours* . . . But he was not mine.

I will say this. That if *whore* is fire, then I am ice. If *whore* is like midnight with no stars or moons, no comets trailing their ghost-light, then I am bright. I am milk-white.

Jane

I walk where she walks, and see what she sees. What a gift. I write this in my room, as always. But she speaks so richly of her wild life, of living in heather and moss and rocks, that I feel I am amongst it. Is this bewitching? This skill? What she says stays with me. I walked along the loch tonight, yet I thought it was the river Coe, and that the houses I passed by were mountains. I walked into this room, and in spite of its fire and hangings, and my books, I half-wished it was starlit and far from here. It feels like magick, how she tells her tale.

I suspect this is partly my homesickness. I am vulnerable, I think. There was a hope and strength I had in Edinburgh that I lack here, somehow. No matter that Corrag offers me what I had hoped for, about these deaths—I carry a sadness, a weight I cannot name. Perhaps this sadness is what makes me fall so deeply into her tale. I will agree with her that the natural world— the seasons, the rain in the earth—is a healing thing. We can be too far from it.

On to Ardkinglas.

Indeed, he is the sheriff. Colin Campbell of Ardkinglas—a short, plump man with a very pale skin which is even paler than most skins are, in this country. I wondered, as he received me, if he was ill at all. There were shadows beneath his eyes which warranted me to ask, am I intruding, sir? I can return . . .

But he shook his head, said no, no. Come in. I have time, always, for a man of faith, as you are. Your voice tells me you've come a long way?

What fine lodgings, he had. If I had ever doubted there was money in the Campbell name, they were cast aside by his parlour which was finer than

any I've seen in Edinburgh. A huge fire, Jane! I might have roasted a pig
upon it, and it cast a pleasing glow upon the glass and wooden walls. He
offered me a whisky, which I graciously declined—for the drink can souse a
man's wit, and I need all that I have, I think. He poured himself a glass—
but I will say that neither the dram nor the fire put any colour in his cheeks.
He was ghostly-pale.

How may I help you? *he asked.*

I gave my false name and false purpose (God forgive these lies—but they
are spoken in His name and for the sake of the nation). I gave a lengthy
account of my wish to rid the world of the unfaithful, of heretics and hea-
thens, and that it is God's path for me. I was earnest, of course. I am not
without a little cunning of my own, and I said that I had heard of his own
pious nature—that I was assured of his most courteous help.

Indeed, *he said.* I will help where I can. We can all hope for a
civilised world.

I noted, at this moment, that he finished his whisky and poured a
second one.

Might I ask, sir, on Glencoe?

Well, Jane—I saw him wince. Indeed, wince *is too mild a word—he*
grimaced, he bent at the waist as if the glen was a blow to him. He swal-
lowed, straightened himself. If it is darkness you wish to rid us of, it is a
shame you were not here a month before.

I hear there was a massacre, there. By the King's men?

He eyed me. His face, then, softened. Aye—I cannot hope to think
that those deaths will not be spoken of—such as they were . . . Brutal
business. No creature deserves an ambush of such a kind . . . What
can warrant it?

I asked about the oath.

Oath? *He nodded. He drank the whole glass in one mouthful.* Oh
they came. He came—the MacIain. He came to swear allegiance to
William, as decreed. I had him here—here! Where you sit now! Poor

man . . . He'd been through mile after mile of wretched weather, and he'd barely eaten, and he was not young, sir. Not young.

He was late, I hear?

He was. He went to Inverlochy on New Year's Eve. I was bad-tempered with him, Mr Griffin. I scolded him—I said, "why Inverlochy?" It's well-known that Colonel Hill at the fort is a friend of the Highlanders, and tries his best by them—but he could not accept the oath! It had to be myself, sir! My task and mine alone! And yet the MacIain rode north . . . *He filled his glass again. He looked into the whisky, rocked it in his glass.* For all my life, sir, I will never forget how he looked as he stood here, in this room. Snow on his shoulders. Tears—

Tears? The MacIain cried?

Ardkinglas nodded. He begged me. To accept the oath—no matter of lateness. He said, "the snow has hindered me! But my people and I are the King's servants now." He begged. It was a sight—a man of such stature and fierceness, a man of such reputation, weeping before me.

You accepted his oath?

Aye. I did. We shook hands, and he departed—thinking he was safe. That his clan—*he swallowed*—was safe . . .

Why weren't they safe? If you accepted their oath? Surely a little lateness might be forgiven . . .

Ardkinglas said I think they saw their chance. To rid the world of the Glencoe men.

They?

But he spoke no more on it.

It surprised me—to hear of the MacIain's sentiments. Tears? From a warrior? But as Corrag would assure me, we are all human, and can feel all human things. He loved his people, I am aware of that. He was a man of humour, also, from Corrag's tales of him.

I will suggest that Ardkinglas did not drink as he does, before Glencoe.
I'll suggest he was never this pale.

On leaving, I said Sir, forgive this impertinence. But the prisoner?
The witch? Must she be burnt? It feels as merciless and uncivilised
an act as any Highland war. Might she not be spared her death? Or
hung, at least?

He nodded. I know. I've heard no proper case against her, sir. But I
do not keep her there.

Are you not sheriff?

I am. But do you know a man called Stair? *he asked.* The Master
of Stair? John Dalrymple? The witch is imprisoned by his orders.
It is he who orders her death—and I do his bidding, as he does the
King's . . .

So she must be burnt?

She must. *He took a mouthful of whisky, swallowed.* As if we've not
seen enough blood . . .

At least, Jane, I tried. I have done my best to save her. I asked the sheriff
for her life—what more can I do?

Write to me again? Of small, daily things. Of the flowers that you put in
vases, and where these vases are. In the drawing room? Or the table in the
hall? But I am foolish—for what flowers might there be, at this time? It does
not snow with you, you say, but it is still cold and unkindly. The bulbs are
still tight in the earth.

Write of your tapestries. Of how our sons sound as they eat their sup-
pers, in a line, like they do. Write of your nightly toilette. Of what you think,
before blowing out the light.

                                                                    C.

VI

*"They say a wounded man that eats mint, his wound
will never be cured, and that is a long day."*

of Mint

When we have no skies, we think of the skies we did have,
once.

I know this, because I have no sky in here. It is stones, and damp;
it is a broken cobweb no legs are left to mend. So I think of my old
skies. Of the best skies I have seen—by which I don't mean only blue
ones, or summer ones with clouds all blown away. They are good. But
they are not the ones I think of, in my chains.

I think of Scottish skies, always. I saw some sovereign sunrises in
my first, English life but I was young, and did not gaze upon them like
the heart-stirred woman does. In Scotland, I was heart-stirred. I had
wiser eyes, and a need, and it was as I rode north on my mare that I
looked up and stared, for the first time. In the betwixt-and-between
times, we would see such skies that I thought they were a gift—that
they were a promise of some kind, in airy form. We trod through a
wet, Lowland mist to find a red sun, rising on a marshy land. A red and
dark-grey morning. I can see it now.

Or the split sky of Rannoch. Rain had been and gone, and its last
clouds were broken by a thick ray of sun which slanted down onto its

lochs. It made the lochs silver-bright, in places. I watched. I thought
keep this—as if I knew I would have no sky to gaze upon, one day.

The blustery glen sky.

How a hundred thousand stars were flung across the dark.

And I think of the sunset that we saw from the Pap—Alasdair and
I. I did not look at him, but I knew his face was lit by it. I knew the
light was red, that it was in our hair and that if I was to turn, and look,
he would glow, and if he was to look at me I would also be glowing,
and my eyes would be bright. I thought *look at me. Turn—for now, very
briefly, I am pretty. I rarely am—but I am at this moment. Standing by you.*
But we both had our sight on the sunset. The line of the sky was gold,
and red.

He said *the western isles are out there, somewhere. My ancestors' land.*

I remember.

HEAR the *drip . . . drip . . . ?*

It gets worse. It gets louder. I reckon the market place is truly
thawing now. The snow will be coming down off the ropes, the barrels, the stake, the wood.

Not long said the gaoler. He is drunk today. He slipped by my door,
and fell, and cursed. I've heard some cursing but his was the worst
of all. He said some dire things on God—and I am glad you weren't
here for it.

Which is worse? To blaspheme, or to plot against the King?

Is *witch* a worse word than *Jacobite*?

I don't know. It's your kind, sir, that William hates and wants to rid
his nation of, but it's me they'll take for burning.

Those MacDonalds. Their cause, which is your cause. What will
happen, with *Jacobite*? Will James ever sail back, and be king? The
future will tell us. It knows. One day—in a hundred years, or two
hundred, or three—people will say *Jacobite* and know what it meant,
know what it caused. They'll know how it ended—if it ended at all.

We'll be gone by then. You and I.

I will be gone sooner, of course.

* * *

Politics hummed like the bees did, in June. It was in the air, and I heard it—whispered on the river-bank, or called out on the braes. The word *Achallader* thrummed, so that even my stag shook his head, and stayed away from me. I spied him, on the tops. He had lost his branches, but I still knew it was him. He stood very still, with one hoof up.

I didn't know that word. I was too busy to—for I had quite a farm by then. I had seven hens, for one of my girls had passed by a cockerel and that was that. Three of the eggs did not hatch. But five did, and at first they were yellow, scurrying chicks which threw themselves under their mother's behind when a cow trod by. But they grew. They did their own scratching in the dirt, and laid their own eggs. They all roosted in the hazel tree, in those long summer nights.

And I had my goats, by then. I was given two goats by the man at Inverrigan, in the woods by the bend in the Coe. They were a gift— for I had been on toes' tips at a bee's nest, being gentle with a stick, when I heard a boy calling out my name. *Corrag! Corrag!* He tugged at my sleeve, spoke Gaelic. When I shrugged, said *I don't speak Gaelic,* he flapped his hands, then pointed at his tooth—so I knew. I took lovage to Inverrigan. His father was lying down, and I've seen some blackened teeth in my time, and smelt some putrid breath, but none so black or putrid as his. I winced at it. He winced as I prodded his gums. But he winced even more when I plucked the peg out for there was no cure for a tooth like that. I packed lovage about the hole, and picked about with my nails. He was sore, after. But within two days I had two goats dozing by the hut, resting their heads on each other's backs, and I knew they were a *thank you*—that the man at Inverrigan was eating his meat again. Also, I had honey—for the boy found me again at the bee's nest, and showed me how to steal it without hurting the bees.

He dipped in his finger, sucked it, beamed at me.

So I had hens and goats, and a stag. Cobwebs in the eaves. The owl outside was wild, but it hooted in the dark like it was mine. All those stolen cows.

And in the long, warm weather I wandered more than I ever did. I set out early, and came back late. I went far to the north, where the greatest of all mountains was—snub-nosed, and mist-covered. I went south, to the sea. In the glen itself, I snagged through the buttercups, the knee-high grass, and when a stalk caught between my toes, and broke with my tread, I'd bend down and save that flower. I'd put it behind my ear, or take it to my hut. For why let it wilt upon the hill? So my hut, in summer months, had flowers in it—dried, or nearly-dried, and mostly yellow buttercups which shone like proper candles do, so I might sit beneath my thatch and pretend it was a palace, and how well my hall was, how finely it was lit with golden light.

Buttercups, ragwort, sage. The early summer brings the sovereign healing herbs—which was good—because the MacDonalds were for-aying more than they did before. Maybe the heat warmed up their blood. Or maybe it was the word *Jacobite* which boiled them up and made them roar—I don't rightly know. But I had several wounds to heal, from blades. One of the bears could not fit in my hut, so I tended to him outside. The MacIain was with us. He bent over as I stitched the bear and said *those stitches are smaller than the ones you gave me. Do you like him more? Or dislike me?* And winked.

He was also thieving, like he was never wounded. Six months or more, since the gash on his head which I'd sewn, by the fire, and as he mounted his garron before me he said *what would you have me do? Let myself rot in a fireside chair? Not go to Achallader?* I worried that my work would undo itself, as he rode, or that a fallen branch or casual blow would burst it all, and he'd die. But *I'm a MacDonald. I'm from the line of Iain nam Fraoch who fought the Fionn . . .* and I knew he'd not sit by the fire.

So he went to a place called Achallader. I saw him go. Him, and his two sons, and a handful of men. Nine of them walked beneath me in the warm June sun, with insects in the air, and grass scent.

But only eight walked back.

Iain came for me. He spat into the bushes, breathed hard, said *Hurry,* he said. *It is a bloody wound . . .*

It was. I came to it, and found more blood in the grass and on his clothes than was left in the man. I recognised his face. He had brown hair, and a clefted chin, and he'd raised his hand at me, once. He'd waved, and I had waved.

Can you save him? Iain said.

The wound was to his leg. A dirk had been twisted into the thin, bluish tissue behind his knee, and the vein had been undone. I grappled with cloth. I pressed rupture-wort as firmly as I could, and I tried, and tried. But his eyes were fixed on the sky. His breath was gone.

I shook my head. *No . . .*

I remember it. I remember how the women bathed the dead man in silence, how the water sounded as it moved in its bowl. Gently, they bandaged the place where he'd been cut. They closed his cold eyes. In the soft summer twilight they carried him out from the house by the loch, and the pipes lamented him, and torches were lit, and all the glen's people went down to where the Coe met the sea. I wrapped my arms about myself. They laid MacPhail on a boat, and it moved out across the water. An island waited for him.

He will be buried there, Alasdair said. *On Eilean Munda. It is sacred ground, and for the best of our clan.*

I watched. The last of the light was spread out in the sky.

As if he knew my mind he said, *it was not war, Sassenach. Not a raid.* He shifted. *We were called to Achallader to meet with other chiefs, to talk with a Campbell . . . He offered money. Our allegiance to King William is worth a princely sum, it seems.*

A bribe.

Aye. But we did not take it. And there was a brawl . . .

I felt sad. I could not have saved him, I knew that. But I still felt a sadness which was deep, in my bones—deep, and with no words to it. All this loss.

The piper stopped his tunes, and a breeze came in.

We stood. Sarah trod neatly to us, with her hand on her belly. She kissed me twice, said *there was nothing to be done, Corrag. We all saw the wound. Do not blame yourself.*

They asked me to go to their home, for bread. But how could I have done that? I was not that strong. I always thought my heart was strong, but it was not strong. I'd always thought I did not fight, that I was not a fighter—but maybe I'd always fought. I just fought in different ways. They went, and I waited into the darkness until the boat came back—the body gone, buried in the island's salty earth.

Achallader. Write it down. A man died from a wound, in that place. A bribe was thrown back, and dirk was pushed in. I don't know much more on it, but that is enough—that speaks enough. It hastened the trouble that came from it.

I grieved for him. For MacPhail.

I did not know him. But we had raised our hands at each other, and I had been leaning over him as he died—I heard his last breath. I felt it, upon my cheek, and they say a man's last breath is his truth, his soul.

I sought the sea. There was a small comfort in it—in how it never ended, how there were other lands beyond it that I would never see. I tried to see the realm, like that. Like the dead people had only gone elsewhere, to a place I could not see—a place just over the sides of the earth, which is as real as the beach that I sat on. By Loch Leven, I thought this way. There were gulls, and white tips to the waves, and Eilean Munda looked back at me. I did not think of kings. I did not think of Catholics, or God, or Jacobites. I only thought of loss, and love. Of the *lap lap* of tides, and of his widow who had wailed as the boat came back without him. The sound of the water in its bowl.

Sarah found me there.

She lowered herself beside me, said—*truly. You are not to blame.*

He waved, I said, *at me. When the others just passed by and said nothing, he waved.*

I know. He was a good man. A heart as big as his body was—but you could not save him.

I nodded. I knew this, deep down. *Why is nothing simple? Or good? It never is.*

Sarah nodded. *I know. It feels that way. But it will pass, in time—it cannot be like this forever. And,* she nudged me, *this is not you talking. Don't you see the good in every little thing? My husband says you do.*

We looked across the water. A gull called out from a weedy rock, and in the distance I could see the little ferryboat, moored for the evening. The sky was red, and grey, and light.

'Tis a fine place to be buried, she said. *It has a small church on it. They say St Munda walked upon it, made it a sacred place. We bury the bravest souls on there. The beloved ones.*

I liked this. I smiled. *It was a calm crossing for him.*

It was. That was the Lord accepting his death. They say that high waves and a bad crossing would mean the world was mourning, raging, and not wanting the person leave it behind. Two geese skimmed the water, and she watched them, and said, *I am yet to see a stormy sea. The tenth MacIain was buried this way. The rain was so hard it broke stones—so Alasdair says. He saw it, as a boy.*

I don't think we truly leave it, I said.

Leave it?

The world. Here. I whispered this. *I don't think we go too far away.*

Sarah smiled. *There. That's your proper voice speaking again. Alasdair told me you spoke such things. He loves how you speak—so do I.*

As we sat, we saw the herrings flash. We felt a small breeze, and we were two women, sitting side by side. I asked *how are you? Both of you?*

She blew out a breath. *Tender. Big. Ready.* And, she added, *tired of talk of kings . . . It's all we have in our house. 'Tis all my husband talks of, or it feels so—wars, and James. Why talk it over as much as they do? I tell them this—but what good is my word? I'm only a woman . . .*

I gave a small sound as I smiled—not a laugh, but nearly. *My mother said that if women did the politics there'd be more calm in the world.*

I'm with her, on that. And Sarah made a throaty sound, as she did so. *These are difficult times,* she said.

But you will give birth soon enough.

She shook her head. *Not the child—I do not mean the child. They are difficult times for all of us. They are difficult times for the Highlands, and for all men who are faithful to James. Alasdair is troubled. He says less and thinks more. Sometimes he does not sleep, and goes walking with his thoughts. He doubts his cause, I think, and what can I tell him? Me? I was the enemy once.*

I frowned, and she saw this.

Campbell, she said. *I was one. I was raised in the south.*

I stared. *You are a Campbell?*

Was. By birth. My father is an Argyll man whom the MacIain always hated—and truly, my father always hated him. So it was. But neither man's a fool and they tried to make an alliance. We were the alliance—Alasdair and I.

I blinked. *It was politics?*

She laughed. *That word! See? We are plagued by it! Not politics—but nor did we marry for affection. We had none at first. I thought him too hasty. I thought he was a wanderer by heart when I am not—and far too blood-hungry! Always with a blade . . . But love has come by us, in its way.*

I thought *Campbell*. When all I had heard in this glen about the Campbell men was unkind, or resentful. Mistrustful. Sarah was one, or had been. She kissed me, when we met, and had said *how are you?*—like the answer mattered to her.

A cloud's shadow moved over us—dark, and light.

Do you not miss home? I asked.

The people, perhaps. But home is where I am now—with Alasdair, and this one inside me. I was a Campbell by birth, but I'm a MacDonald now. I don't know if she felt my quietness. I think I hide my feelings well, but perhaps I don't. She tilted her head lower, as if to catch my gaze, and said, *not all the people here are Glencoe born.*

No?

No! Plenty are not.

Are they not all called MacDonald?

She nodded. *They are, mostly. But if you serve a clan, and love them, and walk under their flag, then you may take on their name. So it works. If a soul is willing to fight for MacDonalds, then they are one of them.* She eyed me. *See?*

I saw.

MacPhail? Whose bones are out on that island? He's not a MacDonald by birth, nor is his from these parts. But the Highland way says it's who you say you love, and who you serve, which is of worth. Not some title that is passed down upon you by tradition. That's the English way, and the Lowland way—

but who can be born a nobleman? Nobility is earned. She stroked her belly. *'Tis our choices that make us,* I say.

SHE was kind. She was wise, and good. She had never feared *witch* in all her days, and told me so. Sarah took my hand, placed it on her belly and I felt her child move—his child, moving—and it was like how dreams flinch beneath us. They turn and press themselves against our skin, so that we feel them, and how can we control them? Our dreams have their own heartbeats. Our wishes do.

I wanted to say, *please forgive me. I think of your husband all the time. I wish I did not, but I do.* But I did not say this.

Instead, she spoke. *Corrag?* We stood. We were ready to leave each other, to go back to our homes, when she said *will you attend me? When the birth comes? I should like you there.*

I stared. I said *me?*

Aye. With your herbs, and calm. They call you a curewife, did you know that?

I didn't know that. It was another name to tie to myself, and carry. I said *yes. Yes, I will be with you.* And I was happy that he had such a brightly-lit woman, such a generous one, for he deserved no less than that, and I was glad she had a man who could see the beauty of an eggshell, and carry it in his pocket, for she deserved such a man.

It is a good match. The right match.

I told myself these things. Made myself hum a tune as I wandered back through the thick-heat, the insects, the rumbling skies.

⁕———◆———⁕

Death and a coming birth. The two together, in one day—but that is life, I reckon. Starts and ends, and the rest of us are living between them both, living as best we can. Living a life of peace and contentment, if we can, before our death comes for us and says *it is time, now.*

Mine comes. I've always known it would, for I'm not like many people, but I am still a person and my body won't always last.

The eggshell he gave me, and pressed into my hand? I think a death's like that—a broken body with the best part out, and free. I knelt over MacPhail. I saw the grey hair in his eyebrows, his teeth, his cleft chin, and I felt his last breath on me—warm, and tired, and wise. And his widow, later, wept with her fist against her heart. *He is gone* is what she said. But as she passed me, a week later, I whispered *may I speak? He is not gone. He's not.*

Here is what Cora taught me, and the mare's soft death, and the bones I'd find in the bogs, and here is what the mouse in the claws of an owl cried out, as it was lifted up, up. That we may fear the manner of death. We may fear the pain, and I do—so much. But the word *death* is like *elsewhere*—it is some other place, where others are.

At the very least, sir, there is this truth—that there will always be the signs that a life was lived. Children, tales, words they said. Places they named. Marks they left in dust, or on bark. People they loved, and told so.

I KNOW all this is true. I believe it fully, and remember it. *I will always be with you* said Cora. And so when I die, I will always be in Glencoe— for there is nowhere in this world I have loved as much as there.

But all the same, I am sad. I fear the burning, and I am sad—for the realm may be waiting, and it may be fine, and quiet, but I will miss Alasdair. I will miss the earthy, little things. I will be so sorry to leave.

In the days after MacPhail died, Alasdair came to my hut and said *how are you?* to me. He searched my face for the answer. He stayed for a while, and we spoke about the world—how we saw it, him and I. I told him of the mare, of England, and wild skies. Of my mother's hanging. He told me stories as old as his clan, and drew a map on my hand of the western isles, and when he stood to leave he said *how do you live with it all? So much hardship has come by you.*

I smiled. *Others have had worse.*

Some. But most have far better. Most do not live alone, as you do.

I knew this. And I said, *I've had my sorrowful days. My lonesome ones. Sometimes I wonder how the world can turn, with such loss in it.* I shrugged. *But there is beauty, too. Plenty.*

He stared. He said, *there is no-one like you.*

There must be.

No.

And he went. He went, and I climbed up onto the tops to watch him go—into the gully, along the glen floor. It rained, so that my hair flattened down, and my clothes grew wet, and as I watched from the peaks my head said *go now, get indoors*—but my body did not want to move. It was like two creatures—the head being the master, leading the heart away when the heart is not done yet with the mountains, or the rain. *Go now. Go.*

YES I will miss him. More than all other things.

Jane

*She has no politic sense. She can talk of herbs or instinct—but ask her of
kings and she sulks, shakes her head. She does not understand it, nor cares
for it, and she has a manner of pouting behind her mane of hair which is
childlike, and gives her a very innocent air.*

*She is both child and woman, Jane. In size and form, she is girlish—
when I hear that the Glencoe men called her a faery, of some kind, I can
almost believe it, for she is uncommon in appearance and might be thought of
as a trick of the mind, or a strangeness of light. She is quick, in her movements. She has a habit of tugging her toes, and feeling the skin between
them, and this reminds me of all our boys when they were very small—
playing with their own bodies as if they'd never seen them before. There is
also, of course, her voice. It is how a faery would speak, if they lived—high,
shrill.*

*But Jane, there is no denying that the life this creature has lived—the
treatment she has endured (and still endures) and the feelings she has har-
boured—are far from childlike. I know few people who have undergone such
a solitary life, and one of such suffering. Moreover, I believe she is in love. I
hear her, sometimes, as I walk up to her cell. In the dark, I hear her whispering, and it is his name she speaks over and over. Alasdair, she says—in the
breathy, high voice of hers.*

*How he felt—or feels—about her is beyond my knowing, this far.
He was a married man, and therefore I hope he adhered and respected
God's laws, and his own vows (although who can say what is respected, in
Highland parts?). But I will say this to you, Jane—that for all her smell
and strangeness, I suspect she could incite strong feelings in a man. I have
them—I do, as a father does. I recognise them—for when I see her raw*

wrists which the shackles have given her it brings to mind the cut knees, the bloodied noses and the grazed hands of our little ones, as they learnt to walk or ran too fast. I wanted to kneel down to them, each time—and so it is with her. I want to soothe her, as a father does. But might she have stirred up more, in Alasdair? It is hard to say. She is like no other soul I've met.

I have written to this Dalrymple, Master of Stair. I asked him to think upon his conscience. I wrote, too much blood has been shed.

So I wait. There are a mere five days for my letter to reach him in Edinburgh, and for him to reply. But greater feats have come to pass, in this world—such as us. You and I. Are we not a great work? A blessing?

How I wish you were here. The snow softens, the birds sing a little more.

Charles

VII

"It is as gentle as Venus herself."

of Peach

What I would give to be back there. To be there, and not here. When I pushed my hands into the sand, I'd have the sand beneath my nails for days, or weeks—and I wish for sand, now. I have an old scar, from this time. Here—see? I caught a thorn on the Keep-Me-Safe. I was running, and it tore me, and I bled through two leaves of dock. It is moon-white, now. I have healed. But I wish the wound was fresh again, and bleeding, and red, for this would mean I was back in Glencoe, and unchained, and it would mean he was still near enough to be seen—on peaks, or by water. Or in the corn—for they harvested it, and I saw him. The kiss had not happened, and was still to come.

My eyes will never see him, Mr Leslie. Not again.

I know I talked of what we leave behind—and of not fearing death. But last night, I wanted him with me—I wanted his face to be here, by my face, and for him to teach me those Gaelic names. *Aonach Dubh. Coire Gabhail.* Missing him is like water—it comes in waves. It rushes in upon me so that I'm soaked with it. It is like being grabbed. It leaves me gasping like how the herring did, in their nets. Just now, I felt it. Just now.

You were pressing a penny into the gaoler's hand, in the corridor—I heard it. I heard him grunt. And it rushed in, then. Fear rushed in, grabbed me by the neck so that I could not breathe, and I thought *I want to see Alasdair,* and *I do not want to die,* and I cried—I gave a sob—and *look.* I still have my tears coming down. Still a torn voice, like rags.

Sit near me?

Give me a while to wipe my face, and be steady.

What a poor welcome for you. A filthy crying thing with no cloth to clean herself. You deserve a little better than that.

WHAT were my last words? A man had breathed his last breath. *Mac-Donald* was a name to be earned. His child rolled beneath a freckled skin.

I could not sleep in those nights. Those were the summer nights which did not feel like night. There was too much light—too much grey and pale-yellow and deep-blue in the sky, too much silver on the lochs. I called them *half-nights.* I called them this, for what else could they be? I could see my own hand, in them. I could lie in my hut with a ghost-blue light outside, and not sleep for it—so I would wrap my arms about myself, tuck up against my knees. In my knees, I found a darkness.

Yes, sir. Half-nights. And if I still could not sleep, I would take myself high up to the northern ridge and sit, and smell the damp, earth-clean smell of summer nights, and dew, and feel the slight breeze, and watch the strange half-light upon the rocks, and trees. I thought of the clan, sleeping. I thought of my goats, curled up. Or half-dressed, I lay in burns—with their water coming down on. I felt the world turn, and time pass by. I took myself up the Dark Mount, on such a night—very quietly, testing each stone before I trod on it. On its peak, the women were sleeping. They lay about like children—neatly, and on their sides, with their mouths open. I heard them breathe. I saw how truly human they were—their knotted hair, their dirty hands. Doideag's feet were wrapped in her shawl so I thought *her feet get cold at night,* and I felt so sorry for them, then. What lives had they had? What life was this?

I walked and walked at night.

And once, Mr Leslie—just once—as I crouched on the ridge as the nights drew in, and an autumn air blew in, I saw a green light. It was frail, and very faint. As a moth's wing does, it fluttered where the earth met the far sky, and I looked at it, and looked, and wondered if I dreamt it. It was like no other thing. I said *Cora?* For I thought of her. I thought it was a trick of hers, perhaps. Or I thought of her sitting, on that cool half-lit ridge beside me, her hair drifting as mine drifted, and watching this green light. I asked her, *what is it? This northern light?* But she could not answer. She was in the realm.

The MacIain spoke of it. Once, by his hearth, he spoke of this green light—so I knew it was real, and seen by other folk. He said God was with the Glencoe tribe, and with all Highland men, and this was His word to be seen, in the sky—a gold-green breath, a moving light. *See it, and be mindful. Of God's power.*

So he said.

Me? I was mindful when I saw it. I was mindful of all my fortune, all my special days. I nestled there, and knew that to see such light, to see any strange and secret beauty is a gift, softly given. I reckon there is beauty in knowing this, as well. I am not much, sir—but I felt very beautiful sitting on the ridge, with the night breeze shifting and that greenish, northern light. I felt wise. Blessed.

I thought *Cora,* briefly.

But mostly, I thought *him. Him.*

. . .

LATE summer. The goats, like me, couldn't sleep. Their tails thumped the dry floor, and I felt the draught from them. I heard their tails, and I heard my name.

It was Iain, and I knew what this meant. *Corrag.*

I said, *yes.*

We hurried. Maybe that was the fastest I'd ever moved without my mare—the ground was quick beneath me, and I did not slip or slide or worry I might. His plaid snapped back on himself as he ran, and we ran through the shadows, between the walls of rock.

Their house in Carnoch was hot, and low-roofed. The room was dark with peat-smoke, and people—and I said *where is Sarah?* Alasdair was there. He stood by a cloth that hung from the thatch to the floor, and he came to me, said *the child will not come . . .*

The child will, I told him.

Sarah was lying on her back in her shift, and was whimpering under her breath. I pushed the men out. I was sharp with them, said *I want you gone* even to Alasdair. I pushed them back towards the door and pulled the cloth back down to give Sarah some secrecy. It was only her, me and Lady Glencoe with her white cap there. This was a woman's place now like all birthing chambers should be.

Sarah, I said, *let me look.*

I tended to her. I took out my herbs and moved through them, and said to Lady Glencoe *will you burn this?* Or *put this in water. Make her drink.* And we moved together, we moved easily, and she brought in more candles which I laid by Sarah's feet, and her waist. Sarah let out a wail. She was wide, and sore-looking, and I said *I will help you. I promise I will.*

Lady Glencoe asked me, *have you been at a birth before?*

Once. A dog's.

A dog's?

I glanced at her. *It is enough. You are here, and I am. We will help her. A dog's?*

Lady Glencoe was a good nurse—how she took the herbs I asked for, ground them or watered them as I asked her to without saying a word at all. She pressed poppy onto Sarah's gums for the pain, and we together washed her parts. She burnt lavender in the candles so their smell cleansed the room and might make the mother some calmer. *Rub her belly softly* I said, which she did. And I said *you must try to push now, Sarah*—for inside her, I could see a little chick-wet head. It was dark-coloured, and bloodied. She pushed very bravely. She pushed and I said *that's it* and Lady Glencoe stroked her hair and whispered in her ear and poor Sarah wailed more than I ever had in all my life—such a despairing wail too like she was done with it all, this breath was all she had left in it. I said *push,* and I felt sorry to see all that blood, but the baby must come out. And then, it was there! There it was, the head, and I could see a little ear, and I called out *I can see the head, Sarah! You must push again* to which she said *I can't* and both Lady Glencoe and I said *you can* so she took in a huge breath and cried and this push was silent, with her jaw clenched tight and she raised her head up so I saw how damp and pale she was, like she was cold but I knew she was burning hot and I put my hands about the tiny wet-haired head and whispered *push* and then out it came, pup-slick, and I was holding a baby. I was holding a pink and filmy thing with its cord by its side as it is meant to be and it had a face, a tiny screwed-up face with a nose on it and a little mouth and I pulled it up to me, held the boy against my own chest like he was mine, like he fitted very well against me so that for one small moment I was his mother and he was my son and I tapped his back and rocked him back and fro.

Cry, I whispered to him, *you're here.*

Then it came. It was a frail, bird's wail, like he was lost and frightened and wanting his proper mother. He wanted her smell, and to be held by her. So I carried him to Sarah. She was half-dead, desperately pale, and I placed her son in her arms. I said *Sarah? Look. You have a son.* She had life enough to see him, to smile in a way I have seen no person smile. She brought her arm forwards and took him.

WE BURNT more lavender. I daubed gentle herbs upon her, and I did a little stitching. I think my work must have been very sore for her, but she had her son. I reckon all the pain in the world can come to you and you do not mind it once your babe is safe.

She slept. Her eyelids went down and she looked very peaceful and Lady Glencoe rose, took the bowls of cloth and blood away.

I did not hear him. But Alasdair came by me very slowly, his breath very shallow like he feared his breath might wake the pair. He moved beside her, crouched gently down. I have never seen such a look on him or any person—like all he had ever thought of as beauty had been a ghost of this. Every starry sky had been a shadow of his tired wife sleeping with their son on her breast.

This was not my place to be. Not now.

I finished my stitch, lowered her shift down. I crept to the curtain and as I pulled it behind me I saw him put a kiss on her, on her cheek. The chamber was a tender place now, and made for the three of them—no one else. I knew this was right, and slipped away.

A DANCE followed. A fire was lit—the greatest fire I'd seen in all my life was lit in the field by Achnacon, and I heard them shouting from home to home. And out came the cousins, out came the clan. There was laughter, and ale, and drums.

Lady Glencoe said *we celebrate life most of all.*

I understood. She touched my arm, briefly, and then she moved out into the field with the fire's glow, the sparks.

I watched, from the shadows. I felt like being alone.

But a breath came down upon me. I felt a man standing near, so I turned. *I have reason to thank you again, I think,* he said—and he put his hand on my shoulder like he knew I was good, and had done a good thing. *It's a fine son she has given my son* he said. *You'll have a drink Corrag.*

I said *thank you but—*

He pointed. *You will drink!*

And I did. I had a drink that took my breath away, but there can be no denying how soft it made me feel. The MacIain roared by the fire, with his men, and Iain was kissing his wife by an ash tree. So I carried my cup amongst the other people. I slipped by unseen by most, for they were dancing—but a few put their heads on one side and looked at me. In my head I thought *witch,* but none said it. Instead they called *it is a boy* out across the townships, and a man with a snow-white beard was sent to light the fire on An Torr to spread word of their child's safe coming into the world. It was more of a festival than I had ever seen. Out in the field by where the river came down through its rocks they lit a fire also and families came down from their houses, from Achtriochtan where I'd taken the pot and spoon and Inverrigan whose eggs I'd lifted. I saw great Ranald with beard, and his pipes. I saw the man from Dalness in the next glen who was lifting a boy up by his ankles, so that the boy laughed, and the red-haired family from Achnacon were dancing together—all dancing together. Some nodded to me. One lady who carried an infant herself passed by me, and smiled. She spoke no English, and my Gaelic was small, but she put her hand upon my cheek which had a thousand words in it. It was a *thank you,* I reckon. It was what a person does when they want to see a face more clearly—truly *see* it.

I'll always remember how she did that.

Drunk? No. But many were. The women faded to their hearths, in time, with their children and left the men bawding and bragging of who fought most well, most likely, or who sang most, who had robbed the most Campbells. Iain was smiling wider than I'd ever known him to. A tacksman danced alone to the piper which made them call and cheer, and stamp their feet.

I will say this. That I think they danced to celebrate a new life, yes—but also to celebrate life, all life. For theirs was a deathly world. Winters alone could kill them, and their feuds and plots did too. So when life came in, they were glad of it.

I left my cup on a stone.

I tucked up my skirt to make its bell-shape for the climb to Coire Gabhail and had one backward glance to the house where Sarah slept and then to the moon which was shining very brightly, and then to where the fire was with the men laughing by it. Alasdair was there. He was no longer in the chamber, but was standing by the fire. He looked on me. He wore a smile, which I knew was not from seeing me, but a smile from a joke his father told and which had not yet left his face. But it left his face as he looked on me. We stared for a moment, he and I.

I knew he thought *thank you*. I could feel it, in his stare.

This is what I told myself, as I made my way home. I skirted the bogs and brushed through the trees, and thought of how he'd kissed her cheek—a slow and proper kiss. I looked up at the stars. By my hut, the owl called out to me, saying *all is right, and is as it must be*—which it was. A new life was in the world. A woman was a mother now. A man was a father.

I CRIED a little, in my hut. Only a little. I was tired, and to see a birth is so wondrous and strange that most of us cry, at it. It is beyond words, I think. It is what all the beauty is, in the whole world—that. New life.

I slept by the goats, and one of them licked me, and this made me cry a little harder. But in time I found my sleep.

It is a comfort—it is. It is a comfort to think of that birth, when there has been so much death. So much death came, to Glencoe. There was so much blood, later, that I trod through or knelt in, and it made me think of the first frail call of their son. His voice took its place in the world. It became part of it—as much as wind, or soil. And I will always remember how he felt, to hold, how he fitted against my collarbone, like there had always been a space there that only a baby could fit, or fill.

He survived the massacre. Sarah strapped him to her, with a blanket. I saw her running into the blizzards with other women, other bairns, and Iain shouted *Hurry! This way!* I saw them, and thought *they are safe* . . . But then I thought *where is Alasdair? He is not with them* and *he is not yet safe*.

I race ahead. I go too far.

WHEN I hear MacDonalds of Glencoe I think of the fire by Achnacon, and the dancing. I think of what I felt amongst them, which was how they were one being, one creature, and just as I had helped to birth Alasdair and Sarah's child, so I had delivered a child which was all of theirs. It felt that way. The joy of it was in that field. The knowing that death was always near, but here was a life, made it joyful. I will always think of them like this. The fire's glow, and the pipes.

In the days afterwards, he came. I was standing in my valley, feeling the first drops of rain. At last, it was raining, and the thunder rumbled out, and I looked down to see him walking through the grass.

His hair was wet, and his shoulders were, and he said such things as *he is beautiful* . . . *His feet* . . . *His eyes* . . . And when he spoke of his boy, he held out his hands, as if he was holding him. I was glad. I was glad of his happiness—for he was bright with it. I was glad that all was well.

I said so. I said, *I've never seen such beauty as that. Him. You are lucky.*

Yes. Thank you, he said, *for what you did.* His hair grew dark with the rain.

Alasdair left, and as he left I thought, *what a light you are. What a gift—to where you are, to the ones who are with you.*

I felt it very simply—no grief, no deep wish.

Yes I shall be fine. I've heard myself today, and I know I've not been spirited or talked like I mostly have. I've been low in my heart, like a stone. It is not my death which lowers it, or not so much—it is the loss. It is the simple loss of what I never had, and will not have.

But I will be fine. I will think of what did come to me, and this will hearten me. How can I be ungrateful? You have come. I am so grateful that you've come, and so I will think of you for a while, and then perhaps of rivers, or sunsets in Glencoe. Of my mare.

Have I ever thanked you? I do, now. I am grateful, Mr Leslie. I am glad you found me, for it makes all less hard.

Be warm tonight. Stay warm.

Jane

I will not write of her tonight. I will not tell you what she spoke of, for it will take up ink, and time, and light—and I have little of these things. What I will write of is what I should have written of long ago, or spoken of. We are two trees with out branches entwined, you and I—yet there are secrets we do not talk of. One secret.

My love. I do not want to distress you. But tonight all I have thought of is you, and our lost girl. Our little girl, whose birth and death was almost five years ago. I know—that you have asked for us to leave her be, and not mention her. You have said that to keep her unmentioned is to lay her to rest—but we think of her, do we not? I remember. Don't think that my faith and duty have taken my memories of her away. They have not. I did not see her as you saw her, but I remember your own face. I saw your shame, and sorrow. We have never spoken of it.

We are fortunate to have our sons alive and well *you said.* Most women lose a child or two. It is God's way.

But why did we not speak more of it? Why did you feel ashamed? What shame was there? In the days and weeks that followed you shook at my touch, like my touch pained you—or you felt that I should touch other, better things. Lives pass on, Jane. Our daughter came in strangled, and blue, but some must. Some fail in our eyes, but not in the Lord's.

Did you ever think I loved you less, for it? I worry that you think so. It was hard to speak of our loss to you, for I feared to speak of it may widen your pain beyond all measure. But I will write it now. I will write what I did not say, in words, and should have done from the moment we knew: I do not love you less. I love you more, Jane, for it—for your firm little face which you showed our visitors, when your heart must have been broken. You were so frail in those weeks. But you still lifted up your chin, offered tea.

There is no blame. I know you, my love—I know you blamed yourself. I saw you in the garden, staring at the grass, and I know you saw it as your fault that our daughter was born sleeping. It was not your fault. It was God's will that the only life she knew was tucked up, beneath your skin. That, alone, is a good life.

Speaking of a death does not worsen it, or change it. Our daughter does not suffer again, when we speak of her. Our girl is gone—but let us talk of her? Let us give her a second life, of some kind?

Be gentle with yourself. Do not try to understand God's mystery, or wisdom—which none of us can know. Do not count the years, as I know you do. We have four sons of such strength and curiosity that I thank the Lord daily—more than daily. Four sons, and such a wife as you. I can ask for no more. I never even dreamt of half of this, half, of you. Jane, be gentle with yourself.

I read my Bible in a different manner, these days. The pages are damp which makes the business harder. But whereas I have mostly looked for guidance, it is not guidance I seek now. I look for proof—that my secret thoughts are noble, worthy ones. For I am having strange moments, Jane—I think as I have not, before.

"The Lord's unfailing love and mercy still continue, fresh as the morning, as sure as the sunrise" (Lamentations 3:22–23).

I will eat supper now, and to bed.

My everything is yours—even from here, in Scotland.

Charles

VII

"If the virtues of it make you fall in love with it (as they will if you be wise) keep a syrup of it to take inwardly, and ointment and plaister of it to use outwardly, always by you."

of Bugle

I talked of births yesterday. I spoke of a new life as my own is nearly done. I talked of all the blood and mess, and out he came—a new MacDonald, with his mother's cloudy eyes but the red hair of his father, and I was so glad he was living. I was glad of his tiny pink hands.

I am not so low today. And I did think of all the goodness I had seen, and felt, in my other lives. I counted them, and passed the night this way. I told myself that I have saved lives—I said *make for Appin and do not trust these men,* and those words of mine saved life after life after life.

But I race ahead. I have not spoken of that, yet.

Births, and a little one, and did I ever hope for that? I can't remember doing so. I have no memory of dolls, in Thorneyburnbank, or of listing names for my ghostly, unmade child. I do not think I ever thought of being a mother—for love must happen first. A man would have to love me, and take me as his wife, and undress me by a fire—just him, and I. That is the way. He would have to move upon me, and fill me, and we would put so many kisses on each other we would have to stop and smile. This is what I hoped for. I hoped so hard that I might know love, and feel it, but I did not think it would come to me. I never thought of children. It felt like a hope too far.

But now that I am dying, I am allowed to think of it. Can you imagine it? Me? All round like a blackberry with a baby inside? I doubt I could walk. I would stand, and fall forwards like old folk do. And how would I push the baby out, as I am? I am tiny. I am a mouse. The Chief MacIain said *why does a child tend to me* because he thought I was a child. Most have thought it, too.

I reckon I was not made for it. I have to tell myself this—that the world did not give me a shape for mothering. A heart and a head, yes—but not a body like Sarah's body was. It makes me a small part sad. But I nod, and understand it—we are not all the same, and I am glad we're not. I like the differences. I liked the plum-faced Mossman, and my tooting horse.

But I imagined it, and do. I dip my toe into fancies which will never come to pass, but what harm can come from it? Chained up? I had a daughter whose ear I would whisper stories to. I'd show her a dewdrop caught in leaves. Her father would dangle her by the feet till she laughed, and laughed.

I am not a mother. I will not be one. And that is a world I'll know nothing of, which makes me ache a little in the empty hours, in the rainy days. But it does not make me less of a person, less of a girl, or a witch. I pulled Alasdair and Sarah's baby, into the world. I saved lives, which will make more lives, which will make more. In a hundred years, there will be many people who would not be living were it not for me. *For Corrag.*

Who?

She was a small thing that lived in the hills. They burnt her on a stake in Inverary for her words, for helping us. Those wild goats come from her goats.

So she died for us?

She did.

Maybe I am the mother to a hundred thousand things.

⸎

I kept from Carnoch that month. I chose my own company again, or that of my goats. I hoped for the stag, but these were airless days, with the rocks being warm to touch and the heather in bloom. So he kept high up. He kept where a thin wind blew the flies away, and I did not see him for a long while.

Perhaps I missed him. Or maybe the wild creature in me wanted the wind and the wide views, too—for I was often up, up. It was the time for scrambling—for the old summer light was clear, and sharp, and every rock seemed bright to me. I could feel them, and see them. I watched how their shadows moved across the glen floor. I might leave my hut in the morning, with the dew still on the grass, and not return until the evening was down. I could smell autumn, then. Its cold, leafy breath was on the air.

What a gift you are . . . I thought of him, on my walks.

I thought of the baby, of oaths, of God.

On a heavy day, I went to the Dark Mount. The heather was dry, dying, and it caught my skirts as I climbed its slopes—tugging the bushes, and rustling, so that they heard me coming. Doideag said, *aren't you too kind to be here, with us? Too clean?* Sharp piece. I heard her jaw click, as she spoke.

I look for Gormshuil. Is she here? And like this might open those red-veined eyes of hers, wherever she slept, I said *I have henbane for her.* I showed it—dark-green.

Gormshuil came. She crept out from stones like a beetle, and righted herself. *Henbane?*

Yes.

Then you're after a thing, she said. *Meat?*

Not meat.

I walked with her—not far, and not down, for I liked the breeze and the view of the moor. But we walked, and I felt the silence. I said, *what can you see?*

See?

There is so much I wish I could know, I said. *The child's life—will it be safe, and long? Where is my stag? What will come of this word* Jacobite, *and will the winter be bad, and how might I—*

Stop? What you feel?

I faced her. Wise old crone that she was. With her puckered mouth and her cunning eyes. *Teach me? To have the second sight?*

Gormshuil smiled at that. She showed her pegs, and wheezed. *The sight? To be taught?*

Yes.

It can-ee be taught. What comes will come. What you see is what you see, wee thing, and it will come to pass . . .

What will? Pass?

As if this was a fool's question, she frowned. *All of it! All comes and goes.*

What comes? Tell me? What will go?

She smelt the henbane in her fist. *Kings are back and fro. But I'm not sure Orange will stay Orange . . .*

William? I shook my head.

Och, she said. And she looked away from me as if she was not addled and reeky, and sad. She looked over the moor, briefly. *It is not always a gift, Corrag. Not when sad things are ahead.*

Sad things?

She turned back to me. She had the old witch-eyes again, and the mocking look, and she lifted a finger up to my nose, pressed it. *I think a wolf will howl its name. A lion will roar. And that is all I will give you, nosy tiny bairn. You bring me more herbs—and soon.*

⌐⟶━━━◀▮▶━━━⟵⌐

Autumn rolled in. I knew the autumn smells. From my first life, my English days, I knew its sharp, wet, earthy smells—and that this meant berries, and fruit. So the turf grew, the baby grew, and so did the people out on the hills, bent at the waist. We scratched ourselves on brambles, and inked up our fingers with blackberries and sloes, and plucking the mushrooms up from the wetter parts. The women did this. I saw wives and daughters, with their hair tied back. I thought, once, I saw Doideag of Mull with her gums and sad eyes, but the eyes can be fooled in misty weather.

Mushrooms made me think of the mare. I could see her, trying to eat them—her lips curled back from her teeth, displeased. She was for apples, and mint. And so I thought of her, too, with the apple tree. It grew near Achnacon—twisted with age, and heavy, and the freckled man who lived there gestured to me, and the tree, said *pick!* So I gathered an armful, grateful. Left all-heal at his door.

I STAYED from Carnoch for a long time—for weeks.

But Alasdair came to me. He knew, I think, that I was keeping far away—for he did not find me at my hut. I was picking berries on Cat Peak, and was berry-stained, and he was the colour of these autumn hills—deep-brown, and red, and gold. He had freckles from a month of sun. He looked tired. I thought *him.*

He kicked a stone with his boot. *It's been a while.*

I did not answer.

Walk with me, he said.

So we brushed through the heather, and west. October, in the afternoon, with geese flying over and the rocks still warm from summer sun, he took me to the Pap of Glencoe, at the western end of the northern ridge. When he led the way, and I followed, I looked at how his hair was, and how thick his legs were from his life of hills and fighting. When I led, I hoped he only looked at the ground, or the sky—for I've never had the shape that men like. I've never had much that men like, I don't think. I was aware of this, as we went to the Pap—of my smallness, of how he might be walking through the scent I left behind, of milk, and grasses, and how I probably had blossom in my hair.

The Pap was not as high as other hills were, in the glen. It rose up from the sea, looked down on Carnoch's roofs. It had woodland, where the smaller deer were, and he said *careful* as he stepped over fallen trees, and thorns. I smiled, for hadn't I seen worse? Been in worse places? I knew thorns and bore their marks on my arms. I had been cut by rocks, and torn. But he still said, *careful*.

Up—into the air. He was striding with those thick legs, his plaid swinging, but I climbed behind him. I did not stride. I was quick, scrambling, with my hands and feet as animals do, and I had it in my head that I was like Bran, or the wildcat I had seen. He waited, sometimes. He did not look back, but he waited—like he knew I would be slower. I reckoned all folk were slower when they walked with him.

Up, and up, and the wind picked itself up from the rocks and gusted about us, shaking the grass. I felt the wide, green space that was beneath us now, but did not look—not yet. I wanted to wait till we stood on the highest part, with the view at its best—like a gift, as views are. My hair was blowing like a bird, when I joined him. My skirts were *tug tug* against themselves.

I puffed out. I straightened my back and stared.

Nowhere better, he said.

I looked. There were mountains all about us. Loch Leven stretched out below, out towards the peaks which were all red or dark-coloured. There were houses, and streams, and his father's black horse in its field. I saw the Coe—breaking white around its rocks. I saw people, and chickens. In the water, I saw shadows of fish, and weed.

Here?

This view. This hill . . .

I looked at him. I looked at the proud, straight nose and the forehead, which was lined and puckered from his years as a fighter, from hunting and climbing into the wind. His hair was blowing like mine was blowing. Through my dark-brown strands I saw his wet-earth red, its golden ends.

His eyes were on the view. He said, *this is where I learnt to fight, on this hill. Iain and I. We'd come up here with wooden swords . . .* He pointed. *That path leads down to the far side of Loch Leven. We'd swim there, and charge up to this point. I've slept here.*

Slept?

Aye. I've slept all over this glen. We all have. But the sunset from here is . . .

I looked where he looked. West. I always knew west. I knew it in my head, in my heartbeat—maybe our women do, or maybe all people who love the outdoors look west, no matter of their faith. We feel west. Like the mare felt north-and-west, and took me there. I thought of her, for a moment. My hair blew, and the sky beyond the loch was reddening with light.

We looked on it.

I imagined him as a boy. I imagined Cora as a child, on a half-moon bridge. I thought of all the joys and sadnesses wrapped up, side by side.

He said, *I'm a different man to what I was. I know I am.*

You're a parent now.

I am, and I'm glad of it. But that is not why I am different, Corrag. I was different before. I've been different for a year, now. I changed.

With what?

With you. He said it very flatly—not at me, but at the view. *You came. In you wandered with your English voice and grey eyes, and all this talk of the world which I've never heard before—of nature, and goodness. No talk of God, or kings.* He gave a single shake of his head. *I can't recall the last time a person came here, and did not speak of those things.*

I stood. I had no words.

Do you know how I was raised? To be proud. To protect everything I loved, and never give up. The stories we were given, as boys, were all of Red Angus, of warrior men and vengeance, and glorious deaths in war. If I could walk, I could fight—so our father said. And it's true. I could. I did fight. Did you know—he turned to me—*that I was imprisoned as a small boy? For my part in a raid? In Breadalbane lands. I had blood on my face when they took me. I was so proud . . .*

You knew no other way, maybe.

Maybe. Or I had no choice. We have so many enemies, Corrag. The Campbells and the Lowlands, but the English too. William. If we don't fight, we die—or our way of life does. Our hearts die, maybe . . .

We looked out. I could see the tiny ferryboat, moored near Balla-chulish. In the hazy distance, there were the mountains of far places—places I'd never go. A wind moved my skirts. The clouds were blowing over us, and the colours in the sky were growing dark. My hair was lifted, too, and blew about my eyes.

We've been ordered to swear an oath, he said.

Ordered? An oath?

To William. To swear our allegiance to him. He pressed his toe against a rock, and it moved. *He said if we swear it, we will be forgiven for all our past raids, all our past treasons against him and others. We will have his protection.*

And if you do not swear it?

We will be seen as traitors and punished as such.

I thought on this for a while. I felt my hair blowing. I thought how far away such a word as *king* can feel, in such a place as there—the Pap, with clouds.

What will be done?

He laughed. *Ah. Aye. What will be done? That is the question, is it not? Iain loathes this Orange king. He loathes all he is—his race, his faith. He says we must never swear an oath for it kills what we are. My father also thinks this way. I think it, mostly.*

Mostly?

He shifted. *There is a good man at Inverlochy. A man called Hill. He calls himself a friend of the clans, and perhaps he is. And he says we should make this oath, for our own sakes. But I do not know . . . A year ago, I'd have been more against this than all the other men. I'd have taken my sword out—fought them. I believe what they believe and I'll not denounce my faith, or my clan— never. I'll die before that. But this quest of ours . . . This way we serve James, when he's fled away . . .* He rubbed his forehead, sighed. *Are we fools, is what I ask myself. Fools, to be resisting what feels so much stronger than us? Would we be fools—proud ones, at that—to miss this oath?* He gave a wry smile. *A dead man is no good to James, or God. Or to his wife.*

No.

I've fought and fought. And if we do not swear this oath, we will be fighting all our lives—against every single shadow! My boy will be an outlaw before he can even speak a word! We'll be done for, if we fight this king. I can feel that as clearly as I can feel this weather.

So sign it, I whispered. *Make this oath.*

He smiled. *Ah. But what of our hearts?*

Hearts?

Aye. Hearts. Don't you crease up your brow as if I'm not talking your language—I know I am. You speak more of hearts than all of us. You live by yours. How you said you had no king . . .

I was very still. I looked at him. I looked at him for a long time, for I loved how he looked. I loved his face.

We aren't shrewd enough, he said. *As a people. We aren't . . .* And he shook his head, as if he couldn't find the word.

I used to stand in the marshes in England, and look at the frogs. I looked at them so much I thought I knew them, and that I might even be a frog. But then the men came for my mother, and I ran north. I had to. I won't see them again—the frogs—but I know they are still there. They still clutch the rushes. I might not see them plopping in the water but that doesn't mean they don't do it—they do. They still go cleep *in the evenings. They are probably* cleeping *now, as we're standing here.* I shrugged. *I had to leave them. But they are still in me. I carry them, and I know they are as real as they ever were.*

Alasdair looked at me. He looked down upon me as if I was not there—like he was seeing through me. It was a strange look, and a deep one. Maybe he saw those frogs.

I tell you this to say that we all make our changes. Everyone does. I left those frogs, for my own life's sake—but I still love them. They will always lick their eyes with their tongues, like they did. And if you swear an oath, your heart will still be your heart, Alasdair. How can they take your heart away? Or kill it? They can't. I blushed, looked away. I heard my words, my foolish talk of frogs. *That's just my way of talking.*

He said, *Aye, I know. It's a good way.*

It's prattle.

He smiled.

All I try to say is that we change—over and over. But I think our hearts are our hearts, and cannot be governed—not by kings, or oaths. Not by our own heads. I shrugged. *They are too strong.*

In came a wind. I tried to catch my hair, which was blowing strongly now. I caught it, and tied it at the nape of my neck. Strands still fluttered, but I'd tied most of it.

You think we should swear the oath, Sassenach?

I eyed him, half-smiled. *How can I say? 'Tis your oath to make, not mine. All I know is that nothing—not an oath, or a promise, or any king—can change a person's heart. It feels what it feels.*

Aye. Maybe it does.

My skirts snapped on themselves. His plaid shook in the wind, and for a while we stood there side by side, watching the sun sink down. The light was gold and red. It spread over all of Scotland, and shone upon our faces, and I knew how he would look if I turned to him, now. How I might look, if he also turned.

Once, he said, *you said I'd made you feel wrong—for being here, for having come. I never meant that.*

I smiled. *I know.*

And we said no more, but I was happy. I was so close to him that the hairs from his arms brushed my own arms, and we had spoken of hearts, and it was a red-coloured, breezy, beautiful world. I thought *I am meant to be here. Here. I always was.*

He said *what are you thinking? At this moment?*

Of its beauty. Its age. All this age . . .

We looked out at the peaks. We looked, and looked, and I thought of all their wisdom—of the sights and breaths and troubles that had passed beneath each mountain, of the years which had rolled by. More years than I could think of. More sights, and loss, and wishes. *All my places have been old,* I thought. Caves, or valleys. Forests. Sands.

He did not turn. *Age?*

Of here. These hills. They have seen so many lives. They've seen wars, and births, and love, and sorrow, and all the deer. All those feet that have trodden on them . . .

I thought I heard him smile—the soft, quick mouth's sound when a smile is made. *Aye. They're old. And they'll still be here—when we're dead and gone. When we're dust, and forgotten, there'll still be the Pap of Glencoe.*

I looked down at my hands. Briefly, thought of the realm. I thought of the ones I loved, who were in it now. I closed my hands up. I said, *you will not be gone. You live, in your son. You have a line, now.*

Nor will you.

Me?

Be gone. He looked straight ahead. *I'll remember you.*

IT WAS my happiest place. My happiest time. Being in a place of wind, and setting sun, and sun upon the water—and being there, with him. Standing so close to each other that I could feel his warmth, and he could feel mine. The Pap of Glencoe, and us. I have never liked kings or queens, for I think no one person is ever better than another, or not in the world's eyes—but on the Pap, I had felt like it was only him and me. That is was us, and all this beauty. With the autumn, and height, and hearts.

I knew it would not happen twice. It came, and was gone.

In time, he said, *it is late. We must go down.*

I followed him. We took the path we had come up on, and I saw my old footprints in the dust. I saw the bramble he had caught his plaid on, and the rock he'd helped me over, and all these things seemed a long time ago.

When we came to two pathways in the grass, we stopped.

I'll leave you here, I said.

He studied me. He stared, and as he did a wind picked up. It brought in a raindrop. I felt it on my bare arms. Then I felt one on my nose, and my scalp, and each drop seemed so loud—heavy, and fat. I looked about me. I looked at how the rain shook the leaves it fell upon, and how flowers held each drop, and the sky was growing dark, now. I closed my eyes, briefly. When I opened them, he had a raindrop on his cheekbone, and his hair looked wet. He was still staring. He lifted his hand, and brought it to my face, and slowly moved a strand of hair back, behind my ear.

He said, *you* . . .

I made a sound. I shook my head, stepped back.

Be good to every living thing, said Cora, when she lived. I had promised her, and I liked Sarah so very much, so I made my way along the side of the Pap. When the storm came in, it struck the backs of my hands, and dimpled the mud, and the Coe was very loud and white, and when I was nearly down in the glen again, I paused. I looked back. He was so brown-coloured—his clothes, boots, his damp hair and the dirt on his arms—that he looked like the hills. He looked so much like the hills that I could barely see him. He was like the earth. He was part of the rocks and old heather, the old ferns. I could only see him when he moved. When he stood still, and did not move—which he did twice, as I was watching—my eyes lost him, and I wondered if he was not there at all. I wondered, too, why he might slow, and stop. I didn't know. I thought *there is a deer,* or *he looks at the view,* or I thought that, maybe, perhaps, he was looking back, as I was looking back. I was also in brown colours. I was damp-haired, with dirt on my skin.

So. Oaths. I half-believe in them. Or rather, I believe in them if the heart is what makes them—not the mouth. I believe in deep, honest ones. I believe in the ones which you know you had made many years before, in your empty bed.

Do not love. And I'd said *no. I will not.*

But that was my mouth, speaking. That was my mouth saying what she hoped it would, so that she said *good girl,* and kissed me good night. Yet all the while my heart was saying, *I will! I will! I will love, and when I do, I will give my whole life for it. I will give myself up. I will love, and love.*

So I believe in the heart's oaths. They are the ones we should live by—for what life is worth living, with a stifled heart? None, that I know of.

PROMISE me you'll come back to me?

I do not have long. Not long—not now.

Jane

The thaw is quick, and clear. It is truly upon us—burns are running, and I have seen my first bulbs pushing up from the ground, and buds on branches, which are things she would notice and take pleasure in. So I have her in my mind, when I walk.

She talks—we talk—of oaths. She says there are two oaths that we make, in our lifetime—those with our intellect, and reason; and those with our heart. There are the oaths we choose to make—and those that are made for us, by our bodies, or nature, or God. Is she right? Two weeks ago I would have scorned this, and derided it, and called it madness or witchcraft as most people would. But now, I listen to her. I listen to her, for I know she will not last. She will die. And I am the only one who might be left to speak of her.

She swore an oath to her mother that she would never love a man. But her heart made an oath that it would, it would—and no rationale might stop it.

What oaths have I made? Here is a question. She did not ask it of me, but I ask it of myself. I am sleepless, and writing this by a candle which gives a poor light, and I ask what vows I have made in my life, and if they were chosen or not. My faith? I did not choose that. It came upon me as a boy, and for all the troubles that a faith may cause or undergo, I have never lost it—I know there is a God, and I know He sees me as I write this letter, that He also sees Corrag, and that He sees you, my wife, who sleeps as I write this under the blankets in a south-facing room. I did not choose my faith. It chose me, and my heart knows it—and for all my days I will have this faith in God, and in goodness. I am certain of that. But my profession, Jane? That is different, I think. I think it was set before me by my father, and expected, and I chose to enter into it, and to preach, and to write as I do. I made an oath with my head, for when have I ever enjoyed speaking before crowds? My hands shake with it. But I do it, and I am fine with the rhetoric, and an orator who receives such compliments that I almost blush—I am lucky, I know. But did I learn it? Rather than have it, by nature? Perhaps.

What would my father do, at this moment?

How would he feel?

He would not allow his feelings to have come to this, I am certain. He'd have trawled the Bible to find enough to quash any compassion—for King James and God are his purpose, and his faith is written down in ink. He knows, and feels, and it was his head, I think, that made an oath to God— his head, which led him. But I am not him. I am my own man.

Jane—what do I do? My head speaks of law—of the Bible, of God. It tells me not to expect a letter from Stair, nor to hope for a change in Corrag's last few days. I should not want it. I should wish (as I once wished) for the world to be rid of all darkness, and what concern should it be, if that darkness is burnt away, in light?

I should allow it to unfold as God intends it to. She is a prisoner of the law. If she dies, she dies.

But—but!—I am troubled. Sleepless. Missing you. As I take off my wig in the evenings I look at the man it reveals and I barely know him—he is tired, and old.

Pray for me. Pray that I may find guidance, and solace—that I may find the right, noble thoughts.

Charles.

IX

*". . . the syrup helps much to procure rest, and to settle the brains
of frantic persons, by cooling the hot distemperatures of the head."*

of Water Lilies

Tell me of the square. Of the Mercat Cross and how much wood
is there—how much is built. It is this talk of death. It is this talk
of the massacre, this remembering—it has frightened me, and has put
terrible deaths in my head so that I want to think *it was a dream, a
fearsome dream*. Did they die? I know they did. I saw their bodies. I
saw their charred bodies with knife wounds in their backs, and sides—
wounds like mouths, so that as I stumbled by them I thought they
spoke to me. I thought they said my name, these wounds—like I could
have stopped it. Like I could have saved more people than I did.

It is remembering this, that has frightened me. And the man.

A man came.

This morning. I heard his footsteps by my door, and I thought it
was you. I thought *Mr Leslie has come early!* And I was so hopeful, sir,
I was so happy for I like your time—I like speaking to you, and how
you nod, and it is a peculiar thing that I find a little comfort from a
churchman when they have never offered comfort in my life to me,
or to my kind. But all things change, I know that. And I do—find a
comfort in you. I like you smiling. Not many smile, but you do. So

I heard these footsteps by my door and thought *it is Mr Leslie,* and I stood up in my chains to greet you and I had my smile upon my face to meet your smile, which you give now.

But it was not you. It was a man whose name I never got. But he is the one who does the tying up. When it is a hanging, he is the one who does the knot, and then who makes the horse walk forwards and pull the person up. When it is branding like they did to a man who defiled a creature in its stall, he is the one with the branding iron—he pushes it into the flesh, and hears it hiss. When it is a burning, he ties to the stake. He piles the barrels up and gathers the wood.

So he was here. He came in, and laughed. He saw me standing in my chains with my bloodied skirts and laughed.

I did not know what was worth a laugh. I watched him.

He said *we'll be saving a pretty penny, then.* Then he laughed some more. *How did you thwart a plan? You?* He put his thumb in his eye to press a tear of laughter away. *I've seen bigger newborns! You?*

And then, when he was calmer, he spat. Of course. He spat at my face but it missed and caught my arm and I looked at it, very sadly.

We'll need half the wood I thought we would, he said, very properly— like there was a magistrate in the room who he was talking to. *Quick. And cheap. But folk like a show so I'll use even less wood—make it a longer thing. Yes.*

And then his eyes met my eyes, and he lost his proper tone. He hissed at me. He said *you meddler . . . Mr Dalrymple wants you gone, oh aye.*

Then he went away. And if I had wished to hear your footsteps before, I wished for them twice as hard after, for this made me so frightened. It has made me know it was true—that they mean to kill me. That these bars are firm, and these chains won't undo.

I am glad you are here. I am so glad. My death will be a slow one, says that man, and I do not want to die, and I do not want to die that way.

MY HANDS are lost in your hands. My hands are so small, and this was used once as a reason for *witch—she is so small! The Devil's taken part of her!* Like that was our pact, the Devil and I. Like my hands are enough to condemn me when far less is enough—my grey eyes, or my curious name. They have always wanted me dead. I've only wanted others to live so where is the fairness? I've never seen any. Nor did Cora. Nor did her mother as she was drowned in her shift.

My hands are so small in your hands. They have rubbed a grey horse and plucked rushes from boggy parts, and they have mended people. Little hands, but they have held his hands—his. Look? I cannot even see them. But the room is very dark.

Tell me of your wife? Or of your four boys. I mustn't talk, I reckon. I reckon for a little while I must listen, calm my breath.

I will sit.

For a little while, let us fill this room with kinder words than *meddling piece.* Fill it with life.

Maybe it was him—filling me. Maybe it was being on the Pap, and being close to him, and talking of hearts which took sleep away from me. Or maybe it was the first, blue frost which I crawled out of my hut to find about me—hushed, and bright. For this meant my weather, and I needed to be in it—I had missed it, and lay down on it. And I stared at the stars, and did not sleep.

Or it was the roaring. For as I passed the slopes of Thistle Top in the afternoon, I stopped. There was a roar. It was a long, creaking sound, a broken roar, and I thought *what is . . . ?* For it was lonesome, and determined. And when I looked up, I saw him—my stag. He was back, on the braes, and I was glad of it.

What comforts. Winter. My stag, with his thick-furred neck and branches. His coat was still deep and whorled, and he would tread over the tops, eyeing me. One afternoon, as my fire smoked, I looked up to see him coming down the sides. There was a fine rain, and shook himself.

I said *do not go away! Stay!* In my hut I found the apples I had saved for him, for weeks. I took one, rubbed it on my skirt. I saw its wrinkles, and flecks. I saw the small, crisp leaf on its stem, and when I stepped back out I held it in my hand. I stretched out my arm. *Here.*

He was still, for a while.

Then, slowly, he came. He had a world in his eyes—the reflected sky, the birds that flew through it. I saw myself. And I saw more than this—I saw all the hills which he'd walked upon, and all the lochs he'd drunk from. All his resting places. His hinds. His life, and age, and knowing.

Here . . .

He nearly took it. He nearly did. He stretched his neck, tilted back his head so his nose could smell the fruit. I watched his nostrils tremble. But he was afraid of me still, and wary—for his wildness did not yet trust my own, and so he came no further, and did not take the apple from my hand.

Instead I laid it on the ground, nearer him. He took it, crunched, and stumbled back up the sides of Cat Peak.

He drooled his apple drool. At the ridge, he looked back at me, briefly. Then he took himself south, into Glen Etive, and was gone.

Frosts, and snow—and they comforted the loving, wanting me. I roamed and wandered, blew and was blown. My skirts sailed the wind which came from the sea, so I was gusted, boat-like, and was salty-skinned. I sank knee-deep into peat bogs, and when the geese flew over I thought of Cora, and marshes, and I called out to the geese, as they flew.

Him, too—whose heart was a fighting heart, but he was tired now.

Down in the Coe, where there was no ice because of how fast it moved—hard, blue-cold water bursting over rocks, and logs—I bathed. I returned to the Meeting of the Waters where I had first washed myself, thirteen moons before. I undressed, and stepped in. I let my hair fill up with water, like I had done. I tried to be the girl I was. But I was a different girl, in some ways.

It was here that I saw Sarah, with her son swaddled in hide and wrapped against her. She was bright-eyed, sniffing with the cold, and when she saw me she kissed my cheeks and grasped my hair at its roots like people do who have proper feelings for the person they kiss. This is how she kissed me. She said my name. She said *you've not come to us, for too long. How are you?*

I said I was very well. I said, *and with you? How are your family?*

She lifted part of the goatskin to show her son to me, as warm and smooth-skinned as an egg freshly-laid. I smelt him. I remembered how he had fitted me—how he'd fitted himself against my neck, and mewled. Little thing. With his damp-fern hair.

They are all well, thanks to God. We are sleeping more at night—she tickled her bairn, smiled—*and there have been no quarrels with any clans, of late. We have salted pork and are smoking fish for the winter.* She looked at me, narrowed her eyes. *Alasdair left some dry peat for you. Did you find it?*

I did. I am grateful but do not need it. You have enough to care for, now.

She frowned. *I know. We both know. But you're on your own up there. And Alasdair says the winter will be hard. He says the rowan berries are redder this year.*

The child gave a single wail, and she put her smallest finger in his mouth to suck upon. His one wail seemed to stay a while, in the air.

What, I asked, *of the oath?*

He told you?

Yes. A little. Not much, just—

Sarah sighed, shook her head. *We are waiting for news from France.*

France?

From King James. Some of our men have gone to his court to ask that we may be released from our oath to him. Maybe she saw my frown, my tilted head. Too many oaths, is what I thought. *We swore our allegiance to him, once. All the clans did.*

You must wait? You cannot swear an oath to William as well?

Two oaths? To two enemies? Neither oath will hold true, then, and there'd be twice the danger. No . . . We wait to hear from France. We hope to hear soon. MacIain must pledge his allegiance by the year's end, which is only a month—and the weather will only worsen.

I listened to this. They felt like old words, like I knew them.

Will he swear it? I asked.

She rolled her eyes. *With his pride? His fire? It will be hard doing— and he won't make any pledge to a Campbell as long as he lives. But I think he will pledge it.*

I said *good.*

Good? You wish him to?

I nodded. I thought, *I do.*

The child hiccoughed, and then gave a second wail. She shushed him. She put her nose against his nose and breathed upon him, spoke Gaelic words.

We kissed our goodbyes, and I watched her walk away from me thinking, *make the oath, now.* I don't know why, but I felt it very keenly.

And then I was ill, that winter. I took on a fever, which I'd never done. I had swum in the loch, very bare, and brushed past ice as I did so—but hadn't I done this before? And been well? In the evening, my hands shook as I lifted my pot from the fire. I grew hot, and pale, but when I stepped out into the frosty night I shivered—my teeth knocking against themselves, and my skin like a plucked hen's, and I thought *what is this?* For I'd never shivered in all my days. I was winter-born. A hardy thing.

I lay in my hut, breathed in the peat.

In my dreams I said *oath! Oath!*

And I knew that a little mallow would help, or some chervil pressed onto my throat, which was sore—but I was shaking, and tired. I rubbed my eyes at the herbs. I curled onto my side, with my knees to my chest, and I dreamt of Gormshuil's weathered face, her pink gums, her voice saying *now, then* . . . And I smelt a green smell—herbs, and rot—and I longed for my stag, and my big-bottomed mare, and there were Mossmen twirling on their ropes which made me put my mouth to my knees, and I cried. I dreamed. I fevered.

It passed, in time. And I woke to find her rotting smell in my hut, and all my henbane gone. Every last leaf of it. *Thief*—to have stepped over me, as I'd slept, and taken it.

For a long while, I was weak. For a long time, too, I was fretful— the fever's shadow on me, or the lack of hot food. I could not walk as far, or as fast. My head, too, spun on the braes so that I stumbled, and grasped onto rocks and old heather which shook off their snow, and I sent a white bird flying up saying *oath! Oath! Oath!* It called this out. I heard it—was sure. And when I cracked the ice on a pool with my hand, I thought it said *oath,* also.

Down in the glen, I saw Iain.

I knocked against the rocks as I went down to him. He heard this, and stopped. His horse snorted at me, and Iain stared down at me with his fox-bright hair, his moth-white skin. *Corrag?*

I have not been well. But I'm better.

You are?

You must take the oath. Please. A bird flew up from the snow and said so. It said oath oath oath. And the crone through her pegs said Orange will not stay Orange, and this stays in my head. The ice said oath, when I broke it. Take it?

He stepped back. *You're feverish. Rambling more than you tend to. Keep back—I've too much to think of and do, to get the fever from you.*

Will you make the oath?

He said, *we shall. We have heard from James, and he says we may. For our own sakes.*

I nodded. *When?*

We must swear it by Hogmanay. The MacIain will ride out the day before. Now leave me—rest. Keep your sickness to yourself, woman. And he kicked the garron on.

I backed away. I gave a quick smile, turned, and felt like the witch they had always thought me to be—dirty, half-mad—and I scolded myself as I ran through the dark, catching my skirt on thorns and bare branches. *What a fool. Sassenach . . . Rambling . . .*

But by morning, my fever was done with. I woke, cool-skinned and hungry, and calm, and as I checked beneath my hens for eggs I thought *it is Christmas Day.*

THE MacIain did leave, four days after it. I saw him.

I crouched on the eastern Sister, with a thin snow coming down onto my cheeks and the backs of my hands. I clutched my cloak to me.

I saw him below, in the white—his plaid, his thick white hair which was whiter, even than snow.

He left on his horse, and three other men followed on foot.

To the rocks and grey sky, I said *hurry him there. Lessen the snow to let him pass.*

Thinking all was better now, I made my way down, told my heart to hush itself—for I was tired of it talking, tired of its ache. I lay on my front, on my deerskin rug.

More snow came down, in the night.

Well. The MacDonalds of Glencoe saw the old year die away in snow, with a half-moon showing through the clouds. They drank, and kissed each other. In Carnoch, Inverrigan, Achnacon and Achtriochtan they slept by their husbands and wives with their children also dreaming, and thought they were safe. That their chief had written his spidery name on paper, and all would be well. 1692 is a famed year for us, now. For the Highlands. For all who whisper *Jacobite.*

Me? Corrag?

The English one? The witch? The black-haired faery? The Spey-wife? The herb girl who lived in Coire Gabhail?

On New Year's Eve, I was on a rock, not far from my hut. At midnight, I was with the stag. I had hoped for him, and he had come. It calmed me, to see him. Like he was waiting for the oath to be sworn, he came back down, and eyed me. I smiled and thought *friend.*

And maybe his heart was tired, too. Maybe he was cold, or done with being wild—for how many wild things can be wild, all the time? I held my last apple out. I held it, said *come* to him. And as the old year died, and a new one came in, he came closer to me than he ever had before. The snow shone. It crunched beneath his hooves. I held my breath, but his breath steamed, and he stretched out his neck very slowly. When it was stretched, he pushed his antlers back. It meant his mouth was near me, and like two hands grasping, his nostrils smelt the fruit. I saw his phlegm, and wetness. His body leant a little more. He smelt, and smelt, and I saw his mouth begin to move.

There was a moment. We both knew it, and saw it—this one, small moment where he had all his trust in me. He was, briefly, tame. Briefly, he was mine—for as he opened his warm mouth and leant in, and steamed, there was no strength in him. He could not have run. He was bare, tired, and he longed for the apple which I'd saved for him, all this while.

I felt the sudden weight of his teeth upon its skin. There was a crush as he bit it. It broke in half, and he stumbled, took his half away. In that stumble, in how he dropped away, he was wild again, and he clattered on the rocks, up onto the slopes of Beinn Fhada with his heart saying *run! Run!* I held the other half. I had his dampness on it, and I looked at the apple with its small brown pips. I ate that half. For I was hungry, too. It was winter, and the apple would not keep.

He clattered away. He was fire-hearted again.

I saw his outline on the tops, and thought it was fine Hogmanay. Me and a deer. Stars. Deep snow. All this love, and beauty in the world.

1692. It will be marked down, for always.

I think I knew it would be.

<hr />

You know what happened, I think. You know.

The chief of the MacDonalds of Glencoe was six days late. Six.

He rode to the wrong place. Colonel Hill at Inverlochy said *but I cannot help you! The parchment is south of here. You lost sheep . . . You poor man.* Or so I imagine, when I imagine it.

MacIain did sign the oath, in the end. Here, in Inverary to a man called Ardkinglas. But yes, he was six days late.

He returned with reddened cheeks and good news. He called me to tend to his chilblains, and as I crouched at his feet with dock, and warm cloth, he said *I was late, yes, but I signed it! It was made, so bring me a whisky, for that journey has frozen me up*—and he sat by the fire, and told his tale. Of Colonel Hill. Of the ferryman at Connel who said *are you the MacIain,* and trembled as he rowed. Of Barcaldine Castle, in the dark.

It was ripe with trouble, that journey. There are scoundrels out there. Is there meat, woman? But—he sipped his whisky, sighed—*I made the oath. I was there. Tis done now*—*and we are safe from the King's wrath . . .*

WHAT is six days? It is so little.

Never mind that he had written his name—for can't a name be scored out? Six days made it nothing. Six days meant that all who hated the name Glencoe could look up from their bureaus, smile at the news. *Late? By six days? Then they must be punished . . .*

Rebels. Traitors.

That gallows herd . . .

SUCH hatred in the world. Such sadness.

My mother always said there is no Devil. Only the devilish ways, in a man. And she walked in landscapes of wind, and height, and grass for these places could not hurt her—not like people could.

DO NOT *love.* For hate is never far from it.

Like light, it needs the other—the dark—to be called *light* at all.

My darling

She says there are moments which change us. There are. I changed when I came to Inverary, and the red-haired inn-keeper mentioned witch *to me. I changed when I sat on a stool and worried for lice. I changed with the black-smith. With each page of the Bible, for the Lord gives us His lessons every day. Yes.*

Or aye. They say aye here.

I have been downstairs. It is an inn and I am not a drinking man, but there was a chair by a fire. And I was changed on the day I saw you, my love. You were bending down to lift a snail from the path, and you put your parasol down to do it, and I saw all your hair, and your tiny waist as you rose, and I promise you this, Jane—that with all this talk of oaths, and love, and the heart's voice, I know what I felt, as you rose. I envied the snail. I thanked God. Every oath I have ever made to you, or for you, was done with my whole body and heart. Soul.

The whisky is sharp, but I had it. It was golden light in a glass—and did I ever write the word Gormshuil, *for you? She is a woman that Corrag knew. She sounds as wretched a creature as it is possible to be—bones and dirt, and no Godliness in her. She took some plant for comfort, and I understand that now. We all have our woes, and sorrows. It does not solve them—a plant, a drink—but it clouds the mind, and I will sleep my first sleep in nights, I think.*

The landlord saw me drinking. He hung about me, and I knew why— and surely, it came.

How is the witch? The vile slattern? The hag?

I was minded to not answer at all but he would have pestered—some folk are like foxes who tread about another, sniffing for meat. Fearing her death I told him. I said, she will soon be burnt to death, sir. She is not, therefore, too well . . .

Ha! For she knows the Devil will take her soul—that she will burn for a while on that stake, but she will burn ever after for her crimes . . .

So I drank, for it filled my mouth. I had no good words to fill it with.

Tomorrow, she will speak of the soldiers coming in. I know it, now. The blacksmith tells me their captain was a black-eyed, straw-haired man. There were English among them, and Campbells, and mere boys who had no place in such a dire deed. A massacre, Jane! They came in for it. They stayed for two weeks before firing their muskets and pulling their dirks through throats to punish them for this late oath, and I will pray for their souls that they did not know their orders as they sat by the MacDonald fires, drinking Mac-Donald whisky, eating MacDonald bread.

She will speak of this—and I fear it! I do! I, who have seen men hang and have hastened, even, the deaths of guilty men, am fearful of what she will speak of. And I am fearful of seeing her cell with no Corrag in it—just the straw that, once, she lay on.

What a death she will die. She does not deserve that death.

And what a life she has lived. I wonder if I envy it, in part. When have we picked berries from their bushes, and eaten them? Not since I was a boy. And have we ever drunk on our knees, like a cat? It is the whisky writing this. But she has fed a stag from her bare hand, Jane—a rotted apple, but the stag bit down, and took it, and when she spoke of this my heart said yes! And envied it. I have never stood in marshes, or heard an owl call out.

All this from her. All these dreams and longings, and fears, and thoughts, and hopes—from her.

Maybe witch *was always the right word.*

. . .

Am I mad? It is the whisky. Your husband unravels, Mrs Leslie.

I will retire to bed with your letter in my hand. I have my faith in God, but His face has changed itself over the past days and nights. Who is He? He is not what I thought. Or He has not changed, but my own eyes have? Me?

I tell myself the law is the law. And then I pass the barrels which are tied, and waiting for Corrag, and my heart says do not die. Keep living. Little thing.

Charles.

X

*"Have a care you mistake not the deadly Nightshade for this; if
you know it not, you may let them both alone, and take no harm."*

of Nightshade

There is less blue light—much less blue. For the first time I have
seen it—how the cell's daytime light is paler, thinner, and I
know that the last snow is gone now, or nearly gone. Melted. I reckon
there are the small green shoots, the buds like fingertips and an earthy
smell—rich, and cool. And hear that? Not a *drip, drip*. It is a faster
sound now. The snowmelt runs.

I know this running sound. I have heard it before in other, lost
places, and in those places I knew that it meant my season was closing
down for a time, and the spring was flooding into the land—with its
filled burns and flowers. Boggy ground softened. Rocks felt warm.
And I liked these things—these changes, which spoke of warmth and
blue-sky days. But this rushing water and paler light means more than
that. A different warmth. Not blue skies, but black ones—filled with
the smoke of burning me. Fiery me. Me blazing like homes did.

I used to feel a little sadness, at seeing my weather go—at winter
curling up, like furry creatures do when they know that winter comes.
The season pressed its snout to its belly, slept, and I'd think *then goodbye, for a time.* I have knelt in marshes and thought, *till next year*—for

winter always comes back, does it not? Like all seasons? In comes the frost. Then the ice. Then the snow.

I say *goodbye* to it now. But properly. For I won't see another.

When it comes back, will you see it for me? Will you breathe against a wall of ice, and watch how your breath steams back for me? Crunch out on snow? Sit by fires?

Look how pink your cheeks are. How wet your shoes are.

It has been a long winter, I know. In the glen, it was long. It was thick frosts which creaked underfoot, and the *crump* of snow as it fell from my roof. I'd stretch in the mornings, breathe that air.

And the soldiers came in this weather. On a February day they came in their bright-red coats with their polished muskets and cold cheeks. Knocked on the Chief's front door.

WHAT was on my mind that day? I think nothing was. Or maybe it was the small things I'd been looking at—my clouded breath, and a cobweb with droplets on. I know a thin snow was blowing, pricking my face, and my hands were very pink so I turned them over, looking at their pinkness. I was neither happy nor sad. I was just as I was. Sitting on Keep-Me-Safe.

Then, I looked up. In the distance, I saw a line of red. It moved along the shores of the loch, past Ballachulish, and on. I squinted, and thought *what is so red? And moves like that?*

And I knew it was redcoats.

Soldiers.

How did you know it was soldiers which would murder us? Who has told you? Or maybe the whole world knows, now—that it was soldiers who came to the Glen of Coe. With muskets. With smiles.

It changed the glen, of course. All those tall, redcoated men with their Lowland voices and snowy boots which they stamped, in doorways, and with their jokes which I did not hear, but I heard the laughter from them. I was not there to truly see it—how the MacIain greeted them. I was minded to think he'd have roared his dislike and banished them, for he hated all things which had William in it, or by it, and these were William's men. I thought he might draw out a sword or two. But he did not roar. He saw the falling snow. He saw their cold faces, heard their bellies growl.

He welcomed them, Iain said, when I saw him three days afterwards. *Gave them meat. Lodgings.*

He welcomed them?

Aye. What else might he do? 'Tis foul weather, Corrag, and they need quartering.

But they're William's men . . . I did not understand.

And Iain sighed, like he often did with me. Like he had no patience for this dull-witted English creature he said *did we not sign the oath? To William? We're no outward threat to him or his men, now—nor are they to us. And it is the Highland way—to offer shelter when asked for it.* His garron shifted beneath him. *Did we not offer it to you? All those months gone?*

They had. I nodded.

Then you cannot protest.

I turned from him, and went, and I remembered his words. *Outward threats. Oaths.* I knew that Iain's reasoning was proper. *There is no danger* I told myself, treading over the ice. And they were smartly done, I saw that. They had their crimson coats and their shiny boots and some had curled, snow-topped wigs. They clanked with their metal. They blew on their hands as they stood in the glen, looking up at the mountains.

There is no danger. All is well.

But still I was not truly calm. Still, there were so many changes in the glen, so many shifts in its air and light, that how could I like it? This coming of men? What, I wondered, of the rocks? What of the tiny, animal lives? It troubled me deeply, despite Iain's words. With my uneasy sea inside me, slapping itself against my sides, I eyed the soldiers. Holding my breath, I crept like a cat through the snowy parts. I slunk my way to Achtriochtan, and saw a soldier by its loch, making it his privy, and I did not like that. On my dark daytime walks, I saw heavy-booted footprints in the snow by Achnacon where cowslip grew in spring, and would this mean no cowslips? When the spring came in? I chewed upon my bottom lip. I did not see my stag for a week—more than a week.

I worried.

I worried for the glen. I worried for the rocks and water. I worried for the air, and grass, and deer, and that the families would give all their salted meat and smoked fish and turnips to these men, and so starve themselves much later. I worried the way the soldiers called from house to house, through cupped hands, would make a shelf of snow break from the ridge, and thunder down, and claim a human life or two. I worried they would stay, and never leave.

AND I had old dreams, of course. I knew what redcoats were. I thought I had left them behind in the Lowlands, on a summer's night when my mare was still living and my skirt had caught on a bramble, bent, and then freed itself—so they'd looked up from their fire, and . . . I had left it behind. I had not dwelt on it, for why dwell on past troubles? I had survived it all. But now there were redcoated men in the valley below, and I was sore with remembering the weight on me, the *hush now*. The *pop*.

I kept to my hut. Missed my mare.

Not all redcoated men are villains, Mr Leslie. I knew it then, and

I still know it. But didn't Mother Mundy hate all reivers, for always, once her body had been entered on a fiery, autumn night? Not all reivers did what that one had done—but she hated them all anyway. By my hearth, I thought of her. I remembered her face like it was before me—lined, blistered, hairy, sad-eyed. I wondered how she was, and reckoned she was dead, now—her rape and gummy mouth boxed in the earth, and gone.

Such thoughts made me kick stones, and feel lonesome.

Not all soldiers are cruel, Mr Leslie. Most are not.

But I did not like them being in the glen from the start, and that was that.

I stayed in my valley, mostly. I would not take myself out of there, by day—fearing the past, and the future, and all in between. Fearing my own self, maybe—for I would look upon my body in my bathing pool and be troubled by its smallness, its muscle, and scars. I saw my own frailty—like the web that a spider makes in corners, I was strong in some places but gossamer-thin, and gossamer-white, and strange. Amongst the clinking ice, I stared. I thought *Cora made this. I come from her*—and this softened my worries, at times. She had been such a wild, fighting piece. She was in me, and near me, and as the river fell down like glass into the pool, and roared about my ears, I thought I heard her voice. *Be strong. Wise.*

Love the world, Corrag. Concern yourself with trees. Hills.

I shall.

Good girl. My ghost-baby.

I tried. I made a dish from my hands beneath the waterfall, and drank. I brushed my goats, and spoke to my hens. And, once, I stood at the end of my valley, where a thinner fall of water had frozen blue, and its coldness made my breath steam back at me as I blew upon it, and I remembered my poor mare's tail which was torn, by that soldier. Whisky, and a redcoat, and she had galloped with me as I'd cried *go! Go!*

I could feel the ice's coldness on my face.

I closed my eyes, breathed. To the waterfall I whispered, *bring Alasdair to me? His face? And words?*

The world hears these little prayers.

So in time, he came.

He came as I trod down the sides of Cat Peak, towards my hut, dragging a branch for the fire. I did not see him. I imagined him, instead. I paused, looked down at my hut and imagined how he'd look if he was standing by it—red-haired and rough-skinned, with his wet-wool smell. He might be waiting for me. He might look up ... I scolded myself, and walked on. *He is not there*—only a chicken was, and the hazel tree with its branches of snow, and the dimpled snow beneath it where some had fallen from a branch when a small breeze had come.

But when I reached the hut, he was there. The real him, the breathing one.

You've kept away, he said.

And I saw his half-smile. Smelt the wet-wool.

We sat inside, where the fire was strong, and he took a cup of water which was hot with herbs in it. I thought he looked tired—as if the bairn was taking sleep from him, or he had his own worries. His hair was long, now—thick, and loose upon his neck. The long winter had darkened it, so it was a deep earth-red. Nearly peat-coloured. His beard was also dark.

Why are they here? I asked.

They say that the garrison is full, at Inverlochy. They've asked for quarters and food, for a time.

How long?

As long as this weather lasts. Who knows how long?

Do you have enough food for that?

We will make do. We have herring, still. Salted beef. He looked down at his cup. *We have four soldiers with us, in our home.*

Four?

There are some at each house—from our cousin in Brecklet to the eastern end. He smiled. *Some are just boys . . . The weather makes them wheezy. Their sleeves are too long for them, so Sarah has sewed . . .*

He saw me, watching.

You fear them?

I blushed. I looked down at the fire, unsure of my words. When I spoke, my voice was barely a voice at all. *Yes. There are so many. There have never been so many people in the glen before, I reckon . . . Stamping all over it.*

You fear them for what they'll do to the glen? The plants?

Yes.

He shook his head. *The glen has seen worse than some soldiers come by. It's had battles and famine. Rain upon rain.* He eyed me. *You think they'll hurt you?*

Inside me, I flinched. Maybe he saw this.

I spoke to Iain. He said you were fretful. Gently, he said *why?*

They are soldiers.

But they have come peacefully. They are civil-mannered, as are we.

They are the King's men. That word . . .

He shook his head briskly, said *is this the same girl? The one who trusts the world so much? Who talks of heart and faith as much as she does? I thought I was the one who was hasty to judge.*

But—

Alasdair said, *Sassenach. I know. I know what life you've had. I know
that you've run from trouble, and that this trouble has mostly come from men,
but these are soldiers . . . We have sworn allegiance to the King they serve.
Why would they harm us? Why now? Are we not on their side?* He blew
out a hard breath, looked into his cup. *If we had refused to give them
shelter, what then? Our oath would have been forfeited, and we'd have felt
the Dutchman's wrath for it. Or they'd have pulled out their swords, forced it
upon us . . .* He drank.

I know.

It will help you, he said, *to know that they are Sarah's kin.*

Sarah's?

*Aye. The man who leads these soldiers? He is a Campbell. Robert Camp-
bell of Glenlyon—and Sarah's cousin by blood.* Alasdair shrugged. *I'll admit
he's a drinker, and plays cards too much and too badly—but he is still kin.
Still a decent man—or as much as a Campbell can be. Why might he harm
us? Her?*

I looked down.

In a softer voice he said, *when did you stop trusting? I thought that
was your way?*

It is my way! It is. But I have met soldiers before.

He paused. For a while there was no sound but the fire, hissing. In
a darker, slower voice he said, *And they hurt you?*

I thought to say *yes, they did.* I thought to tell him that it had been
a redcoat who had grappled me, and tried to take me against my will,
and who had manhandled my mare whom I'd loved, and he'd put a
blade to my throat, and how much I had cried afterwards—and how
fearful I was of it happening again. I wanted no claiming. I wanted no
stranger's weight on me. I wanted none of that—no man's touch, or
not from them, and not that way, and I felt my eyes feel hot and wet
as I thought of this. But also, I thought of Sarah. I saw how tired her

husband looked, and how much worry was in him, and I did not say it. What right had I? To say it? I kept the secret to myself. *No. They did not hurt me.*

Alasdair leant forwards to me. *I am with you in this. I do not like them being here—eating our meat, and burning our fuel. But we have no choice. And my father prides himself on being a host, and a fine one too . . . Perhaps we'll be rewarded for our kindness, in time?* He winked, touched my hand. *They'll be gone with the first thaw, I promise.*

He left, a little later. The hazel tree was heavy with the snowfall, and it creaked, and all night I listened to it—creaking, in the dark.

Sarah's kin, sir. Write that down. Campbell of Glenylon. Sarah's kin.

Like me, she did not go far, in such weather. Unlike her man, she did not wander the snowy hills or leave their house for much more than fetching water from the streams. She cared for her guests very well. She cut the salted pork, and roasted roots in the fire, and one evening she took the pork bone out into the dark for their dog. She called his name. She called it twice, and he gave a low, throaty sound, and caught the bone as she threw it.

I saw this. I stood near the river which was quiet with ice.

Alasdair had been right. I did not judge—I never had. Or if I ever had, I'd been cross with myself for it. For I had been judged all my life and loathed it—how tangled hair or a high-note voice had made them stare and talk behind their hands, and how Cora's wild beauty had made *witch* come out. I'd been so black for that, always. And when I'd found the plum-faced man and his Mossmen in the woods, I'd learnt how truly wrong it is—to judge too quickly, or to judge at all. He had been so kind to me. I'd thought *Mossman,* and *trouble,* and been scared, at first. But then I'd sat by their fire and mended their wounds. The plum-faced one told me tales of Scotland, and his life, and maybe that lonely thief was the kindest man I'd met, for years—yet *Mossman* was all he'd be known for. They'd say *thief. Devil.* None would remember him as part of the world, with a beating heart. A friend.

So I would not judge the soldiers. I told myself this. In a pail of water I reasoned with my ghostly eyes, my thin face. *Only one ever hurt you. And that was years ago . . . There will not be trouble here.*

In a dark afternoon, I took out my herbs. I found elderflower and coltsfoot, and put them under my cloak. And off I set, passing through the boulders which hid my valley from the glen below. I skirted the burn, and the birches, and I sang an old song as I went through the knee-high drifts. It was a childhood song, which Cora would sing. She'd sing it under her breath as she stirred her pot, or brushed her long hair.

The glen smelt of peat-smoke and men. Leather. Metal, perhaps—a cold, sharp smell. I passed Achtriochtan, and I moved beneath the Ridge Like a Church which glowed in the half-light and stared down at me. Some soldiers were by Achnacon. They watched me as I passed.

It was evening, and dark, when I reached Alasdair's house. It looked like homes do, or should—with smoke drifting up, and candlelight coming from it, and the low sound of voices. I heard a man's laughter. Outside, a dog scratched his chin with his hind legs, and settled down. It was a good, human sight. I watched, from the shadows.

Sarah came out. She was fire-flushed, with a bone in her hand. I heard her call and she threw the bone, and as she turned to go she said *Corrag? Is that you?*

I came forwards. *Yes.*

What are you doing? Standing in the dark and cold? Come in!

I shifted. *I only came with herbs. Alasdair said the soldiers had wheezes, so I've come with elderflower, which helps—*

Never mind what you came for—come in! Warm yourself. And she held out both her hands.

Inside, there were many faces. It was a hot, peaty room which made my eyes prick, and I rubbed them. I took down my hood, for it was hot in there. And I saw four, young-faced soldiers sitting in a line, with meat which they gnawed upon its bone. I saw MacDonald men, also—two from Inverrigan, and the balding man of Achnacon who had said *will you dance?* to me once, at Hogmanay which felt like a long time ago. They also ate. There was whisky. The fire smoked, and in the dark corner I knew the baby slept, and Alasdair leant against a wall, away from the fire. His head was back, as if sleeping. When I came in, his head lifted up.

Sarah said, *Stay. Eat a little food.*

I only came with these . . .

Like he knew what my herbs were for, a soldier coughed. He wheezed into his fist, swallowed hard. He blinked a little, and waited— for perhaps his lungs would wheeze again. But they did not, and he went back to his meat.

I heard that they had coughs, and elderflower's fine for that. And coltsfoot—bruise it and put in water, and drink it, and—

She thanked me. She took the herbs, bustled. I shifted by the door with the soldiers looking at me.

A man from Inverrigan said, *you have fuel enough? In that hut of yours?*

I smiled. *I do. Thank you.*

Food?

Enough.

A soldier said, *English? You're English?*

I nodded. Alasdair rose then. He stepped over pots, and boots, and a cow-skin rug, and came to me. He said, *you've brought herbs for them?*

Because you were right. About judging them. They're people, and they have coughs, and not all folk like the winter months. I was wrong.

Behind him, the Inverrigan men spoke Gaelic to each other. The soldiers spoke English. The baby gave a single, bird-cry.

Stay for food. Come by the fire.

I shook my head. I shook it once, quickly, as if a leaf had fallen on me. He understood. He knew I could not stay, and he knew why. When I looked past him, into the corner, I saw Sarah lift their baby up and heard her say *little bird . . .* —and I am hardy, but not always. I looked back at him and said *I must get back now.*

Some things are hard, even if they are right. Even if you know they are the proper, decent way. I was glad to have left herbs for those men whose lungs and minds had not known Highland winters before. It was kindness. And kindness is worth showing.

My hearth still glowed in my hut. This small, thatched home of mine smelt of chickens, and a soft herb-smell. It felt like I had been away from it for longer than I had.

I TOOK herbs elsewhere, in those last days. I went to Achnacon, with lavender, for I knew the lady there was fond of its smell. In a thick blizzard I went to Inverrigan with rosemary—for it cleanses a room very well, and I knew they had plenty of men in there. The boy who had shared honey with me was asleep on the floor, mouth open, and there were muskets lined up by the parlour wall. The captain, this man called Glenlyon, was sitting at its table with Inverrigan's sons, and they played cards amongst them. His eyes were button-dark. He looked up at me, as I entered, but I did not look back. Instead, I pressed the rosemary to the lady of the house and whispered its uses to her. She nodded. She looked tired, and old, and I thought *be well* as I left her. *Cleanse the air. Be well.*

And I took eggs to Achtriochtan. The wife of Old Man Achtriochtan took them in her hands, nodded, and she ushered me into the heat of the room. I did not seek this. I did not hope for food—only to provide it, for I knew they had killed their last hen for these men, and Achtriochtan's bones were old. But she pushed me to the fire, kissed me, said *eat!* I counted seven soldiers there. Achtriochtan took his pipe from his mouth. He boomed, clapped his hand on my shoulder. *Sassenach!*

He smelt of oats. I remember that.

He told his poems by the fire, and it did not matter that they were Gaelic words. I felt I understood them. I knew enough. I felt enough.

I left a fistful of peat outside Iain's house. It was not much to give, but it was a little—and little things can help more than we know.

I WAS soothed, for a while. I looked at the wide, white, empty Rannoch Moor and thought *yes. All is well.* I found a comfort in the simple tasks—milking my goats, or stroking the oily coats of them—or in the simple beauty of short, winter days. Deer left their tracks. An eagle feather showed itself in the snow, and I lifted it, kept it.

They are Sarah's kin . . .

I knew this. And I had seen their faces, heard their coughs.

But still—despite it all—my heart felt unwell in the dark, silent nights. Still, I did not like these soldiers being in the glen. I did not mean to judge them, and I try to like all living things until they hurt me—for bitterness is a sad, pained thing. But I did not like how the beasts the clan had hoped to keep living for another year had been killed, to feed the soldiers, or how much fuel was being burnt. I did not like the redness of their coats against the snow.

I liked the MacDonalds, though. So I gave them gifts—in their final days.

Coltsfoot. Peat. An egg.

One more thing you should know, sir. One more.

It was late, late in the day. The snow was thick, with a crust upon it so that it glinted in the dying light. Like eyes, I thought. I had been by Loch Leven. I'd picked seaweed from the shorelines, slipped shells and razor-clams into my pockets, and I made a basket from my skirts which I filled up with weed. Gulls wheeled. I stood and looked, for a time—for the mountains were very black, against the sky, and the loch was silver-bright. Eilean Munda slept, and I thought of its buried people. For a while, I was peaceful as I stood there.

I turned for home beneath a winter sky.

Every window I passed was candle-lit. The air smelt of smoke, and the soldiers' leather. Their horses shook themselves in the byres.

And with my clinking shells and wet skirts, with a few frail snow-flakes drifting through the air, I thought of Cora. I thought of my birth, in such weather—how she must have steamed, and hissed, and how she heard the church folk singing as she roared, so that her voice split. I had come out. And she'd looked down, said *witch* before my true name.

I held my skirts up, with the weed in them. And as I went, I heard a voice. Not Cora's. I was past the Carnoch woods, and near the river's bend. The light was nearly gone, but the farm at Inverrigan was high on the hillside, bright with life, and candles, and soldiers' songs. I stopped. I listened to it. Was the voice from there? But it came again—much nearer.

It is here. To my left.

I stood very still. I waited.

The voice came again. It was a man's voice—a frail, singing voice, so frail that I wondered if it was a dead man's soul, as I've heard they can whisper.

I heard branches rustle near me, and a clap of water like a foot had tripped into the Coe. I heard a curse. A hiccough. A Lowland voice.

Not a soul. A real person.

And I thought *go, Corrag. Get home.*

But as I hitched my skirts a little more and set off towards my hut, he called to me. He heard the *crunch* of my feet, and said *who is there? Who is in the dark?* He spoke plaintively, like a child. He struggled as he spoke, for I heard the trees shifting, and snow came down from them. I stood very still, did not speak. I held my breath, half-frightened.

Are you a spirit? he asked. *Are you here to mock me? Are you here to punish me further in this*—he tripped—*snow?*

We were both silent, for a moment or two.

Then I heard a branch break, and he stumbled, made a boyish cry of pain. There was the soft, heavy thud of a person sitting down. A sniff. A sigh.

You're a ghost . . . he said. *I cannot see you, but I can feel you . . .*

And as I stood in the darkness, he cried. I heard him sob a deep, drunken sob—a heartfelt sob, and it had loss in it, and sorrow. Those were the sobs of a lonely man, a drunk, and we listened to it—the snow, the rocks and I. We heard him say *Glenlyon . . .* We heard him say *maul,* and *fire.*

I took a step to him. I peered into the dark, and saw him—his clouded hair, his button-eyes. In his left hand was a bottle. In his right, I saw a parchment—dark, amongst the snow, and in a spidery hand.

I left him.

I crept away. I trod through the whiteness with his song in my ears—his drunk, mournful song and his heavy breath. There are old songs which Cora said the last of people sing—the last, the lonesome. It is their way of grieving, of soothing their cold hearts. And I thought *he sings such a song,* I was certain. I pitied him, as I made my way up to my hut. I pitied him, and his heavy song. I thought *keep him safe. Calm him.*

But it was more than pity.

In my hut, I could not sleep. I still heard his song. My heart sang it, over and over, and I stared at the fire thinking *why am I still troubled? Why does it not leave me, this feeling?*

I had heard *maul* . . . I had seen his bright, black eyes.

OH THERE is always sadness. Always grief. I have heard folk say this life could be all hardship and sorrow, if we let it be. If we let our hearts seal over.

I should have stayed, perhaps. Nestled by Glenlyon and spoken with him, for a while. But what might it have changed?

Men have their orders.

LATER, a wolf howled.

I stood in the snow, and closed my eyes. It sounded so sad to me. And the howl echoed. It came from Bidean, to the south, and yet it rang about the Coire Gabhail as if the wolf was with me. It echoed inside me, somehow. I felt it. I widened my eyes.

Gormshuil. Once she had said *come to me. When the wolf calls.*

Listen to your heart's voice, little thing. And I knew I had to be with her. I knew that she was the one to see—so I left my seaweed drying in the eaves, and my goats sleeping with their heads upon each other, and I ran, and ran.

———————

Is it not all there? Are the signs not all there, Mr Leslie? Oh they are now. They are clear as rainwater to the backward eye. The wolf's call, and the stirred heart. The silence of a snowfall, and the black ink in his hand. My stag had gone—he had taken his branches and wise eye and he'd left across the tops, trod out across the moor, and hadn't the bats streamed out from their roosts under a half-moon bridge in the days before my mother was taken, and tied thumb-to-thumb? And when did I last hear the owl? It had not called for nights and nights.

The world whispers, and we must hear. And when we don't hear, we find ourselves running through waist-high snow, with a drunkard's mourning song in our ears, and I knew what the truth was—I was certain of it. And the morning star was shining, and the trees had broken their boughs with the weight of the snow and *you will come to me, after the wolf. You will.*

I went. I ran to Gormshuil. And I was fast, that night—fast, as if the wolf's call had woken me, so that I ran down my gully over the rocks and frozen pools. I ran east, with my heart going *thump thump* and my breath going *in and out, in and out, in and out,* and I ran onto the lower slopes of the Dark Mount thinking *be there, be there*—for what if she was not? What then?

I hauled myself onto stones. I slipped, cut my knees.

But she was there. She was sitting neatly. Waiting.

Ah, she said.

I fell down. I fell before her, and put my hands on her knees, not caring for their scabs or her clotted smell, and I said, *Gormshuil, I heard the wolf—I heard it call. It called, and it sounded so mournful, and so wise . . . And I came to you—*

She smiled. *Why did you come? To me?*

Because you told me to!

No—she shook her finger at me. *Because you know it is time, do you not?*

Time? For what?

I looked very earnestly at her. I looked, and thought, briefly, that I

could see beyond her, beneath her skin—that I could see the truth of
her. Mistreated, lonesome, haunted thing. Wise. Half-lost.

I looked about me, then. The peak was so quiet, so I said *where is
Doideag? Laorag of Tiree?*

The snow was thin, small. It hovered in the air. It did not fall—it
hung about her face, and caught itself on her pale hair. *Gone.*

Gone where?

She pressed her lips against themselves, half-smiled but with lonesome eyes. *Fled.*

Fled? Why have they fled?

Gormshuil breathed out, shook her head. *You know. All your talk of
second sight, and how you think it's my henbane that talks when I speak as I
do. All sour. All green-handed . . . 'Tis not the herb that's speaking.*

I don't understand, I whispered.

She wiped her nose on her arm and looked away. She looked across
the top of Dark Mount, across the empty hearth and animal bones,
and the rags, and the dirt, and for a moment she looked so very sad
that I wanted to touch her arm, to comfort her heart. But I did not,
for she turned. She licked her teeth. *Blood comes, Corrag. It is coming. The
girls spread their wings and flew from it—for it's more blood than they know,
or wish to. It comes. A man comes.*

Blood? A man?

*Oh aye. A man. He'll write a word or two on you. You with your shiny
iron wrists . . .*

I looked at my wrists. My wrists were fine—flesh, not iron.

*He'll come, he will. And it won't be cold too long, for you. It will grow hot.
It will grow fiery hot . . .*

I did not understand. I did not know her talking, and stepped back
from her, and gave a small, single wail, for I could feel the snow in the
air, and the truth I could not grasp, the strangeness, and I said *I am lost
with this! I can't understand . . .*

She took my hand. She held it.

I stared at this—my small hand in her blue claw.

You can. You do. Haven't you always listened to your heart's voice, bairn?
Did it not bring you here? She leant forwards. *Listen to it now. Listen to*
it now . . .

I looked upon her. I looked upon her human face, with its hollows,
its bruises. I saw the sorrow, the hard living, and I saw my own eyes
reflected in her eyes. And as I looked at my own eyes, I saw grass, and
a dandelion day, and as the dandelion seeds drifted through the air a
man was drowning kittens, and I *knew*. I had known. My heart had said
run! Save them! And I had listened to my heart, and run across the grass,
and I had saved five grey cats which had been meant for drowning—
but they lived! They lived. And I blinked, and kept looking at my eyes
in Gormshuil's eyes. And I saw my mother, then—not twirling on a
rope but standing in her skirts, her hands behind her back and her
hair blowing out, and in the last moment before the door went *bang*
she'd seen the autumn skies and thought of me—of *me*. I'd been her
last thought. I'd been her one, all-feeling love—and she smiled as she
died, because she was thinking of me. I knew this. I was sure. I had
crouched in the dank, border wood and thought *she is about to die,*
and I'd sent so much love to her from those woods that she'd felt it,
on her scaffold—she'd felt her daughter's love. I knew she had! And
what else? As I knelt before Gormshuil I saw the Mossman's face, his
plum-mark, and his mouth, and I saw the shape his mouth took when
he said *Highland* at me. *Highland . . .* And my heart had said *yes* as he'd
said it. *Yes! There! That is the place . . .* And I'd heard my heart speaking,
and I'd kicked the mare on. And when I'd breathed the night air of the
mountains, and knelt down to feel the cold, sucking peat in my hand,
hadn't my heart and whole being said *yes* to it? *At last. Here.* Hadn't I
wept, as I knelt? Hadn't I always known *Glencoe*? It had called me. It
had sung my name for all its years and years, waiting for me to walk

onto its earth with moths in my hair, and thorns on my skirts. It had waited, and called for me—and I came.

And *him* . . .

I knelt in the snow and looked at her. I looked at her eyes, and saw my eyes. And I thought *him*—*Alasdair.*

Of all the things my heart has known, it has known *him* most of all.

Never love a person. And I had nodded at Cora as she'd said this. I'd whispered *I won't.* But even then—even then! As a child!—I had heard my heart shaking against its ribs, shouting *you will love! You will! You will!* And many years later, in a room of beeswax candles with the rain outside, I saw his face, and knew.

Gormshuil said, *you want the second sight? To be taught it? Half-mad thing . . . You have always had it.*

And she was right. I had. I knew it, as I knelt there. I had always had it, for we all do—all people born with a heart have it, for it is the heart's voice. It is the soul's song. I have had it with every starry sky, with each bee that knocked against me as it rose up from a bloom. I've had it with kindness—mine, and others'. I've had it with the hairs on my arms standing up, at the sound of a clan singing a fireside song, or with my eyes filling with tears at a simple, lovely sight. For it is in these moments that the heart speaks up. It says *yes!* Or *him!* Or *left* or *right.* Or *run.*

We all have it. But I think it is people like us—lonesome, in love with the blustery world—who hear the heart most clearly. We hear its breath, feel its turns. We see what it half-sees.

We sat for a moment like that. My hand in her hand. The snow coming down.

Then she leant forward. She put her mouth by my ear so that I could smell her breath, and feel her damp hair against my cheek, and she said the word I've said to myself, all my life—a word which a witch's heart sings over and over, night after night. A second-sight word.

Corrag?

Yes?

You must run.

※ ———— ✦ ———— ※

I did. I ran. I left her sitting in the snow and ran down the mountain, sliding on the ice, knocking my bones on the rocks. I ran along the glen floor thinking *faster! Faster.* For I knew. I did.

It is not what the eyes see—no. I thought it was! I had thought the second sight was a dream, or a vision, a sudden rush of breath. I had thought that the truth might step into my hut, like a ghost, and says its name—that I might find it, if I sought it. But Mr Leslie, I was wrong.

You will know it, in time . . .

I knew it, now. And I knew it was a feeling—deep, in the chest, or in more than the chest. It was a feeling in the bones, in the womb, in the soul. It was the animal that hides in us shaking its coat, pricking its ears, and telling us *run!* Or *fight!* Or *love!* Or *hide!*

And I thought *go go go.*

I PASSED the Three Sisters. I passed beneath the Ridge Like a Church. I hauled myself through the snowdrifts, and brushed under trees, and ran.

It was dark when I came to Alasdair's home. The sky was gone—there was only snow falling down now, and the dark. There was no wind in the glen, and before I knocked on his door I paused, and breathed. I heard the hush. All about me, there was quietness. The smoke rose tall and untroubled. The house was asleep.

But he opened the door like he'd not been sleeping. *What is it?*

We took ourselves to a darker place, by a tree. I could not talk for being breathless, and I leant forward, breathed hard. He put his hand on my back and crouched down beside me, and said, *what?*

The red men, I said.

The soldiers?

Yes.

What of them? Corrag?

They will try to kill you. Tonight. All of you. I looked in his eyes—his huge, blue eyes which were shining, so that I saw my own eyes in his eyes, and he did not say *no . . .* Or *you are mistaken.*

He said, *how do you know? Who has told you?*

I took his arm. *No one has told me. But I know—I know!* I beat my chest with my fist. *I know . . .*

Corrag, he said, shaking his head, *why would they harm us? We are their hosts—their hosts! We have fed them, warmed them. My father is playing cards with Glenlyon at this moment . . .* He shook his head more slowly, and then stopped. *What reason would they have?*

But I stamped my foot. I took his other arm so that I was before him, looking up. *I know. I know what your head is saying—I know. But trust me? Please? Trust what I am saying, even if it seems strange? Did I not help your wife? Bring out your son? Didn't I mend your father when I barely knew him and was so desperately afraid—but I still mended him? I don't know why they will hurt you, but they will, Alasdair. Tonight, they will. I am more certain of this than I have been certain of all other things, in all my whole life. My heart knows it—here.*

He stared.

I know what second sight is, now. I have it, I said. *We all have it. We are born with it, as all creatures are . . .* I calmed myself. *Please—listen to me.*

The snow came down. The snow was on his hair, and his plaid.

He said, *what do we do? We have no arms—or not as they have. And now it snows . . .*

Go. Flee.

Flee? In this weather? It will kill folk. Perhaps just the men will flee. The women can stay for they surely won't be hurt . . .

No—all of them. Take all of them.

Women? And bairns?

Yes. Go. Make for Appin. I don't think a single living soul is safe, tonight.

He stepped back. He looked at the ground and made a sound like he was tired of this, of me—like he did not trust me at all, after all. He turned his back. He put his hand in his hair, and I thought *please listen . . .*

There was a moment which was my breath, and no other sound.

Yes, he said. *Yes. You talk of what the heart knows? I've felt this trouble in me since they came—here,* and he felt his chest. *They have smiled, and sang, and we've fed them, and yet . . . I'll find my brother. I'll tell him, and I'll go to Inverrigan and listen at the door.*

Waste no time. Get as many out as you can.

Yes. He stared at me like I was new, like we had never met before. He was all eyes.

I must go.

He stepped forwards. *What? Where to?*

To Inverlochy, I told him. *I'll run there. You say the Colonel Hill is kindly, and a friend of the clans, so I will tell him. I will tell him they are killing the people of Glencoe, and he will come back with me with horses, and men, and save us. I must go.*

I wanted to say *be safe* to him. *Do not die.* I wanted to speak of how I felt, which was huge, and beyond all words. But I said nothing.

He spoke instead. He called to me, as I set off to the north. He said,

I will see you again, Corrag. And like he had had faith in my words, and my truth, or like he also had the second sight in him, I believed his.

I smiled, briefly.

Then I ran.

I ran. I ran.

Take my hand? I am running. I am sitting in a cell, in chains, but I run. I run north to Inverlochy. I run to save their lives.

Tomorrow I will tell you of the Glencoe massacre. The dead, and the living. Him. Me.

Hold my hand? I am running. All my life, I have run.

Jane, my love

Forgive my last letter. Whisky was in it, as it was in my blood. There is none in me, now.

It is beyond midnight. In the dark, amongst the dripping and the other water-sounds, I stood and looked upon the place where she will die. I saw its stake, and the many ropes. They have more ropes than they will need, for she is so small.

She speaks of second sight. With her dove-grey eyes and girlish voice, she speaks of what she knows in her body—her stomach, her bones. I listened. Once I would have backed away, hissed, prayed. But tonight, I listened to what she knows, and loves, and believes.

What do I believe? In God. In His goodness. I believe that by knowing Him, a person's life is richer, and brighter, and is spent with better purpose. I have always believed in that. But I also believe, now, in the recognition that others might also think that—of their own gods, their own religions. She dreams, perhaps, of a day when all folk know the skill of herbs. Or (more likely) she believes very firmly that there is more light than dark in the world, more kindness than woe, more beauty than any violence can destroy, and maybe she longs for others to also see this—to not seek to change what is. I will confess she has shown me beauty. I only ever saw it in piety, and you. But a mountain has beauty. A loch does, at night.

We do. We have it in us. That is her speaking, Jane, but also—it is me.

I went to the forge. I sat in its warmth, watching him at work. I looked at his tools, hanging in their proper place, and I wonder if he believes in the heart's voice, and the soul's heart—for he did not ask a thing of me. He did not ask me to leave, or why I was there. Perhaps he knew, or did not care to know.

I read and read. "He that loveth not knoweth not God; for God is love" (1 John 4:8).

I love you, Jane. Whatever happens, now, know that I love you—that of all my life's blessings, you are the greatest.

Charles.

Four

I

"Venus owns this herb, and saith, That the leaves eaten by man and wife together, cause love between them."

of Periwinkle

Sir. Mr Leslie. Who she saw, coming.

Do not sit on the stool? Crouch with me. Crouch on the floor, and wrap my hands and my chains in your hands. This is a fearful telling. What I will speak of is such wickedness that I am afraid of speaking it. I've not breathed a word, till now. I've kept it inside.

You're so warm. See?

Once, once, you were so offended by my dirt and my eyes that you did not sit. You eyed that stool like it was a trick. Remember? And now you settle on straw, by my bars.

We all change, I told Alasdair—*but not our hearts.*

Not them.

I HAVE never run faster than I did, that night. Even in snow, with drifts that were shoulder-high to me, I had never run faster in all my life. I was all legs and arms, like a spider. I was wings, like a bird, and when I startled a hind that was crouching by rocks she ran alongside me, until she grew tired. I ran faster than her, in the falling snow.

There was no wind, at first. When I came to the ferryboat at Ballachulish, and the man rowed me across, the snow came down thickly, and straight. It came onto my hair and nose and hands, and the loch itself was dark, metal-coloured. I said to him *go, now. When you have dropped me on the other side you must flee. Do you hear me?* He stared. He had a kind face.

I fled. I climbed ashore, and ran north, and I ran so fast that the air I breathed had snow on it, in it, and so I had snow in my mouth and lungs. I thought of my mare. How fast she would have carried me. How white she would have been in the falling white.

So I ran. I ran from the water and I ran through the hills. I ran through fields and over ice, and I ran, and ran, and I did not know the way to Inverlochy—or my head did not—but my heart knew, my second sight said *north,* and *this way,* and *turn left at this drifting.* And so after some long, long, white hours of running, I came down through snowy trees to see the fort before me. It was such a good sight. It was the best sight, and it made me hopeful, and I slowed. I thought, *I am here, I have made it. All will be well from this moment on.* The fort was very black. It had torches staked by its gates, and lights in its thin, slit windows that warmed me just by seeing them. As I came to its gates I thought I could hear the wood hiss as it burned, that I could smell meat cooking, and I thought for a little time *be calm, now—be happy* as I was here now, at Inverlochy, whose governor had promised to protect the Glencoe men. *You have done well, Corrag* and in the yard of the garrison I saw many soldiers gathering with pikes and muskets, and I held on to the bars of the gate, pressed my forehead against it.

I called out.

The guardsman approached me very briskly. He said *what's your business?* He held a torch up in the snow to see me better and walked forwards, all muffled up and heavy from his damp coat.

Please. I am here to see Colonel John Hill very urgently. It is of grave importance. People are in danger and I am here seeking his help.

I breathed very hard through the bars. He looked on me like I was talking in a whole new tongue, like I made no sense, and I thought *hag* was in him, that he might say *hag* or *witch*. I would not have him say it—not when I needed Colonel Hill, as I did—so I asked again. *Colonel Hill? Very quickly?*

The Colonel sees no-one tonight.

I flinched. *No-one? Why not? He will hear me, sir. Go to him and tell him I have a message from Glencoe and he must hear it at once. It's a very dire matter and he must see me, he has to—I've run from there tonight in this weather.* I looked sadly at him. *Please?*

His look was different now. It altered as I talked—from one of contempt for me, this bunch of rags at the gate, to a look of proper worry and discomfort so that he looked very quickly into the shadows either side of me and then glanced back at the soldiers who were blowing on their hands.

He said, *Glencoe?*

All of Scotland knew its name. I wondered if he thought I might rob him of his purse or pull a musket on him. But I was very small and my hands were holding the bars of the gate very firmly, and I was no threat that I could see.

I said, *Yes. Please tell him.*

He was gone, then. I saw his great coat grow lost in the snow as he passed the soldiers with their arms, and in his absence all I could do was stamp my feet and practice in my head what best to speak to Colonel Hill, so I tried the words to myself and shook my hands to warm them, and I saw from the yard a man with a fine overcoat buttoned to the neck was eyes on me, very warily. I eyed him back. His staring was no matter to me now, for I was very certain of Colonel Hill receiving me—a young woman on her own in snow on a night of such foul weather. Colonel Hill was good—the clan said so. They said he understood them, kept his word.

I was calm. But when the torch and frown of the guardsman came back through the white to me he was gruff, strong-worded, and said *Be gone. Like I said, the Colonel is seeing no-one tonight.*

None? This was dreadful. I was open-mouthed, very afraid, and I grasped the bars harder and said *but he must! A terrible thing is going to happen! And is he not a friend of the clans?* But the guardsman spat into the snow, and scowled, and I heard some foul words come from him before he turned and was lost in the snow again. I did not rest, or go. I shook the gates, called *Come back! He must see me!* And when I saw the scowling man would not return for all my hollering and pleading I decided to shout so loudly the Colonel himself somewhere would hear me. Inverlochy was a mighty garrison, I saw that—very big, but not built so soundly that it might keep all noises out. On such a night also when the streets were muffled with the snow and the only men abroad were soldiers who gathered very quietly so I only heard the clink of their pikes on the frozen ground, and their boots also, he would surely hear me by his fire with his supper at his side. So I shouted out his name. I said, *Colonel John Hill! Colonel Hill of Inverlochy! I have come for your assistance! Will you hear me?* Through the snow I shouted. *I have come from Glencoe!*

I shouted very much. I screamed *Colonel Hill! Colonel Hill!*

Did he hear? I think he did. I think he heard me crying out—that maybe he thought, *is that the wind? Or a ghost?* For he came to the window to see. As I shook the bars, I looked up to a thin, high window in the west tower, which flickered and glowed with a fire's light. And as I cried out *Colonel Hill* I saw a darkness move across the glow—a man-shaped darkness, and it stood there in the window so that I saw his wig's silhouette, the shape of his nose. He looked down into the courtyard. He looked at the girl who waited at the gates, calling his name, and I let go of the bars. I stepped back. I felt rushed with fear, for I knew he would not let me in.

He knows, is what I thought. *He knows what lies ahead.*

Which he did. He must have done. For the King's orders always pass from hand to hand. There are parchments signed, and passed on, and signed, and passed on, and I reckon Colonel Hill found this order on his bureau which said *maul and cut off the branch of Glencoe,* and what could he do? What choice did he have? But sign it? What choice?

I do not blame him. I blame him no more than I blame the hangman who put the rope about Cora, breathed *sorry* to her. I blame him no more than I do the rain, on rainy days, which drowns fledglings in their nests—for it is the clouds that make the rain. It's not the raindrops' fault.

So Colonel Hill looked down. He saw me in my rags. He saw the snow thickening, and perhaps he thought, *it is too late.* Or *may God save their souls.* Or *may God save mine*—for they say he was a man of faith, with a good heart, and there was a manner to his silhouette which was sad-looking, and old.

I nodded.

Then I thought *run*—and I turned and ran, back through the snow.

ON AND on. I ran back past trees and rocks which had seen me before, and I saw my old footprints in the snow which made sorry—for what good had it served, in coming north? I saw them and said to the ghost of me *turn around turn around. Don't waste time.*

It was the worst of all weather, and the worst of all feelings—to long for a place, to be dreadfully afraid and to want to get home yet for each leg to sink deep into drifts of snow, and the heart panics at such sinking but panic makes it worse by far. I fell fully down. My skirts and cloak were drenched from the snow and stuck to my skin, and I couldn't see for the blizzarding—I could not hear at all for the wind howling round. I thought of Alasdair. I thought of how he said *what harm could they do us? They are our guests*—and those seemed very gentle words, and wise words, but I'd not believed in them. Even though he'd said them—him, with his freckled hands, his eyes. I loved how he said my name and how he'd held back branches for me as we'd walked, and as I ran through the snow I said over and over *let all be well, let all be well* . . . I tripped, I cracked ice and fell into pools. I fell against a rock, and struck my jaw, and I tore my skin on thorns so that I bled and left red on the ground. But when we want we find a way, we do, and I said to myself *up! Get up!*—for all I wanted was to be back in Glencoe. I knew trouble was coming. I knew what lay ahead.

Blood is coming, Gormshuil said.

As I ran, I said *I am hardy. I am winter-born. I will reach the glen before any blade is pulled through flesh, before the byres are emptied. Or I will come to the glen and find them all gone—all those I love will have fled, and be safe.* I hoped this so much. And I charged like garrons do. I was mud-shot and blue-skinned. My hair slapped my back as I ran.

I came to the shores of Loch Leven and I saw the boat was gone. There was no ferry, now—so I went east along the bank to the loch's far end, behind the northern ridge. From there, I knew there was a pass—high, and airy, but it was the only pass I knew of that came across that ridge, and down into Glencoe. It was all I had left, so I ran to it. I had no food in me, no warmth. But when we must, we must, and we manage it, and I tripped on my hem so that it tore but hems never mattered. I climbed the steep pass through such heavy snow that it made the Inverlochy weather like a mild dust of snow. It was chest-deep on me. I used my arms like swimmers. My head was all I had left to feel—my body now was gone. If I had sat down on the high pass I reckon death would have swung down and caught me. Despite my December birthing. Despite being hardy, and small.

I did not stop. Only when I crested the blustery ridge did I pause—for I heard Lowland voices. In the white, I heard men's voices. I blinked. I thought *hide.* Two redcoats were coming up the pass towards me, so

I crouched down. I dug into the drifts with my hands, and crept in, and I clutched my hands to my mouth to keep in my ragged breath, as they passed. They hurried. One said *I will not be part of such business! I will not! I cannot*—and the other said *it is against all laws I know of!* And they were as anxious as I was, those two escaping men.

They went. And I said to myself *go! Run! Run!* So I pulled myself out of the hole, and I tripped as I came down into the glen which made me fall, tumble down the slope like a stone would, and it made me very sore and wretched but it was a quick descent, which was all I wanted. Then west, west, west into the glen by the way I had first ever entered it, on a silent moonlight night, and as I came to the Meeting of the Waters which were frozen, and blue-bright, I looked down into the glen and saw beauty. All was white. All was hushed, and bright.

I slowed.

I stood very still. At that moment, as I breathed, and as the snow fell very softly, I wondered if I'd ever seen such beauty as this—this, here. Now. It was a glinting world. It was gentle, and sleeping. The hearth's smoke from Achtriochtan drifted up, very straight, and the trees bent down with snow, and I saw deer tracks about me. Icicles shone. The morning star was out.

I thought, *I love this place. Deeply.*

Also, as I stood in all this silence, I thought *have I been wrong, all along? Is there no death coming?* I almost smiled at this. I almost laughed, said to myself *look at all this beauty. How can there be murders here? Look how wrong you have been, Corrag—how wrong . . .*

I believed it too full of light, for any darkness. Too loved.

But then there was a musket shot. It cracked the glen open. And I ran thinking *no no no no no no no no.*

In I went. Snow-shod, and bloodied from rocks.

I went in, panting, and I saw a bright, orange flash in the west, and burst of grey smoke. There was a second flash, and a third, and I heard

the *bang* of the muskets echo back to me, from the heights. I thought
of the legends—of these ancient warriors who slept beneath the hills,
who may rise up with their swords to protect the glen, and I thought
*rise up now. Now is your time, to rise up and fight. Your people are in danger.
Your glen is being plundered and set alight, and inked with blood. Rise up!*
And yet they slept. So I shouted *rise up* as I ran. I said *rise up now!* For
I could not save the MacDonalds of Glencoe on my own. I knew I
was too small and too slow, too human to save them on my own, and
I was praying to all things, now—the sky, the snow, the eyes in trees,
the eagles, the rocks, the shadows which moved as I passed them, and
the ones that did not move—to be with me as I ran, to quicken my
feet and strengthen my hands. *Rise up* I asked them. I had never been
so afraid.

I came to Achtriochtan and they were already dead.

It was an awful sight. Their chimney still smoked, but they were
not beside it, sleeping—not now. Old Man Achtriochtan was face
in the snow, hands outstretched, and his skull was blown away. The
back of his head was not there anymore—instead, there was redness,
and a thin line of snow settled on his hair. I thought I saw two of
his fingers move, briefly, as if had only just been shot—but when I
crouched down beside him there was no breath, or heartbeat in his
wrist. His eyes were shut. His mouth was partly open. Beside him, was
his brother who was half-lost in the snow. I gasped, and looked up.
Behind the house, I heard another shot. I thought *that is his wife. She is
also gone.* And as I thought this, I saw three redcoats dragging her body
out. Her apron grew redder as she was dragged.

She had kissed me twelve hours before. Said *eat* to me.

Run. I left Achtriochtan—for what could I do? What could be
done? He could not tell his poems, now. He could not nod, as I passed
him by, and she could not sing, and I wiped my eyes, said *do not mourn
them yet—run west, run west* and I ran to where the sky was flashing,

and dark with smoke. Here, there was screaming. There had been silence, before. As I'd knelt by the dead old man, I'd heard no sound till the *bang* of his wife. But now, it was noise—screaming, and crying, and the muskets were so loud their sound was breaking the snow on the highest peaks so that it came down with a roar, and bringing rocks with it. I saw a person fleeing up into the heights, who was buried in it. Lost in the snow.

I shielded my eyes. I had to peer through the smoke which stung, and look for faces—and I saw some. Amongst the snow and smoke, I saw the red-headed family from Achnacon were hurrying through trees with their cloaks tied up, and bundles pressed to them which were maybe food, or bairns. I watched them flee, and thought *yes, go!* And I saw a grey-haired couple making their way up the slopes, hand in hand, and I thought *hurry—do not stop till Appin.* As I moved on, a redcoat came out to me. I wailed—but he had no sword or musket. He was weeping. He was a boy—so young, and pale—and he knelt down upon the snow and wrapped his arms about himself. Just a small boy.

I rushed to him. I grabbed him by his arms and said *why are you killing us? What is this? Talk!*

He shook his head. He mumbled *there is a dead man over there . . . His face . . .*

I shouted *tell me!*

There was mucus running from his nose, and he sobbed, said *they were the orders.*

To kill?

He nodded.

To kill who?

The Chief. His eyes closed up. *All of them—but mostly the Chief. His sons . . .*

I let go of him. I stepped back, said very quietly *why?*

He wailed. He opened his small, pink mouth and said *the oath was late. It didn't count* . . . And he pressed his face down to his knees like a child, and I left him—for he was not killing. He was as scared as me.

I hated this. I hated how the snow was melting in the heat of houses on fire, so the grass was showing itself, and old ferns. I hated that Achnacon was blazing, as I came to it, and its flames were so fierce that I could not be near it, and had to run by with one arm up, shielding me. Its sparks fell down with the snow. Its ash came down upon me, and I heard men's voices. I heard one say *there! That woman!* And some tried to grasp me as I ran. One fired a musket. I heard the *bang,* felt the rush of air as it passed me, and a bite, and the smell of powder, and later I would find a blackened streak upon my bodice where the shot grazed me, and some blood.

I yelped, at this. I felt a pain.

But I did not stop. I wanted to make it to Carnoch—to save who I could, to warn who was left. Alasdair would have warned most of them, but all? Perhaps not all. *Perhaps Carnoch does not burn yet.* So I left burning Achnacon—but as I did, I glanced to my right where the midden was. A shape was on it. It was a star-shape, so I cried *no* . . . I tumbled over to it and grabbed the body and hauled the man over. It was Ranald the piper who had once picked blackberries with me. Very dead. Run through the neck with a blade, so his head was almost a hat for his neck—half-raised in *hello.*

I retched then. I vomited up on the midden.

I vomited again as I pulled what I could of Ranald from that place, for he deserved better. A midden is no dying place.

I closed his eyes, and re-settled his head. I tried to make him look like it was a gentle death.

Keep him safe, in the realm. Give him a peace that he deserves.

There! There! It was an English voice. And I turned to see soldiers pointing at me, saying *there! Her!* And one of them I recognised. One of them was the cloud-haired man with the button eyes—the one who had wept in a ditch, talked of ghosts, and I had felt so sorry for him, as I had passed that ditch. Now? I did not feel sorry. I felt so black for him, so desperate, so that I screamed out *how can you do this? They were your hosts! How could you?* He heard me. I could tell from his face, and he lowered the hand that had pointed at me. Others said *there! Get that one!* And I had to run on after that.

I ran over the body of a woman, musket-done.

There was a hand, in the snow. A hand, on its own.

I took myself to Inverrigan. The house in the woods, by the bend in the Coe. Where once I had mended a toothache. Where there had been a dog who'd lie on her back when she saw me, to have her belly stroked, and I ran to it. I moved in amongst the trees. There were many soldiers there, packing their muskets with powder or cleaning their blades, and I felt arms try to catch me as I ran through, smelt their breath and sweat, and blood, and when one hand caught my hair, and grasped it, I spun to face the man. I screamed with all my power. I flashed my eyes and bore my teeth, and I think Cora was with me at that moment—she was in me, roaring. She was stormy-eyed and bloodied. She made the soldier let go of me, back away, say *witch* . . .

When I came to Inverrigan, it was too late to help.

The house was not burning. It stood as it always stood—but behind it, in the snow, were all the Inverrigan men. They were tied up, and lying down in a line. They were shoulder to shoulder, all on their back. All were dead. The last of them was a child—the jug-eared boy who'd shared honeycomb with me.

I sobbed. I stamped a foot weakly, and wiped my nose on my arm. Why did they not go south? And flee? Why did they not heed Alasdair, for he would have told these men. He would have knocked on their door, said *run* . . . I made a sound like a dog—a howl—and I could not see well for the tears which pricked. Alasdair had said *I will warn them.* But they were tied up and lying down, and dead—even a boy. I saw his dead face, and remembered it when it was living—laughing, with honey on its chin.

You cannot help them now, I thought. *Carnoch. Go there now. Save them.*

I turned. But a man grabbed my arm. I scratched, and fought the man. But he was saying *Corrag! Corrag ! It is me.*

It was Iain. He was wild-eyed, and his hair was grey with ash. He had a rash of blood upon his cheek, as if someone had died near him, and he took me by the shoulders and said *run. Don't stay here. They are killing everyone—women and children are dying.*

I tried to speak.

Go, he said. And then he glanced behind me, to where the nine lives were gone. I saw his eyes widen. I saw how sad he looked, and as he looked upon the bodies he whispered to me, *get yourself away, Sassenach.*

Why are you all still here? I asked. *Why? I told Alasdair! He said he would warn you all!*

And he did. He warned us. But some did not heed him.

I kicked the side of the house, sobbed. *Why did they not heed him? Why not?* I said, *you must run, too. They are after you, and your father—a soldier said so. Make for the coast. For Appin.*

We go there now. Come with us.

No.

They will kill you, Corrag. They are killing every living soul . . .

I must save who I can save, Iain. There must be some who are still hiding, or who are hurt. I must save them . . .

Corrag! There are three-score of them! With muskets and blades and what do you have? Your heart? Eyes?

I shook my head. *Iain,* I said, *will you tell Alasdair? That I have stayed? Tell him why I have stayed, and that he must keep his family safe, and himself safe—for always? In case I don't survive the night? Tell him?*

Then he stepped back from me, let go. He gave one hard breath. He glanced about the trees, said *I cannot. He is not with us. He will not come.*

I stood. I stared for a moment. Then I bent at the waist, like it hurt. *He has not made for Appin?*

No. He's still in the glen. Somewhere . . .

I vomited again. I did it in the snow, by his feet, crouching. I wiped my mouth, and whimpered, and when I straightened, I said *why? Why did he stay? He said he would flee! He told me he would flee . . .*

Briefly, Iain put his hand on my shoulder. He opened his mouth, but had no words.

I ran from him. I pressed my teeth together, and charged through the trees, and felt so cross at his wet-earth hair and wide smile and his stubborn ways for he was meant to be safe, and yet he was still here? In the glen? It was the fighter in him. His nature, his ways—and I charged past some soldiers. I ran through a herd of goats which had broken free, and were bleating with fear, shifting their eyes. I fell out into the fields where once there had been fire to celebrate a birth, and dancing, but the fire was houses blazing now. I slid on melting ice. I slid straight into two soldiers and feared they would draw out their dirks and finish me, so I grappled with them, said *let me go,* but they backed away and did not hurt me. They said to me *don't stay here.* And they looked more afraid than anyone I'd seen—more hopeless.

Not all soldiers murdered that night. Note that down.

But I did not note it. I noted nothing, for all I had was *let him still be living* in my head. I said it loudly, into the air. I hoped Carnoch might not be ablaze.

But it was. Of course it was.

All its houses were burning. There were cows roaring, rolling their eyes, and I called out his name above all the noise. I screamed it. I heard a dog barking, and Bran came to me. He licked my face as I knelt to him and I asked him where Alasdair was—*where is he Bran? Good dog. Where is he?*—but he did not know. He left me, and galloped west, to the loch.

Their house had fallen in on itself. There was nothing left to it. I prayed that Sarah and her baby had made their way south-and-west, and was sure they had. Surely they had. He would have warned them, and they would have fled. Then I went to the edge of the Coe where the great house stood, and its stone and glass was not fully burning yet, but inside I could hear a clattering and a breaking of things, and I saw there were redcoats inside. Looting. Taking his silver and cow-horn drinking cup. His books. His antlers from the wall.

I saw him, too. The MacIain.

I took myself about the side of the house. I stumbled, anxious, and I came upon a window which was broken, and its wall torn down. There he was. There was the MacIain—and I am minded not to tell you how I saw him. He was a man of dignity in life, of grandeur. But he was not so in death. He was shot as he climbed out of bed to meet his guests, who must have walked into his chamber with false, dark smiles and their muskets hid behind their backs, and what might he have said? *Gentlemen! Welcome! What troubles you, at such an hour?* Maybe. But I know he was lying on his belly, a hole in his back, and his trousers only halfway up. An ignoble death. A wrong death. It makes me doubly sorry and sick, in my heart, to think of it.

I knelt down to him. I kissed him on his brow, where I had stitched him once.

Outside, tearful, I trod upon a thing.

I looked down.

It mewled, like a cat.

It was Lady Glencoe. She was lying in the snow, half-bare. They had stripped her of her top clothes, and she was shivering, still living, but with gruesome wounds done by a blade all upon her. Her fingers were bloodied, with teeth-marks on them. I gasped. I dropped down. I said her name over and over, and stroked her, and I took off my cloak and laid it upon her for warmth and a dignity which her husband did not have. I said her name again, said *can you hear me?*

Very faintly, she said, *Corrag?*

Yes, I'm here. Why are you here? Why did you not run to Appin? Didn't Alasdair warn you?

He did . . . Too late. They shot my husband . . . And she closed her eyes, opened up her mouth in a long, silent howl.

I said *ssh* to her, and smoothed her hair. I said, *I will take you from here, and mend you. I will find herbs that—*

No . . . she breathed. *No herbs will do. I'm dying. I am dead, Corrag. He is dead, and I am stabbed . . .*

I can lift you, and—

Let me be, she murmured. *Mend other ones. My boys.*

I laid my face beside her face, so that I could see her eyes. I said *Lady Glencoe, I have seen Iain. He is well. He is making for safety, and will survive. But where is Alasdair? I must find him.*

She shifted, and made the small sound of a surprised creature. She said *he did not find you?*

Find me?

*He went to look for you. At your hut. Corrag—*and she sighed, she breathed out a long, tired breath and spoke, as she sighed.

And then her eyes clouded, and her jaw lowered itself, and she was dead in the snow like her husband was dead in his chamber. I brought her eyelids down. She was all good and had never done badness that deserved such a death as she had.

I DID not care for the soldiers who were still stalking the glen, who had their muskets and swords and were looking for more Glencoe men to cut down, or root out. I did not care that they saw me and grappled for guns, or snatched at my hair. I did not care for them at all, or what they might do for me, for I had him in my head—him with his hair, him with his hands. *Him! Him!*

And when we run very frightened it is a fast running and a numb one for the head can only think of why you run, and where you are running, and not of wounds and pain upon yourself. I felt no coldness. I felt no hurt where I was bleeding—I only ran along the edge of Loch Achtriochtan which was black with ice in it, through its marshes, and I ran past the fiery house of Achtriochtan where the men still lay outside on the snow, with a coat of snow upon them, and his wife's red apron was glowing through the dark.

To my valley. To my hut. To home—and as I crossed the Coe I remembered how Alasdair had kissed his Sarah's head as she was sleeping, with their newborn son upon her breast, and how it had felt, to see it. How I had cried, quietly, that night.

That, I thought, was my time. *That was my time*—like how Cora's time had been on a half-moon bridge as she watched her mother bobbing in her ghost-white shift, and drowning, for that time changed her life for always. It altered all her life. Like Mother Mundy's time had been as she was taken by a reiver on a night not far from this night, with fire and so much crying, and had she looked at the sky that was coming through the burning roof and known she was always different now? That she was changed, and none might ever know it but her, for all her life? The plum-faced man's life had changed in Hexham, that winter—with his brother's neck being stretched.

We all have our moments that change us. But some change our lives, also—the life we are yet to live. And mine had been as Alasdair had kissed her hair, like all the world was there for him, in that bed asleep—for I'd wished to be her. I'd wished that. To be a mother and wife—his wife. Just that.

Still. Our hearts stay our hearts. They are as they've always been.

I thought these things, as I ran through the snow.

· · ·

IN THE gully that led to my hut the muskets sounded far away, and the snow was not as deep for the trees by the burn were wearing it, in their branches. I moved quickly. I prayed *let him be well,* and it was as I hurried on the path with the valley nearing me that I saw it—a sight I knew, which was dark stains on snow like ink on parchment can be, or like stars, darker at their middle and paler at their sides.

I wailed. It was an owl-cry, the hare's cry when the owl finds it.

It was Alasdair's blood—I was certain. I knew. And I ran on to find only more of it, more on the path like a giant man had thrown the blood out from a pot and here was where most of it had fallen—a smattering of it, not just the snow but the rocks also. I put my hand on a rock and lifted my hand back to find it red, and wet. I wiped it on my skirt. There was too much blood here for one man to have lost. There was so much.

He was lying on the path ahead, under a birch tree.

He was not on his face but on his side, with one arm out above his head and the other resting down across his chest. I thought *he sleeps like this*—though I didn't know, I had never seen it. But maybe he was sleeping now, like people do after walking far and after fighting. He said he slept for many weeks after Dundee died, at Killiecrankie, and so here he was—sleeping with the snow drifting down. I made my way to him carefully, like I thought my feet might wake him and I did not want that—he must sleep. His bed was snow and blood. I knelt down. I said his name. I said *Alasdair* and he was so cold to touch and so pale that his hair like ferns looked black against his face and I said *Alasdair* again very sharply.

He did not say *Corrag* or open his eyes.

He stayed as he was with his arm on his chest and I made a cry, a shriek. I pressed my thumb against his neck to feel for the heart that should beat there. It took my eyes closed tight to feel it. I felt it. One beat. Two. He was not dead, but there was blood on my skirt from my kneeling by him and we could not stay in the snow like this. My hut was not far. My herbs were not far.

Hardy Corrag always, and he was three or four times my size, and I could not drag him—but I would not let him die. I would not let his heart stop beating in his neck under a birch tree like this. *Wake up* I shouted and I took his arm, laid it around my neck like it was meat to carry. I roared, and I pulled him up—up across me, so my shoulder fell from its bone again, it dropped out of its socket with its old, proper hotness and its *pop,* and his chest lay down across my back, and his head was by my head so that his hair was by my face. I wailed at the pain. I hauled him up the gully towards the guarding stones. *Wake up* I screamed, and we trailed blood behind us like I once trailed branches before I ever knew him.

He coughed thickly in my ear.

Some fluid came from him down onto my arm and I shouted *wake up* again and I loved his thick cough. I did not care for my shoulder or my soreness, only for his cough which I wanted again and I shouted *wake up* and *wake up* but he gave no second cough.

We made it to my hut, my hut of mud and stone and heather. It was snow-hid and very silent, so still after the glen. My fire was still lit. My goats were still sleeping, by it, and my hens clucked gently. I took Alasdair in, laid him down upon my bed of deerskin, and moss. He groaned, like the mare did when she lay down years before. I turned from him, briefly. I bit my bottom lip, arched my back and pulled upon my shoulder until *pop*—and it was righted.

Alasdair? I knelt by him, and tapped his face. His eyelids parted, so I could see some blue. I put straw behind him for his head to rest upon, and looked at him. He was so pale. He was deathly-pale.

I said *you are safe. You're with me, and shortly you will be well again.*

I cut his jerkin away. It was bloodied, and his shirt under it was also very wet with blood—I cut this from him also. He winced. The shirt had stuck itself tightly to the wound and I pulled it too roughly, pulled at his skin. I thought then to find poppy for deadening his pain and set to finding it. There was not time enough to make a tincture of it, so I put a seed or two into his mouth and said *chew on them. They will help.*

His chest was hurt from a small blade. It had sliced him, and the blood was very red. But when I tore my skirts to make a cloth, and wiped the blood away, I saw the wound was very shallow—it was not enough to kill a man. I packed comfrey straight on it, which helped. But I knew that there was a greater hurt upon him, somewhere—one that had bled out onto snow, like stars.

I whispered *there must be more.*

He shifted.

I looked down. His plaid was wrapped upon his leg like it was part of him. It was sodden. It was so wet with blood that when I touched it, blood rose up out of the wool—like the wool was full with it. His blood was on my hand. My hand was glossy, by firelight. He must have seen my face for he breathed, *how bad?*

I have to look.

He nodded. I crouched lower. I took his plaid, and rolled it very gently. I rolled it like I might roll turf—slowly, neatly. It showed his pale skin, his reddish hair. It revealed his knees to me, and the old scars on them, and as I rolled the plaid above his knees I saw the blood. On his left leg, his skin was not pale anymore. It shone with wetness. It was red, and dark, and there were clotted parts of blood. And I rolled the wool up a little more until there it was, there was the wound.

It was terrible. It was not wide, but it was deep—like a blade had been thrust very harshly, and turned whilst in the skin. It was a hole, in which I could see his inner flesh, his muscle which was cut right through, and the very tender parts of the body we are never meant to see.

He said again, *how bad?*

He knew enough. I said *it is not good.*

I found my herbs. I set about him like he was not Alasdair Og MacDonald who I loved but a man I did not know at all, not even his name. I used whisky to clean it. I lit my single sheep-fat candle and brought it close to his leg so I might see the wound clearly, and tore more of my skirt. I pressed a poultice of horsetail and betony and rupture-wort directly on it and held it there. His eyes were shut as I did so. It was like he was sleeping again—still, pale.

Wake up I said.

He parted his eyes a little and looked down on me. I kept pressing the poultice onto his thigh so it might both deliver its herbs into the wound and also stopper up his blood by not letting it leave his veins anymore, pushing it in, and he said *Corrag.*

Yes.

You're bleeding.

I said it was his blood on me and for his tongue to stop wagging for he needed strength elsewhere.

It's yours. And he winced as I pressed harder and he said more than this but very quietly so I did not hear.

I looked down. He was right—there was my own blood coming through my bodice. It was mine, I knew that—for as I eyed it, it grew. Also, on seeing it, I felt a sharp ache, and I remembered the musket's *clap* at Achnacon—the rush of air, the bite.

It bloomed like a rose, this blood of mine.

We cannot help others if we need help ourselves, and do not give it. I wished this wasn't true, but it was true.

Alasdair? I took his hand, said *press this to yourself. As hard as you can.* His hand was stiff with cold and I pushed it down upon the poultice, and I remembered its freckles, its marks and scars. I remembered holding his hand all those months ago, before I truly knew him. How strangely, I thought, the world can echo. *Keep it there.*

Then I set upon myself by cutting through my bodice strings to rid myself of it, for it was too knotted to be untied in the normal way. I threw it away. I crouched down. On my waist my shift was ragged. The skin was chewed and black-dappled, and red.

I made my own poultice from my torn skirt. It was wet enough to seal itself onto my body with no hand needed to hold it there.

You had moths . . . he said.

This was the poppy talking like poppy can. It was the broken talk of shock, and loss, and a man whose blood was more out on the snow than inside him. I took my needle from my broth pot and threaded it by the candle, held the needle in the flame to cleanse it with the heat. I said *moths?* Then *don't talk.*

And I lifted his hand from the poultice, and when I took the poultice from his thigh I saw how worthy of its name rupture-wort was, how red and tender and huge the wound was but it was bleeding less, there was no dirt inside it. I dabbed it. I pressed the wound with a herb or two more, and then pinched the sides together. I took my needle. I pushed it through his skin which I felt him tighten at but he did not wince and I pulled the needle through. Slowly, like this, I began to sew.

He said, *do you know when I first saw you?*

I said nothing. I wished he would be quiet, for he needed all his strength, but I did not say this. I sat and sewed.

It was early evening. You had moths in your hair . . .

I breathed. *You saw me?*

You stood in the waterfall. Laid the moths onto a tree, by me. His mouth made a sound.

You saw me? That day?

I did.

Outside it snowed. Inside the fire lit the walls of my hut and his face which looked on me as I worked. I thought of how he had carried two hens through darkness, and how I'd later touch those hens thinking *he's touched them. Held their legs.* I walked where he had walked. Said words he had spoken, as if they had a taste.

I looked up at him. *Why did you not flee to Appin? Like I said?*

He smiled. *You know why.*

I don't, I said. *I don't! I thought you were safe! All the while, I thought you had fled. And look at you now—how wounded you are!*

Hush, he whispered. *Hush yourself. How could I have gone there without you?*

I wanted to cry. I blinked, and pressed my lips against themselves, and I thought how curious our lives are—how sad, and strange. How—of all sunsets and tiny beetles, making their way on a leaf, and of all the blown grass—this was the greatest beauty. Now. This love of mine, for him.

Corrag, he breathed, *I'm dying.*

You are not.

Very gently, like he was speaking to a child who did not want the truth to be as the truth was, and thought she could alter it, he said *I am.*

You're not!

You can't change how the world is.

I can stop your bleeding and sew. Feed you. Warm you till you're mended up.

Look at me he said.

I did not. I had to sew. I blinked hard, cleaned the old blood from him so his skin was white again, and I sewed the broken part of him.

Look, he said, *at me.*

I slowed. I sniffed. I put my needle down, and straightened myself. I did not look at his eyes, but he took my hand and shook it very lightly, as if to say *look at me* again. So I did. My eyes met his eyes.

Sassenach . . . he smiled. *The oath? Which we made? It was not for kings . . . It was never for kings. It was to keep our loved ones safe. That's why we made it.*

I looked at him.

I wanted you to be safe. You . . .

We looked on each other then as if there was so much inside us that no other soul had ever seen but we could see it, we could see it very clearly. I thought of all the years gone by. I thought of how much loss there had been—so much loss, and sorrow. I had walked amongst death all my life, and felt it, and I had seen more in the glen this night than I had ever seen before—and such painful deaths. Such lies. Every death in this glen, I thought, was a lie—just as politics was, and money, and laws.

What matters has never been money, or laws. It is people.

Come closer, he said.

He put his hand against my cheek, felt it. I made a small sound, a child's sound.

Ssh he whispered. *Little thing* . . .

I cried. I felt his hand upon me, and I looked at his face. It was such a face. It was his, his face, and I cried to see it so close to me   so close our breath was on each other's face. I saw how blue his eyes were, each hair in his beard, and I saw the creases by his eyes from all his days of laughing or from squinting through the rain. I saw the lines in his lips, from talking. I saw his straight nose, the soft pads of his ears.

It is people that matter—them, and their hearts. And I leant very slowly. I leant like the stag had done for my hand—gently, and in silence, and with shining eyes, for it is so hard, so very hard, to give all your trust away to another life, to put your nature down and be fragile for a while. I was partly scared. All my life, I had been partly scared.

But I was tired, now. I was so hugely tired—in my body, and mind. I
thought of the stag's thick fur. I thought of his life of sideways rain,
and rock, and how he'd turned upon his hooves, and run. He had also
grown tired. I'd seen it—how he'd trodden closer, and closer. I'd seen
the half-close of his eyes, as he came towards my hand. His mouth had
opened slowly. His breath had been so warm, and like the stag's breath
was warm, mine was warm. My breath was on Alasdair's face, and I
held my mouth above his mouth, breathing his breath in. We were
frail, then. We hovered, sharing breath. We were eyes, and breath, and
fear, and need, and that was the moment—the small, bare moment—
where it was too late to turn, to pull away.

I was done with fighting.

I was done with *witch*. Done with being hardy.

He was half-lit and half in shadow. The fire hushed beside us,
and outside there was snow, and he was what I loved more than all
the mountains and all the skies, all the windy places. When my nose
touched his nose, he smiled at it. When we kissed, it felt known—like
this kiss of ours had been waiting, all along.

⸜⸝────◆────⸜⸝

I watched the doorway lighten. I lay with my cheek upon his collarbone. I heard his heart beating, and I thought of the red winter sunrise
over Rannoch years ago, and wished he'd also seen it.

I'd dragged *witch* all my life. I'd cried from it, and felt alone. I'd been
bruised and chased because of it, and spat upon, and my mother had
been murdered, and her mother had been. But it had brought me here,
to this moment—to being with him.

We spoke no more of love. We had no need. We'd known what
it was, when we came upon it. I'd known it, when he said to me *it's
raining*. He'd known it, when he'd crouched by a waterfall one night,

and seen a tiny woman, standing very naked, with moths and cobwebs in her hair.

Love is what saved him, in the end.

Some might say it's what saves all of us, but I know none of that. I only know of him. I only know that my mother's loving heart said *north-and-west* to me, and my own loving heart said *Glencoe, Glencoe*—and look what I found there. This. Him.

So love saved Alasdair, and others of his clan. And he would love his wife, and son. He would live his life with them, tell them tales, bring in peat for their fire and make more children by that fire's light, and how could I mind that? I could not mind it. He was living. And I had loved him all my life.

Alasdair sighed. I felt his chest rise up, and down.

He put his mouth against my head, and kissed it.

I smiled. His fingers held my fingers, and it looked like a single hand.

⸻

We are the magick—we are. The truest magick in this world is in us, Mr Leslie. It is in our movements and in what we say and feel. I learnt this from the second son of the twelfth chief on the snowy night their people were slain so cruelly in their glen. His father had died, and his mother, and the Highlands were dying also in their way, and yet still he came to find me. He held my hand, and when we kissed, he made a sound like he could rest, now—like he had imagined that kiss a thousand times.

In time, I heard a horse outside, and I knew whose horse it was, and I knew whose feet they were that came across the snow.

Iain looked tired. He saw his brother, knelt.

He is sleeping, I said. *He is very wounded in his leg.*

He felt his brother's face, said *we must go. Alasdair? There are soldiers in the glen who are looking for us. You and me. We have to leave here now.*

So they left. They left me. Iain carried Alasdair out into the daylight which was very white, very clean, and he hauled his brother up onto the horse. They sat astride it, both of them—a brother with dried ferns for hair, and one with wet ferns, wet hillside, and wrapped in my old deerskin. Iain sat behind with the reins in one hand. The other hand held Alasdair against him, pressed him in.

I saw his face. His blue eyes.

Iain said, *Thank you.*

I nodded. I pressed all my herbs into his pockets, filled his purse with them. *Boil them and press them on his wounds.*

Aye. He gave a ghost-smile, a sad one. Then turned his horse and kicked her on.

AND SO they were gone. I watched them pass up the steep sides of my valley, onto the back of the Three Sisters and over the ridge, out of view. I stood by my hut for a while after, and looked at how the morning was—the sky, the hazel tree, the snow.

After this, I took myself back into the glen. I moved through the blackened grass, the empty byres. I held the hand of every frozen soul, and prayed for them, mourned them. The light was pink, and gentle. I sat by each one, for a while.

Where Carnoch smouldered quietly, I found Lady Glencoe. She was cold and dead beneath my cloak, with all her jewellery gone. I stroked her hair, and told her that her boys were safe—both her boys.

The ruined house was smoke, and ashes. I blackened myself on its timber, and burnt my hands on its walls. Under stones, I found the old chief's sword. I dragged it out. I hauled it outside, and it ploughed a black line into the earth. On the shores of Loch Leven, I made a wish. I wished, with all my soul and heart, that such nights were over—that no such lies or treachery or blood would come again. That the men and women and children of Glencoe would not die like that again— not ever. I wished. I prayed.

I threw the sword into the loch.

We bury what we hate to keep it from us, Cora said. *We burn it, or drown it.* And I watched how the water settled back down, sealed itself back over the sword.

So it was.

So it was meant to be, all of it. I had done my best, for always, and a single snowflake drifted down. Then two flakes. Three.

THE soldiers came. By the water's edge, they circled me. *That's the one. She warned them—she did.*

This tiny thing?

It was her. Bind her up.

How did they know? From the dead, I think. I think the dead told them, before they died. I think that as a blade was held above their chests they were asked *who told you? Who warned you of this?* For most of the clan were gone, and safe. Most of the beds were empty, for their sleepers had risen up and were in the hills already, with their hoods up and their children's hands clutched in their hands, saying *run, now. Don't look back.*

Who told you? Who?

The Sassenach did . . .

So they knew. A calm-eyed soldier found me, with blood on his neat hair. He wiped his face, eyed me, said *so this is the English witch?* They shackled me. They put chains on my wrists, and they struck me. They kicked me, hissed out *hag* and *meddling piece,* and the calm-looking one took off his glove, looked at his hand, and then threw his fist at me which cut my eye, and made me drop down. I bled from it. When I looked at him, he was red.

I did not weep.

Instead, as they led me away, I turned. I turned back towards Glencoe, which was burnt, and very still, and high above its trees I saw the Pap. I saw its snowy heights—I said *goodbye* to it.

⚬⊤───◁▯▷───⊤⚬

I was dragged for many nights. I slept in my chains on rocks, or wet sand. They talked of the murders, and who they killed. Of who did the killing. I heard names.

The sons?

I mauled one of them. Put a blade in him—and deeply. But I reckon they both made it.

Stair won't like that.

And I smiled when I heard this—I smiled behind my hair, or into my knees, for what else mattered? Not my musket's wound. Not the bloodied eye. Not where they were taking me, or why.

LATER, on a snowy night, near the castle of Barcaldine and a stirring sea, I heard *what's her name?* They had lit a fire. They were warming themselves, drinking a bottle they'd taken from the ashes of Glencoe, and I lay in the shadows. *That one?* They meant me. They trod near me, and a redcoat woke me from my lost half-dream, pressed his heel on my waist where the musket had hit me, and he rocked me back and fro.

He bent down. In my ear, he spat, *what's your name?*

Witch. That'll do for her.

Devil's whore! Ha . . .

But no. It was never that. My proper name was never *witch,* never, and nor has it ever been *hag* or *wicked piece* or *Devil's wife* or *whore.* When have I ever been whorish, or cruel? When? And yet all my life I had had that—false names, lies, curses thrown out, and I'd had no family name which made them say *whore* even more, and *the Devil's her father as well as her lover, most likely*—and what was that? Lies! Sadness, and lies. But *not now,* I thought. By their small fire I thought, *no more . . . That is not me. That's not my name.*

I rolled onto my back and parted my lips so that a soldier said *she's speaking, sir! Can't make it out . . . There's blood in her mouth.*

Is it English?

Can't hear.

And I blinked at the sky with its scattered stars, at the bare branches of trees, and I felt the blood and a loose tooth in my mouth, and I pushed the tooth out with my tongue, so that it slid down my chin and onto the sand, and I spoke. I said my name very clearly.

What? What did she say?

MacDonald for them—for the people I'd lived for, fought for, saved. And as I pushed my forefinger down into the cool, wet sand, I smiled. I said *Corrag.* For I'd shown them the way.

⊶━━◄▌▶━━⊷

There.

There it is. All you have wanted, Mr Leslie. *My telling of it*—what I saw, and did.

Was it worth it, sir? The long wait?

THE world will speak of Glencoe's deaths. It will talk of the lies, of the blades pulled back through flesh. It will widen its eyes, say *they killed bairns, even*—and yes, it must be spoken of. Speak of their deaths. Mourn.

But Glencoe?

Its name does not mean death, to me. It means him. It means the cold draughts of water which I'd suck up from the lochs, with my hair in the water. How mist nestled in hollows. Ferns. Wind sounds.

A DARK place . . . For now, it is. For now, they will call it so, and shake their heads at it. For now, folk will not go there—or if they do, they will hurry through and not look up at its airy heights. But shadows pass. Before shadows come, there is light, and what follows them is light—for how else can there be shadows? If there is no light?

So *a dark place*? Briefly. But Glencoe will always be bright.

Jane

I will not write much. There is no need—for you will read this when it is over. You will read this when all will be done, and I will be gone from Inverary, and there will be stories of an Irishman who came, and rode away. Of a witch, who is no more.

But I will write an apology, my love. I write to express my humble, deep and inexpressible love for you, and how I regret the hardship that my duty puts you and our boys through. I came here to serve a king. I came here to serve him by proving the sins and misdemeanours of the man who took his place—and I do this in God's name. I feel it is right, that I'm here. But I am aware of what is beyond the sea, without me. I am aware that you must walk the gardens on your own, and hear our boys read without your husband at your side. They grow, with no father to teach them. And I am sorry to you all for how this is the truth of it.

Forgive me. Understand me when I say that I do not pretend this is easy—for you, or our sons. I know it is not. I know you support me, but I know that there must be times when you stamp your little foot at me, or shake a fist, and wish me to return. I will return. I will.

I hope it is a comfort to know that I don't do this for James's sake alone. Nor do I only have God in mind. I think of you, Jane—with my fight for the Stuart cause, with my hopes for a better, safer world I have a longing to make you proud of me. I would love—dearly love—for our sons to become men who speak of their father with pride, and affection—that they might say our father, Charles Leslie, made a difference to the world. Imagine it . . . I try.

Jane, how I miss seeing your face.

Tomorrow I will go to her.

I will get her out.

II

⟨decorative divider⟩

*"[It] may be properly called Heart Trefoil, not only
because the leaf is triangular, like the heart of a man,
but also because each leaf contains the perfection of a heart,
and that in its proper colour, viz. a flesh colour."*

of Heart Trefoil

ever love a person. Do you hear?

N So Cora said. Cora, with her blue–black hair like a raven's wing, and her herbs. She'd taken my face in her hands and said *for they won't love you back. Or if they do, that love will be taken from you—see?* And she stepped away, smoothed her hands on her skirts. *No-one loves ones like us.*

Love the ice, and wind, instead. Mountains.

And I loved those things. I loved the whorls of hair on my goats. I loved how the wind met me at a peak, and it wrapped itself about me, shook me like a friend. I loved sky—every single sky. How the wolf was, when it called.

But Cora was wrong. *Never love* was wrong. It makes me sad to think it, for I think she had a heart which longed to love, and love. I think she dreamt of it—for I heard her whispers, at night.

Can she see me, now? Oh yes. She sees me, in this cell. She spends these final hours with me, and says *I am with you, Corrag. The realm is near, and waiting, and I am not far away.*

MR LESLIE. I knew you would come. I used to think you never would, that my dirt and voice and *witch* would send you away, and keep you there. I'd think, *he's gone,* and be sorry—but in time, my heart would whisper to me *no, he'll come back, he will . . .* And you did. Each time.

So. No quill, today. No leather case.

Come closer?

I would like my last words with you to be as we hold hands.

❦———◆◆◆———❦

I have names. I have names from that night, and will give them. Barber. Drummond. Hamilton. I know that there were some Campbell men—not many, sir, but some. I know that Glenlyon who wept in a ditch—*forgive me, Lord, forgive my soul*—was not haunted by his past sins, as I'd thought, as I'd crept by. I'd thought *poor man . . . So lonesome. Look how he regrets his old ways.* But he prayed for his future ones. His orders had come, from the King.

Maybe *poor man,* still—for his weeping was soul-deep, that night. It hurt my own, to hear it. It made me think *find your comfort . . . Forgive yourself.*

I also have the name *Stair.*

Stair. A curious name. But it's the name I heard, when they shackled me. After they'd struck me, and spat, and knocked me down, I heard them say *she warned them.*

Stair should know it.

Stair will not be pleased at this. Stair's plans have been ruined by her.

And a soldier crouched down to my ear, said *he'll not take kindly to you . . .*

He didn't. Not at all. The Master of Stair came here. He rode from

Edinburgh to see the grey-eyed creature who unpicked his careful stitches, saved that thieving tribe. Through the bars he watched me. *Meddlesome piece,* he said. *The world would have done well to be rid of that clan.*

And him? Would he have done well? To have been rid of them? No doubt. I lost him a title, I reckon. Favour. A little land.

But what have others lost? What was lost, in snowfall?

It will be a vengeful burning—that is all. But *witch* is the reason they give. *Witch* is why they will kill me, or so the townsfolk say.

Who will you burn?

Hag. Witch.

It has always tried to kill me—this word, this life of mine.

⸻⸻

I do not have long, sir. Not long, now.

Tomorrow they will come, and take me out. They will lift me up, tie my hands behind the stake, and a rope about my neck to hold me straight, to stop me crouching down and quickening my death—and who thinks, this way? I could hiss, and say *what world is this? That has such treatment in it?* But I will not say that. I will not die thinking of the dark parts, or the pain.

Sir? Mr Leslie?

Have I been so hard? Have I been a hardship to visit, every day? I hope not, very much. I hope I have been worth the crooked stool, and this *drip . . . drip . . .* and I hope that I've given you some sovereign help with what you call *my cause.* You know I'm not for kings. I never was. My heart says that there is more blood—far more—to come for James's sake, and I hope I am wrong, and I hope this blood isn't yours. Be careful? No war. Fight with your pen. Give your battle-cry in ink, and mark your dreams down on a page.

And truth . . . Tell them the truth. Speak of my story, when I am

gone. Say *witch? Devil's wife? She was not those things . . .* Do your best?
Please? For the only ones who knew me, who shared their broth
and sang with me, are Highlanders—and who believes their words? I
know tales will rise up, like ghosts—of wickedness, and spells. I know
that some will always hear my name, and cross themselves. But pass
a whisper on, sometimes? Say my name? For speaking of the dead
makes them less so.

I hand my telling to you. I pass it through the bars.

And go to Appin, sir. Ride your way north, along the coast. And
in its coves and little homes you'll find MacDonalds there. Speak to
them, and they will give more.

CALM? No. But Cora is waiting, and I miss her. I will try to make her
proud, and I will not scream as I am burning, or clench my feet as the
flames find the skin between my toes.

Hardy Corrag, wasn't I? I must be again. I must be hardier than ever,
and look out across the houses and the loch, and bare trees, and think
I am ready, and *I do not mind,* for look at all the beauty that *witch* has
brought me to, and *he lives, he lives,* and have I not been lucky? Have
I not been blessed to have lived such a blowing life? My heart spoke,
and I heard it. I let it sing its song. I trusted my own self, and I had faith
in the world—for why shouldn't we have faith in it? If a tiny seed can
be a tree, in time, and if birds know where their old nests are, and if
a mare can know *north-and-west,* and *go,* and the moon push and pull
the silver sea, then isn't it worth our faith? I think it is. I always have.
And for all the times I wished I was not me—*fool! Clumsy thing*—I
know I would not change me, for I've tried to be kind, and I love the
windy world, and even a solemn churchman with buckled shoes can
sit with me, and smile. Look at us! You and I! Did you ever think it? I
never ever thought it. Cora never did.

I prattle, as I always did.

But I have one more request.

Watch me, as I burn? I am so sorry to ask it—I am. It's a dreadful asking. But when the fire is still small and I'm waiting, waiting, and I'm twisting at my ropes and still wanting to live, I know I'll whimper, and be afraid, and I'd like to see your face amongst the faces saying *witch*. I'd like to see your spectacles, your wig, your wrinkled brow, and it will be a friend's face that I can look upon. I will be less fretful. I will think *I'm not alone,* and you cannot hold my hand as I burn, but you can smile fondly and it will be the same.

Maybe say a prayer? As my soul unties itself? We are different, yes—but we both pray, or make wishes, and our prayers may drift in different ways, and roll out like cold breath, but I reckon they meet up in the same place, in the end.

SAY you'll remember me. That you're glad a snowy road led you to this cell.

Say you'll not think of me as a girl on fire, or a shackled one—but as I was, when I was happiest. In Glencoe, with my hair blowing out. With Alasdair by me.

Say *yes* to this?

Say yes?

But you say *no.*

No, Corrag, no! You will not die.

We all die, Mr Leslie. The realm waits—

In time, yes—we die. But you will not die tomorrow. You will not die this way.

⸻

Once, just once, I thought I saw my death. I was knee-deep in English marshes, with the frogs saying *cleep,* and the wind in the reeds. It was early evening, and as I looked down I saw my face in the water—and it looked strange, to me. Still my face, but very old. My hair was grey. I saw the geese also reflected, and sky, and I thought *there. That will be your face, when your life is nearly done.* And I waded out, and wandered home.

An old, quiet death. Was that what I saw? I saw an old woman, drinking from a wild pool. I saw a quiet life, at least. Quiet, and long.

I'd forgotten. All these years, and I'd forgotten that.

Do not love. But it is all I've ever done.

Stop talking, you say. *Open your hands.*

And in my ear you say *come with me, Corrag. Come with me.*

Five

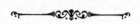

Jane,

It is done. It is over. The man I once was is dead, now—and I am standing in his place.

There are so many words I have, to tell you. So many moments, and thoughts. How can I write of them all? I can't. I will keep most of them inside me—or I shall, for now. I will tell you of them, when I can see your face, and have you by my side. Perhaps we can walk in our gardens after rain, so that the air smells of earth and wetness, which is how all of Ireland smells to me. Perhaps we can sit, you and I, on the bench beneath the willow tree, and I can tell you how I lifted up the large and fearsome file from the blacksmith's forge and tucked it underneath my coat. He had many files. I trust he'll not miss it—or I hope he does not. "Thou shalt not steal," Jane—but also what of the Psalms, which the moths have eaten in your Bible? "Who is like the Lord our God, the One who sits enthroned on high, who stoops down to look on the Heavens and the earth? He raises the poor from the dust and lifts the needy from the ash heap; he seats them with princes, and the princes of their people" (Psalm 113:5–9)—and am I not His servant? Is she not in need?

She speaks of love being all that truly matters. Love is the heart of faith, I think.

If I took from the blacksmith, I gave to the gaoler. Love, for him, is whisky—he has always smelt of it, and spoken like it's in his veins. So I gave him a bottle—as thanks, for his help, over these past weeks—and as soon as I left him, I heard him uncork it, and drink. It was the strongest I could find. It would lead him to a stupor, if not to proper sleep.

Who is this man in me, who did such deeds?

Corrag was so wide-eyed, when I found her. She sat by the bars, waiting, and we were quiet for a time. She spoke of her death. She held my hand, and was brave, Jane—so brave, in her talking. She did not rage, or curse the world, and I thought, as I sat with her, she has never asked for help. She has never asked for me to write to Stair, or get her out.

I gave the file to her.

I will speak of her expression when I see you—to see yours. But perhaps, you can imagine it. She looked at the file and looked in my eyes, and I saw a thousand things in her little face. As she filed at her chains, her hair dropped down about her, and I thought of your hair, then. How it curls, at its ends. My love, through all of this, I thought of you.

The chains broke. Corrag held them, briefly, in both hands. She looked upon them, felt them, and I think she said goodbye in that small moment— a farewell to her chained, tollbooth life.

I hated her, once—didn't I? I wanted her burnt, and gone. But tonight, when she tried to fit between the bars, I said push, *and* turn, *and I wanted her out. I pulled her arm, and twisted her. I tried to press the bars aside— but she shook her head, stepped back.* Try again, *I said, but she could not slip through, and so I said* try again *very sharply. And then? Next? I saw her close her eyes. I saw her take hold of her other wrist, and tug, and there was a sound, Jane—a* pop, *a tongue's click. Her shoulder rose up. It shifted high, and over—like a wing. Her mouth was wide. She longed to scream in pain, I think, and she came towards the bars with this new shape of hers. She bit her lip. She held her breath, shifted through. And when Corrag fell against me, she was so light and so warm—like a cat, or a bird. Then, a sec- ond* pop. *A frail mewl came out, and I saw her eyes were wet. But she was standing by me, and was human-shaped again.*

She wiped her nose, and looked at me.

I carried her out. I stepped over the gaoler who was talking in his sleep, and I carried her out without holding her: I bore her, with her fingers grasp-

ing tightly to my clothes, and her legs fixed very tightly about my body, and I held my cloak about me with my hands on such a night—such a wet, unruly night. I carried her. I walked up into the streets, feeling this life clinging to me, her face against my chest, those fingers clutching on, and when I passed others I hoped they only saw a man in a buttoned coat, hurrying home at such an hour, and in such rain. I hurried. I looked down. When I came to the chestnut cob by the inn I mounted very gently, and I heard a small whimper against me, as if I had leant upon her.

The cob had new shoes, and two weeks of rest. He took us well.

And I rode, and thought *what is this? What life is this? My heart beat so strongly I thought it may burst*—as if she was clutching to it, and might pull that organ out. *My lungs breathed very quickly, and my back ached, and I thought how are these hands mine, and these legs mine? I had our daughter's ghost with me, Jane*—and I rode, thinking of you.

By a cold line of trees, I slowed the horse.

Inverary was behind us, and the smell was wet pines, wet horse, wet earth. And it was there that I set Corrag down.

For a moment, she stayed as she was. In the heavy rain, she stood with her arms held up, and fingers bent, and her eyes were tightly closed as if she was afraid to open them, and see. But she opened them. She brought her arms down, and she filled herself up with rainy air, and looked about herself, and blinked, and I will not forget that, Jane.

What words will I use, in our garden? When I speak of that moment? I don't know. I don't have the ways to speak of it, yet. We looked upon each other. Her hair was wet against her face. She took my hands, then. She held them, and did not say a single word to me—but what a look was on her. It was grace, and wisdom. She pressed my hands, let go of them, and that was her thanks.

She ran. My last sight of her was her ragged skirts, and hair. I stood by the trees. I stood for a long time, until my horse shook its mane, and all her tiny footprints had been filled washed away by the rain.

I will leave, now. It is nearly dawn, and when the sky is lighter I will remount, and go. Appin is not far, and I will be welcome there. I will whisper Jacobite. *Perhaps I'll say her name.*

What follows, I cannot say. A half-drunk gaoler may stagger in the streets and say she is gone! Flew away! *Perhaps they will find another soul to burn for some other deed, or burn it anyway. If they try to chase the Irishman who went to her, each day, they will chase a ghost—for Charles Griffin has fled. Like a dream, or like magick, he has slipped away.*

Jane. My love. I hope you read this letter, fold it, and place it on your lap with a small, true smile. I hope you are proud of this man—who thought to serve God, but who knows, now, that the best way to serve Him is to serve all others well.

Daily, I have missed you. But you are in all beauty, which keeps you near me.

I am coming to you. Imagine me, walking up the path to our door. Look out of the window every day, and picture it—me, with my spectacles and calf-leather bag, the pink roses by the window in full bloom—and one day, one day, the picture will be true.

On to Appin, and to serving the world. And on, on, on with loving you.

Charles

I

"... let no man despise it because it is plain and easy—
the ways of God are all such."

of Cinquefoil, or Five-leafed grass

I ran. I moved my legs, and they carried me. I ran across wet earth, and old snow, and I made for a line of trees. When I reached them, I turned. You were still standing there. The rain had darkened you— your wig, your waistcoat—and I thought *remember his face, remember it for always. Remember him who saved you.* You saved a thousand things.

We did not wave, did we? No.

And no words—for what words were there, that could say it all? I had clung to you. I had pressed myself against you, closed my eyes, breathed your warm, human smell, and when you wrapped your arms about yourself, they were also about me. Who had ever held me? Pressed me in, like that? No father ever had. Only Alasdair—sixteen nights ago.

I smelt the sea, as you ran with me. I felt your bones, and clutched at your clothes.

Thank you, I said, as you mounted the horse. And later, by the line of trees, you smiled at me. You smiled, looked up at the rain, and held out your hand to feel it. *Remember him, standing there.*

Mr Leslie. Who serves God, and lost a daughter, and is the kindest of all men I've ever met—all men. Who loves his wife. Who misses home.

Remember him, Corrag.

Then you turned, and left.

WHEN I came to a pool I knelt in its mud, and drank, and drank. I washed beneath my arms. I cupped the water in my hands, lowered my face to it, and I took the blood and dirt away. Ash was in my hair. My hands had lines, and bruises, but I thought *they will live. They will survive, and not be burnt—not now.*

By the pool, I cried.

Not for long, and quietly. But I cried—for I was living. I was in a wild place, where I was meant to be. I cried for my iron wrists. For the death I nearly had, but did not. I cried for those who were yet to die that way.

For the MacDonalds who were gone now. For all the magick, tiny moments which pass by and die, unseen. For my mare. For Alasdair.

For not seeing you again.

Who we were is not who we are, these days. What was a lie, is no longer full of lies. We changed. Blood and love changed us. And words did—*north-and-west* and *make for Appin* changed my life, and other lives. So did *witch,* and *Sassenach.* So did *little thing . . .*

And you? When you first sat before me, with your goose-wing quill, you loathed what you saw. You saw *witch,* and would not move the stool to me. I think you feared for lice. You thought my burning would brighten the sky. But then you heard my story, and you took a blacksmith's file from your pocket, passed it through the bars. You said *hurry.* You also filed my chains, on and on, till they broke. You said *hold on to me,* and you carried me into the rain.

My story, which I thought would die with me. For who would tell it? Who knew what I had seen? What I had felt? And done? But both of us are unshackled now. Both my story and me can wander, and be lifted up with the wind.

WHAT was dark will always be dark, I know that. Death is still death. Hatred will never be far, in this life.

But also, there is light. It is everywhere. It floods this world—the world brims with it. Once, I sat by the Coe and watched a shaft of light come down through the trees, through leaves, and I wondered if there was a greater beauty, or a simpler one. There are many great beauties. But all of them—from the snow, to his fern-red hair, to my mare's eye reflecting the sky as she smelt the air of Rannoch Moor— have light in them, and are worth it. They are worth the darker parts.

It is in us, too. Cora said so. She spoke of inner light, and I believe in that. It is the soul, perhaps, or just our thoughts, our heart and lungs and liver keeping us alive. The flush of life. Magick. Our pulse, our loves, our hopes and dreams. When I kissed Alasdair, we passed our brightness on—his into my mouth, and mine into his. So I carry his light in me, now, and he has my small light.

Cora. She died—but I have every tale of hers in me, every laugh. How she loved blackcurrants. How she cried to see a rainbow, for it seemed so lovely to her—too lovely, as if she had no right to see it being *hag,* and tangle-haired. But she had every right. The rainbow was no lovelier than she, my mother, had been.

So I say this. Speak of them. Speak of those that died. Speak of all those who ever died—in all the world's history, in its wars, and long-lost days. Speak of those who met their deaths in Glencoe, in snow—not of their deaths, but of their lives before them. Not of how they died, but of how they bent to pat a dog's head, or what ballads they could sing, or what their skin was like by their eyes when they smiled, or which weather was their weather—for it keeps them living. It stops them being dead.

To do this—to speak or write of them—puts breath back in their mouths. It lifts them up from their earthy beds. It shakes off their worms and brings them forth, and they stand by the side of the one who speaks of them; they walk out of the pages of those who write them down. From the realm, they smile upon us. All the dead people—only, they are not dead.

THEY will always call me *witch*. That will stay with me. I doubt the tale of me will always be truthfully told—for it will be told in time by men I've never met, who have only heard rumours of me. They will say *evil*. They will say that the Devil came for me, in my cell. Changed me into a beetle, or an owl, or a cat, and I flitted away with him.

But Charles Leslie of Glaslough knows the truth. He knows it, with his Bible on his lap. A blue-eyed MacDonald, the old chief's second son, knows the truth as he rocks his son to sleep by a hearth, singing an old Highland song. Every bird that skims my hair now, for the rest of my life, will feel the truth rise up from me and call it out— *Corrag! Corrag!* And this is enough. I am alone, now—like I always was. But I have been a mother, a lover, and a wife. I've been kind, or always tried to be. And these things are enough.

This is my fifth life. I wake when the sun does, and I watch it change the sky. I watch it, and feel grateful. I feel my arms, my bones.

These days are hushed, and long. Like the days I once knew, they are simple. I sleep in warm hollows. I sink my heels into bogs, and watch the tiny droplets on the tips of bright-green moss. I crouch down by lochs which are so still that they have their own mountains, their own moving sky. Deer tread in a line, and I follow them. I came upon a hind giving birth, two days ago, and watched her—the bluish bag, the silence, and how her nostrils went in and out. She knew her child when it came, and it knew her, and as I watched it try its legs I thought how well the world was. How well.

The evenings are slow-coming. Sometimes I sit upon a rock all day, and watch the sky—how its light moves from east to west—and those are well-spent days. No day is like the day before, on Rannoch Moor.

WITH all these things, sir, I think of you. Of your face, and spectacles. Your voice.

I hope you are well, Mr Leslie.

I hope you are happy, wherever you are. I hope that, when a breeze moves the trees you walk beneath, you close your eyes to hear them. That you think, *they move for me. In my honour.* For they do—for a good man like you.

In my cell, I thought that I would meet my death saying *I love one man. I love Alasdair*—and I do. I always shall. Daily, I think of how my hand looked in his hand, or how he moved my hair on a red-coloured day—and I miss him. I say his name, to hear it. I feel the parts of me that he has felt.

But he lives, like I live.

And I love more than just one man, these days. I reckon I love two.

I THINK this, and look up.

It is evening. The moon is small, and new. There are stars, and a stream's sound, and I can hear the wings of insects, in the dark. I think *what gifts we are given*. Such gifts—every day.

I wrap your coat about me, breathe. Smile.

I WALK out beneath the sky, across the moor.

Afterword

In May 1692, three months after the massacre, a pamphlet entitled *A Letter from a Gentleman in Scotland* appeared in Edinburgh. It gave an intimate account of the deaths in Glencoe, from soldiers and survivors alike. Whilst the pamphlet is seen as Jacobite propaganda, it remains the most substantial source of information on the Massacre of Glencoe. Published anonymously, its author was almost certainly Charles Leslie.

Leslie himself went on to write numerous religious pamphlets, and continued to fight for the Stuart cause. In 1715, he joined the court of the exiled James VII/II in Italy, where he remained for six years. In 1721, at the age of seventy-one, he was finally allowed to return to his native Ireland, where he died. He is buried in Glaslough, near his family home.

News of the massacre brought national outrage. In 1693, an inquiry was ordered into the deaths, but this proved ineffective. Two years later, a second inquiry found John Dalrymple, Master of Stair, accountable. He was stripped of his title, but was soon reinstated. In 1701, he was promoted to Earl of Stair.

After sheltering for several months in Appin, and the mountains of Argyll, the MacDonalds of Glencoe returned to their glen. Iain, their new chief, re-signed the Oath of Allegiance in August 1692—ensuring his clan's safety. No more is known about Alasdair Og.

King William himself reigned for a further ten years, before being succeeded in 1702 by his sister-in-law, Anne. Despite another fifty years of trying, and several bloody rebellions, the Jacobite cause never succeeded and no Stuart ever returned to the throne.

THE LAST execution of a so-called witch in Britain was in 1727. The Witchcraft Act of 1735 put an end to the generations of fear and persecution. Over the previous three hundred years it is estimated that over 100,000 women—mostly knowledgeable, independent, old or outspoken women—stood trial, accused of witchcraft. Torture was widespread, as means for confession. Across Europe, as many as 40,000 were put to death.

As FOR Corrag, there is still a story to her name. Her wish to protect the people of Glencoe from the sword has passed into folklore. It is rumoured that no local men died by the sword in battle for over two centuries. Only when a sword was found in the Loch Leven, in 1916, and brought ashore, did any local men die at war; the Battle of the Somme was the next day.

There is no account of Corrag's own death—although legend says that she was an old woman, when she died. It is also claimed that she was buried, with highest honours, by the MacDonald clan. In the 1930s, a tiny skeleton was accidentally unearthed by road-builders on the shores of Loch Leven. Believed to be Corrag's, it was taken, and re-buried. Although her grave is unmarked, her new resting place is still by the water. It has a good view of the Pap of Glencoe.